"What have you become, Tiernon?"

"I am an Adept, Mother, in the ancient Orders of the Seven. I am a Priest. I have seen colors that do not exist on this world, and I've created fire from my hands. I can call the wind up at sea. No poison can touch me. I can call armies of spirits from the earth and fire to be my servants and do what I command. I have done these things. And I have very little personal stake in the outcome of the political games at the Court, and the only political end I serve is the fulfillment of the Prophecies."

"FIRST AND FINAL RITES is an outstanding piece of work . . . a clear picture of an alien civilization and a fascinating plot of court intrigue."
—*Andre Norton*

"Shariann Lewitt has the ability to move into an alternative world and take the reader with her."
—*Madeleine L'Engle*

"FIRST AND FINAL RITES adds a new dimension to fantasy—Scimitar & Sorcery."
—*Susan M. Shwartz*, editor of
HECATE'S CAULDRON

Other Fantasy Books from
Ace Science Fiction & Fantasy

THE FACE IN THE FROST, John Bellairs
ARIEL: A BOOK OF THE CHANGE, Steven R. Boyett
JHEREG and YENDI, Steven Brust
THE LAND OF LAUGHS, Jonathan Carroll
LYREC, Gregory Frost
HARPY'S FLIGHT, Megan Lindholm
THE DOOR IN THE HEDGE, Robin McKinley
RUNES, Richard Monaco
THE ANUBIS GATES, Tim Powers
BARD, Keith Taylor
THE REVENANTS, Sheri S. Tepper
THE SEVEN TOWERS, Patricia C. Wrede
SORCERER'S LEGACY, Janny Wurts

FIRST AND FINAL RITES

SHARIANN LEWITT

ACE FANTASY BOOKS
NEW YORK

FIRST AND FINAL RITES

An Ace Fantasy Book / published by arrangement with
the author

PRINTING HISTORY
Ace Original / September 1984

For information address: The Berkley Publishing Group,
200 Madison Avenue, New York, New York 10016.

ISBN: 0-441-23998-6

Ace Fantasy Books are published by The Berkley Publishing Group,
200 Madison Avenue, New York, New York 10016.
PRINTED IN THE UNITED STATES OF AMERICA

For
Freda Blum
who deserves much more

✑ ONE

CATAIA LAY ON the stone slab altar waiting for the ritual to begin. Mother Daniessa, her Initiator, lightly dusted her face with powdered gold and arranged her limbs as one dead. Then she gilded Cataia's palms and the soles of her feet. The young woman lay unmoving, only the pounding of her heart giving away the secret that any life lodged in that body.

Behind closed lids Cataia could visualize the chamber quite clearly, the dark stone masonry, the empty space, the shadowy green-robed Priestesses circling the altar. It took every ounce of self-discipline she had learned to remain still, to wait for the opening words. She was aware of the light breath of fabric around her, her Initiation robe, the most important ritual item of all. She resisted the impulse to push out with all her senses to take in the preparations.

"Your feet are on the corridor that leads to life, for we live in illusion and all things are illusion," Mother Daniessa intoned.

"Life and death are illusion," Cataia replied, a cold shudder going through her as she realized she might very well die

1

here in the next hour, the coming night.

"Have glory and triumph, be guided by the truth, be guarded by knowledge," the Priestesses chanted in unison.

"The truth and knowledge are one as all things are one," Cataia responded. She felt the hardness of the stone under her head, the cold of it, felt the drafts in this subterranean chamber breathe moisture on her skin.

"As we take the symbol of the sun as it rises," the chant circled around her.

"To the East." She imagined a great solar disk at her head, behind her, and extended her inner self, striving to reach it.

"And as it sets."

"To the West." Again she reached out, opened, expanded to meet that great red disk beyond her feet.

"As the burning sands of the desert and the cold mountains."

"To the South." Cataia felt herself rise up, up above the chamber until she watched the earth from a distance, until she was the desert and the mountain range that was the southern border of Avriaten.

"And the sea."

"The Dark Mother who is my Mother in all places," Cataia responded. She was utterly involved in the ritual itself, yet distant, floating without any point of reference. She waited again, spread out, thinking.

"Cradle her in your bosom."

The words sounded far away to Cataia, very far, but she felt the response within her, the warmth glowing, a single point of light before her. It doubled on itself, reflected, and she was at the Door, the great nighttime beach with sand tinted the green of her Order. Before her lay the great bitter water, the water of the Planes. She rose in this place and began to walk down the beach, drawn by the lapping of the waves.

"Bitter Mother, accept this for your halls, a daughter."

Cataia heard this final chant not as the speech of her teachers, but as the singing voices of the Planes themselves gathering to bid her off on her journey, the journey she had spent ten years preparing for.

She entered the dark water of the Planes and felt it like ice, numbing her feet and ankles. The Initiation robe wound about her legs, weighted by the water. Deliberately, step by step, Cataia entered the vast sea, entered the Planes where she would be accepted as a Priestess Adept. Or die.

The space around her was infused with green flowing light and she heard the music of bells. Around her forms swirled, those things that belonged here. They did not challenge her. Enclosed in a sheath of glowing power, she walked on down the gentle slope into the deeper regions.

She came to a stop. The cold no longer bothered her and she had adjusted to the strange light, all color and shadow. Before her stood a gate, two stone pillars topped by a third. She reached out to touch them and found that her arm did not move. She watched. In front of her, between the pillars, a shadow was beginning to form. It drew substance to itself and solidified into a monster that guarded the gate. It opened its jaws, and in the soft turquoise light its fangs glowed like rubies.

Terror, anger and disappointment filled her. And then, behind her, distant on the motes of light, she heard again the sound of the bells. She strained to hear them, the clear, high sound coming closer until it infused her being.

Laughter welled up in her and the monster dissolved in the mist as Cataia passed through the gate.

The terrain changed, the downward slope becoming more pronounced and the light both thicker and clearer. Before her, in the distance, a glint of light played. She felt drawn forward, compelled to reach that light, the safety at the end of her voyage in this place. She no longer thought of why this was happening, or that she herself had chosen it, but only that the next step and the step after that must be taken. She felt no weight at all, floating in this heavy flux of force, permeated with a radiance not of the physical world she had left far behind. Lines were crisp and clear and the edges of things glowed with their own power. In comparison, the world itself was but a dull reflection.

She found herself following a path. There was no marking in front of her feet, but she felt its even, packed hardness beneath her. Forms materialized, lining the path, elemental wraiths with sad eyes and seaweed hair. They drifted just within her vision, but as she made the sign of her grade, they floated away from her. This was not their place.

She found herself on a high terrace of grey slate battered by the winds. The light had dipped, hidden behind something far beyond and she could no longer see it. The path ended. In front of her rose a great structure of energy, colored threads woven tightly into a bright net. Below, the rock shimmered, the grey sparkling dull silver where she had passed. There was no sound but the rustle of the wind of the Planes. She stood and studied the structure before her. There was no fear, only a deathly certain understanding. She was facing 'Kleppah, the enemy, the always-enemy. This place was Tyne as it was on the Planes, and not its pallid reflection in the physical world.

At this juncture in the Planes had two Adepti sealed 'Kleppah, the evil, the unclean, and ended the war that had sunk half a continent. A thousand years ago they had succumbed to the temptation of power the Master of 'Kleppah had offered them. They had sealed, but not destroyed it. And here they had permitted themselves to be condemned for eternity, for the great structure in front of her still pulsed with a life of its own.

She heard a slight moaning as she surmounted the rock face that rose behind her, floating softly up the sheer cliffside. A man, a Priest dressed in the robes of the Orange Order, knelt as a suppliant. His face was contorted in pain. Behind him rose a thing more fearsome than anything she had ever imagined. It took something like human form, the face merely skin over bone and large yellow eyes burning through all they beheld. Its hands were almost human too, but the fingers terminated in great claws, held as if in a blessing over the Priest's head. Most awful of all, its bloodless lips were pulled back in a grimace that mocked a smile and there was thin laughter emerging from its throat.

Cataia was frozen with a blast of cold. The demon, for demon she knew it to be, had turned its gaze on her. "Little friend," it said, "have you forgotten my name?"

She shuddered. She knew, suddenly, what this was and that knowledge frightened her more than the thing had itself. "Lechefrian, the Eater of Souls, the Laughing Master," she whispered in terror. If it wanted to, she knew, it could devour her then and there, and nothing she could do, no power she could command, would make the slightest difference.

"You forgot one title, little Priestess," the demon replied softly. "Master of 'Kleppah. And we will have a good time, all of us, my minions. I have plans." He hissed and began to dissolve into the mist. Behind her the energy structure glowed more brightly, the threads shimmering against the darkness that enveloped them.

She turned her attention to the man. He was still, his jaw locked as if carved in stone. She was surprised that he was so very beautiful. She reached out a hand and found that the thick waves of hair were fine and soft, not carved of stone at all.

So this was Tiernon of the Seven, the great traitor, the arch-villain. It was he who had been tempted by the demon, he who had not resisted the promised power of 'Kleppah. Something in her opened and she felt a great flood of compassion for him, still tortured, still bound here on Tyne. She raised her hands in the Sign of Blessing and murmured softly. The image of Tiernon faded.

She turned again to face 'Kleppah, and in the net of energy woven around the island was imprinted the face of the demon master, many times, laughing. Something in her wanted to grieve for it too, for the bondage, but she dared not look too long. The enemy was ancient, true evil, deliberate and conscious. Again she turned her back on it as a symbolic gesture and yet another figure stood before her, this one far more shattering than any of the three she had already faced.

It was her mother.

Keani rei Aandev, aunt to Eltion the Queen. Keani, the accused regicide, the suicide in the Council chambers, the reigning beauty of Avriaten. Again there was a spark of anger in Cataia. When the Queen had been found dead in her rooms, it was the proud and powerful Keani who had been accused. Keani had cut her own throat in haughty rejection of the Council's allegations. But her defiance had been seen by many as a confession. Because of her mother's actions she was soon to be presented to Court as the Crown Princess and not Queen, as should be her right. It was thought Keani's daughter might well be a traitor too.

Cataia shivered and stepped back. The woman who was her mother held out a long, shapely hand with the nails lacquered gold against the golden ivory skin.

"It's not me you need to fear, daughter," she said softly. "Beware of Bertham, the regicide, the servant of others."

In a moment Cataia softened to the sad-faced woman before her. Yes, Keani had been high-spirited and spoiled, had not always controlled her temper, but she like Tiernon was obviously suffering. Cataia took the hand that was offered and found herself embracing the stranger and crying.

Suddenly she found herself engulfed in a brilliant white light. No longer alone, or even separate, she pulsed together with a Mind, a thousand minds. Everything that lived and breathed was within her. Centuries happened, worlds were born and died, the stars whirled through her. She was everywhere and all around her, inside of her, were the thoughts of the Unity. Cataia no longer existed. She was with them, one of them all, of and in that singular being and non-being that was symbolized by the blazing sun. Joy echoed through the chambers of the Unity, through her.

And then she was back on the altar. The stone still felt cold under her shoulders and she was stiff. Her body had been rigid for a long time and the muscles had locked. Experimentally she opened her eyes and then blinked as they became accustomed to the light.

The chamber was blazing with banks of candles and the Priestesses of the Abbey surrounded the altar, ranks of them arranged in quiet contemplation. Mother Daniessa stepped forward and placed her hands on Cataia's forehead.

"Welcome back to the world, Lady Priestess, daughter of Ge."

A thrill ran up Cataia's spine. She had succeeded, then, had become one of them and acquired the power of her Order! She felt Mother Daniessa's hands under her shoulders assisting her to rise. Another Priestess helped her place her feet on the floor and the two of them supported her as she stood.

For all the exertion, Cataia did not feel in the least tired. She permitted the Priestesses to help her up the stairs onto the main floor of the Abbey, but insisted on entering the rectory unassisted.

Even this place, so very familiar, seemed somehow different now. There was the slightest hint of dark-grey light coming in through the intricate wood carvings set in the windows, and she could hear the birds outside. She was led past the lower tables up to the dais, where the finest, thickest cushions had been arranged around the grey-green lacquered table. The resident Priestesses each had her place at this table. The others of the Order were out in the world at their assigned tasks, just as Cataia knew she would be by the time today's sun was full on the horizon.

A sumptuous feast was laid out on the fine table, large steaming bowls of flaked fish in sauce and warm bread, trays of brightly colored fruit and, best of all, honey pastry from the shop just down the street.

She and Dacia, her best friend, had gossiped about the traditional Initiation feast, but Cataia had discounted it. As long as there was pastry, Dacia counted anything a feast.

And then Cataia realized why it all seemed so strange, in this room where she had eaten almost every meal for the ten years of her novitiate. There were no novices, and she was at the other end of the room. It felt strangely empty, the large space being taken up by only herself and the twelve resident Mothers of the Abbey.

"You must try to eat something," Mother Daniessa said firmly. "There's still enough time before you have to change, and you have a very long day ahead of you."

So even if she was a Priestess in her own right she was not above being chided! She finished her pastry.

Very casually, Mother Daniessa tapped her on the shoulder and handed her a small box. "This gift is traditional in all the Abbeys at this time. It will identify you to your brothers and sisters in the world, but we like to think of it as something to remind you especially of this night, and of your home here. No matter where you have to go or what work you must do, the Abbey is always your home."

Cataia opened the box and found in the folds of green velvet a ring like the ones she had noticed on the hands of all the Priestesses. The band was made of seven different-colored metals, braided together in an intricate pattern and set with a single green stone. She had nothing to say. She slipped the ring on her right hand and found it a perfect fit.

"Now run along and get dressed," Mother Daniessa said before Cataia could utter a word of thanks. "The Guard will be coming to escort you to the Palace soon, and they can't find you like this!"

Cataia went to her own small room and looked around carefully as she slipped out of her Initiation robe and packed it in the open trunk. No doubt her room in the Palace would be far finer. She tried to quiet her mind and concentrate on buttoning up the stiff, high-collared blouse that was proper attire for a member of the nobility, and arranged the great katreisi of Aandev-white over everything, making sure the folds draped gracefully across her shoulders and down her back. The gold trim set off her skin, the same golden ivory as her mother's.

There was a discreet knock at the door.

"Cai? I wanted to give you a little present. Just something to remember me by when you're in the Palace."

It was Dacia. Ignoring the careful drape of her formal

clothing, Cataia ran across the room to embrace her friend.
Dacia had entered the Abbey at the same time she had, and
they had been friends ever since. "I have about a zillion questions to ask you, but they told me that you don't have time, so
here." Dacia thrust a book into Cataia's hands and raced out
into the hall.

It was a volume of the Prophecies, calligraphed and illus-
trated by Dacia herself, a magnificent volume. Dacia was a
promising artist, and soon to take Initiation herself. Cataia
felt tears forming in her eyes. Leaving the Abbey was hard
enough, leaving Dacia was almost impossible. After all the
silly things they had done together . . .

She heard her name being called. Quickly she straightened
her katreisi again and smoothed the stiff pleats in her pants,
and went down to meet her honor guard. Crown Princess and
Priestess, she acknowledged the captain and climbed into the
litter that would take her to the Palace.

There was so much color in the formal reception room that
it made Cataia dizzy. Some Salsatean designer who specialized
in brothels must have been responsible for the geometric patterns on the ceiling painted in red and overleafed with gold.
The varicolored hangings, depicting the gardens at various
times of the year, clashed with the brilliant red, purple and
orange hues of the guests' cushions. Only the single great rug
that covered the entire floor suggested fine taste, its azure
ground patterned with gold and amber kyrili blossoms, echoing the shades of the tapestries. Heavy lamps scented with
kyrili oil picked out glints of gold threads woven into the deep
pile.

Cataia found herself seated on the second step of the azure-
tiled dais at the far end, just under Lathanor, the King Regent.
He looked Aandev, with skin to match her own and thick
black hair neatly caught back at the nape of his neck. The
scent of Four Blossom oil was heavy on him, but under it
Cataia detected a whiff of stale brandy and drew back a fraction.

In neat rows facing them the courtiers were seated, the
members of the Council of Avriaten and the representatives of
the Reis, Major and Minor, as well as ambassadors from Salsatee and the five Nestezian tribes. These last were seated
apart from each other to prevent bloodshed during the presentation ceremony. She wondered which of those in the first

rank was Bertham. Her mother's warning nagged at the back of her mind as she surveyed those politely formal faces.

A scholar read the Aandev genealogy. Cataia stared fixedly at one of the more horrible arabesques painted in pink on the ceiling, and rubbed her thumb against the braided band of her ring, trying to control her anxiety. The old woman's monotone droned on and on, Tamane the first and Tamane the second, each with her record of deeds, real and imagined. Cataia wondered if the others were as bored as she was. The faces before her were politely blank.

There were still a few hundred years to go. Cataia breathed out in a controlled count and began focusing energy at the base of her spine. She would need all the energy she could gather for what lay ahead, the presentation to the Council and the Reis and the ambassadors and the feasting and entertainment that would follow. Slowly she pulled the energy up her spine, lighting the centers as she went, until it reached her head. There, now she just might be able to keep her eyes open during the interminable ceremonies.

She gazed out again at the sea of faces, still wondering which one was the Bertham her mother had accused. Ayt, the High Priestess of the Star Temple, the State religion, was easy to pick out in her black robes of office. And Tiernon lar Asirithe rei Bietehel, Third Councilor and representative of the richest Rei in the land, was obvious in an indigo katreisi. He seemed exhausted, even more so than she.

Tiernon. She had to remember not to smile. Funny how propaganda worked sometimes, that the populace who knew nothing about the real struggle of the Seven Adepti against 'Kleppah had made that Tiernon a hero. Even now, a thousand years later, the name was extremely popular, perhaps the most common in the language. The Orders had done their work well.

Thank goodness there were only fifty more years to go! Cataia yawned in a ladylike manner, flaring her nostrils but otherwise not moving her face. And then, finally, the reading was done.

Ayt rose gracefully to deliver the benediction and bless the Crown Princess. Like the genealogy, the benediction was in the ancient ornate style, and was even longer than it was ornate. Cataia spent the time it took studying Ayt. She was amazed by Ayt's grace, unusual in so tall and strongly built a woman. Ayt would have been tall even among the desert

tribes. Irreverently, Cataia thought that she had missed her
calling. The Star Priestess ought to have been a general at the
very least.

Then the Council came to greet her individually, their richly
colored katreisis heavily embroidered in precious metals and
gems proclaiming rank and lineage. First Bertham, and she
kept control, not flinching when he touched a dry palm to her
hand. She did not need to remember her mother's warning
about him for his presence to worry her. In his almost too
regular deep-copper face, the pale-blue eyes burned with
something almost akin to fanaticism.

Fear mingled with shock as she heard his formal recitation.
He was so solid, so very substantial here in the flesh, and
Cataia felt overpowered by him. Only ten years of discipline in
the Abbey kept her from bolting from the First Councilor's
overbearing presence. Then she realized that what frightened
her was the desire flaming on his face. Desire for what? That
would be the key. She filed it in the back of her mind and
sealed it with an image to examine at a better time.

Nikkot, the Second Councilor, was introduced next, but she
acknowledged the ancient scholar only perfunctorily, her
mind still on Bertham. Or rather, on the chill Bertham had left
her with. She couldn't help but smile warmly, though, when
the old man with wisps of white hair patted her hand more like
a daughter than a monarch.

The Third Councilor was called, and as he rose Cataia was
struck by something even stronger than she had felt with
Bertham. It was a type of recognition, but she couldn't place
it, as if there were a power link. Her stomach knotted as Tiernon approached the dais.

Cataia was immediately confused. The fine fashionable
brocades he wore and the silver streak in his black hair at the
left temple seemed to mark him as the Court fop. But when he
placed his hand on hers she felt more than saw the ring. Seven
braided metals with a tawny stone, a match for her own.

When she finally trusted herself to meet his eyes, the
recognition was reflected back to her with a wry smile. She felt
at ease, comforted, although there was no comfort in that
face. It was all sharp lines and angles, like a hungry cat, at war
with the heavy-lidded eyes of sensualist. Not black, she saw,
but eyes so deep a blue that it matched his Rei indigo, and
behind the sensuality she read the stern reserve and control of
an Adept.

Cataia did not know if she should be relieved or worried. There was already too much here and her mind was reeling. From the tawny stone she knew his Order, the Orange, one of the six, like her own, with a color and an Abbey on Dier Street. His presence here shook her more deeply than she wanted to admit. Adepts did not meet by chance.

The rainbow hues reeled around her and the perfumes threatened suffocation. The soft, cultured voices murmuring flowery pat phrases seemed poised to drown her.

Others were being called. Again she drew on stored energy to sustain her through this ordeal, until there was nothing left within.

She took a breath replete with the odors of sweat and stale drink, and followed it down into her lungs, to the base of her spine, and then down further into the earth itself, into the very rock below them. She began to pull slowly. The effort expended almost as much as it gained. But it should be enough to pull her through the feasting.

Servants entered with small red lacquered tables loaded with food, and placed them beside each guest. Poems were chanted at length, and each of the ambassadors had to make a speech. Cataia was too tired even to eat, and the food smelled cloying and heavy after the simple Abbey fare. Oil ran over each dish, and there were too many wines. Every moment felt like eternity.

And then, just when it had become so unbearable that she thought she might scream, a gong sounded. The guests rose and filed past, bowing. It was over.

An old woman in a rose katreisi came and bowed low to Cataia twice. Cataia bowed to her cousin, the King Regent, and then followed the woman to her suite.

There, far from the feasting and the crowd, all Cataia could see were the heavily piled sleeping rugs. She barely had the strength to undress before she sank down into blessed unconsciousness.

Tiernon, lounging on the sea-green sleeping rug, was analyzing the latest vintage wine from the Tersoneat region. The color was a deep ruby and the flavor, under the youthful tannin, promised richness and subtlety. The underlying tartness, which offended the palate and permeated the bouquet, would mellow with age. In truth, a fine vintage, and he made a mental note to order seven or eight barrels in the morning.

Quite unlike the wines of two years ago, which he kept in his cellar to serve guests he did not particularly honor, this vintage would be saved for his private table. Finishing the glass, he put the wine from his mind and turned to the events of the day.

The Crown Princess had stood up well under today's ordeal, he thought, especially given what must have happened the night before. For a moment he let himself remember his own Initiation, and then firmly dismissed it. She was very young, too young to handle the present situation alone, and she could not possibly suspect what he did about Bertham. If only she were strong enough to help on that score.

There had been something else about her too, something that played around the corners of his mind like a face or name one should be able to place and couldn't. He closed his eyes and hoped that it would come. Unlike the others in the Abbey, he had never remembered a past life, no matter what techniques he used. But he had often thought that something, a face, a taste, a building, might recall them to him, and the stirrings he felt when he saw Cataia indicated a clue at least.

Perhaps it was simply the Aandev. Cataia certainly looked like a member of the ruling family, with her golden-ivory skin and her black almond eyes. He lingered on the image of the elegant narrow wrists, the stately neck and the masses of the blackest hair he had ever seen. With a start he realized that she was more beautiful than her mother had been, although in what manner he could not place. Yet image after image brought no information, and the sense of inadequacy nearly overpowered him just as it had fifteen years ago when he was a novice.

Again he had to force his mind back to the subject at hand, the implications of an Initiate Queen. Above all, Bertham must not know—and Cataia must be warned as soon as possible.

Before he even considered telling her his suspicions, and informing her to rely on Nikkot, the old man stumbled in and exercised the prerogative of age, sinking down on one of the thick cushions without waiting for an invitation.

"Ah, Tiernon, I'm glad to see you're still awake. I need some advice, and you know about such things as what ladies like and all."

Tiernon smiled indulgently at the old man and poured two glasses of wine. "This pressing is still young, but don't you think, with maturity, it will be worth a barrel or two?"

"That's what I need to ask about. There is the matter of the dinner I'm giving tomorrow night to honor our Princess before I leave on the excavation. I assume you received my invitation? Good. Now, what would be the most elegant, stylish, impressive dinner I could serve? Something really unusual. Should I have the clear soup and the tiny shellfish in sauce?"

"No, Nikkot, Bertham served that last week and I assume you want to outdo him. Why don't I have a menu sent down to your cook by tomorrow sunrise?"

Nikkot seemed greatly relieved. "With you making up the menu, I'm sure no one will be able to say anything about old Nikkot not being able to keep up. Thank you, my friend. And thank you for this good wine too, although I'm a bit too old to buy for a cellar anymore. The wine will live longer than I."

"I'll see you at supper tomorrow, and I'll send you a bottle of this wine, just to see if you outlive it."

Tiernon insisted on escorting Nikkot to the door himself, giving honor to the old man. Indeed, Tiernon mused, Nikkot deserved it more than most. After all, why should anyone laugh at scholarship, even in an obscure field? And the man had most definitely contributed much to the understanding of the earliest days of the Aandev line. He resolved to lend his cook for the supper tomorrow as well as the menu: Nikkot's party should be worthy of praise.

"And now," the elderly Councilor said, "it's time for me to go off and tutor our illustrious First Councilor, even this late at night. The hours you all keep."

Tiernon smiled as he closed the door behind Nikkot, but he hated to be reminded of Bertham's study. Ancient languages was not exactly what one would expect of the Tonea'Rei's son. There was something devastating here that he dared not even suspect, and yet it nagged at him. Bertham was not what he seemed, Tiernon thought. And neither am I. But Bertham, what is Bertham up to? The question circled around and around in Tiernon's head as he picked up the wine again.

As he ushered the old man in, Bertham knew very well what he was doing, but he kept his countenance sober.

"But why don't you come to the University?" Nikkot asked. "It would not affect your duties here, and there are other manuscripts and other teachers. You might prefer to study with Herian Astrivo; his treatise on Nestezian verb forms is quite impressive."

Bertham shook his head and offered a bowl of fruit that had been carefully kept chilled in one of the deep wells. "No, Nikkot, I can't. You have given me some of Astrivo's work, and I have found it less useful than what we are doing. Now, here, I have a translation of that poem we were discussing."

Nikkot looked it over carefully, checking against the original. "Adequate, but you have used the familiar agreement on the nouns."

Bertham sighed and began to reread very carefully. Tiresome as this study was, it was vital, at the very heart of his plan. "Nikkot, I have something to ask you."

"Yes?"

"You know I'm financing this excavation on Tyne, and I'd like a small consideration in exchange. If there are any manuscripts, could you keep it quiet until I have done the translation?" He glanced down at the pale-green fruit in his hand. The past months of study with Nikkot had taught him just what to say to the old man, although how anyone could be so stupid as to really think that scholarship alone was important was beyond him. "You see, I'd like to be the first with something of this nature, a scholarly work that no one has duplicated. You can understand?"

Nikkot almost patted his hand. "Of course. I myself would love to be first with a new translation, but I do have my jars and candlesticks to study. There may even be some scraps of cloth, imagine. And it would be nice to outdo Astrivo at least once. No doubt he'll find errors in your translation. Be warned."

"And you won't tell anyone?" Bertham asked quietly. "I want this to be a surprise. I will, of course, mention you in the credit."

Nikkot was practically beaming. "And you will come to my dinner tomorrow? I spoke to Tiernon, and he's helping arrange the menu, so you should be pleased."

"Of course I'll come," Bertham said. "I must admit that I admire Tiernon's taste, although I can't help but resent him a little."

"Come now, why? You two are so alike I'd think you were destined to be great friends."

"Oh, just that he's Bietehel, always had everything. Always knows where to get anything, and then he corners the market." Bertham laughed amiably. "Have another geri, Nikkot, they're in season and unusually sweet. I managed to obtain a few before my erstwhile fellow Councilor cornered that market. I'm really not that jealous of him, he actually told me to buy geri now before the price went up. Do you know,'' he said, trying to change the subject, ''I'm quite excited about your new excavation. I have the feeling that it is going to yield some wonderful things, maybe a really rare manuscript.''

''My fondest wish,'' agreed Nikkot. ''But tonight we had a long lesson, and I have the party tomorrow. Young people can stay up all night, but I must go home before I dishonor myself by falling asleep right here.''

Bertham had to laugh out loud, for while he knew that at Nikkot's age anyone with less than great-grandchildren was indeed young, he had reached what most people called middle age himself. He gestured for a servant to show Nikkot out.

Once he was alone, Bertham's smile faded quickly. There was still much work to be done. The tiles of the Wheel rested in their case under a small carved table, the thirty-two tiles of divination that had served him so well in the past. One by one he took them out of the case, caressing the enameled glass.

They were old, how old he did not know, only that such glasswork was no longer done. The tiles, just the size to fit in his palm, were of a deep smoky-grey and the patterns on each were incised deeply and overlaid with bright enamel in not only the green and red and yellow of the modern tiles, but in purple and blue and gold and a strange dusty-black that he had seen nowhere else. The outlines were of silver and gold, inlaid in the heavy glass, and the surfaces were polished smooth from both fine craftsmanship and many years of use. He ran his fingers over the faces of the tiles, amazed as always at their soft texture.

He placed them all face down on the smooth surface of the wooden case and swirled them, concentrating deeply. Eyes still closed, he chose tiles and laid them out in the Wheel pattern, one in the center, twelve around it in a circle, and two cast off to the side.

The Bright Bird, the Snake at Rest, the Double Eclipse, the Garden at Midnight, and, in the center, the Snake Striking, his own tile around which all the others pivoted. Could the Bright Bird be Cataia? She was right for the Bird, light and beautiful and so very young. The Snake at Rest he had always read as Tiernon, an unknown quantity whom he felt was always ready to strike but had never shown his true colors. Then the Double Eclipse—both of them defeated, perhaps? And the Garden at

Midnight, a garden not alive, but not dead either. Usually the books read it as the reincarnation of a soul. Bertham was almost worried that the interpretation seemed too exact, too positive to be believed. After all, prophecies were usually fulfilled in strange ways, but this seemed so direct. He copied the pattern and dated it before he broke down the tiles and returned them to the box. The reading might well bear more meditation in the morning, and he was too tired to check the books right now. Still, he felt a kind of warmth, an afterglow from the reading that led him gently to sleep.

It was still early enough to be cool when a fiercely grand-motherly woman, Cataia's lady-in-waiting, presented the Princess's first caller of the day. Cataia found that she had to ask more than once before the Lady Valnera would leave the room, so she and Tiernon could have some privacy.

"Well," she began, "I have never met a brother of your Order, but I assume we have certain things in common. I also assume that you are here at Court for reasons other than the obvious. Please correct me if a direct manner is offensive, but it seems wrong to be otherwise."

"Agreed." Tiernon matched her businesslike tone. "Why do you think there is some purpose for my presence, other than to simply observe and represent Bietehel?"

"Don't play games," she snapped, testing the limits of the freedom he had granted. "I might be young, but the Abbey has made sure that I am not naive. First, no matter what your rank, or mine, neither of us would be here without reason. The Orders place Adepts as they see fit in the universal sense. Even a novice knows that. Second, I was not informed that you were an Initiate, although otherwise the information on the members of the Great Council appeared quite complete. Therefore, there is something going on, something involving the old struggle."

The tension turning Tiernon's neck to rock relaxed. "Very good. What was your information about Bertham?"

"Spotty, compared to most," she replied. "Collateral branch of Tonea'Rei, came to Court as soon as he came of age, and has been active in politics ever since. An advocate of the judicial jurisdiction reforms, opposed to public domain of unsettled land, owns a vineyard in Sherkon."

"His wine isn't very good," Tiernon added. "Were you

told that Lathanor is drunk most of the time? And Bertham is his best friend at Court. When Lathanor claimed the throne in a provisional regency, he named Bertham First Councilor, passing over Syleria and Nikkot, who are senior to him. He's the one who accused your mother, and he studies ancient languages with Nikkot.''

"So?'' Cataia asked. "What does that have to do with 'Kleppah?''

"A great deal,'' Tiernon said. "A very great deal. Doesn't his preeminence in the Council and Lathanor's alcoholism suggest something to you?''

"You mean, he rules Lathanor,'' Cataia said softly. "Very tidy arrangement.''

"And his study of ancient languages with Nikkot. I assume you studied Eskenese at the Abbey.''

"Of course,'' she replied. "Most of the major works on magic, from the time of the Seven until about three hundred years ago, were in Eskenese.''

"And it is still necessary to translate back to get the numerology correct, isn't it? And guess what language Bertham studies. I don't suppose I need to tell you,'' he remarked dryly.

"Circumstantial evidence, Tiernon. It wouldn't be admissible in court. Besides, many of the scholars at the University know the language quite well, Nikkot among them.''

"Are you going to be continually resistant to any advice? Bertham is dangerous. It's not simply the language study, or even his manipulation of Lathanor, but something much more subtle. I haven't touched him on the Planes yet, but that could be because he doesn't use the Orange at all, or that it wasn't the time, or any of a million reasons. Besides, unless there is a real meeting there, how often do you bump into your sisters?''

She chose her response carefully. "Believe me, I understand your warning and I will be careful. I have dealt with renegades before. I was on a hunt against a Priest from the Star Temple a few years back.''

"I remember it. But he wasn't very dangerous, just one of those misguided sorts who stumbles on a few techniques and can't resist trying. Most of them don't even believe that the magic of the Seven works anymore. Bertham is in an altogether different class. Also, the Wheel tiles have been indicating danger for weeks now.''

"All right. What do you think he is up to?"

"I don't know yet," Tiernon said evenly. "He hasn't shown his hand. But some nights I get the strangest focus points in my meditations, and I've seen him in dreams."

"Plain old dreams?"

"When I can't tell the difference between a plain dream and a real dream, I will burn my Initiation robe and be renounced in the middle of the Order refectory," Tiernon said, truly angry now. "Why are you trying to fight me?"

"I'm sorry," said Cataia, and she meant it. He was really trying to help, and she knew as well as any of the Adepti that sometimes there were indications that something was amiss that were not easy to verify. Besides, she thought ruefully, even the report said that he'd been at Court for over ten years, which meant that even if he were sent directly on his coming of age he would have been an Initiate for longer than she had been a novice.

"Why don't we start over, ator?" she asked, using the Eskenese term, the most intimate word she knew for an Adept. "Thank you for the warning. I will be careful."

"Good. I don't normally like to be so abrupt, but the indications of the Wheel have been extremely consistent, unusually so. Besides, atore, it has been a very long time since I could talk about these things, a very long time."

Cataia smiled as Tiernon rearranged himself in a comfortable position on the deep cushions. It was vaguely pleasant, being alone with a man. She had never had much to do with men in general, and certainly never with one who had any understanding of her secret.

She found herself staring at him, more like an art critic than anything else. In an objective sense, the composition was lovely. He had draped himself luxuriously across several pale-amber cushions, and his dark katreisi flowed across the heavily patterned rug like a waterfall of ink. His hands were at rest, so utterly so that they seemed molded from bronze. She noticed that the silver in his hair was natural and there were the beginnings of tiny creases at the corners of his eyes. A young-old face, she thought, beautiful with that even color, sorrowful even in composure.

"There are other things I think you should know," he started slowly. "Bertham may be your most dangerous enemy, but in her time your mother was disliked by almost the entire Court. You'll have to walk between the ocean and the sand."

"To walk between the sea and sand,
To drink the nectar of a stone,
To feel the fire and take the brand
And reinstate the Eastern Land
And only then can we atone."

Cataia quoted the final prophecy of the Oracle of the Caverns, who had once been Chevaina of the Seven.

Tiernon looked thoughtful. "I always thought it strange that I was named for the founder of my own Order, and he a villain at that."

"It's a very popular name. Most people don't even realize that he is the villain of the story. Most people think that the sealing of 'Kleppah was a heroic act. They don't know that it could have been destroyed. The Orders have managed to keep the truth well concealed," Cataia said, reflecting on the Orders' passion for secrecy.

The deep heat of the day was beginning to seep through the delicate carvings in the windows as they sat contemplating those moments, which, had they been different, would have made their present lives unrecognizable. It had been a shock to Cataia when she first realized that it would have been indeed been possible for the Seven to destroy 'Kleppah and that Chevaina and Tiernon had sealed it so that they would be able to draw on its power later. There were stories in the Abbey that every novice was considered by the Priestesses to see if she were Chevaina, returned to repay her debt and finally destroy the evil power that had resided on the island for so long. Every novice hoped it would happen soon, preferably on the eve of her preliminary examination, and should Chevaina appear they would be the very last to be informed. Probably not until after the poem was published at the earliest.

Cataia wondered why the war between the Seven and 'Kleppah had been fought. Oh, she knew all the traditional answers, the truth of the unbalanced forces existing as long as there was an existence. And she thought she knew why people could be tempted to serve them—there were moments in her own training when she had wanted power and felt an almost overwhelming pride in her rapid achievements and her position. Even more now, with Lady Valnera to wait on her, living in seven large rooms in the Palace with rich wall tapestries and patterned cushions, she could understand a lust for luxury. It would be very easy here to forget the discipline of the Abbey, the four Chants to the Sun, the daily meditations and the fasts. She wondered how Tiernon had managed over the years. Mother Daniessa had never mentioned that part of it.

"Oh, you'll learn to manage," Tiernon said, seeming to read her mind. "You never do get the Abbey out of your system." He laughed, but there was a tinge of bitterness to it that Cataia couldn't understand.

After Tiernon had left, Cataia was surprised when Valnera brought in another visitor. If yesterday Nikkot had reminded her of a kindly grandfather, today his bearing and grave face made him seem more like an old soldier. Cataia took him out to the enclosed balcony overlooking the river, where they might enjoy a cool breeze.

When she sat on one of the cushions, Nikkot came over, bowed, and then took her hand, kissed it and touched it to his forehead. Cataia shivered. It was the respect gesture given to a reigning monarch.

"My lady," he said softly, "I have a great deal to confess to you. First, I have brought steel into your presence." He took out a long package wrapped in fine blue silk. He nodded and Cataia unwrapped it, finding a narrow, businesslike stiletto with a finely etched handle.

"It was your mother's. I knew Keani from the time she was a child, knew her well enough to know that she didn't kill Eltion." He chuckled sadly, lost in memories. "She was fine and proud, but she loved Eltion like a little sister, especially after you had left the Court for school. She was proud, but honest. She would never have stooped to poison. And, she was in my rooms all that night. She never left."

Cataia's eyes widened, but she said nothing. Nikkot was too deeply lost in his own memories, his own shame, for her to interrupt. Tentatively, she reached out with her mind for the other sight that she had learned at the Abbey, watching the ghostly shadow of his energy field, and she knew that he was completely open to her.

"My sister's son, the second-born of Batter'Rei, was visiting and Keani had taken a liking to him. I knew even then, but I was afraid to speak out, and it all happened so quickly. I was going to say something, and then it was too late. For my shame.

"I am an old man, too old to bear this shame. There is very little I can offer you. You are of age. Yesterday you became

Queen by right. I hold the title Councilor, but it has been a very long time since I've exercised any of the real power that accompanies the title. It has never been my passion.''

"You have given us great wisdom and understanding, Uncle," Cataia said.

Nikkot looked up and met her eyes evenly. His were steady and clear in his lined face. "This morning I came to a decision. This excavation on Tyne will be my last. I have already written my resignation to the University. Make your bid, Cataia. I still know how the paths of power work, even if I no longer walk them. And there are others who will be behind you. My sister is Mother of Batter'Rei, and she is not without influence elsewhere. I suspect that there are many others who would aid you as well."

Cataia gasped involuntarily. Nikkot reached over and patted her hand.

"Our country is in trouble, little Queen. I have been in retirement far too long. Let me wipe out the old shame. When it is time to move, you can count on me. I ask only one thing. See that my pyre is lit in Volenten."

Cataia felt the tears welling up in her eyes, and her throat had swollen, making it difficult to talk. "Thank you, Uncle," she said.

"Do not call me 'uncle,' " Nikkot replied. "Had I spoken before, it would have been your coronation yesterday, not merely a presentation. And now I must go. I have some hopes for this party tonight."

After the old Councilor left, Cataia sat rigid as stone. Fear contested with the possibilities; the awareness of what Nikkot had implied immobilized her. Inside, the knowledge welled up, overpowering her. "Make your bid," Nikkot had said. And Cataia knew that she would have no choice. It was what she had been trained for, to be Avriaten's first Initiate Queen.

🎵 Two

"WHAT IS THIS, how could this have happened? It's utterly unreasonable. I demand from Lathanor that more patrols be sent out on the roads." Cataia was trying not to scream and was only marginally successful. "And why wasn't I told immediately?"

"Highness, I don't think that either notification or more patrols will be of any use," Syleria said dryly.

Ignoring the interruption, Cataia continued. "First of all, when one of the members of the Royal Council is murdered, it is imperative that the Aandev know. Immediately. Second, if the roads aren't safe for a Council scholar, who are they safe for? Answer me this, Bertham, who killed Nikkot?"

It infuriated Cataia to see them all so calm, so assured, when Nikkot had been murdered. It had taken all the Princess's reserve not to break into tears when the news had been announced at the Council meeting. "Nikkot was harmless. He didn't crave power, only knowledge, and he was old. What good would it do anyone to have him dead a few months sooner?"

"Nestezians," Bertham commented.

"Perhaps, my lord, you did not listen closely enough to what was said by the guard who found him. His rings and his money had not been taken. The desert men don't leave goods of value lying around. And why was I not informed?" Cataia fumed.

"The Aandev was informed. A report was sent to Lathanor as soon as we had any information. May I remind Your Highness that it is he and not you who holds the throne."

Cataia bit back a retort to Bertham's vicious reminder of her position. She looked to Tiernon, hoping for some support, but he seemed to be concentrating on the half-eaten geri in his hand and totally oblivious to the whole debate.

"In any case, there are far too many brigands on the roads and I want something done about it. Ayt, do you have anything to add?"

Ayt smiled sadly and said, "It must have been one of the nomad bands. They've been getting bold lately, and no one else would harm Nikkot. I agree that we need better security, more patrols in the area. And I will pray for him."

"Can we close this meeting?" Tiernon asked lazily. "There are some new rugs in from Salsatee that I want to examine."

"No, we cannot close this meeting!" Cataia screamed. "I want to know why Nikkot is dead, and I want more patrols on the roads, and I want to know where we're going to find the money to pay for them."

"What about the Royal Treasury?" asked one of the younger Councilors.

"Thanks to our King Regent, the Royal Treasury is nearly empty. The harvests in Aandev'Rei have not been good this year and taxes have been late because Aandev'Rei was not the only place hit by late rains."

"We could borrow from Salsatee. They can't refuse us, they need the food," Ayt suggested helpfully.

"An avenue we could pursue. I'll summon the Salsatean Ambassador this afternoon," Cataia agreed.

"Princess Cataia, I'm afraid you're overstepping yourself," Bertham said silkily. "If we're to borrow more from Salsatee, you'll need the King Regent's approval, and I'm afraid he's off on a hunting trip today."

"Bertham lar Nisria rei Tonea, First Councilor, what is your advice on this situation?"

"It has been my opinion all along that this is an isolated incident. Perhaps the roads aren't very safe, that may be true. But I haven't heard any complaints before now, and we do not have the money for improved security. Perhaps," he said quietly, "we should invade the Nestezi. Then the desert would no longer be a threat, and we'd have their jewels to replenish the Treasury. It is an option."

"And what makes you so sure we'd win?" Tiernon asked with an edge of sarcasm in his voice. "Wars are terribly expensive, and the Nestezi is desert, in case you'd forgotten. No food, no water, and the Nestezian tribes have a reputation for being fierce. And there is another problem. The Nestezi is large and the tribes are nomadic. How do you propose to find them? Magia?"

Bertham snorted and shook his head. Cataia was pleased that Tiernon had pointed out the holes in Bertham's logic.

"What about the funeral arrangements?" asked Ayt. "I think a state funeral is in order, given Nikkot's service to the Crown."

"He asked that his pyre be lit in Volenten, although there will be a memorial service here, of course," Cataia said softly.

"Since this matter seems to be concluded, can we move on to other business? The Salsatean trade agreement has to be discussed, and it's almost time to eat." Bertham spoke almost sluggishly, and the others assented.

"However, there is still the matter of another Councilor to replace Nikkot," Cataia said.

"Lathanor will appoint one, no doubt, Princess."

"Then, my lord Bertham, I will leave it in my cousin's hands," Cataia conceded, biting back her bitterness. Her face was completely controlled as she continued, "Perhaps we had best go on to the trade agreement before it becomes too hot to think."

At twilight the roof garden of the Palace was deserted. The special preserve of the Aandev was forbidden to all but the Royal Family and their invited guests, so the yellow kyrili and the pale-blue mosaic fountain hid no unfriendly ears.

"All right, Tiernon, what did you make of that charade this morning? I appreciate your need for public neutrality, but honestly, had Bertham said one more word I would have killed him myself."

Tiernon paused a second before he replied. "I'm puzzled about Nikkot, more than puzzled. First, he was not robbed.

Second, we both know that there are very few Nestezians who kill and don't rob. Generally they prefer it the other way around, with a nice fat ransom in the bargain. Third, Nikkot was on Tyne, the site of the last battle of the Great War, and you can see 'Kleppah from there. Fourth, we have reason to suspect that 'Kleppah is involved, so far as the Wheel and several meditations indicate. Fifth, who knew where Nikkot was?''

''I'm not sure I understand,'' Cataia said.

''Listen, then. Does it make sense that Nikkot was murdered by nomads? All the evidence points away from it. Nikkot was on Tyne, looking for artifacts. Anything he found on Tyne would be of as much interest to 'Kleppah as to ourselves.''

''You mean Nikkot found something, and he was killed to keep him quiet? So the question becomes, what did he find and who killed him?''

Tiernon smiled and dipped his fingers in the cool fountain.

''You know,'' Cataia said softly, ''I'm going to miss him. Besides you, he was the one person here I knew I could trust.''

''I know. It would be nice if we could manage to get another Councilor we could trust to take his seat. Do you have anyone in mind?''

''I was going to ask your advice.''

''Nia of Zyster'Rei or Sethen.''

Cataia thought quietly for a moment, lines wrinkling her brow as she considered the possibilities. ''Sethen, I think. Nia will be a Rei Mother, she won't be objective. Will you help me plan a small dinner party, Tiernon? The wine list is especially important in this case, I think, and do you think you could find some of that potent Nestezian brew?''

''For Your Highness, all things are possible.''

The sun had almost set and there was little light now, and what there was flamed bright-red and reflected through the water of the fountain. In the strange light, Cataia thought Tiernon looked almost out of another order of existence. The brilliant red ran across his face, highlighting the angular planes and filling the hollows with abrupt shadows. Softly he began the Third Chant to the Sun, and Cataia joined him. In moments the red light was swallowed by indigo, and they left the garden.

It would be a small party, Cataia decided when Tiernon had left her in the rooms, small and select, and Lathanor would have to come. Sethen, Tiernon and herself made up the remainder of the guest list. Bertham would be angry when he found out, but Cataia hoped he would find out too late, after Lathanor had signed the documents of appointment for her choice. For all she knew, Cataia mused, Bertham could already have managed to manipulate Lathanor and her efforts would be useless. This she banished from her mind, knowing that negative thoughts had a way of coming true. Instead, she concentrated on her plans for the party. She ruined three pages of paper writing Lathanor's invitation; even her calligraphy must be perfect.

"Oh, Your Highness, a party! I'm glad to see you a normal girl some of the time. A girl just come of age shouldn't be too serious, it's bad for the complexion," Valnera admonished. "But what an awful guest list. Why anyone would want Lathanor at a party I don't know, and Sethen is such a dour fellow. Successful, I'll admit, but not the kind of company a pretty young Princess should keep. Now Tiernon Bietehel is another matter, but my dearest bud, are you aware of his reputation? He's a rake, an absolute libertine. I'm sure he's never read the classics. And you've been spending entirely too much time with him. Exclusivity is not healthy. A girl your age should have several lovers. Three at least, and none too serious. It's important to know the qualities of many men before you select the father of your heir."

"Oh, Valnera, it's only matters of state. The Treasury is a mess, and Sethen might be useful."

"Cataia, I'm almost ready to give up on you. My own daughter studies medicine at Volenten, not the most frivolous thing to do, but even she knows how to enjoy life a little. Come. Tomorrow morning a cloth merchant is coming from Salsatee and we can choose some new brocades for you."

"Valnera, I trust your judgment. Order whatever you think appropriate."

"Honestly, Highness, I don't know how Lord Tiernon manages with you or you with him. He at least has a sense of pleasure. Maybe he'll teach you something." Exasperated, Valnera sighed and walked out.

Bertham had locked the door to his study, not a particularly unusual occurrence, so it caused no gossip. The manuscript lay on the low carved table in front of him, and he stroked the heavy leather, richly tooled and embossed with precious metals. It had been well worth the price he had paid to underwrite the expedition, he reflected, and the even higher price he had paid for Nikkot's death. Thank all the Powers that be that he wouldn't have to tolerate that dried-up old fool any longer!

He was pleased to realize that, with some concentration, he could read the blockish letters of the Eskenese language. The Rituals and System of Lechefrian had been carefully drawn on the first page, embellished with strange drawings and sigals whose use he could not determine.

The entirety of the knowledge of 'Kleppah was there. It had been well worth the tiresome hours spent with Nikkot to be able to read this.

He could not remember when he had first been convinced that the magia was not dead. Maybe it was when those cold-looking men in the orange katreisis had come and talked to him, and longer to his mother. Maybe it was simply the fact that if it had once existed it could not have been entirely wiped out. It might have been his strange dreams when he was still a boy in Tonea'Rei, when he knew that his will alone was sufficient for a thing to be done.

Old Nia, whom some had thought crazy, had taught him simples before he had come to Tsanos, the capital. All of them had worked. Queen Eltion had fallen in love with him, or at least enough in love that he had been able to kill her. Her brother Lathanor, who was basically a decent man, was easily kept out of the way, and lacing his wine with one of Nia's spells had served Bertham well. High commissions to the sellers of rare manuscripts had yielded more pieces to the puzzle, but nothing had ever been complete enough to use for his grand plan. Now it was possible, now that this particular manuscript had been found.

He fingered the pages lightly, lovingly, with an avid worship as he read the series of rituals. The System, he thought, was very good. It had been unbelievable that the unconnected rituals would yield results. They had to be part of a system to have any real value. Old Nia hadn't known any better; she had deserved what she had gotten. His Wheel tiles, and the knowledge of how to read them, came from the old woman. Old Nia. Old Nikkot. If only they had any idea of what he was using their knowledge for, they would certainly writhe in whatever hell was provided for the boring.

The first steps of the System were simple, almost too simple to be bothered with. Meditate on the sigal of Lechefrian every day for a long lunation, preferably after dark.

Tiernon had dismissed the servants for the night. He was sorry to have refused the young man's offer, but tonight there was no choice. It would have been more pleasant to lie in someone's arms and forget everything, but tonight other things had to be done. The young jeweler had been an engaging companion on several evenings past and would probably not come again. That, however, was not very important now. The bath had been set steaming, and if he delayed any longer it would be miserably cold.

Lighting incense, Tiernon passed it over the water, and then emptied several cruses of herbs and powders into the large tub. The water slowly turned a shade of pale yellow, and as he stepped into the hot bath he firmly closed the door in his mind to the cares of the day, the state and the young man who would not come again. The heat relaxed him, and he helped it, going over his body muscle by muscle, commanding each to lose its tension. He imagined the water drawing out all impurities, making his mind, his real self, undisturbed to walk the Planes. Any residue of lower thought, any moment's lack of concentration, could be fatal there. It was not yet time for him to leave the material world permanently. He let his thoughts scatter, float, drift, until nothing was left. He was unaware of the fact that the bathwater had turned tepid.

By rote, Tiernon moved from the bath through the corridor and found the catches behind the wall-rug. The panel sprang open and he entered an octagonal room painted black. It was bare save for a large black mirror at the far end and a central slab of stone, waist-high and just large enough for a man to lie down upon. There was also a small chest beside the door, which Tiernon opened to draw out the thin Orange robe, the robe of his Priesthood. The robe, the link belt, the circlet —each brought out another Tiernon, a Tiernon he had built since he had entered the Abbey. No longer was he in a state of being; he was aware of the magician who dwelled within. He anointed his hands and forehead, recalling the night of his Initiation, and lit the bronze oil lamps that rested on the altar.

Kneeling on the hard slab, Tiernon concentrated on the image in the dark glass, willing himself into it. There was a moment of darkness, a moment of disorientation, and the image in the mirror became the man and left an unoccupied body kneeling in the small temple. Then the image retreated to its own place.

The Orange Plane was a great clicking abacus occupied by beings that arrived as thought. Tiernon, a part-time denizen of the place, found it all familiar. He set out to search for Xchin, a Master on the Plane who might help him, might have some clues as to why Nikkot was dead and why Aken was involved. Something appeared before him, but Tiernon didn't have to look to know it was not Xchin.

Bitter laughter possessed the thing, chilling Tiernon as the insanity of that cold, humorless chuckle echoed around him, disturbing the unity of the place, breaking it up. The clarity of the colors around him muddied, and Tiernon realized that he was on the other side of the Plane. The thing, whatever it was, had drawn him through.

"Maybe I'll eat you, my little magician. Or maybe I'll let my minion do it for me. He is quite good, little magician, like you once were. How pleasant that meeting of old friends will be."

"No," Tiernon replied. Rapidly he built the images of the great abacus, the clear Orange Sea, the bright, shining colors that indicated the right side of the Plane.

"Not so simple, is it, little magician?" The thing laughed again, hideously.

Tiernon tried again to refocus, tried to bring back some shred of brightness; tried and failed. The stench grew around him, penetrating into the outermost reaches of the mirror-body.

"We'll have none of that. Now, now, it's not so uncomfortable, and we can have a little chat. I haven't seen you for a very long time, and it is so nice to catch up with old acquaintance. And you must admit, your vices haven't changed considerably. How boring." The thing reached out a filmy tentacle, encircling Tiernon's waist. "I can eliminate Bertham for you, if you wish. A simple task. No, I can tell, you don't need that. How about power?"

In a nauseating swirl of color, Tiernon found himself in the center of a great unconsuming fire that pulsated with raw energy.

"To use as you wish, my friend. Think of what you could do with it. Rule the world, gain knowledge, destroy your enemies. Power, pure and simple. Or maybe you would prefer to stay soft. Think of it, the power to feed all the hungry, to eliminate disease; does that appeal to you?"

The flame grew and intensified. Even charged with the vast energy now flowing through him, Tiernon felt strangely distant. His mind muddied and he began to pull away from the flame, from the form in front of him. Couldn't concentrate. Only the strongest force of habit, reinforced daily since childhood, prevented panic. Panic was sure death here in the Planes. Panic was final failure. There was nothing to fear. The words of his old Master at the Abbey ran through his head. "What is real in one place is illusion in another. Go to the place where it is illusion, and it cannot touch you. Evil can destroy you only if you permit it to. Illusion, illusion; it's all illusion." He had repeated it many times after Master Teordin. Illusion, illusion, it's all illusion.

It did not dissolve. The flames died in a sibilant hiss, but the thing that floated just before him had not changed, and the heavy murk still permeated the atmosphere.

"Illusion?" the thing screeched. "And is this an illusion?" It moved too rapidly to resist, a claw shot out from the film and raked his torso. Cold. It was very cold. He could see the soft puffs of pale energy-patterns leaving him. Life-stuff, going out, being absorbed by the smoky figure. The cold was restful. He relaxed and drifted. There were sounds far away, laughing sounds, and he wondered vaguely where they were coming from. No more strength to see. No more thinking. Thinking hurt. Just drift and sense the little puffs floating off. Some small remnant of consciousness told him that this was death, the real death, but he no longer cared. No panic. But where was Chevaina? Chevaina should be with him when he died. He remembered that much.

Cataia awoke suddenly with a start. Something was wrong, very wrong, and she quickly began to control her breathing, quieting her mind so that she could focus on the dilemma. Long count breathe in, quiet the mind, relax the body, hold the breath, concentrate on the feeling, breathe out long count. She could feel herself touching the Planes, long count in, and permitted herself to rest, letting the feeling, the call, draw her. Hold a count of four, there was confusion, rapid change, a barrier, and the call was strongest at the barrier, long count out.

There was no longer a need to count. The barrier was clean

and smooth, shaped like an egg. Cataia concentrated on the barrier, on its feel and shape, and then began to imagine the other side. The call was becoming weaker, but she forced herself to the barrier, to the other side. Glimmers now, the imagined inside was dark and quiet, the barrier not quite so warm or smooth. Detail by detail she built the image and in a sudden thrust it became real and she was inside. She saw a shadow and moved to it cautiously.

Were it possible to gasp on the Planes, Cataia would have. As it was, she halted a good distance away and watched. A strangely incandescent, filmy replica of Tiernon floated and spun lifelessly in the enclosure. There was no more call, no more feeling. She reached out to touch him, but the image decayed even further, as if her fingers were acid.

Gingerly she built a sheath for the frangible image, carefully modifying the energy to meet the almost nonexistent vibrations and protecting it from further fading. Now, if the body wasn't dead or too badly damaged, if the consciousness could be lured back to the body, and the image remained cohesive, it was perhaps possible that the Third Councilor wouldn't die. Cataia knew the chances were slim, knew that Tiernon had lost too much energy for her to be optimistic, but he couldn't be left here to bleed to the last drop. What had done this, she wondered, locking him away from the proper places of death?

Quickly, surely, she tethered the sheath to herself and started to pull the consciousness back down the line to the body, that thin, tenuous connection that still assured her he was in some way alive. Careful, pull, she thought, careful, slowly, slowly, no more trauma, gently, gently home. The colors around her changed gradually after she managed to take Tiernon through the barrier, fading from Orange to Silver as she followed the connecting thread. Here was safe territory, territory she knew well and had traveled frequently. Ever more carefully she guided, until the shapes and images of Tsanos became clear and they were all the way down, down to the roof of the Palace, down to Tiernon's hidden room.

His body was still kneeling before the mirror, and here Cataia could no longer lead. She pushed the image, trying to force it down the last few inches over the altar, but there was resistance. Some shred of consciousness must remain! Hopeful now, but confused, Cataia shoved again, still gentle and careful of her wounded advisor. Again there was resistance.

Puzzling, she thought, his body was not badly damaged.

There were three gashes on his chest, and blood, but the cuts were not deep enough to affect any of the organs and not too much blood had been lost. Then, suddenly, she remembered a story told by one of the Priestesses when she had studied healing.

Once an Adept had endured a serious fall and had left her body, sure that it would die, as any Adept would in a physical trauma. A physician from Volenten, however, had been present, and the body of the Priestess had been repaired as best as was possible, and would heal fully given time. The Priestess still refused to reenter her body, and one of the Healers had been called in. There was, the Healer had said, no reason to reenter from the Priestess's point of view. Non-Adepts didn't have this problem because they were afraid of what would happen to them when their bodies died, but Adepts are not particularly concerned about bodily death. So the Healer had flowers put around the woman's bed and had called her lover to hold the body, not the woman. The minimal energy of the flowers held the physical body together while the Priestess, wanting the attention her lover was giving the vacant body, reentered it. At the time, Cataia thought it was a neat trick.

She would have to return here, to this room, in her body. Realizing that she didn't know where the room was, she exited by the door, noting its locking mechanism and placement in the apartments before she raced to her own body.

Throwing a katreisi over herself, Cataia cursed the fact that she couldn't move as quickly here as she could on the Planes. She ran through the corridors, ignoring the shocked stares of those still wandering the Palace at this late hour. The groggy servant who opened the door to Tiernon's apartments looked at her inquisitively, but she ordered him brusquely to leave her alone. Within seconds she was in the miniature temple, and there she stopped, confused.

In the Healer's story there had been some emotional link to call the Priestess back. Here she could not call anyone, even if there were someone her advisor cared about. It was definitely time to employ the next-best rule.

Next best. Well, Cataia surmised, she would have to do as a lure. Simply being loving wouldn't be enough to draw Tiernon back; he was used to admiration, and besides, he needed physical care. Now her mind was brimming. Nursing was perfect. What could be a better lure than a Crown Princess taking care of him; surely it would appeal to his pride. Besides, maybe an Adept taking care of the body would convince him that it was important to get back into it.

She laid him on the altar, casting her eyes around the room for some substitute bandages. Nothing. Without a second thought she began tearing strips from her katreisi, thanking both Valnera for making sure it was clean and herself for choosing a soft, simple fabric.

She spoke aloud as she worked, hoping desperately that some consciousness remained to speak to, to hear her. "Please come back, Tiernon, please. I need you. I need your help. You can't help like this, please. I need you here, with me."

Suddenly she became shy. She realized there was more, much more, that she wanted to say and didn't want to say. Frightened and lonely, she didn't notice the tears that were gathering in her eyes. His rhythmic six-count breathing frightened her. He was alive, but it was the breathing of the trance.

"Why don't you come back? Your work isn't done, it can't be done, mine isn't done, don't leave me alone. Am I so terrible? Am I so ugly? Why don't you want to come back?"

She began to massage him gently, slowly bringing the circulation back to his hands and legs. Running her hands over the long corded muscles, now frozen with abandonment, she let the emotion grow until it engulfed her. She wanted him. She permitted herself to feel the fine smoothness of his skin, the hardness underneath, and imagined him back. She admired the proportions, the narrow hips and the long fingers, which she chafed to bring back the warmth. She let herself want him, that body glowing softly golden in the oil light; nothing else mattered. Nothing else existed. Emotion overwhelmed her, defined her, until she could no longer contain it and a long, heaving sob broke from her throat. Crying the hard, gasping way that would leave her with a headache the next day, Cataia continued her massage, coaxing life into the cold limbs. "Please, please, for me."

There was a shudder and a groan, and at this sign Cataia cried even harder, from relief. He had returned.

She would have to get him back to his sleeping rug somehow before sending for a doctor. Cataia was exhausted, and Tiernon far heavier than anything she had ever tried to lift. It would be impossible to carry him. It had been hard enough to lower him to the floor. Abandoning the better grip under his arms for fear it would open his wounds, she grabbed him by the ankles and dragged him to the deep pile of his sleeping rug.

Pausing for a moment to catch her breath, Cataia walked slowly through the two large rooms separating them from the sleeping servant. He was awakened a second time and ordered to fetch Chervan rei Batter, physician to the Aandev. The servant stalked away, muttering something about crazy nobles and physicians who didn't like to be gotten up in the middle of the night.

Cataia returned to Tiernon, wondering what she would say to the doctor. This would have to be kept quiet, and while Chervan was a model of discretion, it might occur to him that there was some crime involved that ought to be reported. And here she was right in the middle of what appeared to be an assassination attempt. Oh, would Bertham just love that. Crown Princess or no Crown Princess, Bertham could not have created a better way to start her down the road to the pyre if he had planned it himself. Her position was clearly incriminating if the evidence were twisted, as it had been in her mother's case. Turning away from such thoughts, it struck her that she ought to remove Tiernon's robe before the doctor arrived. It was difficult to remove the garment without moving Tiernon, and Cataia resorted to her knife again. She hoped he had not been wearing his Initiation robe, or he might not quite forgive her for cutting it to shreds. Tired and working too quickly, she cut herself in the process.

Having done what she could for Tiernon, Cataia began to suck the small cut on her hand. A cut. He was cut. Attacked. An idea began to form and Cataia acted. There was going to be talk all right. She only hoped there would still be enough time to set the scene before Chervan arrived.

No one would question her spending the night with Tiernon. Indeed, most of the Palace believed she did, so it would not look out of place. Please forgive me, she thought as she smashed one of the delicately carved window insets. Two small bronze statues were dropped carefully on the floor. She found an enamel vase of kyrili and carefully dumped it over, hoping that the water would not stain, and that the wet area looked authentic. Gingerly she tipped over the fine lacquer table, praying it wouldn't be scratched. She threw open the two trunks in the room and artfully strewed clothing across the floor. She turned back and surveyed her work. If no one bothered to notice that nothing was badly damaged, it was quite believable that a fight had taken place here.

Now for the final touch of authenticity. Gritting her teeth, Cataia took her knife and inflicted a small wound on her thigh. By the time Chervan arrived, Cataia was seated in the middle of a shredded cushion, trembling. In the dark, she couldn't see if it had been one of the finer ones she had shredded; if it was, Tiernon might well be furious in the morning. She pressed her leg, now bleeding convincingly, and wondered if she could get Bertham blamed for the apparent attempted assassination.

"You were lucky, Your Highness. If anything, this assassin was certainly incompetent. The wounds are not deep, not deep at all, more like a claw than a knife. Did you see the face? Could you recognize your assailant?"

Cataia shook her head. Tiernon was sleeping now, naturally, and he was as comfortable as the doctor could make him. Cataia sported two very neat professional bandages, feeling half-guilty about receiving such concerned care for her self-inflicted injuries.

"May I assist you back to your apartments?" the doctor asked. "Doubtless, both of you will rest better alone tonight, and rest is what you need."

Nodding wearily, Cataia leaned on Chervan and pulled the indigo Bietehel katreisi closer around her body. Hot as the day would be, these predawn hours boasted a stunning chill, and the wide halls and large Palace rooms were drafty. She wanted to sleep. She wanted the total oblivion that would move the memory of the last few hours from their current horror to unreal dream. She wasn't even aware of Valnera spreading a thick quilt over her shivering form, and if Chervan had said anything more, she would never remember it.

❧THREE

"OH, MY LITTLE PRINCESS, weren't you frightened to death? A Nestezian spy, right there in the room. Of course, someone said that one of the servants beat off the attack, but I corrected him." Valnera was talking faster than she was preparing Cataia's bath, and Cataia was restless. She hadn't slept enough, and what sleep she had gotten hadn't been restful.

"What else are they saying down in the kitchen?" Cataia asked, more because she knew that Valnera wouldn't stop talking than because she wanted to know servants' gossip.

"Well, someone said that Bertham, our very own First Councilor, said that the Nestezians ought to be punished, that's what."

"Oh?" Cataia's head jerked up.

"Oh, yes. First Nikkot, and now you, or Lord Tiernon, it doesn't really matter to those savages, does it. Well, Bertham thinks we ought to go in there and clean them out, and after what they did to Lord Nikkot, too."

"What do you know about the Nestezians?" Cataia asked cautiously.

"Only what everyone knows, Lady. That they're a bunch of

36

bloodthirsty, unwashed savages who can't abide civilized people, that's what." Valnera said this with special emphasis as she tested the bathwater.

Cataia stepped into the bath and let the warm water caress her and the scent of the soap sink into her skin. The soap stung a little where she had cut herself, but she ignored it. Her plan had worked, and all too well, it seemed. She cursed under her breath. She had never meant Bertham to use it to his advantage, yet she knew Valnera's attitude was completely normal.

Slowly, she let her thoughts wander back to Tiernon. She had taken a chance last night, a terrible chance, and had set something in motion that could not be set back. But she couldn't watch him die like that, not the death of the spirit where his innermost self would have evaporated. Perhaps he would awaken normally this morning, with only the unimportant pain of the clawing; but Cataia doubted it.

She did wonder what had attacked Tiernon, and why. She could almost hear Tiernon's voice saying, "Aken is interested." This attack would certainly be the kind of thing that Aken kept watch for. Too many threads and not enough patterns.

For the first time in her life, Cataia resented Aken. They knew and they weren't telling. Always she had thought of Aken as the protector. It was rarely discussed, this seventh Order that had no Abbey on Dier Street and trained no novices, that remained aloof in isolation on some rocky island in the Western Sea that no one but those of Aken could find. They drew their members from the other six Orders, and their specific task was to guard against 'Kleppah until the time came when it would be destroyed. They were royalty among the Adepti, those shadowy magicians of Aken, and only their Order had a name and no color.

There was another side too, she realized. Otherwise, why would Tiernon have been lured or forced behind the barricade? He had not been helped or defended, even though the hand of 'Kleppah was obvious. Aken saw them all as expendable, Cataia thought. All expendable in the most horrible terms, terms that she could barely bring herself to think about. The death of a body was one thing, but the evaporation of a self was quite another.

Suddenly she wondered about Tiernon. He couldn't know of her plot to pass off the attack as an attemped assassination attempt. She would have to trust his intelligence and ability to improvise, but she was worried. Besides, he should spend most of the day sleeping.

Thinking that, it added to her surprise when, after being dressed by Valnera and stepping into the reception room, she found him lounging on her second-fattest cushion.

"I would rise and greet you properly if I were able, Highness," he began. "But it isn't necessary to pretend here. I have heard that we were attacked by Nestezians last night. I have been asked numerous questions by the Guard about what my assailant looked like. One of the guards told me that they thought it might be the same Nestezian group that killed Nikkot. May I request a favor?"

Cataia inclined her head.

"Would you tell me what happened last night?"

"Would you tell me?" she asked. "Why are you here and not asleep? You were in terrible shape when I found you."

"Always at your command," he said, making a formal gesture of respect, "though I would be fascinated to hear the rest of the story."

Cataia gave in. At the end of the recitations, Tiernon leaned back against the wall and closed his eyes as his features contorted momentarily with pain. Then he broke into a sudden smile. "Well, I'm just glad it wasn't my Initiation robe that got shredded."

"This still does not explain what you are doing up when you should be resting. No one would question the victim of such an attack being unable to move around the next day."

"I beg to differ. It would be inconvenient if certain parties were to know how badly I was hurt," he said.

"It would be rather inconvenient for me if you got some massive infection or bled yourself to death. But I suppose that never occurred to you."

"Of course it has and I shall do neither," he said glibly.

"Stop talking like a courtier."

"I am a courtier."

"There is something you aren't telling me," she said softly. "I would prefer to hear it now. I hate surprises."

"Highness, my apologies. I should tell you that Chervan Batter has done a wonderful job on me, and the wounds look far worse than they are. This attack is, as you've no doubt surmised by now, tied in with Aken and something else. I'm not sure what, but displaying weakness at this time to your enemies could well be dangerous. Besides"—he grinned—"if you must know, I didn't walk. There is a carry-chair outside in the hall, if you want to look. I don't believe in taking chances."

"Not good enough, Tiernon," Cataia said quietly. "I'll accept it for now. I don't want to strain you."

"No strain. I never find it difficult to talk to a beautiful woman, especially after she saves my life."

Cataia remained silent for a moment. Something in what he said, light as it was, had stirred a suspicion. "Wait. It was too easy. Whatever attacked you just let me drag you back. No real complications, except from you."

"What do you mean it was too easy?"

"Tiernon, if you don't relax I can't tell you anything. All right. Why was it so easy for me to slip behind the barrier? Why didn't this thing wait around to finish you off? Why could I pull you through the barrier? The whole thing was too easy, and that bothers me."

"Why should it?" he asked, smiling. "Did you want it to be harder?"

Cataia stared at him with unabashed exasperation. "You're totally useless."

"I was taught that making light of difficulties was the best way to assimilate them, and the mark of good humor besides. There is also the fact that, much as I am worried, I don't like exaggeration."

"Will you be coming to my dinner tonight and playing the noble martyr, or will you be sensible and rest?" she demanded.

"Being sensible, Highness, is something of which I am never accused, and I could not resist playing the noble martyr in front of our beloved monarch. It may play into our hands. How could he refuse me?" Tiernon's voice became serious. "I also think I'll be needed. Lathanor may be an irresponsible drunk, but he isn't stupid, and this will have to be handled gently."

"I believe I am capable of that, thank you."

"You take offense too quickly. I simply meant it would be easier to handle him with two of us. Atore, please be careful. Lose your temper in front of me and I can forget anything, but there are others who don't seem to have that type of memory. So for your own safety, please stay calm."

Carefully controlling her features, furious at his presumption—temper, indeed!—Cataia managed to speak smoothly. She'd show him. "Yes, thank you. If you are going to be in any condition to assist in our plan for the appointment of Sethen tonight, you'd best get some rest. Already you look tired. Please?"

It pained her to see the way he moved, so different from his normal fluid grace, as he rose and braced against the wall. Still, it was a great relief not to have to pull off the delicate manipulations necessary to secure Sethen's appointment alone; but as Tiernon walked to the door she could see that his visit had been sheer idiocy.

"Now, now, my Princess, my beauty, you must sleep a little before it is time to prepare for your guests. There's hot milk out on the balcony just waiting to keep away the bad dreams while I change your quilt, and then I'll rub your back."

Cataia pressed Valnera's hand gratefully and went out to the balcony. Glancing back to make sure that Valnera was safely out of sight, Cataia dumped the cup of hot milk over the ledge. She hated hot milk, and even the best of intentions could not induce her to drink the stuff. Valnera, however, managed to provide a glass every evening, and while the Princess abhorred the superstition she appreciated the thoughtfulness of the action.

Valnera wakened Cataia in plenty of time to prepare for the evening, although the older woman looked vaguely distressed. "I don't know why you wouldn't let me take care of things for you so you could sleep longer. You are hurt too, you know."

Cataia only smiled gently. There were other arts, learned at the Abbey, that could influence a man's mind as much as alcohol. Color, a musical arrangement, light incense in just the right balance could be a subtle influence on Lathanor's thinking, and these skills she dared not leave to anyone else's possibly muddled interpretations.

It was not magic, although some would call it that, but simply the influence of environment. The pale-blue and sea-green of the hangings had been carefully orchestrated when she had moved in to soothe and to aid the digestion. The patterns were very subtle, shading one into the other without firm definition, a flowing of color that gave the room the air of being deep under water. The cushions were a deep dull-green and the low central table of Nestezian lacquerwork was a rich, satisfying cinnabar with dully glowing bronze inlays. All blended together to create a feeling of ease and opulence without overwhelming.

The musicians, having been contracted for and given the appropriate music when the plan was first decided, were not on Cataia's mind, but the incense definitely was. Of all the weapons in tonight's arsenal, scent could tip the scales of the battle. Nothing astringent to awaken the mind, or bitter for awareness, or deeply spiced and sensual, it would have to be formulated to relax her guests and render them totally pliant, totally open. A woods scent, with tones of green things and dark earth and a few half hints of flowers—that would be correct. From an abundant collection of little jars and boxes she sniffed and mixed and selected with great concentration until she was certain that the results would produce the desired effect.

She dressed carefully in her simplest garments, choosing the soft, gathered pants that were informal, not the stiff knife-pleated design more proper for Court. The pale rose silk of her outfit gave her a young, flushed look and was quite definitely not Aandev-white. Over it all she arranged a full-cut katreisi of soft pink bordered with deep-green.

She studied herself critically in the mirror, and approved. She looked very young, very innocent, and not at all the Aandev heir with a plot of her own. Lathanor must never suspect, must not even think about the documents she hoped so strongly he would sign and not think to read. Then it was time to wait for her guests' arrival.

Sethen appeared first, just as the water-clock indicated the correct hour, and Tiernon came in just behind him. Lathanor was late, as fitted his rank. They all bowed to the King Regent, and Cataia led them into the dining room. Out on the balcony, the musicians were playing a soft, elaborate moon-song.

Covered dishes had been placed on the table. Tiernon had told her that servants were unwelcome in the late night suppers that dominated Court life. Cataia served Lathanor as Tiernon poured the wine. Then the others served themselves.

"I am glad to see you well," Lathanor said, and Cataia bowed her head. "I've heard you were attacked by Nestezians, and some of us are of the opinion that they ought to be disciplined."

"Thank you for your concern, sir," Cataia said in a guileless voice. Tiernon poured Lathanor another glass as Cataia held his attention. "It was nothing of any importance, and you can see that neither of us was seriously harmed. I should hate Your Majesty to be troubled on our account."

"But I am troubled. The Nestezians have been getting too bold lately. And the harvest from the eastern Reis, Aandev'Rei among them, will not be good. This is the third bad year in the east. The peasants say they are under some kind of curse."

"Oh?" Cataia was all innocence. Tiernon changed glasses and wines.

Lathanor smiled softly, and Cataia could read the mild intelligence there. "Of course the Nestezians aren't responsible for the bad weather, or the blights. But there isn't going to be very much food this year, and the stores are low. The Nestezi will provide some diversion. It is better that they blame the desert folk than the Aandev."

Cataia nodded, trying to assimilate what he was saying.

"I must ask your opinion of this wine, Majesty; do you think it appropriate for your birthday celebration? It may still be too young, of course, and I wouldn't wish to offend your palate. On the other hand, the Tersoneat does lack some body, and of course I have saved the best for last, although it might seem bold of me to recommend the vintages of my own Rei. There is a vintage of Bietehel pressing that may be more to your taste, and with due modesty I must say that our climate is unusually ideal for cultivation."

Lathanor drank from the proffered glass, drained it and then held it out for more. Cataia had lost count, but Lathanor's coordination seemed just a bit off. Tiernon was keeping him supplied so smoothly that he didn't seem to notice. Cataia was grateful that he had come; she couldn't have handled Lathanor as well.

"And Sethen, what brings you to Court? I thought you were only interested in the money you could squeeze from Salsatee."

"Majesty, I had hoped to be of some service to you in the matter of the Treasury," Sethen said, remembering to keep his voice light and congenial. He had been carefully coached by Tiernon prior to arriving, Cataia knew. Tiernon had not had time to tell her what kind of pupil Sethen had been, but it seemed that he would manage.

"I don't want to mention that matter," Lathanor said, "or it will ruin this lovely wine."

"Oh, but cousin," Cataia jumped in, ignoring Tiernon glowering at her, "the matter need not be disturbing. Sethen has a talent for turning sand into jewels and bare rocks into money, and you'd never need think about the Treasury again."

Lathanor gave Cataia a stony glance.

Tiernon immediately picked up his own thread. "We were sorry that your grief at Nikkot's death prevented you from joining us earlier. Here, will you try some of our Bietehel red? I would truly appreciate an honest opinion, as the softness in the flavor is not pleasing to everyone."

"It's so upsetting. No one could ever replace Nikkot," Cataia moaned quietly. "I do not envy the terrible task of naming his successor."

"I have given thought to the matter," Lathanor said gravely, his words barely slurred. "I have been considering Teth rei Maddigore."

"A most wise decision, Majesty," said Tiernon. "He's such a pleasant person, and quite an able warrior."

Cataia bit back her words as Tiernon gestured with his left hand across the wine cup. Tiernon knew the Court far better than she did, and Lathanor as well. Cataia decided that she had no choice but to trust him.

"Quite," Lathanor said. "An able warrior. Tiernon, I approve of your Rei's wine greatly. I would taste it again."

Tiernon poured, his face a mask. Cataia studied him against the King, and she had to admit she was confused. It seemed as if Tiernon were giving in already, just when Lathanor was getting really drunk. He was changing the script on her, and she didn't like it.

"Cousin, would you like some of the liqueur now? And while you are here, after you have given us your opinion of the Salsatean brew, there's a minor document I'd like you to look over," Cataia said, earning a hard stare from Tiernon.

"Not more legal documents, Cataia, please, not tonight." Lathanor's voice had an edge of command to it still. "No, no documents tonight. Come, let's have some more and drink to good fellowship and forget our worries."

It was over, she knew that now. All the careful planning, all her hopes, were dashed for the time being. Inwardly she seethed at Tiernon, who hadn't backed her up according to plan.

Sethen knew that it was over too, although he hadn't really

had hopes. "With your permission, I have noticed that the hour is quite late. I am very tired, and as I must deal during business hours, I beg your permission to retire."

"Very well," Lathanor said graciously. "One day I would like to hear about your plans for the Treasury."

Sethen left, and Lathanor turned to Cataia. "Cousin, ask the musicians for some hunting songs. Let's pretend that we are hunting in the mountains, and not in this stiflingly hot city in the summer."

Cataia nodded miserably and they sang. They sang until the slightest early chill wafted in through the carved windows.

"It is time for me to go," Lathanor said lazily. "There is early Court tomorrow. I thank you, cousin, for your entertainment, and you, Tiernon, for your wine." With that he rose unsteadily, Cataia and Tiernon on each side of him. Gently they kept him upright until he was settled into the carry-chair waiting in the corridor, and bowed him on his way.

"What were you doing?" Cataia demanded once she and Tiernon were back in the privacy of her reception room.

Tiernon seemed to study her carefully. "Didn't you notice? I have observed him for a long time, and I had suspected this."

"Would you tell me what you're talking about?"

"Cataia," Tiernon said gently, his face looking haggard, "it isn't the alcohol. He drinks, yes, but being drunk alone wouldn't sway him. Did you notice his energy-net, or were you watching? There was a seal of some sort there."

"What do you mean?" Cataia asked, too tired to try to solve Tiernon's riddles.

"Drink alone cannot make a man go against his true being. It can barely nudge him, the way Lathanor's been nudged. Hypnosis could at least begin this process. Binding someone magically could complete it."

Cataia stared at Tiernon with shock. "Only an Adept could do that. And no Adept would. We were taught only as self-defense."

Tiernon nodded sadly. "I told you that Aken was involved. And if Aken is involved, we also know that the other side must be involved as well. We couldn't have gotten Lathanor to do what we wanted, but we gained other information, just as valuable."

"But I don't understand about Teth," Cataia said, yawning. "He's young, and he's never shown any sign of being one of Bertham's trained ferri."

"That's what we've learned."

Cataia's eyes grew wide. "So whoever is doing this mind-bending is confident that Teth can be bent later. And then it's perfect. He's pleasant enough, but he doesn't seem to have a lot of character."

Tiernon nodded. "Now, if we're going to be at Court tomorrow, we'd better get some sleep."

Full Court, Cataia thought, was a useless waste of time. Unlike Council meetings, where final policies were argued over and finally made, or the late private suppers of various factional groups, this formal display was simply the public form of announcement. Nothing could be done, not with all the protocols of who could speak and when.

First, Ayt started with the usual blessing, and then Jerwyn, chosen chief lector because of his strong voice, said, "Anyone with business to bring before the Court of the King Regent, take notice. His Majesty is open to petition."

Cataia noticed that several people in the back squirmed. Theoretically, the Court was open to all the nobility, but few Reis had the resources to keep a representative in Tsanos fulltime. Several younger daughters watched with interest, but they knew better than to speak. If any petition was to be brought, it would be through a Rei Mother herself, or her eldest daughter. These younger ones were here simply to learn protocols. Cataia remembered when she had sat in the back, before she had gone to the Abbey. Then the glitter of the room itself, with its varicolored hangings and brilliantly painted ceiling, the sonorous voices and the fine phrases had been enough.

Jerwyn repeated his call three times, and there was no answer. Cataia wondered how long it had been since that traditional statement was answered. Surely no one would bring up business that had not been thoroughly discussed in Council. That was what the Council was for.

Lathanor nodded to Jerwyn and handed him several large documents. "A representative of Hasmra fi Cleindelle, Comfres'Rei."

An older man without the noble's katreisi came forward, kissed Lathanor's hand and raised it to his forehead. "The Aandev grant you charter to the unsettled territory ten marches from the charter town of Hasmra fi Cleindelle,'' Lathanor said. Jerwyn handed the charter to what must have been the headman of the town, who pressed the King's hand to his forehead once again and returned to his place.

Cataia watched, keeping her face as still as stone. Two or three grants like that followed, all of them decided, she was sure, before she had come to Court. None of them dealt with contests between Reis, but jurisdiction that Reis themselves should hold. The grant for that town, for example, Cataia thought, should have come from Isna Rei Mother. No matter that Comfres was Minor. Isna still held rights there. The more she thought about it, the more Cataia was sure that the Rei Mothers must have some opinions about the Aandev, and she made a note to ask Tiernon about it later. Old Nikkot had told her to make a bid. She had few enough allies here at Court, but if the Rei Mothers had found too much of their power eroded . . .

Lost in her reverie, Cataia didn't notice the sudden hush in the large audience hall, the almost palpable tremor of excitement. The faces of the Council members in the front row had changed from polite boredom to anticipation. When Lathanor stood, Cataia snapped back into the scene around her.

''. . . therefore, with great pleasure, we appoint our honored servant Teth lar Tieri rei Maddigore to our most illustrious Council of Advisors, may the Stars guide him.''

Teth, looking innocently surprised, came forward, flanked by Ayt and Bertham. Yes, the High Priestess and the First Councilor had to be the legal witnesses.

''Is there anyone present who has knowledge that Teth lar Tieri rei Maddigore is unfit to serve?'' Jerwyn cried out. No voices were raised. Cataia knew the procedure. Now Jerwyn asked who would speak for the Maddigorean, and both Bertham and Ayt said that they would stand witness.

Boredom fought with rage in Cataia. It had all been prepared well in advance. They had been too late last night in any case, and she wondered how and when Bertham had gotten to Lathanor since his return from hunting.

Teth's right hand covered a large diamond that Lathanor held, called the ''Stone of Ronarian.'' Supposedly, the leader of the Seven who had founded Avriaten after the Great War had used the stone as a pledge, and Cataia understood why an Adept would do so. It magnified fields, and helped the magician check the honesty of the speaker. Strange, that the outward forms of the magia were still here when all the substance was gone. And she knew that were she holding that diamond, she would be able to use it to intertwine her own field with the speaker's, locking that person to the truth. But there was no flicker of power from Lathanor and Teth.

". . . to speak of what I know, and to learn of what I do not. And the whole of this land, from the mountains to the seas, shall be to me as my own home. So do I pledge to the Aandev, so do I pledge to the Stars."

It was over. Still flanked by Ayt and Bertham, Teth turned to the assembly, who gave him a polite half bow in acknowledgment. It was over. Cataia managed to smile and nod graciously as Teth took his seat on the empty cushion among the Council, as servants slipped by like ghosts preparing the feast that would mark the appointment.

Lathanor, for all he might be a drunk, was not a dupe. The evening before had shown that all too clearly to Cataia, and she wondered if Bertham really could have bound him as Tiernon had postulated. Surely it wasn't the wine. And while Teth was a reasonable choice, he was by no means the best that Bertham could have made, and Bertham always made the best choices for himself. Therefore, there was something about Teth that no one knew, or Bertham was playing his tiles very dangerously.

Cataia noticed that Teth, placed between Bertham and Lathanor for the feasting, was thoroughly enjoying the event, his lightheartedness not entirely concealed by his grave demeanor.

On her right, Tiernon hadn't said a word. Carefully arranged, he ate delicately with the tips of his fingers and drank as though the wine did not quite meet his expectations. His eyes, however, were dull and his face totally unanimated.

On her left, Cataia caught a few words from the rapid, quiet conversation among Lathanor, Bertham and Teth. She was sure she had heard some reference to the Nestezi, and she groaned inwardly. Already it was beginning.

Suddenly she found herself looking straight into Bertham's eyes. The expression on his sharp-featured face showed clearly that he knew she had been listening and that it would be better for her to be silent.

For all the heat and wine and spices in the food, Cataia felt cold and vaguely ill. She wanted to remove herself from this tightly packed table of conspirators. She wanted to be alone in her own apartments where the air seemed fresher and there was quiet. She needed to think and to rest.

Here in the great audience chamber, hung with its amber kyrili-patterned garden rugs, its deep pile cushions and highly burnished bronze tables inlaid with imported wood, here where the air mixed the scents of rich perfumes and varieties of rare spices and the grease of roasted meat, she felt an overwhelming need for the order and cleanliness of the Abbey. Cataia was homesick, tired of the confusion of the Court. She wanted to return to the silent meals, the long meditations, the cool and soothing pastels and the fountain in the courtyard. They seemed like a dream of perfection which swiftly grew to a need. Home, where there was rest and laughter and simplicity. Home, where there was Mother Daniessa who could help solve any problem, Dacia and Edryn who scolded and made you eat boiled torrigon. Even the boiled torrigon seemed preferable to this feast which lacked no delicacy conceived of by the culinary mind.

Then Cataia locked the homesickness away. There was a meeting with the Weaver's Guildmaster that afternoon, she reminded herself firmly, and the audit of the Reis to finish before begging the Salsateans for another loan. A review of the Palace Guard followed tomorrow along with an audience with the Council of Merchants. No, there was no way home yet.

Tiernon barely managed to get back to his apartments before he collapsed. Physically it had been far too strenuous, though necessary. He had not doubted that Lathanor would appoint Teth at the Court, although he had forgotten just how long the appointment meal could go on; and though the wounds weren't deep they were painful. He lay back on his sleeping rug, breathing heavily from exhaustion. The weakness was overwhelming, and for a moment the room spun violently before he could catch the corners and settle things down.

He hated this weakness, and wondered for the tenth time that morning why it was so bad. It was far more than merely physical. He had been attacked. Certainly the entity had drained off more than he could spare, but by now there ought to be some recovery, a regaining of strength in the past two days. Except for the times with Cataia and the public Court that morning, he had remained abed since the attack, but even the rest had not seemed to help.

Then, through the pain and weariness, the answer started to come. Whatever had attacked him had tied him. Perhaps he was never meant to die, as Cataia suspected, but to be forced as Lathanor was being forced. Ancient, the Thing had seemed, referring to an old bargain, a bargain he had once accepted.

Why was he so weak? The bargain, he had said no this time, he had said no, but the thing had drawn his energy, his blood, and had bonded him someplace in his mind that he could not discern. And there it was still fighting him, offering and pushing and wearing him down.

A slow revulsion grew in Tiernon, revulsion and fear. It was already within him, and there was no way he could break the link, not in his present condition. Nor could he ask Cataia to do it for him, even if he would consider such a request.

There was one place he knew, sealed, in the ancient city of Aandev'Rei. It was the retreat house, mentioned only briefly at the Abbey, which was sealed from all influences. There he could learn to be free again, but it was six days' ride, and he could barely walk.

Still, the understanding and the possibility of hope strengthened him, and he managed to write a quick note to Father Prethed at the Orange Abbey asking permission to go.

Bertham's rooms were glowing from an attractive collection of oil lamps as he hosted a very private late party to celebrate Teth's appointment. Pale-ivory cushions glowed almost golden in the soft light against the very deepest amber-colored hangings. Amber, the color only great wealth could buy, was the main theme of the room, shades ranging from the almost-white to yellow so deep that one could feel the earth in the tones. The lamps and the table were bronze, gleaming dully in this dark room, and the deep-red patterns seemed to move across the floor rug in the glinting light.

The party was very private indeed, for Teth and Lathanor were the only guests. Even the servants had been dismissed until the party was over.

"You must show him, Bertham. It's really very amusing," Lathanor said.

"No," Bertham demurred. "I'm not sure. It takes a great deal of trust."

"I'd trust you with my life!" Teth exclaimed. Bertham looked him over carefully. The young cub! His mop of blond hair indicated many generations of inbreeding with the desert tribes, and it fell wildly out of the narrow ribbon that should have held it at his shoulders. Not at all sophisticated and young, very young, but Lathanor liked a young Council, and Teth's youth served Bertham very well. Open, honest, a little brash, he reminded Bertham of Lathanor years ago when they drank down on the wharves.

He had been planning this, but not quite so soon, and certainly not with a witness. Still, it might be useful to appear to have been forced by the King; it relieved him of unwanted responsibility.

"If you are certain," Bertham said dryly. "As you know, the Seven who bound 'Kleppah believed that the soul has lived before on this earth. Although this is not taught openly in the Temple of the Stars, the Priesthood still instructs the few. The Councilor High Priestess Ayt might be willing to discuss this in depth with you, but you may be sure that you are not violating orthodoxy in this little experiment."

"And what is the experiment?" Teth asked eagerly.

Lathanor closed his eyes, bored by the long explanations, but Bertham kept on. "Sometimes it is possible to recover your past lives by means of a technique used by the Star Priesthood and also some of the doctors of Volenten. The procedure is simple. You simply lie down and think as I tell you. Bit by bit we go deep back into your life."

"Is it dangerous?"

"It is not dangerous," Lathanor interrupted. "I myself have done this experiment, although we didn't get very good results."

Bertham smiled, remembering the first step in taking Lathanor's will. It was so very simple, given Lathanor's trust, and now it barely took a thought to control the actions that had grave effects on the country. Still, he hesitated, considering. It was not good policy to use the technique on too many. Some were just resistant; others would be suspicious. And there were few on whom the entire bonding process would work. Bertham had been rather sure that Teth was one of those. Pliant, amiable, with no strong religious background, Teth should be easy to hypnotize. From that point it would be fairly simple to bring Teth closer and closer, using the old simple he had used on Lathanor, until the final bonding could be achieved. Still, he did not like having Lathanor in the room. Even at this stage in the process, he didn't want any witnesses.

"All right, if it would please the King. But you must do exactly as I say."

Teth nodded eagerly and lay on the floor rug with a cushion under his head.

"Imagine that you are at the top of a staircase. See the stairs, the large flat grey stairs, going down. Down, down, down they go, down into the darkness, down into your past. They have numbers on them, bright-red numbers, and you are standing on step two hundred. Now step down. Go down the staircase. Don't think about anything but the numbers and my voice. Listen to me and go down to the next step. Let your mind rest. There is nothing to think about, nothing to worry about. Everything is fine. Go down to the next step."

Down and down Bertham guided Teth. It was the slow way, but effective. Later on it would take only three words, and after the final phase just a thought, but now he would have to be careful.

He need not have worried about Lathanor, though. Long before Teth had gotten to step one, Lathanor was in a deep trance. Bertham was satisfied.

The next morning, after a particularly infuriating session with the Salsatean Ambassador, Cataia found a small painting in the uniquely glowing colors of Dacia's palette and a note from Dacia.

"Oh, Cai," the note began in Dacia's artistic script, "please forgive me for not writing in all these moons, but with my Initiation, and Mother Jitrain ready to leave incarnation, I have been so busy. I am to remain here at the Abbey, teaching art to the novices and painting. Did you know that I have sold two of my paintings to some desert chief, or Si, or whatever they call them? Anyway, I have sent you a small portrait of Mother Jitrain, although she always despaired of you ever learning to draw. I thought it might be pleasant at the Palace to be reminded of us. Please come to visit if you can, although I know you have so much to do. I won't even yell if you interrupt me at work, and you know what a big promise that is. I miss you."

The miniature, like all Dacia's portraits, seemed almost alive with Mother Jitrain's spirit. Tears, running down her cheeks unnoticed, dropped and smeared the ink. Lucky Dacia, able to spend her days in her studio, relaxed with the whole Abbey. If only there were time to visit, to be able to talk freely and even enjoy a moment's hilarity. The tone of the note sounded as if Dacia hadn't changed in the least, and Cataia wondered how her old friend would react to the changes that four long moons of being Crown Princess had wrought. More than anything, though, Cataia was aware that no one since Dacia had called her Cai and laughed with her.

Then she realized that she dared not go—not too soon, at any rate. It would be too hard, to be back and not belong, to bring the stench of manipulations and plots and decadence into the atmosphere of the Abbey. Dacia would probably laugh when she learned that Cataia hadn't even had one lover yet, though she had considered several, and would tell her that she wasn't working hard enough. And Dacia would roll her eyes at the Court garb and draw a funny cartoon, and then, with great drama, extract two half-stale, paint-stained seed pastries which always tasted better than they did in the refectory minus the paint. For as long as Cataia had known her, Dacia had always had an unending supply of red, blue or green seed pastries. And then the Palace would be worse.

Dacia wouldn't understand, anyway. Dacia had never understood things that weren't beautiful and well ordered.

Perhaps, Cataia thought, she would get used to it in time. Perhaps in a few long moons she would be ready to spend an afternoon visiting, if the Council settled down and the harvest was good and the Treasury didn't go bankrupt.

"Oh, my poor Princess, don't cry. I'll get you some nice ripe fruit. You'll ruin your pants, please don't cry. Besides, Lord Tiernon is here, just waiting for you in the public room, and you don't want him to see you with your eyes all red."

Cataia snuffled and wiped her face with the edge of her robe. Valnera patted her on the shoulder, and Cataia went to the largest room of her suite.

Tiernon stood near one of the crimson-glazed pillars. Against the deep color of his katreisi, his face seemed paler than it should have, Cataia reflected. But she saw that his expression was cool, distant, as if he were already beyond her and the Palace.

He bowed to her almost perfunctorily. "Highness, with all due regard, I am here to inform you that I will be leaving Tsanos within the hour."

Cataia was frozen with shock. "You're in no condition to travel. Where are you going? Why? What's the need? You're still too weak after that attack."

Tiernon's face was a mask, closed to her, and she could read nothing.

"I'm afraid that I'm not at liberty to disclose that at this time," he replied evenly.

"So why did you come here at all?" Cataia demanded, her anger rising, blood coloring her cheeks.

"Duty demands that I inform you. Have I your leave to go?"

"Certainly. Please. Leave. I can't stop you," she said, her voice dripping sarcasm. She wanted to throw something at him, something to make him stay. It surprised her all the more when he simply bowed and withdrew, accepting her words at face value. It took her more than a moment to recover from the surprise, and by the time she heaved a cushion at the carved door, it was as if he had never been there. Cataia collapsed sobbing in the middle of the floor.

"Oh, my poor beauty," Valnera said softly, running in when she heard Cataia's heaves. "You should never trust a man. Who ever taught you anything? They're all weak and fickle and rotten as a geri in autumn."

Cataia pulled away from Valnera. She didn't want sympathy now, not when her anger was high. "So, he doesn't think he needs to tell me where he's going or for how long. Cataia can just stay in the hot city with fourteen factions and no Treasury and no harvest in, but Tiernon has to go on a lovely holiday."

Cataia marched straight into the bathroom, where the hot, scented bathwater had been prepared, and climbed into the tub. Valnera was not sure what to think until she heard the first crash.

Cataia, being somewhat vain, had jars and jars of ointments and scents and lotions and other female paraphernalia laid out around the tub. Another crash followed, and moments later the strong, sweet scent of kyrili oil permeated the room.

"I'd light your pyre with you on it alive!" yelled Cataia, and Valnera started to the bathroom to see if she could talk to the Princess. Before she had quite gotten to the door, she heard three more crashes in rapid succession. Believing invisibility to be the better part of valor in this case, Valnera took her needlework and a copy of one of the latest romantic poems and retired to the balcony. It was quite late when the demolition job was done and a sobbing, slightly soggy Cataia found her way to her sleeping rug.

.❧FOUR

As THE BRIDGES of Aandev'Rei came into sight, Tiernon became anxious to disembark. The days spent at sea had been good for him, sitting out on the deck and watching the crew maneuver the great sail, but now he longed for the peace of the retreat house, for the rarefied silence that would help him to rest and understand.

He almost had to laugh, wondering what the Court would think of him, the libertine, if they knew with what ferocious desire he craved a discipline that outwardly would look too cruel to impose on even a condemned murderer. Nine days of fasting, nine days of silence, nine nights of little sleep and long meditations—it would shock the Court to know what he was doing.

The carry-chair had left him at the door of what seemed to be a small, walled house in a neighborhood that reeked of middle-class obscurity. It reminded him of Dier Street, the rather untended flower vines creeping up the plastered corners of the houses, some of them chipped, and the yards definitely overgrown. Children who looked to be ten years old played out in the street, on the stoops of the houses, but they were respectful and well behaved. On Dier Street, they would have been the youngest novices in the six Abbeys.

Tiernon remembered how simple the Abbey had seemed at first, after the splendor of Bietehel, how at first he had chafed at the discipline and the strictures. It had been a struggle there to learn to sit completely still, the way the Fathers insisted. And then it had become normal to him, and later natural. The last two years, as a senior novice, were his most cherished memories. He had been good at his studies, the best in his class, and had dreamed of going to Volenten to further his studies of medicine. That was one of the great callings of the Orange, as art was in the Green or war in the Red.

After morning meditation he had studied living things, and with three others of his class had even gone out and assisted the three Father physicians in the House. There had been the long quiet hours of meditation, those last two years honing the skills he had mastered. On evenings when there were no rituals to be attended to, he had been free to practice his music, and sometimes sing with others in his class. Three or four of them would go down to the kitchen after the midnight Chant to the Sun and put together snacks with youthful creativity. Once he remembered, smiling, they had even tried to bake a cake in the alchemical oven and it had come out bright-red and hard.

And nights when there were rituals, oh, those were the most fiercely awaited, seeing which of the senior novices was going to assist. Those nights, in a fresh robe with a light overmantle, he would journey down to the crypt with the Orange-clad Fathers of the Abbey, chanting as the room changed around him.

When he let himself think about it, even surrounded by the Court, he ached for the quiet and order of the Abbey. Home was neither the Palace nor the Great House of Bietehel, but the overgrown, fading Abbey hidden behind its walls and un-pruned trees on Dier Street.

Here the house was older and the street not so wide. He entered the gate, remembering that he wouldn't speak or eat until he passed it again on the way out. It seemed like the gate of freedom. He was shown to his room by a young Adept whom he remembered vaguely from his novitiate in Tsanos, and was left alone.

Anros, that was his name. So he had passed his Initiation! Tiernon smiled happily, thinking of how, during his senior years, he had tutored Anros, who was newly come to the Abbey. Of all his class, of all the people who had known him, it was Anros who had patted his shoulder and looked forlorn when Tiernon was told that he would go to Court, not Volenten. He remembered how he had forced himself not to cry that day, to accept the decision of the Order. He knew that the Priests must have a special mission for him. Yet he had felt his whole world crumbling inside when he'd stood before Father Prethed. "Are you the master of yourself, or your own slave?" the old Priest had asked sternly. Tiernon had meditated on that for three days. In the end, he came to accept it, except when he saw Chervan practicing medicine in the Palace. Then it raked through him again.

Tiernon surveyed the room, which took little enough time; it was almost bare. A thin, clean sleeping rug had been unrolled near the shrine niche, and a single cushion had been placed by the wall. There were no hangings, no colors, no patterns to distract him, he noted with satisfaction. It was very much like his room on Dier Street had been, and it made him feel warmly returned home.

Quickly he shed his garments, the indigo katreisi proclaiming the nobility of his clan, the light brocade shirt embroidered with pearls, the full pants and the high Nestezian-tooled boots. He dressed in the single Orange robe of his Order bound with a rope cord. His head and his feet were bare. As before any ritual, he took a small vial of oil and anointed his forehead and the palms of his hands, the final sealing of the Initiate before the walk on the Planes. Then he knelt facing the wall and began his first day in retreat.

Casting his mind back, Tiernon began to relive the previous days on the boat, long, salubrious days when he'd been beset by strong wind and worries. Even now, images of the Court kept crowding back at him and filling him with disgust, the large obscene feasts, neat little teeth tearing at roast flesh with eyes that looked like they were doing the same. He saw himself there, languorously improving the image he had created of himself, created so completely that it was incorporated into his personality. And here, in this clean, silent place, it made him sick. He wondered how he could have come so far from the youth who had passed Initiation, the Court fop, the spoiled, luxury-loving, word-bantering, cutting son of the richest Rei in the land. It had been a hard Initiation, harder than most, so the Priests had said. He wondered now that he had survived at all, although only two had failed in all the ten years he'd been a novice.

The wall was blank in front of him, pitted in places, and he studied the pitting, trying to relieve himself of boredom and hunger. Acute hunger, the beginning of the fast, was overtaking him. His stomach turned and knotted on itself and he felt even weaker than he had before. He tried to turn his mind from it, but his body rebelled. He ignored it; he had fasted before.

The afternoon light threw shadows on the wall, and from some point just above his belly he wanted to scream, to hear a sound. There was no sound. He began to hate the wall, unchanging, almost laughing at him in its total blankness. The hunger came again, in waves that seemed like pain as the wall slowly faded with the sunset. The horrible half-light hurt his eyes. Insanity.

Anger, rebellion, the pain; he felt each reaction. The Priests on Dier Street had once taught him that the inner parts of magia consisted of controlled insanity. Emotion is energy, Father Vodrian had said in the class just after lunch. Tiernon felt himself sixteen again, sixteen in a world without women. Emotion is energy. It is energy that makes any magic work. Magic is to change consciousness, to change awareness, in full control. Insanity is what happens when the control slips. The changes occur. Part of his mind, stiffly trained, held back, watching. Still insufficient.

He let it grow, the frustration of the wall and his stomach and the moments that dribbled by and did not change. It would be pleasant to let his fingers, now lying relaxed on his thighs, curl into tight balls and feel the nails in his flesh. To feel anything but this constant grinding of nothingness, or unchangingness, of unbeingness, tempted him. The cataloging part of his mind smiled and maintained rigid control, coiling the emotions still tighter until the final moment of release when the break would create another state of being, totally conscious and without pain.

The insanity was growing, needing to sneer at the pain, needing to laugh for no reason and cry and let the aching muscles in his back relax. Still Tiernon held on, grasping at the emotion and letting it rise pitch by pitch until it overwhelmed him, pressing in even as he observed his own reaction.

Only then did he take the emotion and compress it until it was no longer emotion but raw energy. And when it had been completely transformed, he let it loose.

There was no time, no place, no beginnings or endings or neat lines. Here only being itself, pure and undefined, had existence. In this being could Tiernon think, realize, analyze, and be, totally, before he could know the nature of the bond that held him and the means by which to undo it. He was alone but not lonely, not with the horrible, fearsome isolation he had known since he had left the Abbey. For the first time he felt exposed, known, accepted.

Quietly he considered the attempts to assuage that loneliness in the Court. The involvement with Ayt, over long before Eltion's death, had been the most painful attempt. He had hoped that, as a Priestess, she could understand, that he could stand fully revealed, but the Star Priesthood was not an Order. Like his mother, she never understood his needs, and he could never tell her of the feel of real power, raw, radiating in his hands, the insanity that was not insanity and the fully clear vision that came with it.

Until he was ten and entered the Abbey, he had thought it was normal for his mother to speak to his sisters and not to him. They were, after all, her heirs. And he had been content, he thought, learning to fish with the children of the Rei, hidden away reading in his secret places. It hurt again, even now, to remember the laughter and games of the other children on the fishing boats, making secret plots that he was never privy to and getting into mischief where he was never invited. And after ten years in the Abbey, he had forgotten some of the cruelties of the world, and the essential isolation of the Adept. Yet the younger courtiers did not fall into the easy companionship he had learned at the Abbey. Their light conversation and frivolous concerns bored him even as he ached for their acceptance. But none of them understood, none of them could see. Even Ayt lacked the vision that the Abbey had given him. In the thirteen years since his coming of age, no one he would choose for a friend could accept him and acknowledge what he was.

Only Bertham, his most trusted enemy, understood, and that only too well.

Since that time he had rejected anything but physical closeness, knowing that no one could ever know him, and that physical closeness left him lonelier and more bereft than before. Yet he was never alone, as if the presence of warm, speaking beings could hide him from isolation.

It was the isolation that had given birth to the thing, the other needs that permitted the attacker entry. At that moment, the final knowledge of a true destiny that could be taken without pride, without attachment, came to him, a thing apart. He called through the Planes for his attacker, sending out vibrations that must draw it in and reveal it where it could do no harm.

Cataia sat immobile, letting Valnera fuss and fume, but the Princess would not respond. Her anger spent, Cataia had simply cut herself off, mechanically reading through a large pile of judicial decisions, and Valnera was determined to know why.

"But my beauty, is one man worth it? And such a lovely letter from your friend. A visit might do you good. You don't look healthy. Please."

To dissuade Valnera, Cataia smiled wearily. "It's just that there is so much to be done. Why don't you go to the market and I'll read for a while. That's good recreation, isn't it? I'll read that new book you've been trying to hide from me."

Valnera sighed and picked up her things. It would be impossible to move Cataia, she knew, and if the Princess wanted her gone, she would go. It was a quiet day, anyway, and it might be nice to visit one of her other friends in the city.

It delighted Valnera that she was thought well of by those so highly placed. The next Queen of Avriaten and the Priestess of the Temple were certainly worthies to be considered, and Valnera enjoyed the opportunity her position offered to hobnob with the great. It was even Ayt's intervention that had secured her the position of lady-in-waiting to Cataia, and Ayt had invited her to the Temple privately, as a friend. Now, for the first time since Cataia's arrival at Court, Valnera could find time to visit again.

Slowly she walked across the mosaic-tiled square that separated the Palace from the Temple, two great twin structures forever staring at each other through an expanse of fountains. In the brilliant midday light, the deeply carved arabesques that decorated the portals of both buildings were dimmed. The sound of water splashing in the four fountains defied the heat. The two on the Palace side had grisly histories. There was the ornate iron Traitor's Fountain, where the heads of traitors were hung for the public to view. Keani's head had hung there not so many years ago. The larger but far simpler Blue Fountain had originally been built of bleached bones, the Nestezian dead of the Great War. There were rumors that when the Nestezian prophecies were revealed, which no one ever believed would happen, the spirits of the Fountain would spearhead the Nestezian thrust.

The Temple fountains were more modern, carved of white stone that glittered in the light, representations of the Stars in human form. Most people considered it much more fitting for a holy place.

Valnera considered it quite appropriate that these two great powers of Avriaten glared at each other warily across the polished ceramic tiles of the square.

She was ushered into Ayt's private chambers by a guard in the midnight-blue uniform of the Temple. Once or twice she had seen units of them marching across the inner courtyard of the Temple and had wondered where they had all come from. It never seemed as if there were more than ten of those in their solid dark tunics and pants, leather belts crossing their chests, the leather and weapons always polished brightly. As if their function were only for show . . . It never occurred to Valnera that the Temple might be in any danger.

"Lady Valnera, my friend! It has been so long since I have seen you. Come in, sit down, one of the servants is getting us a mint drink. Tell me, how do you like the Palace? The Princess? Everything?"

Valnera blushed lightly at the interest of the High Priestess. "Well, I must thank you. In general, things are going very well. But what can you do about a girl like that?"

"What do you mean?" Ayt asked with real interest.

"Well, I'm not sure. She's almost too perfect. Headstrong, but all the Aandev are, and she won't get angry, not the way a normal person does. The poor girl just bottles it up until she can't stand it, and then she throws things."

"Does she ever talk about the problems we've been having, with the Nestezians, and the Reis and the harvest?" Ayt said in a merely conversational tone.

"That's all she ever talks about. And, no matter what happens, even after that dreadful attack, she won't say a word against those desert savages. Not one word. And when I asked her about the attack, she only told me that it wasn't a Nestezian no matter what they said in the kitchens."

"And the Reis?"

"Well, I think that Tiernon has something to do with that. Just the other day they were talking, and she said something about how Lathanor is taking too much of the Rei Mothers' traditional powers. Like with some village or something, I don't remember. And Tiernon said that his mother, Asirithe Rei Mother, doesn't like it one bit, and Cataia asked how many Council votes they were short."

"Ah," Ayt said quietly. "And how many short were they?"

"I forget. No, no, two, I think. Do you see what I mean, though? The poor girl's given only one party, and that was for Lathanor, Sethen and Tiernon. And she said it was only matters of state, because the Treasury is such a mess. Now, what kind of normal young girl won't entertain a charming young person like Teth? But she won't invite him at all."

Ayt's face sagged, with boredom, Valnera thought. Surely a Council member didn't need to hear it all a second time, even if it was bothering Valnera.

"And what about you? Your children and grandchildren? And weren't you working on a birth-rug for your son? Were there any others presented, or is it sure that the next Rei Mother of Lesnahal is your granddaughter?" Ayt asked.

Valnera launched into an excited recitation about her family, Ayt nodding and encouraging her.

After Valnera had left, Ayt paused to consider. So it had not been a Nestezian attack. She had thought as much. And there was the problem of jurisdiction. She knew about those two votes. She would have to talk to Tiernon about her plan, perhaps sometime a bit sooner than she had thought. In any event, she was satisfied. Valnera was proving as useful as the High Priestess had hoped.

Cataia was walking across the room. Fifteen paces across the short end, twenty the long way, she was trying to work off energy. With Lathanor in the Palace it seemed evident that no real work was going to be done. Teth was closeted with Bertham and the King for hours making plans that Cataia could guess at without much doubt as to accuracy. The harvest was not in yet, but the deep heat of summer hadn't been as oppressive as usual, which was a bad sign for the farmers.

Avriaten lived on farming. Mother Daniessa had taught that the first year of the novitiate, and even Dacia could explain that they traded with Salsatee for goods and the Nestezi for materials. It was food that had kept Avriaten a power in the world, the ability to grow it, the power to withhold it. And for the third year in a row the harvest didn't look good.

Something else was disquieting. Lathanor had "invited" her to stay in her rooms "for a few days," as he'd put it. Of course, it had been couched in terms of catering to her safety, making allusions to the outbreaks of pestilence in the city. She did not have to wonder why Lathanor did not trust her. She wouldn't trust herself, if she were in his position. On the other hand, he had no reason to lock her in. An heir to the throne would find it a bad precedent to kill her predecessor.

Suddenly she began to wonder if the long meetings between Bertham, Lathanor and Teth were simply pipe-dreaming plans for the improbable invasion of the Nestezi. She remembered what Tiernon had said about the bonding. There were two ways to do it, the way they had been taught at the Abbey and the way they had been told to avoid. In the first way, each magician is the center of a circle, and as the circles touch they merge to form a figure eight. The other way was that the controller sat in the center and threw out an energy circle around the one to be controlled, who sat just inside the perimeter of the circle. Cataia wondered again. Lathanor certainly didn't seem an idiot, and he wasn't easily controlled when he was drunk. She had ample experience with that. But the second form of bonding chilled her. She didn't know how to get free from that, if there even was a way. Mother Nisria hadn't seemed to think so.

The curiosity overcame her. Valnera should be gone for a while; it always took Valnera a long time to go shopping, and the Wheel case lay just within reach. She spread the tiles, mixed them thoroughly, selected and drew them into a pattern. Then, one by one, she turned them over. The Snake Striking, the Two Moons, the Dark Bird and, in the center, the Garden at Midnight. As she turned the last tile, she gasped. The Eater of Lives.

Cataia took a deep breath and forced herself steady. She tried to focus on the entire pattern, and commanded herself to be positive. The central tile was the Garden at Midnight, perhaps the most beautiful tile of the whole Wheel, the promise of life and rebirth. That was the center, the whole thing. So, no matter what the Eater of Lives represented, it would lead to a new life, a new birth. Well, it would be best to work with the easy ones. The Two Moons were probably Tiernon and herself. The moons regulated their magic, and the tile was often read as two magicians. The Dark Bird, an unknown force, and the Snake Striking, an enemy. Well, she surely had enough of those! And the Eater of Lives. Most people read that as death, but in the Abbey Cataia had learned to see it as a challenge, a difficult lesson to overcome, which would result in a death of an old part of the personality. It was a very positive tile, really. So there would be a difficult lesson, from which they would both emerge into the Garden. So far, so good.

Something else nagged at her, and she couldn't banish it. The Eater of Lives. The Eater of Souls. Cataia started to tremble. No, it couldn't be that at all. The tiles referred to stages of development, not to demons and people, and things the way the carnival-readers said.

She broke down the tiles, swirled them and placed them again, this time choosing only four and laying them out in a new pattern. This time the Fountain came to the North, the Garden at Midnight to the South, the Garden at Dawn to the West. She hesitated before she turned the last tile, the Eastern tile that defined it all. Again, the Eater of Lives.

The Eater of Souls again ran through her mind. To the East. The island of 'Kleppah lay to the East. It was the Eastern Reis that were having such terrible problems with their taxes and the harvests.

Intuitively, Cataia knew. The Eater of Souls, the Laughing Master as she had seen him in her Initiation, Lechefrian was loose again. After a thousand years, he was spreading his claws into the land.

The chill began to shake her. She didn't need the tiles to see; it was becoming a pattern, falling into place. Of course. She had seen it at her Initiation. Lechefrian had claws, and hadn't Chervan said that Tiernon's wounds looked like claw marks? The Master of 'Kleppah was responsible for the attack on Tiernon.

It was strange, she thought, trying to keep her mind calm, that he would have the same name as the traitor to the Seven. It always seemed that the names Lechefrian and Tiernon were bound to one another. Yet it seemed as if the demon had planned Tiernon's escape. The Eater of Souls. He had eaten part of Tiernon, absorbed it. What did 'Kleppah want with Tiernon? What could one Adept do against Lechefrian? After all, they weren't in the days of the Seven.

She could almost hear Tiernon saying, "Aken is interested." If she was right, no wonder Aken was interested.

But how had Lechefrian managed to get out of 'Kleppah? The seals were still strong, Aken made sure of that, and even if the Seven had not destroyed Lechefrian they had certainly curtailed his realm of activity.

It had been the Adept Chadeer, Chevaina's older brother, who had unleashed Lechefrian's power, Cataia remembered. He had been the head of a group of eighteen Adepts, the traditional number for the greater moon, and so for magical groups. No one was aware of it for some time, the story went; they had all been blinded by dedication to him. Just how Chadeer released Lechefrian the first time wasn't really known. There were traditions that said that he had been doing experiments, and that he had not observed the correct precautions. Other traditions told that he had become corrupted by the leadership of the group itself. Ronarian, his working Priestess, was the first to spot it, and she broke away from the group. Four followed immediately. Chevaina and Tiernon were the last to leave. Mother Daniessa had said it was because they loved Chadeer and hoped to turn him, or clean up his experiment, whichever story was true.

Only eighteen magicians and one demon, Mother Daniessa had stressed. There were no armies, except those of the Planes, and the elements of the earth itself. The very land had opened and heaved from the stress of that elemental battle, many of the Easterners fleeing west as the floods, and then earthquakes hit. They had driven the Western population into the desert, into the Nestezi. By the end of the war, almost a third of what had been the East had sunk beneath the sea. But the Eleven who pledged to Lechefrian were badly weakened. Two had been killed in the flooding, and had been eaten by the Laughing Master. Three others had tried an oblique attack which had been reflected back on them. They were in the citadel they had built on the top of the mountain, now an island, called 'Kleppah.

The Seven knew that it was time to attack. The Citadel had remained secure, but those in it had been without supplies for a long time. They had prepared a mountain, and found themselves on an island. That night, the Seven slept in a hall in

Aandev'Rei, a city even then, planning to face the Citadel from the neighboring island of Tyne at noon, when Lechefrian's powers would be at their weakest.

Mother Daniessa speculated that Chevaina and Tiernon had never really planned for what happened. Perhaps they still hoped to rescue Chadeer before the final attack. But they arrived on Tyne at dawn. Lechefrian still had the power of the night with him.

Tiernon bargained, Mother Daniessa said. He bargained for the life of Chadeer, and the power to repair some of the damage that the population had suffered during the three years of war. Chevaina had tried to dissuade him, but for the life of her brother finally agreed. Together, they wove an energy-net around 'Kleppah, using the energy and power Tiernon had bargained from the demon itself. They had sealed it with Tiernon's sigal, completely neutralizing it. Nothing could get out, but nothing could get in, either. Ronarian and the other arrived, and found that they couldn't pierce the net Tiernon had woven.

He had asked for Chadeer's life. Tiernon and Chevaina took a boat to the Citadel, to bring back the survivors. There were none. The ten magicians who had followed Chadeer, along with their leader, had starved to death, their souls eaten by Lechefrian. It was Lechefrian's own life he had promised Tiernon.

Only the original Tiernon of the Seven could break that seal, or loosen it enough to let Lechefrian function, unless the demon himself had managed to find a way. After all, it was the Eater of Souls' own energy Tiernon had used to weave the net. With the right pull on the other side . . .

Cataia was really afraid. Lechefrian had access to Tiernon, and he could have access to anyone he chose. The Abbey must be warned. Lathanor had not issued her a direct order, and Dacia was on no political lists. Indeed, her growing reputation as an artist protected them both. It would be normal for a Crown Princess to commission a portrait of the King for his birthday.

But now, Cataia was too frightened to move. The knowledge of Lechefrian's freedom forced her to think about her own. Lathanor was capable of rather unpleasant action if his wishes were disobeyed.

It was difficult to write the note to Dacia. In case anyone else happened to read it, she had to use the language of command that, as an Aandev subject, Dacia could not disobey. On the other hand, it seemed low and dirty to command an old friend, truly the only friend she had after Tiernon's betrayal. She would explain to Dacia when she got to the Palace, and Dacia would understand, Cataia convinced herself. For her own safety, for the Order, Dacia must understand.

Just outside the barrier of infinity created by the safety of Tiernon's beingness, it began to materialize. As the dark, glistening energy patterns resolved themselves a familiar figure began to emerge, and Tiernon felt terror rising in him, the beginnings of a panic that he knew could envelop and destroy him.

The energy glistened bright as the stars. The demon wore the shape of a man, mostly. The energy that created it glowed with the crimson and grey of 'Kleppah, giving the whole being a skeletal and bloody cast. The eyes blazed ruby, laughing with an insanity older than age.

"Has my friend forgotten my name?" the thing sneered.

The barrier that was the retreat house, unassailable by force, was still vulnerable to the bond that could be seen sparkling between them, the two unembodied beings with the appearance of bodies, neither of them real.

"I cannot believe that you really do not know who I am," the figure taunted. "Surely in your Abbey you must have remembered me."

Almost, almost Tiernon felt a vague flash of recognition, but it faded before he could resolve it. He cringed, casting about, knowing that without the memories of some former life he was crippled. And he knew that the demon before him knew, and gloated over him. He tried to disentangle the gleaming threads of energy from around the universe contained in his solar plexus. Unwind, redirect, change, use.

"I am Lechefrian," it said simply. It was vastly old, Tiernon knew, and vastly powerful.

"We cannot remain balanced, you and I," it continued. "One of us must fall, and rest assured that if it came to that, it would be you. You know that. Look. Have you disarmed me?"

Cold horror swept Tiernon. He had concentrated, pulled, unwound, and yet the bond remained, shimmering dull red, burning and enfolding him in its web.

"Join me!" the demon said. "What do you have to lose? Do you want to know who you have been? Do you want to know why they were so harsh to you at the Abbey? Why they have never given you anything but pain? Because you are mine. Once you had a chance to destroy me, did you know that? Once you could have. But you are corrupt."

Just outside the barrier, images began to form. The rocky barren island of Tyne, set in a grey sea, looked out to the even greyer fortress of 'Kleppah. He was on the island, swept by the hard, hot wind and oppressed by the heavy moisture. It was near dawn. In front of him stood Lechefrian. The Eleven were dead. Only their Master had survived them. Tiernon saw himself spinning the wall around 'Kleppah, spinning it to protect this thing, to protect himself.

The others did not understand. They had never come so close, felt so much, been at one with the power of 'Kleppah. He understood the Eleven now, understood Chadeer. Tiernon knew the exhilaration, forming, embodying, being that much power, and Lechefrian had offered it to him in return for a wall. He had thought of the good he could do with that power when the bargain was struck, but he did not know what he would do after. The image did not last.

The fading of the images was a relief to Tiernon. Suddenly he knew that it was all illusion and that he was not Tiernon of the Seven, but simply a Bietehel, which was far less and far more. He had made no bargain with this thing, this terrifying, soul-eating demon.

The demon began to laugh, and that joyless hilarity froze Tiernon. He could not remember. He didn't know what to do. Panic began to fill him and he fought it down, a second enemy as bad as the first.

The bond glimmered between them, making him this Thing's being more than any pledge. It could not be unwound, Tiernon realized. It had to be severed.

Power blazed around him, clear and golden, focused and healing. There was a sword, held by an unknown hand, which breached the chasm and flared momentarily through the red cord, cauterizing it, cutting Tiernon free.

"You will find," Lechefrian said from far across the blazing golden abyss that separated them, "that I keep all my bargains. All of them."

The tendril of energy seemed to fade uniformly as the an-

cient Master retreated, leaving Tiernon confused. He didn't
know that he had called for aid, or who had given it, or why.
Tiernon was convinced that the only reason it had worked was
that Lechefrian hadn't expected it and had been caught completely off guard, as he had himself. He cast around to thank
whoever or whatever had been responsible, but there was only
emptiness, silence, the feeling of long abandonment.

Returning to his body, he found himself still facing the wall,
his legs and shoulders badly cramped from the long days of
sitting unmoving. There was bright light streaming through
the window. Just beyond that pool of light stood Anros bearing a pitcher of water and a cup. The younger Adept's face
shone with joy the color of the sunlight on the stone.

He understood then and, remaining on the cushion, bowed
to the floor. He was glad of the rule of silence. There were no
words he could have used.

Anros smiled sadly in acknowledgment, and poured the
water into the cup. Setting both on the floor in front of the
door, the young Adept disappeared.

He drank some of the water slowly, feeling it slide down his
throat. There was no hunger, no desire even for the water, but
Tiernon knew it was necessary to drink. The water had a quality of ambrosia to it, sweeter than the lightest wine. Anros had
saved him. It was the second time someone else had saved him
from Lechefrian, Tiernon acknowledged. There was something there that bore meditation, but he was too tired to think
about it.

For the first time since the attack he felt true tiredness, the
healthy body's need for sleep, and not the strange ebbing of
his internal energies. Even the thin, worn pile of the sleeping
rug seemed a luxury, and a wave of contentment drifted over
him before he fell entirely asleep.

Waking refreshed, Tiernon felt better than he had in a very
long time. Almost since he had left the Abbey, he thought.
There was some pattern to the whole thing, he knew, and he
relished the challenge of finding it.

Tiernon of the Seven had indeed struck a bargain with
'Kleppah, branding himself the greatest villain of any of the
Orders of the Adepti. Tiernon had often wished, after entering
the Abbey, that his mother had not seen fit to name him for
the archtraitor; but she had not known. It was considered bad
policy to let the people know that the purpose of the Seven had

been thwarted and that the Orders still preserved certain forms that drained a great deal of energy, in order to stave off confrontation until those who could fight Lechefrian's power took incarnation.

On the other hand, it would be like Lechefrian to set him up. That made good sense, and the Eater of Souls had a reputation of toying with his intended victims and confidants. Make him believe that the blank his memory could not break concealed the original Tiernon of the Seven, make him believe that he was so corrupt that there was no possibility of escape, delude him into the narrow margin between pride and fear and then close in for the kill. Lechefrian liked to play, and Lechefrian's games always involved suffering. He, or rather it, had long since outgrown any attraction of physical violence. Doing violence to the mind was far better. And what better way to corrupt him, Tiernon thought, than to seek him out and try to convince him. After all, the original Tiernon hadn't been able to resist Lechefrian's offer, so if he believed that he and the founder of his own Order were one and the same, he could not resist either.

It was neat, Tiernon had to admit, but he wasn't going to accept it. If he understood the laws of reincarnation properly, and they had been etched into his fiber by his Priest-teachers, Tiernon of the Seven would come back to a miserable life, endure terrible conditions, and die quite young. Certainly he would never be born into a major Rei. And Tiernon had to admit that, in general, though lonely, his life was quite pleasant. Most Adepts were lonely and he had more, and more interesting, lovers than most, could afford to surround himself with beauty and refinement, could enjoy the exercise of the mind and pursue his studies with access to facilities open to very few, and wielded as much power as anyone not born an Aandev could possibly aspire to. In short, his life was as totally successful as anyone, even a Bietehel, could imagine, and therefore it was impossible that he could be the original Tiernon of the Seven, even if his mother had given him the name.

Besides, the name was common. Children were constantly named for the Seven, and there had even been another Tiernon at the Abbey when he was studying there.

Relaxed, contented and full of energy, Tiernon poured himself another cup of water, admiring the rough glazed texture of the ceramic piece with his fingers. The hunger had changed, and it was no longer painful, but the light, floating sensation of true fasting. It was pleasant. His body had stopped demanding food for now, and he was content.

The cup in his hand and the warm water in the back of his throat were acutely sensual. The deep rays of twilight turned the room a rich amber, throwing the small uneven places in the wall into high relief. It amazed him that he had not noticed it before, the barely perceptible fluctuations of the summer air, the faint elusive undersmell of a garden somewhere. He smiled at his old companion the wall, and shook his head, wondering how such perfect peace and total freedom could have tormented him so deeply on that first day.

Looking out the small window, he realized that he didn't know what day it was, or how long he had been sitting in front of the wall. It could have been only a few hours, or it could have been four or five days. He didn't care. He was content, fulfilled. Anros would knock when it was time for him to leave, and he would be content with that, too.

Then he realized that there was no pain in his chest. Curiously, experimentally, he started to peel the bandage away from the uppermost wound, fully expecting it to be bleeding gently. For as long as he had been bound, the wounds hadn't healed. Now only a thin pink line of new skin marked the place—soft, real skin and not the unchecked bleeding of these past many, many days. From his window he saw a flock of birds crossing the sky, the late sun dyeing their feathers rose and amber across the indigo of the approaching night.

ஃFIVE

TIERNON WAS AMAZED by Cataia's coldness when he
presented himself at her rooms. Valnera had given him stern
looks and Cataia had remained unmoved even after he had explained his experiences at the retreat house.

"You could have explained when you left. I understand
about Lechefrian; my Abbey, at least, is warned. But you
could have told me where you were going."

"I . . . well, it involved only myself," he replied, equally
icily.

"It did not, and you know it. You called for me when you
were attacked, and it wasn't particularly easy for me to coax
you back into your body."

"There was nothing else I could do. I was worse than useless
in that condition."

"You could have told me," she repeated, at a loss for
words. He wasn't behaving as she'd decided he should. "I
could have been prepared." It was all wrong, Cataia thought.
He should be happy to see her, guilty for having abandoned
her. Confusion and anger replaced her anticipation.

71

"Are you going to call the Court of Aken? Or can we forget it?" Tiernon asked snidely. He knew she was right in part, but anger wasn't getting them anywhere. There were moments when she could be so immature. He hardly remembered that she was far younger and a good bit less experienced than himself. She had turned her back on him, and this gesture hurt.

"I apologize, Highness. I should have explained fully. I will be more thoughtful in the future."

She turned back to him when she was certain the pain and confusion she felt were not plain on her face. "Good. Please do so. I feel that Bertham is still pushing for a war in the Nestezi, which is sheer idiocy to my way of thinking. Still, it looks likely that they will begin to set things, perhaps another tax which the people can't afford, so that this will be feasible within perhaps the next year and a half. Obviously, we must stop it."

"Obviously."

"Can you talk to Ayt? The Temple preaches peace, and they have power. And you do have some influence with her." The last Cataia said in a tone calculated to hurt, and to prove her indifference. "Use any means possible to win her over firmly. Any means." She gave him a knowing half smile, and Tiernon had to suppress an urge to spank her. His affairs were his business, and if she had none that was hers.

Still, he couldn't resist saying, "It is true that I am your advisor, Highness?"

"Yes."

"Then if I may be permitted to give you some advice. I believe it would be in your best interests, and the country's, if you gave some thought to a lover. People will think you're cold and selfish if you don't. Besides, an heiress to the Aandev would secure your position."

"Are you suggesting yourself? I am totally uninterested."

"By no means," he replied. "Bietehel does not need any more connections to the throne. By your leave . . ."

"Please go."

After he had left, Cataia stomped angrily around the large room, making as much noise as possible. Didn't he know when to disobey her? She wanted to break something, but she had exhausted her supply of cosmetics in her first anger, and the efficient Valnera had managed not to replace them with anything breakable. She was sure she hated him. So many times during his absence she had fantasized this meeting—his

abject misery for having offended her, her gracious acceptance—and then he had the gall to try and defend himself.
Even in her pique, she realized that she wanted him to return
and tell her that he had discovered some feeling for her, and
that he couldn't face Ayt with that knowledge.

So, his advice was to take a lover. Well, it was good advice.
She would take it. At least, she would look. If it were known
that she, a Crown Princess fully of age, was still a virgin, she
would be laughed at in every tavern from Aandev'Rei to
Volenten. It was what everyone looked forward to most on
coming of age. Even Dacia had been shocked, and Dacia was
on her side. So be it, then. She would make use of the first
reasonable opportunity.

When Tiernon returned to his own rooms, he moved immediately to the private dining room. It was his favorite room,
with the deep-burgundy-and-sky-colored hangings, the softly
scented carved fountain and the four graceful fluted columns
that seemed to drift lazily to the ornate arches. The low divans
were covered with sprays of white cushions, and the table
matched in an unusual white lacquer. It was different, and
quiet here, the nearest he could get to the isolation of the
retreat house.

Tiernon wondered what to do about Cataia's command to
influence Ayt. He could do it, he knew, there was no problem
there, but the fact remained that he did not want to. He had
respect for Ayt, far more so than for other members of the
Council, and it would be immoral to use a long-dead relationship to further his aims.

It was at moments like this that he most regretted Nikkot's
death. Nikkot would have stumbled in on him and talked
around ancient history, and not only would have suggested a
solution, but would have convinced Ayt himself. He did not
expect an impromptu visit with Nikkot gone, so it was with
great surprise that he heard the servant telling him that a
visitor had arrived.

"How happy I am to see you in good health," Bertham said
smoothly. "You can hardly imagine how worried we were
when you left. Some of the Council thought that perhaps the
assassination attempt had destroyed your nerve. How glad I
am to see it isn't so."

"I thank you for your concern, Councilor, I had no idea
that you were worried," Tiernon said. "But I am forgetting

my duties. Would you care for wine?''

"One would have to lack a tongue and a throat to refuse your wine, Tiernon. How pleasant it is to have you back.''

Tiernon did not pour the wine himself, a gesture that Bertham noted with something akin to approval. Enemies must be as loyal as friends, he thought, or what is the use of having enemies. It was strangely refreshing to be here, facing Tiernon openly. The smell of hate under the words was as intoxicating as a chill running through the deep summer day, and bittersweet enough to invigorate the moment.

Bertham took the enameled wineglass and drank slowly, savoring the perfect richness and deep flavor. It was gratifying to drink with someone who had too much class to try to poison the wine. He had truly worried when Tiernon disappeared. It would be unfortunate to lose the only courtier in the Palace whom he respected. There were even moments when he regretted that it would eventually be necessary to destroy the Bietehel Councilor. No one else would ever stock so much good wine and so much cunning. It would be a pity to lose both.

"I am sure that it was not an inquiry as to the state of my health that brought you here, Councilor," Tiernon began.

"I must admit that there were a few matters to discuss, provided I found you in such good condition. But why rush things? I'd be most anxious to know where you've been all this time, hiding from us. It has been most disturbing.''

"I was at sea.''

"At sea?'' Bertham raised an eyebrow. "A strange place for a Council member.''

"Salt air and sunlight are marvelous medicine for wounds, especially for one who has grown up sailing.''

"But you did not inform the King?'' Bertham's voice held the slightest threat under his carefree manner.

"The King Regent, I believe, was informed that I was taking a holiday, on the orders of my physician.''

"Oh, yes, of course," Bertham demurred. "Still, it must be pleasant to be back at Court.''

Tiernon merely nodded, sipping his wine.

"I was wondering if you would care to join Teth, the King and myself in my apartments tonight? Of course, if you are not feeling up to such a gathering, it is more than understandable.''

"If it is simply a social visit, I don't see how I can, although

I am greatly honored that you came to ask me personally," Tiernon said. "You see, after a holiday there are so many reports to read, so much to get in order, that for the good of the kingdom I can't indulge myself, much as I am tempted."

"Why, Tiernon, I would never think to take you from your duties to Avriaten," Bertham said, feigning shock. "Indeed, isn't that our whole life, to see to our country's needs? No, I'm afraid that this isn't a social occasion, much as I wish it could be. In fact, it's going to be dull as dust. We must do something about the Treasury."

Tiernon laughed. "But Bertham, I'm best known for spending money, not making it."

"But you do know something about economics, if I'm not mistaken."

"Only in theory. In practice, I never had to worry about such things. But I will come and give you the benefit of whatever is the current rage at the University," Tiernon said flippantly.

"I would be entranced if you would be so good as to come and share your knowledge with us," Bertham said. "Now that I have secured your presence, I have some other business to attend to. You are not the only one who is behind in reading reports."

They both smiled politely, and Bertham rose to leave. In a strange way, he hoped that things would not go well that night. He knew how useful Tiernon could be to him, to his whole plan, but he disliked the manner of it. There had to be one enemy one could respect, could trust, could even love.

But much as he enjoyed Tiernon's enmity, pleasure was not important, not compared to the dream. Emperor of the World was his title in his fantasy, and it could be so. He had stared at the sigal of Lechefrian every night, as instructed by the book, and he wondered if the change he was feeling was real.

There was power there, power that seemed almost to ache to be flexed. Poor Tiernon, he thought. He doesn't know what he's up against.

Bertham thought of all the times Tiernon had laughed at him for his belief in the magia, that even today one could actually harness it. Tiernon didn't even go to the Temple of the Stars. A materialist was at an extreme disadvantage against the system of Lechefrian, Bertham knew, and no one at Court was more of a materialist than Tiernon.

When Bertham had gone, Tiernon chuckled to himself. It

was a duel, and of course the challenge had to be delivered in person. Thank goodness that Bertham was not some sloppy minor adversary. Bertham had poise, had style. He had been gratified that Bertham had known him well enough to drink the wine without hesitation or trying to exchange glasses.

Bertham knew the rules. Destruction was a delicate business, careful, respectful and very precise. Only an amateur would stoop to mere annihilation.

Keeping Bertham's sense of propriety in mind, Tiernon dressed carefully for the evening in rich- but somber-colored clothes set off by a single dull chain. He wore a katreisi with the design of the Bietehel Tree subtly worked around the borders in silver, a quiet reminder to Bertham of Tiernon's rank. Only immediate relations of the Rei Mother were entitled to wear the design, and then only after certain documents were signed denoting representative powers after coming of age. He spoke for the wealth and loyalty of the wealthiest and most loyal Rei in Avriaten, save Aandev'Rei itself, and he wasn't going to let Bertham escape it. Bertham, a mere second cousin to the heiress of Tonea'Rei, still resented his position relative to Tiernon in the ordering of the old nobility, and on occasion Tiernon wasn't above rubbing his nose in it.

There had been times when Tiernon had thought that Bertham was a mirror of himself, had he been born a cousin in a poor Minor Rei, and had he not been chosen for the Abbey. It was unsettling to see all the "what ifs" personified. He wondered if Bertham saw him the same way, and then rejected the idea. Bertham couldn't afford to think "what if," couldn't afford to wonder what life would have been like. It would destroy him, and that was why Tiernon carefully chose to wear the chain and katreisi of his rank.

Arriving only barely late, Tiernon paused to admire Bertham's taste yet again. The contrasting ambers and ivories of the hangings and cushions were blended in delicate patterns, and the beaten brass table was inlaid with calligraphic inscriptions from the Prophecies and quite obviously antique. The enameled plates were as fine as his own, though the enamelwork was fanciful design, as Bertham did not have the right to use one of the high crests. The doors to the balcony had been opened, the view overlooking the Traitor's Fountain providing a lightly scented breeze to cool the company and a richly clear night sky to complement the decor.

Lathanor and Teth were already conversing, tasting wine

and cold meat before the meal, a pleasant way to spend the minutes that were not yet business. They stopped speaking for a moment as they noticed him, and Bertham gestured lightly to him to enter.

"How good it is to see you with us again," said Lathanor. "I hope you aren't planning on leaving again soon."

Tiernon heard the undercurrent of sarcasm in his voice. It had already begun, before the first course had arrived.

"If no one attempts to assassinate me again, I will be happy to remain where I am. However . . ." He let his voice trail off in a meaningful manner.

"It was probably a Nestezian spy," Teth volunteered quickly. "You have no idea how underhanded they are. Living in Maddigore, we have all kinds of thefts and murders committed by Nestezians. You know, they actually believe that Avriaten will belong to them someday. They have prophets . . ."

"Can't we talk after dinner? Work tends to dull the palate," Tiernon said.

"Has the Princess spoken to you lately? Our King asked her to keep to her rooms, so that she might be better protected," Bertham said, complying with Tiernon's request.

"Cataia?" Tiernon asked. "Why should I know any more than our King, whose cousin she is? After all, it isn't necessary for us to talk too often." The slight rise of the eyebrows, the vaguely condescending manner and the apparent unconcern made Bertham suspicious.

Bertham knew that Tiernon had influence over Cataia, and if he could use that influence, well, it would be better than approaching Cataia herself. Bertham had never figured Tiernon out exactly, but it was easier to work with a known entity. The Princess was far too complex to use as he had used Teth. His bitter experience with Eltion, his inability to manipulate her precisely, was not forgotten. He could gain access to Cataia only through Tiernon. It was going to be amusing, no matter what turn events took.

"My compliments to your chef, Bertham," Tiernon began, a shade too light to be completely trusted. "Is the fish Bietehel, by any chance?"

"With a Tonea sauce, and it is the sauce that makes the fish," Bertham replied in the same tone.

"True, very true," Tiernon agreed. "It dresses it, as clothes the man, but it does not change the fish, as a katreisi will not make a noble of a commoner, or a stupid man wise."

Bertham nodded archly. The fish was ignored until a servant took it and placed a dish of lightly steamed spiced steema and roasted meats in the central dish. With great delicacy Lathanor scooped some of the steema with two fingers and a thin slice of meat. After he nodded his approval of the dish, the others began to eat. Tiernon schooled his impatience. It would not be so bad if there were interesting foods to sample, but Lathanor's taste was strictly pedestrian. At least the wine was palatable, and that was a relief. There were still two desserts to go, but Bertham had a reputation for his pastry. Tiernon was sure they had been bought on Dier Street, and had frequently wondered how a non-Adept could ever find the place. He decided the best way to find out was to ask.

"Spies," Bertham responded laughingly. "They followed your servants around those back alleys into that terrible, crumbling neighborhood, and what did they find? Heaven!"

"Spies could be better used against the Nestezi than to find some pastry shop," Teth said.

"The Nestezi, the Nestezi, somehow we always return to the Nestezi," Tiernon said. "Personally, I think it's rather uninteresting. After all, who cares about a bunch of unorganized nomads and a few sand dunes? If you want war, why not Salsatee? At least they have something worthwhile, and I'd be much happier not to pay their dyer's tax."

"They might not be important to you," Teth said, "but in Maddigore those tribes are a constant nuisance. And wouldn't you rather be spending the summer in the mountains instead of Tsanos? But we can't. And remember, they have those jewels, which wouldn't hurt the Treasury."

"But Teth," Tiernon replied, trying to mix just the right degrees of sarcasm and mock innocence, "the Nestezi is a big place. You don't expect them to lead us to the jewel caves and say 'Here they are, help yourselves,' do you? As for their being a threat, I repeat, they're disorganized tribes, nomads, primitives. The only way we could see them as a threat at all is if we permitted them to become one. Remember too that they hate water. They won't cross a river or use a boat. How could they be such a threat to Maddigore, which has mountains on one side and the river on the other? A few incidents now and then, that's all there ever has been, and that's all there ever will be. As for the problem of going to the mountains, it's not worse than in other years. Do you think the Batter are worried?"

"I'm not concerned with the Batter, only with Avriaten, and from Maddigore's point of view they are a threat," Teth retorted.

"What concerns me is the Treasury," said Bertham. "A war would win us new land for people to settle and cultivate, and the jewel caves. I believe that we could find the caves if we tried. And we have nothing at present. Do you know how bad the State debt is?"

"Of course," Tiernon said smoothly. "Bietehel holds most of the notes at fourteen percent interest, I believe."

"Usury!" Teth exclaimed.

"Usury?" Tiernon replied. "The Batter hold notes at twenty-one and the Tersoneat at twenty-eight percent. My mother, Asirithe Rei Mother of Bietehel, will not extend any more loans."

"Suppose, for the sake of argument, that we join with the Salsateans against the Nestezi," Bertham said. "They have as much to gain as we do, and we could split the jewel caves. The Nestezians don't confine their raids to us, you know."

"Suppose we did, Bertham. The Emperor of Salsatee is looking for an Empire and, unlike the nomads, he could pose a real threat," Tiernon said, the mask of the fop discarded.

Then Lathanor spoke for the first time. "I believe that the Emperor and I could come to some sort of agreement. We both have the security of our people to look after, you know, and these tribes are trouble. They're primitive, as you said, and that makes them unpredictable. With the Salsateans, we know what we're dealing with."

"I'm not convinced," Tiernon said.

"Tiernon," Bertham said, "I would like to speak to you plainly. We need this war, and we need your support."

"You mean you need Bietehel's support. Asirithe Rei Mother has said no more loans, not until the four hundred thousand zertin are paid off, with interest. We simply can't afford it."

"No, not Bietehel money, Tiernon, you," Bertham said. "Look, the Nestezi is an outlet. The brigands, the beggars, the peasants whose lands haven't yielded well, we send them out of the country. They either get killed or carve out Reis of their own. The Treasury gets the jewels, which means that the loans, including the Bietehel loans, are paid. It's you we need, Tiernon."

Bertham looked at him slowly, openly, and Tiernon felt the tension between them shimmer. He and Bertham were mirrors, dark and light eyes, leaning gently on ivory cushions, katreisis spread like dark ink in the flickering light of the oil lamps. Bertham's hand played almost idly with the wine cup inches away, half smiling.

It had always been between them, Tiernon knew. Perfect examples of their types. And yet, and yet . . . Once, when he had first met Bertham, he had dreamed of it, of stroking that taut skin, that curly hair. And in the dream, under his hands, it had turned rancid, decayed, full of maggots; but even the revulsion had never lessened the attraction. Bertham met his eyes and shifted, subtly inviting as he had always invited. Another thing between them, like their hatred, and just as pure.

"And after that?" Tiernon asked, his voice husky.

"After that? Why, we enter another golden age, of course. Besides, the land is traditionally ours." Bertham's voice was low and full of undertones.

"I see," Tiernon responded. "And you would join with Salsatee on this?"

"Yes. They're already equipped from the explorations. It would be best to appear allies."

Tiernon shivered as Bertham held his eyes, fascinated both by the beauty and the corruption, and the open invitation. It would be interesting, Tiernon thought, and Bertham was so very much the dark image of himself. . . . And then he thought of Eltion. There was no proof, of course. Bertham had been too good to leave any behind, but Tiernon had made some discreet inquiries. The Wheel tiles had made the picture even more clear.

Eltion had been a truly fine queen, sometimes a bit headstrong, but a gifted administrator who could bring differing factions together on issues. She had had only one blind spot: Bertham. And it had killed her. She had favored Bertham greatly, listened to him at length, but he had not been able to manipulate her as he did Lathanor. Thinking about it, Tiernon knew that her strong will made her a poor candidate for any of the mind-bending tactics he had learned at the Abbey. Even though Eltion had usually been a good judge of character, she failed with Bertham. She rarely gave credence to the level of ambition Bertham really had. Tiernon knew that she had never understood it. She had trusted him, and had died of it, alone in the dark, from poison. Tiernon was not about to make the same mistake.

"And my place?" Tiernon asked softly.

"How does Provisional Governor strike you?" Bertham replied. "Wouldn't you prefer to be something more than your mother's messenger boy?"

Tiernon was grateful for the disciplined training he had received, which enabled him to refrain from killing Bertham in his own dining room. "And Cataia?" he asked sharply.

"It has come to my attention," said Lathanor, "that my cousin is rather more interested in my duties than in hers. I have reason to believe that she was in league with her mother, and assisted in Eltion's murder."

"I must point out," Tiernon said softly, "that the legality is highly questionable. The Rei Mothers are not pleased. Besides, Cataia was fourteen years old and not at Court when Eltion was killed."

"But it would not do to have even a suspected regicide Princess in such a sensitive position," Bertham said, emphasizing the word *regicide*.

"And what about the succession?"

"Once she has a girl child, that will be taken care of. Two, perhaps, for insurance. We can afford to wait that long," Bertham said languidly, carefully gauging Tiernon's response.

Suddenly, Tiernon felt not only surrounded, but disturbed. He sat quietly, pretending to consider what he had been told, but he was trying to analyze what was wrong. It was not simply that they agreed on all points, he had expected that; but their words, their manner, were too similar to be natural. This kind of thing could be done by magia, but theoretically it was impossible for a non-Adept to manage it.

He was aware of their eyes on him as he considered the matter. He would have to break away subtly, in character. "You will, of course, give me some time to think about this proposition. I am amazed, I hadn't been expecting anything of this kind. And I would need some details."

"What details?" Teth asked. "Isn't Provisional Governor enough, especially considering the jewel wealth of the area?"

"Well," Tiernon replied, smiling, "it all depends on how hard you want me to work for the money. After all, wealth and power aren't everything. There must be some time to play too, or I couldn't possibly function. And the climate is not really good for the preservation of fine wine."

"There are fine cellars in Maddigore," Teth offered.

"Though I would trust you with my life, I would trust no living being with my wine. If I did, there would be none left for me."

They all laughed mirthlessly.

Bertham was half-pleased and half-confused. There were moments when he knew that Tiernon was not what he seemed. There were moments when he honestly thought the Bietehel snob had actually seen through his veil, but then it always resolved into something like this. And then there were the moments when desire sparkled between them, making the chase, the game, all the more delightful.

If Tiernon didn't accept, Bertham thought, and there was no reason to suppose that he would, it just might be a good idea to send Cataia. She'd go eagerly enough and those tribesmen might kill her off, or she might die of the heat, or any number of things. And it would keep her far from Court and the center of action. It just might be worth considering.

"You will permit me to think it over?" Tiernon asked. "And I must have some idea as to how much work will be necessary, and how large a staff the government would be willing to provide me."

"Of course," Bertham said airily.

"And now, if you will excuse me, I must retire. I am not entirely recovered yet, and such a long period of mental exercise is exhausting. If I may have your permission?" Tiernon bowed in Lathanor's direction.

"Certainly. Please be sure that no more assassins find you before our agreement is settled," Lathanor said.

"I will order a double guard at your door tonight. We must take every precaution," Bertham added.

So, Tiernon thought, they are putting me under guard. It was good of Bertham to mention it. Bertham was playing the game on all levels, Tiernon noted. So? Provisional Governor? He was certain that they had no intention of permitting him that much freedom. Not when it had been countered by the tacit surveillance. There was some reason why Bertham had let him know their plans. The duel had come to a draw, Tiernon thought, but Bertham still had the upper hand.

Pointedly, he ignored the grey-and-green-clad Palace guard who escorted him and flanked his door. These were not the best troops in the house, and obviously there was more than one secret that he was keeping from Bertham. If Bertham thought a few extra guards were enough to scare him, the Tonea was sadly mistaken. It was amusing that Bertham didn't respect his ability with conventional weapons. Tiernon knew that he was a better courtier than he was a warrior, but the Abbey had had excellent Masters, and his scimitar was at hand. For all he had never been attacked openly, Tiernon did not like to take too many chances.

The household staff, knowing his habits, had left writing paper, inks and brushes on the low white table in the center of the room. Exhausted as he was, Tiernon sat straight on the cushions and stared at the writing paraphernalia. More than almost any other, this was his job, to keep Asirithe Rei Mother of Bietehel informed. His mother still used him, although he had not seen her in over twenty years, not since the men in the Orange katreisis had taken him to Tsanos as a young boy. He selected pale-grey paper from the assortment, and ink that matched the color of the Rei. This was formal communication and must be sent as such.

He stared at the finely watermarked paper, thinking hard. Asirithe of Bietehel spoke for the Rei Mothers of Avriaten, and he spoke for Asirithe at Court; that was the base of his power. The Rei Mothers were strong, perhaps the strongest force in the country, even if Bertham wished to deny it. It had only been six generations since the Aandev were the first among equals, when the pressures of Salsatean competition had forced them to centralize. In that time, the Aandev had both gained and lost power, lost their real power by moving away from their traditional Rei lands to the city of Tsanos. The Rei Mothers were fiercely independent, grudging every concession to the central government. In the reign of a good Queen, one the Mothers trusted and accepted, personal loyalty had been important. Eltion had been such a Queen. But Bertham and Lathanor did not understand that these women who held the true wealth, the production of Avriaten in their hands, had never really accepted the Regency. In their eyes it was illegal, just as it was illegal to charge someone not come of age with treason, as had been done to Cataia. Indeed, only the severe problems of flooding and poor harvests had kept them from open rebellion, and if they rebelled Tsanos would not stand.

Perhaps Bertham called him his mother's messenger boy, but in truth he was the representative of the most powerful group in the country, except perhaps for the Temple. It was up to him to find the delicate balance between Tsanos and the Reis, a job made continually more difficult by Bertham's policies.

Tiernon had observed the trend from Bertham, and through his eyes the Rei Mothers had observed it, too. Bertham and Lathanor were trying to centralize the government, to truly make Tsanos the legal center of power. The taxation, the Palace army, were all part of this trend, and it frightened Tiernon. Tonight had frightened him particularly badly.

Purposefully he swirled the brush in the mixture of pigment and oil, mixing the ink to a fluid consistency as he thought of the exact wording. As always he wrote with the assumption that Bertham's spies would read his communication. From what he received in return, he knew that Asirithe wrote the same way. After a moment's deliberation, he applied the midnight ink to the paper in the most formal style of calligraphy.

In the name of those most beneficent and compassionate Stars, may they ever guide your path and light your way, the Third Councilor of the Court of Avriaten addresses Asirithe, Mother of Bietehel'Rei the most noble and prosperous, in the sixth year of the Regency of Lathanor rei Aandev, greetings.

As you have no doubt understood, the appointment of the Maddigore'Reian Councilor still fills our hearts with great admiration for his loyal and martial stance. The barbarian tribes of the desert, which, joyfully, have never touched your lands, have threatened this great southern city. The Regent and First Councilor are deeply grieved by this situation, which they claim is shameful to those of us who call ourselves civilized, and wish to chastise these tribes for their outrages.

Through the blessings of the Stars, which make all things possible, I have been asked to accept the Provisional Governorship of the Nestezi after its glorious conquest, to the greater glory of Bietehel and Avriaten. To this I have responded that I am not worthy of the honor.

The First Councilor assures us that this great conquest will live forever in the songs and stories of Volenten, and that the great jewel caves will fill our now troubled Treasury. I have informed the Regent and the

First Councilor that there is no hope for more loan
money, much as the loyal subjects of the Rei wish to
partake in this great venture, as the harvest is troubled
and not yet in.

The gracious and gentle Princess Cataia, not wishing
to burden her subjects further, is opposed to this heroic
undertaking. Certainly she does not have the experience
or understanding of our esteemed First Councilor and
Regent, but the Princess's compassion for her people is
commendable.

At this time nothing is certain, and any action of
yours is sure to be of great importance. I beg you by the
Stars to follow in all conscience that course which would
secure our fair land by the traditions we all honor. I
shall keep you informed as to all developments, and
thank you for this opportunity to serve you in this, as in
all things.

Tiernon read the letter over twice before he rolled his glyph-
stone in the ink and applied it to the bottom of the page. There
was no way anyone could call it treasonous, but Asirithe
would understand. She would be surprised, too. He had sent
his regular long-moon report just a few days ago, and only
once before had he sent more than one report in a short moon.
That was when Eltion was murdered, when Keani committed
suicide in the Council chamber, when it looked like the fragile
monarchy might be totally eliminated. He had not stinted on
his estimation of Bertham at that time, or Bertham's unprec-
edented rise through the ranks. Asirithe would know what to
think.

Smiling, he folded the letter and sealed it with indigo ink,
pressed with the Bietehel Tree. He rang the soft silver bell that
rested on the edge of the table, and a nondescript manservant
appeared. Tiernon handed him the letter without comment
and the man left, carrying the letter with a tray of wine, sweets
and empty cups. He expected the letter to be read but that
didn't mean he had to make it easy. His servants were experienced in slipping through Bertham's guards.

His duties finally done for the night, Tiernon undressed and
sank into the thick, soft pile of his sleeping rug. Just before he
lost consciousness he checked under the bandages one last
time. Only the faintest scar was visible, a scar that looked very
old and long healed, but he pulled the bandage back into place

before he fell asleep. If Bertham knew he was fully healed, there would be more than minor problems to contend with.

Bertham sat alone. The party had broken up shortly after Tiernon had left, and that was pleasant. He was in no mood to spend the night drinking with Lathanor and that childish idiot Teth. Only one oil lamp was left burning, throwing deep shadows on the pale rugs, easing to the eyes. In his mind, Bertham formed the image of the sigal of Lechefrian, the short heavy strokes and the long, thin, wavy ones, tipped with arrows and circles, and other shapes that he was not sure of. They all meant something. This was the second step, forming the image in his mind, making it his own. He followed the heavy lines and the thin ones, and lastly the letters in the ungraceful Eskenese script.

Complete, he held the black-and-grey image in front of him, making it stronger and more sure than the soft ambers all around. He tried to make the lines shimmer on their own, but they remained hard and black and not quite solid. Harder and harder he tried to make it real, and one night it would take on a being of its own. Then he could go on to the next step, and that would make it final. The next step contained the real power, the raw energy that would be built to release and then Lechefrian himself would come. Bertham did not think beyond that point. It had been left blank in the manuscript. The power that sank half the country, the power that had waited and grown for a thousand years, that radiated so firmly from the ground itself that fishermen knew to stay well away from 'Kleppah—all that power was to be his. Armies would be mere vanities. His weapons would be the land, the sea, the sky itself.

And then he shivered and the image wavered. A second of doubt, that was all it took. Frantically he grasped and tried to hold it together, but already the thin grey lines were gone and the black had faded to dull red. Like always, like every night. The level of concentration the System of Lechefrian demanded was inhuman.

But the rewards, Bertham thought. The rewards were more than human, too. And the image *had* held, if only for a short time. Every night it was getting just a fraction longer, his concentration just a fraction stronger. He would be the first since the time of the Seven to control the magia! Bertham could almost feel the energy permeating his being already.

𝒶 Six

THE COURT WAS GLITTERING for the celebration of the new agreement with Salsatee. Tiny lamps flickered, hanging on long bronze chains from the ceiling lost high above them in the night.

Cataia smoothed her royal white katreisi edged in gold, arranging the drape across the full crimson-patterned cushions. Agreement, she thought, what a charade. It was a debt that would take four harvests to pay, and she seethed inwardly at her cousin's ineptitude, and her own powerlessness. She sipped her wine daintily, sealing the anger off in a place where it would do no harm, as she had learned in the Abbey. *Relax*, she heard Mother Daniessa's voice, *look around you. Take note. Become empty.*

With the discipline of her novitiate, she let her eyes sweep the room carefully, noting details. A flutter of memory threaded around her mind. Hadn't Tiernon suggested that she take a lover? Halas rei Tersoneat, the youngest son of Rothele Rei Mother was there, near the corner, almost as newly arrived as she herself. She gave him her attention.

Yet even from here, something about him bothered her. It was not his looks, although he was young, but, she analyzed, the way he sat and moved. The Green were trained in that, to see indications that others would miss. He lay loosely across the cushions without a hint of the tension that went with awareness. His movements were slow, self-conscious, almost a parody of the elegance he tried to emulate. Compared to Tiernon, he was a country bumpkin playing at being of the high nobility, and she dismissed him with contempt.

Tiernon was on the other side of Lathanor and the Salsatean Ambassador, and as Cataia watched him in soft conversation with Syleria, her resolve hardened. He hadn't been sorry enough that he had left her. Let him see that she didn't need to be alone. Her resolve firmed.

Degevyn, the eldest son of the one of the Minor Reis, was seated near the back, as was proper for his rank. Cataia realized that she had seen him a few times at Court functions, but had never spoken to him. They were almost finished with the sweet, and when it was cleared . . . She made her plans.

The interval between the sweet and the entertainment was the time where people drifted and talked to those on the other side of the room, or made a quick exit if they wished. Servants came in and turned the lamps up, and lit many more, brightening the chamber for the jugglers who were to follow. Lathanor was fond of jugglers.

Cataia made her way through the crowd, nodding and exchanging greetings while she tracked Degevyn with her eyes. It took a little work to move into position, next to him but casual.

"Isn't this boring?" he said, laughing.

Cataia flashed a winning smile at him. "What do you think of the agreement?" she asked. After all, it was the excuse for this dinner.

Degevyn shrugged. "Do you hunt?" he asked conversationally. "The hunting is marvelous at Cei Tahad this year."

Cataia felt lost. She didn't have any idea of what she should say. She knew nothing about hunting, and certainly hadn't had the time to go to Cei Tahad to learn.

"Oh, no," Degevyn said, his face twisting into a mockery. "They're talking about that awful new poem that everyone's reading."

"You didn't like it?" Cataia asked, grasping at straws. She had enjoyed it thoroughly, but at least it was a better topic of conversation than hunting.

"Like it? Who has time for that? The hunting's been fine this season, and we had some dancers up from Salsatee. Well, I guess I shouldn't mention that." He blushed. The jugglers entered the open center of the hall.

"I think I'd better get back," Cataia said softly, no longer smiling. "I think the entertainment will begin soon."

She moved away as carefully as she had gone. He was an idiot, boring beyond belief. There was nothing she could say to him. In less than a minute, he had managed to make even Valnera seem exciting. And compared to Tiernon . . .

She didn't want to think about that. No one had ever mentioned that it might not be easy to find someone suitable and pleasant. By the time she resumed her place, Cataia wanted to find Valnera and cry. Valnera would have good advice about where to look. Or was it always so very difficult? It hadn't been difficult to find Tiernon at all, but then he wasn't her lover yet, and at the moment not ever likely to be.

Miserable, she tried to watch the antics of the performers, reminding herself that any more attempts were useless tonight. Degevyn and Halas had seemed the most presentable of the young courtiers she had seen, and perhaps they would be less distasteful if she hadn't met Tiernon. Under the gaiety of the crowd, delighted by the juggling, Cataia cursed Tiernon under her breath.

Today, again, SiUran thought about his Vision Quest. Not, he reminded himself, because he was an old man who lived in the past, but because he had felt it again, the strange pull that made him feel as if all the waiting would soon be over. He had waited all his life for this vision to become truth, for the Great Ones to be reborn and lead his people from the harsh Nestezi back to their land. Their real land, which had been stolen from them in the Great War, so long ago that many people wondered whether it had happened at all.

Their land had been rich and fertile, with great rivers and streams and wells and whole valleys full of food. Then the War had come and they had been pushed out by the eastern people, pushed south over the mountains to this desert where tribe raided tribe for food and water. They had been promised then, in the ages before memory, that their good land would be returned and that they would have plenty for the rest of their days. It was a good dream, but no one had ever believed, no one but SiUran, who had gone on a Vision Quest as a boy and had seen the Great Ones. And they had given him their promise, to carry anew to his people.

Since then he had waited, trusting that when it was time he would know and would be among the first called. The Great Ones promised him that they would know him and that he was marked as one of their own. But recently, very recently, SiUran knew that the time of waiting was almost over.

Eryah, the leader of the teti war band, bounded between several tents to meet him. He had always been fond of her, as if she were his own grandchild.

"Grandfather, I've been looking all over for you," she said, and SiUran noticed that she seemed a little less open than usual. "Could I talk to you in your tent?"

He smiled at her, finding it hard not to put an arm around her shoulders as he had when she was younger and had often come to him like this. He couldn't do that anymore; she had been initiated into the women's mysteries and was no longer a child. Instead, he said, "Come, there's a nice pot of hot ghena and I've no one to share it with."

They sat cross-legged in the tent as SiUran poured the bitter beverage. Eryah chatted about the war band and about a new pair of boots, and they drained the cups. He poured again, becoming more concerned. A one-ghena conversation had recently been for asking permission for a water raid. The second cup was nearly empty, and Eryah was still making small talk. He wondered what kind of matter would necessitate three cups from one so young. Still, he filled the cup for a third time, trying to appear attentive. Finally, when the third round had been emptied, Eryah came to the point.

"Grandfather, I had a dream. SiUran, War Leader of the Atnefi, will you hear my dream?"

She'd spoken formally, his little leaping one. He had named her Eryah, the leaper, at her initiation, and he was proud of her. He gave the required answer and saw her relax.

"I dreamed of the Great Ones," she said in a whisper. "I dreamed I would be called friend. There was a great desert, a desert of water, and we glided over it like sand in a storm. And, Grandfather, I saw the Caverns. They were not filled with jewels, but with lights. I stood at the edge of a lake and the Great Ones stood on an island in the great chamber, and they spoke to me. They said, 'Eryah, wait for us, we are coming. Tell SiUran it will be soon. Tell your people to prepare. For the Atnefi will lead, but you must join hands. Make peace with the Swanimir, the Qaludi, the Itesi, the Tororer Anerim. They shall be as your age-mates and your grandparents whom you love. We are coming, and the world will be changed.' Then there was nothing and I woke up.''

SiUran poured another cup of ghena for them both. It was not required this time, but he needed to think and the bitterness of the beverage helped with that. It was no longer hot, and he drained his cup with one swallow.

''I think you truly saw the Great Ones,'' he said slowly. ''I think they spoke to you, and I think they told you the truth. Could you find the Caverns, if it were necessary?''

''Yes, I think I could,'' she said. ''Near the Rumbler, to the west of the jewel caves.''

''Good,'' SiUran grunted. ''Then let me tell you something. You, and your dream, are part of the Vision, and you will have to lead the Great Ones to the Caverns.''

''But don't they already know the way?'' Eryah asked reasonably.

''No,'' SiUran replied sternly. ''Don't you remember the Prophecy? They must be led to the Caverns by a warrior whose heart is free from hate. I taught you that verse myself.''

Eryah nodded miserably. ''I don't want the world to change,'' she said.

SiUran felt sorry for her. He had had time to adjust, time to live a proper Atnefi life, and he could see why no one would want that life to change.

''Well,'' said Eryah, ''I guess I'd better go back now. My whole tent is waiting.''

''Come sometime soon, Eryah. Just to sit and talk to an old man whose generation is all dead. We won't talk about the Great Ones or any of the mysteries. Agree?''

''Agree,'' she said, and leapt out of the tent.

It was late in the morning, but for all Valnera's fussing Cataia still had her quilt firmly tucked up to her chin. ''I refuse, that's all. I disapprove. I think it's against national policy and I won't go.''

"But you have to go, Princess," Valnera pleaded. "If you don't go it will look like you're setting up some kind of faction. Besides, everyone will be there, and it's good for you to be seen. They get to know you, and that's important."

"Do you know what they're going to announce today? A new tax. And no one can pay the old taxes, and to be there would mean that I approve and I don't, so don't try to make me."

"Lovey, you might be wrong," Valnera said. "Just this once. Anyway, you'll see Tiernon and all that lovely food, and you could make a speech."

"And get my head chopped off," Cataia said.

"Well, I'm not going to argue with you anymore. It isn't worth it. You're the Princess, and you're going to be Queen, and if it's your decision not to attend a public Court, that's your decision. But don't say I didn't try."

. "You tried," Cataia said. "You tried hard enough to drive me crazy and I want to be alone. We can save face and say that I'm ill. Nothing serious, just a touch of heat, and if they insist on a physician I want Chervan. How's that?"

Valnera left shaking her head. She knew perfectly well that Cataia wasn't ill. It was that stubborn Aandev streak, the older woman reflected.

Cataia counted slowly to one hundred to give Valnera enough time to leave before she rose from the sleeping rug. The cheerful midmorning light streamed in and blended with the cool greens and blues of the chamber, making it look like the bottom of a courtyard pool.

She dressed quickly in a simple blouse of green linen with a plain, collarless neck and full-cut pants of the same fabric. Discarding the fancy, tooled Nestezian boots, she chose heavy boots with low tops and a functional design. There were things she had to do in the city, and it would be better if no one knew.

Not attending the public Court had also been a political decision. They had talked until they were hoarse at the last three Council meetings, and the announcement of the new tax was set for today. Although Cataia knew that Bertham would try to make it appear that she was shirking, it would be worse for her to be there and not say anything at all. And she dared say nothing in front of Lathanor and Bertham. No, she had carefully worded a small announcement of her own, and had shown it to Syleria last night. Syleria was the younger sister of the Rei Mother of Tersoneat, one of the Major Reis, and Syleria would make sure it was passed on. The Rei Mother would know, all slander aside, that her absence was a gesture of protest. Syleria did not have Tiernon's power to speak for her Rei. By tradition, only the Bietehel representative spoke for all the Reis combined, unless there was deep dissension on some issue. Syleria was there merely to observe and report. She'd smiled when she had read Cataia's note to the Reis.

Cataia studied herself in the mirror, then braided her hair quickly around her head, as she had when she'd been a novice on Dier Street. Another look in the mirror told Cataia that no one would see the Princess in this commoner's outfit.

The day was bright and hot, and Cataia decided to make a detour through the marketplace before turning back to her original route. She had loved the market as a girl, although as a Princess she couldn't go there anymore. Now all the finest merchants came to show her their wares in the Palace so as not to inconvenience her, but it was the rush and the smells and the bright colors that Cataia missed. Yet, as she approached the main square, it all seemed less impressive than she remembered it. Perhaps because perceptions change, she thought, and one notices more things as an adult.

For instance, the geri seemed more brown than bright-green and they were covered with dust. Plekas, both the belts and the long, narrow hair bands, hung from weavers' stalls as usual, but the colors didn't seem as bright as she remembered them, although there was no wind to whip them around and make them twirl. Nor did she see any of the tall desert tribesmen in their patterned robes selling precious jewels.

The street seemed dusty in the haze of midsummer. The light dust clung to her hands and clothes as the activity of the market went on around her, grey and sordid, and without the intense excitement she remembered. People seemed weary as they haggled, their voices sad and firm. Perhaps it was subdued by the intense heat and dryness.

"A penny, a penny," a beggar called, trailing after Cataia. She tried to ignore him and walked on. "You've got a penny, lady, you've got a penny." The voice had an odd ring and Cataia turned before she could place it. The accent was Batter, southern and lilting.

"What are you doing in Tsanos?" she asked.

"For a penny I'll tell you," the beggar replied.

She gave him the money, but angrily. He was not old or crippled, and she disliked the idea of people who begged when they could work.

"I farmed in Batter, in the orchards," the man said. "But this year the harvest is rotting from the sun, and all the rest is promised in taxes, you see, so there's nothing left. Now they said there's work in the city, so I come here. I went to Volenten first, but there's nothing there, only more like me from the West, so I decided to come here. Well, you see all the good it did me. Was it worth a penny more?"

Cataia nodded and parted with another coin before she walked away. She found the encounter disturbing because she suspected that the man might have been telling the truth. She had heard similar stories before, beggars were notorious for their hard-luck stories, but Cataia still wondered. After all, she had never encountered a southern accent from a beggar before.

Ringing the bell at the gate on Dier Street, Cataia felt out of place. The house hadn't changed, and this was disquieting because it felt more like a dream than reality. She rubbed the carved wood door, feeling the flowers and leaves in their geometric designs, loving them as she had before she'd left this place. A novice opened the gate and led her into the main parlor, a place that made Cataia feel even more ill at ease, since only Priestesses used this area. The last time she had been here, she and Dacia had been polishing the pale-green tiles on the floor and plumping the overstuffed cushions. Now she sat on one.

Dacia came in, looking no different than she had in student days. True, she wore woman's clothing and a woman's hairstyle, but her large, paint-covered smock managed to cover things quite convincingly and there was a yellow splash on her nose. Unconcerned with the half-dry colors, Dacia immediately embraced Cataia warmly, covering the shorter woman with a light coat of half-dry greens and purples.

"I'm so glad you came, I can't believe it. It was so strange, visiting you at the Palace. How can you stand that place? It's so good to have you home where we can talk. Tell me everything. Are you all right? Why are you here? Isn't there some kind of Palace thing going on today, Court or something? Why aren't you there? Shouldn't you be there? Not that I'm not overjoyed to see you, Cai, but knowing you, you didn't just drop by to say hello. And you don't have to worry about what you told me about Lechefrian. I told Mother Daniessa. Have some fruit. You look half-dead.''

"Let me breathe, first," Cataia said, half laughing. She took one of the ripe green geri and tossed it in the air before biting into it. It was good to be home, and Dacia's presence made everything seem more real. It was as if all the months at the Palace had dropped away from her. Of course, there were things she had to ask, but that could wait. "I didn't go to Court today because I'm sick and tired and bored to death with it all, and besides, they're passing some new tax, and I didn't want to give my approval. They'll know what it means. It's about the only way I can show my disapproval publicly, without losing my head, that is. But I want to know about you. What have you been doing? How is your work going? Are any of your students as hopeless as I was?"

Dacia led her into the studio, a large, open room on the top floor, lit by a skylight. Cataia remembered it from her student days, before Mother Jitrain had given up on her. Around the walls were several portraits that Cataia recognized immediately as Dacia's work.

The colors glowed out of the canvases, brilliant and bold, not the dark colors that were usual for portraits, or the pastels used for landscapes. And there was a movement to the pictures. Dacia didn't let her subjects sit in their best clothes in their best room. There was a portrait of a man with a brimming mug in one huge fist, and another of a woman surrounded by scattered sheets of music, her face the essence of concentration as her fingers curled tensely over the strings of the rebabah.

"It's a series of different kinds of work," Dacia said, her voice serious. "I got interested in seeing people in their natural settings. See, the innkeeper and the musician, and here's that rug merchant in the market."

Cataia paused, hesitated and studied each one carefully. "It's strange," she said. "I've never seen anything like this. It's different. But there's something there, as if you've got the soul of each person. Tiernon would just kill to get his hands on this collection."

Dacia didn't say anything. Cataia knew that she wouldn't. Dacia was serious about only two things in the entire universe

—her art and magia. And it was a pleasure to give the paintings her full attention.

"What is it, Cai?" Dacia asked slowly. "You don't seem right, somehow. Like you're afraid of something."

Slowly, Cataia nodded. She should have known better than to think Dacia couldn't read her easily. As she looked up, though, she saw a strained look on her old friend's face.

"What do you mean?" Cataia asked slowly. "It looks to me like you know something that I don't, or something."

Dacia shrugged. "Let's go downstairs. It's almost time for lunch, and I'm starved."

Cataia nodded mutely and followed Dacia down to the rectory, feeling slightly awkward when one of the novices called her Lady Priestess. After all, these were girls she had shared a hall with not a year ago. Somehow, the food was even better than she remembered, the simple broiled fish and sliced fresh vegetables seasoned with only the slightest touch of salt. And the silence that was required at meals was truly pleasurable. That was the one thing she really missed at the Palace: silence. It was almost painful when the meal was over and she returned to the parlor with Dacia and Mother Daniessa.

As Cataia sat with them, she wanted to cry. It wasn't just homesickness, she realized, but something more. There was no rest at the Palace, no place for her to drop the worries she carried. There was always Bertham, ready to pounce, and the tension with the Reis and the possibility of war and negotiations with Salsatee. There was never a moment to just be.

Cataia looked at the brilliant streak of light creeping across the floor. She couldn't let down her discipline in front of Mother Daniessa. "I've come to ask you about what I should do, both about Bertham and his possible involvement with Lechefrian."

Mother Daniessa's eyes glittered hard at her, and Cataia shrank inwardly.

"It's no secret that 'Kleppah is moving," the senior Priestess said. "That's not the reason you've come, though. Cataia, you are where you are because you were born for it, and you can handle it."

The fish turned to a knot of metal in Cataia's stomach. She had known, they all had known, that she didn't want to face it all alone. And it was necessary to do so, just like Initiation.

Hadn't Mother Daniessa often taught her that life itself was a series of Initiations?

"I am disappointed," her old teacher said softly. "I thought you had more courage than that." Mother Daniessa rose and walked to the door. Just before she disappeared, she turned back. "Come when it's over. It's your final trial, Cataia. When it's done, then you may return." With that, Mother Daniessa left the room.

Dacia threw her arms around Cataia and the Princess began to cry. Dacia patted her back and smoothed her hair, and her friend's concern made Cataia cry that much harder. She needed to hang on to Dacia, her anchor against the waves of fear that were sweeping over her.

"It's not Mother Daniessa," Dacia said softly. "Cai, please, it isn't her choice at all, not really."

Cataia looked up and sniffed. Dacia's face was taut, holding some secret, and that made her even more frightened.

Dacia hesitated. "I'm not supposed to tell you," she said slowly. "Mother Daniessa might turn me out if she knew. But, Cai, we're under orders from Aken. They're more than just interested. One of their Initiates, one of Aken, came here, and ordered us to leave you strictly alone."

Shock hit Cataia so hard that her feelings were forgotten. "One of Aken? In the flesh?"

Dacia nodded. "In the flesh," she agreed. "And he said he's looking out for you, so I'm not as worried as I could be. Only, Cai, please, please take care of yourself."

For the first time, Cataia realized that Dacia was frightened too. She took one of Dacia's hands and squeezed it hard. "I guess I'd better go," Cataia said softly. Dacia nodded, and they both rose.

Suddenly, Cataia felt herself being hugged once again, this time more desperately than reassuringly. And then Dacia opened the door.

Cataia wandered down Dier Street, not wanting to return to the Palace yet, and not wanting to be alone, either. She stopped in the pastry shop and bought six of her favorite honey seed cakes. A group of boys was playing a ball game outside the shop, the kind of children who lived on Dier Street, respectful and well behaved, wearing what had been clean clothes before the game. For the first time Cataia wondered if they were simply children who lived on the street, or the novices of some other Order. Tiernon's Order, perhaps.

She had lived there for half her life, seen people come and go, seen children and young people in clumps seated out on the carefully swept stone stoops, chatting or buying sweets on the corner, but it had never struck her before that they well might be her own. There were five more Abbeys on Dier Street behind the high gates and dusty flowers. It was a well of comfort, to be surrounded by them, each isolated and complete unto itself, but all here. As she walked by, she noticed the houses, each with well-scrubbed steps and plain carvings set in the windows, wondering of each if it were a private dwelling as she had always assumed. Two girls who looked about fourteen years old giggled together as they came out of the shop, and Cataia wondered if they were novices of the Purple or the Black, or just two girls. She felt safe here, and happy, but identified the source. It was just good to be home.

Finally she knew that she had to return to the Palace. If nothing else, the day had given her some distance, a security about what she must do. And there was the information about Aken. Watching her? Idly, she wondered who, and then realized that if Aken wanted to remain hidden, Aken would remain hidden. But after a short taste of freedom, it was hard to return to the pomp and splendor of Avriaten's Court.

When Tiernon invited Ayt to dine with him, he knew that Court gossip would have created a new alliance before sunset, and he was not disappointed. That, however, did not worry him. It was Cataia, and Ayt, and the situation in regard to the Nestezi that was on his mind, and he hoped Ayt could help. She had her own mind and was not easily swayed, a rather good quality for someone in her position.

In her own way, Ayt had as much power as Lathanor and Bertham combined, and sometimes more, Tiernon reflected. He was not such an innocent or purist to believe that, in almost a thousand years, the Temple of the Stars had not acquired some measure of power on the Planes, and their power in the physical world was certainly something to be reckoned with. Even if Avriaten's coffers were empty, the Temple had vast resources from generations of contributions by the faithful, and no one but Ayt knew the full extent of them. The Temple also held the loyalty of the hearts of the people, and held their fears for their souls, quite a power indeed. If confronted by conflicting orders from the Temple and the Crown, most commoners would choose the Temple. Ayt could effectively countermand any order given by the Court, any plan devised by the Council, in a single stroke. Twice in history her predecessors had, and the resulting riots had brought down two Queens. That was why she, as her predecessors, sat on the Council itself. It was far better to know of Temple opposition before it became public than after the fact.

There were all kinds of reasons, Tiernon thought, why he should be careful in this meeting, but above all was the overwhelming feeling of loneliness. He had never really understood why she had recoiled from him after the many long moons of their association. He had just come of age, just come to Court, and he remembered Ayt as she had been thirteen years ago. She was still beautiful. He had been too young, there had been too many mistakes, but the memory still brought him both pain and longing. Firmly he pushed these things out of his mind.

Besides, there were other things that inspired Tiernon's respect. She was essentially practical, moral, and really believed in her role. Perhaps that had been the real problem between them, and one that couldn't be overcome. Politically, she did not owe her power to anyone, and no one could depose her save by assassination, and even assassins steered clear of the Temple. On top of it all, Ayt had quietly built the Temple into a vast private army, loyal to no one but herself, an achievement that Tiernon had to admit was clearly the work of a first-class mind.

He had set things perfectly for her arrival, remembering to order her favorite dishes and to use the pale-blue cut-stone goblets she had given him in another time. In a way, this was less to impress than to express his respect, and his remembrance.

He caressed the smooth cool stone, so smooth to the touch that it seemed like glass. Even as he remembered the occasion on which they had been presented, he found himself thinking of Cataia, wishing she were a little older and a little less Aandev. That would not do. The sun had almost set, and Ayt would arrive momentarily. She was very prompt, a trait Tiernon wished more of the Council members would cultivate. Maybe serving a novitiate, or having to lead services at set hours, would improve their sense of time. He chuckled to himself, knowing that these experiences were ones that he and Ayt had shared.

As if on cue, Ayt entered the room noiselessly. She smiled at Tiernon, a weary smile, as she had been smiling all day at worshippers and courtiers and ambassadors. "It has been a long time since we dined privately," she said. "A very long time."

Tiernon stood until she was comfortably settled on the white cushions, a normal respect for the High Priestess of the Temple and an excessive one for an ex-lover.

"I don't want to deceive you," he said. "The reason for this is strictly political."

"Of course," said Ayt. "I expected nothing else. But let's not mar the meal. We did part friends."

"It was a long time ago. Things have changed and you have become even more beautiful."

"I'm not one of those minor nobles who needs your flattery, Tiernon." Ayt laughed. "Come, let's be honest as old friends should. We've been through the wars and we've both survived heads intact, which is more than can be said for some of our less fortunate colleagues. Let's drink to friends and old times, since the new don't seem very promising."

They raised their glasses together and tasted the wine. "I see that the quality of your cellar has not diminished with time."

They laughed for no reason, or perhaps just to make some noise. It seemed too quiet.

"Come and tell me what this is all about," Ayt began, and Tiernon felt more comfortable. He hated the moments before the subject could be broached and knew that Ayt shared similar feelings. It would be pleasant to be honest, or at least mostly honest, for once.

"Quite simply this, then. Where do you stand on this idea of war?" he asked.

"I support it," Ayt said quietly.

Tiernon was stunned, and it took him a few heartbeats to recover. "But why?" he asked, aghast.

"Perhaps it would be better if you told me why not," Ayt said softly.

It was not the situation he would have chosen, but he had always known Ayt was astute. And it was typical of her to force him to turn his tiles over before she had selected hers. Well, then, the stakes go up. "All right. You know Lathanor and Bertham, and you know what's been happening. Six years of bad government and a bad harvest are telling on the Rei Mothers. They will not support a war effort, at least Bietehel will not and most of the others will follow.''

Ayt nodded. She understood a threat when she heard one, knowing full well that Asirithe had not been consulted in this and that Tiernon had full power to make a statement of that kind.

"One," Tiernon continued, "without the support of the Major Reis any call is going to fail, and since Eltion was murdered the Rei Mothers have been pulling back from any government except their own. Remember, the Aandev were only nominal rulers until just a few generations ago, and many Reis consider them only the richest of the Major Reis run amuck. And moving the capital to Tsanos weakened their position again, removing the Aandev from their base of power. Many of the Rei Mothers would be only too happy to reduce their powers, leaving the Queen simply a Rei Mother with no more than some special influence. With the growth of Salsatee, this would be a disaster. All they would need would be for us to disintegrate into a group of warring Reis, each independent, for them to swallow us up. Quite literally. They can't feed their population, and the problem is getting worse."

"I quite understand," Ayt said. "On the other hand the Reis might have a great deal to gain." Here she stopped, not yet fully committed, afraid to say it aloud. If she misjudged Tiernon by even the slightest fraction, her head would be ceremonially deprived of her body at dawn. It wouldn't be easy, but Ayt did not underestimate Bertham. No matter what the consequences he wouldn't let her live. It wasn't a pleasant prospect. For the first time the words *high treason* ran through her head.

She studied Tiernon for a moment. He was no longer young, as he had been when she had first seduced him, and he had not been innocent then. She had always had an intuition that his loyalty was never wholly with either the Aandev or the Bietehel, although she did not know where to place it and he never talked. Ayt knew that somewhere in Tiernon was a secret so strong, so deep, that it ran like a steel thread through his fiber. It had destroyed their relationship, which she had grieved for, for herself and for him. The secret kept him isolated, but it would remain unbroken. He would kill the Princess himself if she stood in the way of that unspoken loyalty, and Ayt secretly acknowledged that it scared her. Still, she judged that unless her treason conflicted with whatever his secret loyalty was, he would not reveal her.

Sucking in a deep breath, she decided to go on. "You are right. The Rei Mothers are dissatisfied with Lathanor, and with good reason. But by rights and tradition we do have a Queen. One cannot equate mother and daughter. The Regency is illegal. Cataia should have been crowned when she came of age. Bertham has created a legal farce and Lathanor is a pretender, according to our customs and traditions. Cataia has also shown signs of being more capable and concerned than Lathanor, at least to my satisfaction. I think Cataia should be crowned Queen and an end to this business should be made."

Tiernon was awed. In over ten years, no one else had ever left him speechless twice. "But what does this have to do with the war?" he finally asked, the food in front of them growing cold, forgotten.

"Simply this. Lathanor is already in trouble with the Rei Mothers. But if they dislike this pretender of a Regent who would lead them into a profitless war and try to take their power, they would turn to a young Queen who was tied to their interests. After all, they know as well as we the danger of splitting the country. Let Lathanor carry the scimitar to his own execution. There will be no war, except a small internal one, hopefully so small that by the time news of it reaches Salsatee things will be settled down and a new monarch will be on the throne, one who has the full support of the country."

Tiernon was stunned. As had been the case in the past, Ayt had gone one step ahead of him. Move, countermove, play both sides. And Ayt had her own army. Small, yes, but superbly trained and equipped and fed through the resources of the Temple.

"I wonder," Tiernon mused, "if it's possible to have any personal morality in this situation."

"For a question like that"—Ayt laughed—"I would initiate you a Priest in a moment. Do you know what your power would be then?"

Tiernon shook his head. That, indeed, would be the height of immorality. "It would make me suspect by the Rei Mothers.

They honor the Temple as much as any, but they worry about the temporal power. My effectiveness in that matter would be extremely limited."

"I think we understand each other," she said carefully.

"You have certainly cleared up your position. You did mention that there would not be a war in the end. I take that to mean that you are aware of my objections."

"Aware, certainly. They are the crux of the plan. It wouldn't hurt to remind your mother that by law Cataia has been Queen for half a year, and that Lathanor's usurping could be classified treason."

Tiernon smiled. "It's so pleasant when old friends agree about the essentials. Shall we drink to a long and prosperous reign of the true monarch?"

As they lifted their cups, their eyes met. "And to the agreement between old friends?" Ayt asked.

Tiernon smiled and drank, never taking his gaze from her face. Her beauty was not strictly of her features, but of the intelligence that animated them. Her pale skin contrasted with the rich burgundy of the hangings, skin as smooth and soft as a young girl's. Wisps of pale-brown hair curled over her ears. It had been a very long time, he realized, far too long. There was something inviting about the line of her long neck, fluted and white like the delicate columns in the room, and the position of her fingers resting on the stem of the cup. The silvery Temple katreisi was draped to reveal the roundness of her shoulders and hips as she reclined gracefully among the myriad cushions.

"Some more wine?" he asked, his voice slightly low and husky. He reached for her glass and lightly touched the tips of her fingers.

"Please," she whispered, with a smile that was neither weary nor set. Their fingers laced and the wineglass went unfilled.

Bertham cursed in fury at the air. He did not pay spies to be stupid, and this one had been. Asirithe would have that letter in two or three days, and there was no way to catch the courier now. Bertham cursed Tiernon for always sending his messages by ship. Once out of Tsanos, they were as good as in Asirithe's hands, unless a storm at sea could be stirred up.

By the traditions we all honor . . .

Bertham was just glad that the second agent had copied the letter down, or he would have thought the whole thing, if not harmless, at least something of less magnitude. He knew perfectly well what traditions Tiernon meant. The succession, the most sacred tradition of them all. That, and the simple fact of biology that a man could never prove his heir.

It was worse, Bertham reflected, far worse than he had thought. He had not expected Tiernon to move quite so quickly to instigate a coup.

He had to do something about it, and now, before Asirithe could answer that call to arms. Bertham knew that she wouldn't risk outright war against the Aandev; that would only result in renewed hostilities with Salsatee. No, if he would break the link here at Court, the whole disaster could be averted.

It was too early. Bertham had planned it down, finely, so that when the time came, he would be able to have Tiernon and Cataia both, as well as any of their followers, executed as common criminals. It galled him to have his precious plans invalidated. Well, that couldn't be helped. There was no time. If Tiernon could organize the Rei Mothers to support Cataia, he might very well have lost the whole game by the next planting.

Old Nia's simples had come in useful before. Now, now that Bertham was touching the real nexus, the energies of Lechefrian and with that all of 'Kleppah, he did not like to think of simples, taught by an old woman who didn't wash too often and stank. He concentrated, trying to remember the spell. There was one, he knew. One for the removal of enemies, so that it would look like common disease. Yes, that would be the best, untraceable, irrefutable. There was nothing anyone could link to him that way. Something that looked like pestilence.

He remembered Old Nia as she had instructed him, her mouth hanging half-open and her long claw fingers picking at his sleeve, asking, "Now, Bertham, do you know what this part is, do you know what that part is, do you remember this chant?"

The simples were based on very specific instructions, he knew. No elegance was necessary, only the rote steps taken correctly. And they were usually unpleasant.

He sealed off the study, the dark-blue hangings making it

the perfect place to work this spell. In the dim light it would look black. Old Nia had laughed when she'd told him that the darker it was, the better the spell would work. Then he collected what he would need. Five candles, three black and two red; paper, brush and ink; a thin braid of red silk; and a little knife. He set them all on the red lacquer table. Red was one of the colors for this spell, red for blood. A dull brazier held the incense. He hoped he had remembered it correctly. When he lit it and the noxious odor hit, he knew that he had. For the System of Lechefrian, he would have no use for stink in order to make something work, but he still had to work on that before he would receive its power, and this had to be done quickly. Tonight was not too soon. Before that letter had been written would have been better.

He lit the candles and extinguished the oil lamps in the study. Then, concentrating deeply, he drew a likeness of Tiernon on the paper, and then wrote the Third Councilor's name across it in flowing calligraphy to better identify the victim. Fixing Tiernon's face firmly in mind, he began to chant, "Life's blood, heart's blood, fire blood, ice blood, blood to blood I draw your life, flowing from you like the Entelle in the spring. By this blood I burn your life in fever, I cool it as stone. Your soul will be borne by the desert storm and dissolve to nothing at all." Then he jabbed the knife into his thumb and dabbed a drop of blood over the head of the drawing, obliterating it.

Twice more he chanted, and twice more he blotted his thumb on the heart and throat of the picture. Then, with fierce anger, he impaled the picture on the knife, already smeared with his own blood. The room stank. The paper, shriveled from the fluids and torn raggedly, was fit only for the trash.

Bertham was satisfied so far. He concentrated on an image of Tiernon fevered and unable to breathe. Those were the symptoms of the Summer Pestilence. He imagined the parched burning lips of the fever victims and their glassy yellowed eyes.

Keeping this picture of Tiernon firmly in mind, he tied the paper with the braided cord, knotting it eleven times as he worked. Eleven knots, each of them a curse, each a bit of the disease. "Headache, nausea, cramps, dizziness, fever, chills, sweating, choking, swelling, insane speech, death." He held the tied paper in both hands, forcing his own image of Tiernon dying of Summer Pestilence into the fabric of the pulp itself, forcing it until he trembled and couldn't concentrate any longer. Then he threw the paper onto the brazier. The dried blood and paper added to the noisome odor as the paper turned to ash, mixed with the stench of the incense itself.

As he lit the oil lamps again, Bertham stripped off the katreisi he had been wearing and stepped out of the pants. They were full of the incense and made him feel filthy. He would have them burned tomorrow. He wanted a bath. He wanted to erase the memory of having done that spell, as he always felt after doing one of Old Nia's spells. And still, the hardest part was yet to come.

The spell would begin to work immediately, but the full force would not set until it was in the victim's possession. Bertham considered for a moment as the ashes cooled in the brazier, and then went purposefully to the next room. There was a cushion there, not particularly lovely, but suitable for his plan. It was to be presented as a gift from some Bietehel peasant with a petition. Tiernon was hardly so hard-hearted as to destroy a gift that from a peasant would represent the earnings of almost half the last harvest.

He waited a good while until the ashes became stone cold, and then opened the seam along the edge of the cushion. Quickly stuffing it with the ash, he reclosed the edge, wishing he would not have to resew the seam himself and knowing full well there was no one else he could entrust the task to. Sewing was not something a Council Lord did. Even in a Minor Rei there had always been servants to do it for him.

Still, Bertham barely hesitated. The feeling of the ash was not completely clean; there was some residue of oil from the incense that coated his hands. It could not be helped. He stuffed the ash deep into the interior of the cushion, hoping that the filling would absorb the oils. At least the smell had been burned out of it. Then he sewed it shut. He was no tailor, but it would serve. As would the cushion, not lovely, but not of particularly poor design, either.

He wrote a note to accompany the pillow, careful to disguise his own hand, but it was too suspicious to be entrusted to a secretary. Besides, the Court secretaries had fine, schooled hands, and there was no time to summon a public letter writer such as a peasant would use. The whole thing had to be completed and ready before sunrise.

It would be delivered the next day during the noon meal, Bertham decided. Tiernon would be dining publicly with the Council. It would give Bertham a chance to watch his reactions.

Somehow, it was confusing that Tiernon did not believe. Bertham would have thought that anyone with a subtle mind would instantly see the connection between the time of the War and the present, but he didn't begrudge his colleague's materialism. Indeed, it was quite the rage now, and Tiernon was always in style.

Tiernon awoke with a headache, and that bothered him. He didn't often get headaches, and he knew perfectly well that the few glasses of wine last night could not be responsible. It disappeared during morning meditation, which had to be done late on account of Ayt, but came back in full force as soon as the Chant to the Sun had been completed. It would be good to lie in bed all day until the damned thing went away, but there was the Council meeting and Cataia would want to talk to him.

The last thing he wanted to do was talk with Cataia. Sometimes she behaved like a silly child with the famed Aandev temper. Her remark about Ayt infuriated him, and if she weren't the Crown Princess and an Initiate, he would teach her some manners. It was a rotten morning.

By the time he got to the Council Chamber, the headache was worse.

"Oh, Tiernon," Lathanor said, "we thought you'd abandoned us to your pleasures. We have been discussing a treaty with Salsatee."

Tiernon nodded, the motion making him nauseated. The tray of fruit in the center of the table turned his stomach.

"The Salsateans are very actively involved in the Western Lands beyond the sea now," Teth was saying. "They'd probably welcome a nonaggression pact."

"With us sitting on their northern border?" Syleria asked.

Tiernon felt his head spin and lowered himself onto one elbow to keep from falling. The movement was wrenching.

"What do you think, Tiernon? Should we try it, or should we wait?" Lathanor asked.

Tiernon hesitated. He hadn't followed the conversation closely. His head was drumming. Every moment he spent was an eternity of agony. He wanted only to escape. "We lose nothing by approaching them," he managed to say.

He saw Bertham observing him, and his stomach heaved again. The room was too hot and stuffy. The air was sluggish, and it was difficult to breathe.

"I think it best not to approach Salsatee now," Bertham said softly. "We don't want them to know too much."

"I agree with Bertham," Ayt said firmly. "They are already unhappy about the late shipments of steema."

The mention of steema made Tiernon feel ill all over again. He didn't know how he was going to live through this meeting, let alone the meal to follow it. He shut his eyes for a moment, letting the debating voices float over him, and concentrated on stilling his head. It didn't work very well, the pain was too bad to concentrate properly.

"But they've threatened an embargo on textiles," Teth said. "What would happen if they actually did it?"

Tiernon had the surprising urge to kick him, both for talking too loud and for being stupid. Only it was too difficult to move. It was too difficult to think. The voices floated around him, making noise without sense. Then the heavy, ceremonial knock at the Council door lanced through him. It was time to eat.

It took all of Tiernon's concentration to navigate the short corridor between the Council Chamber and the audience room. The smell of food was heavy, making his stomach churn and his senses reel. He collapsed onto his usual cushion, and tried not to notice the small table piled high with delicacies placed next to him. Even the pressure release would be welcome now, that foolproof method against headaches that was more painful than the damn things to begin with.

The Salsatean Ambassador was led to his place next to Lathanor, and Tiernon realized that he had to stand and bow. It took more energy than he could muster. Only will alone kept him from falling. And then the entertainment began, the soft string music that he usually enjoyed. Only now every note screamed into his consciousness, tearing him apart. It was hot here, very hot. It was too hot. He could feel the sweat running down his ribs, the fabric of his brocade shirt clinging to his back.

Father Prethed had said that it was possible to endure

anything and function. Only the will mattered, only discipline. The reason most people failed at what they attempted, the reason those who failed Initiation failed, was lack of will.

Tiernon felt the sweat break out on his forehead and had to control himself so that he was not gasping for air in front of the entire Court and the Salsatean.

The singing stopped and there was talking. Tiernon held on, thinly, to the edge of his sanity, to his will. Then he noticed that people were moving, and he didn't understand. Then it occurred to him that the meal was over. Very slowly he raised himself and began to walk with the crowd, uncertain of which way to go.

In the corridor, a voice stopped him. "I would appreciate it if you would dine with me tonight," she was saying formally. His vision was slightly blurred, and it took a moment for Tiernon to identify the speaker. "I am rather upset that you have not spoken to me this morning, as I believe that certain things are becoming resolved," the voice went on.

Oh, yes, it was Cataia. Why was she speaking formally? He could not remember.

"I can't, I'm afraid," Tiernon said. He couldn't see the expression on her face and he honestly didn't care. The few bites he had eaten during the elegant repast were churning inside him, and the light was too bright.

"What do you mean, you can't?" The voice came back sharper, edged in red through the darkness encroaching around him.

"I'm not well," Tiernon mumbled. "I must go."

"Do you want a doctor? Do you want Chervan?"

The voice was beginning to hurt now, pounding away at his temples like the pommel of a sword. He managed some sort of affirmative answer and staggered out of the hall, careful to remain upright and walking, not to let them know that anything was wrong. He never noticed Bertham's smile.

As soon as Tiernon entered his own apartments, he knew that something was wrong. Even through the headache, which had steadily worsened and was now the only thing in existence he could acknowledge, there was the feeling of something very wrong.

"This was delivered for you today, Lord, from Bietehel. There's a petition with it. . . ."

The servant spoke softly, but Tiernon was overcome by a desire to slam him against the wall for making painful, painful sounds. If he did not, it was not due to generosity, but to the weakness that passed through him with each movement of his head. As he took the cushion in his hands, his vision, already swimming, went black and he began to find it almost impossible to breathe.

Something . . . wrong . . . he thought. *Here, pain . . . burn, burn, burn . . .*

Half crawling, half supported by the wall, Tiernon managed to find his way to the secret room behind the great wall-rugs in the hall. The brazier stood ready, clean and empty from his last working.

Deposit cushion on brazier. Light. Where was there fire?

Shaking badly now, he fumbled through the trunk to find the flint and steel that were kept there for lighting the oil lamps, and struck. Half fainting, backing himself against the wall with one foot at the base of the heavy bronze brazier, he struck spark after spark.

Oil, he needed oil. The lamps on the altar were full. The room was spinning, and he was not sure where the altar was, but that made no difference. On hands and knees now, he groped unceremoniously across the floor. Something primitive in him knew that he must destroy that cushion, although he could not say why at the moment. He didn't care. His whole attention was on the search for the oil lamps.

Luckily the chamber was not large and the altar dominated the center. After what seemed an eternity, he managed to get a lamp and find the brazier again. This time it was almost impossible to get up. With all the considerable strength he possessed, he pulled himself up by the long bronze stem that seemed to burn like cold ice under his hand. His breathing was coming harder, and Tiernon began to feel that there was no air, none to breathe in the whole world.

Later, he never remembered how, he somehow poured the oil over the cushion and lit it. It seemed like his hands must have been too unsteady to have done the job alone. The stench was heavy and sickening, and Tiernon sank to the floor, unable to move any longer. It was almost sunset before he could rise and stagger to his sleeping rug, praying only that he had gotten to the spell in time.

Chervan came and went while he slept and reported to Cataia that he was resting peacefully.

He slept until nearly noon, when Cataia herself appeared, insisting on explanations.

"Someone tried to kill me," Tiernon said. "I don't know who or why, but this much is certain: it wasn't an attack from the Planes."

"Are you sure? Absolutely sure?" Cataia asked, trying to keep the concern from her voice. She was having a very hard time remembering that she was still angry with him.

Tiernon tried to keep himself from glaring at her. There were times when she forgot that being Princess did not make her any more a Priestess. "I am quite sure," he said icily.

"Whom do you suspect?" Bertham leapt immediately to her mind.

Tiernon laughed humorlessly. "The list is very long, and Bertham heads it, although if he is mixed up with 'Kleppah I don't know why he'd resort to simples."

"Crude, but effective, and if only the results matter . . ." Cataia said, thinking of Bertham.

"Yes," Tiernon replied. "Then there's you."

"What do you mean by that?" Cataia's voice became even colder. Fury rose in her. How dare he even think such a thing? "If I did a thing like that, I would have succeeded."

"You know," Tiernon said airily, "you sound just like Keani did when she was charged with Eltion's murder. Those were her exact words, you know. On the other hand, given the way you were trained in the Abbey, I'm pretty sure you don't have much background in the low magia anyway. The thing is, where would anyone have learned it? It's not the sort of thing people at Court usually master."

"Exactly. Anyway, I have your man. And it is a man. Bertham."

"How can you be sure?" Tiernon asked.

"Those things have to hit somewhere, don't they? I mean, they have to discharge. So if the intended victim is protected, then whoever sends it gets the hit, right?"

Tiernon nodded. That was about all they had learned of the low magic at the Abbeys.

"Well," Cataia said reasonably, glad to be able to give him new information, "Valnera told me. She heard through the usual kitchen grapevine that Bertham is too ill to leave his rug this morning. Maybe the whole thing will recoil and he'll die," she added offhandedly.

"Not likely. I took a good hit from the thing. Still, the evidence is circumstantial," Tiernon said.

"Oh, I know it wouldn't stand up in court," Cataia said, "but it's the best we have at the moment."

Tiernon laughed heartily and Cataia stared at him in astonishment. "Frankly," he said, "if I'm going to have anybody try to kill me, I'd prefer it to be Bertham."

"That's not funny." How could he be so cavalier? she wondered.

"Yes it is," Tiernon answered. For a flash he saw the whole thing, the entire ridiculous world from another viewpoint, and he laughed again. The thing was all so pointless. Petty bickering, politics, plots, all of it was edged with a sort of insanity that had no relationship to reality. It was, he knew, the delicious freedom of the retreat that let him see it in those terms, the freedom that wasn't gone and never would be.

Like a burden dropped from his shoulders, he realized that he was no longer angry with Cataia. In veiled terms he told her about Ayt's plans, and a hard look came over her. He was proposing treason. She had to resist, but there was Nikkot's voice in her mind, saying, "Make your bid."

"You know, of course, that I could never give any hint of consent to such a thing. And, if she would do that to Lathanor, why wouldn't someone else do the same to me sometime, if they don't like everything I do? Absolutely not. I do not consent." For a moment he saw the struggle in her cross her face as she realized the full meaning of what had been presented. "Still, you are a free entity. I can't stop you, but don't go too far. I wouldn't want to have to denounce you for treason."

There, he had her tacit approval, although there was no doubt in Tiernon's mind that she would denounce him, and testify, and even hold the sword herself if it came to that.

Poor little Princess. In this stone-grey mood of hers he felt sorry for her, a pity that immediately became amusing when he considered that she was neither pitiable nor particularly vulnerable. He regretted the coldness that she had imposed between them, regretted it more than railed against being treated simply as an exemplary servant. It would take a while for her anger to subside. In actuality, she had all the qualities of a virago and no minor compunctions about using them.

"It might not be a bad idea to eliminate Bertham, if it could be done effectively and without a trace," she was saying.

"And how could it be done without any trace? It would not be good for your image, and any hired assassin would immediately be linked to our camp or to the Rei Mothers, which amounts to the same thing."

"Magia?" she asked slyly, in a testing sort of way.

Tiernon bristled. That kind of death had other implications. To kill a body was no big thing. Bodies weren't very important in the whole scheme of things, but a magia death devastated the soul. Besides, something inside of Tiernon naturally rebelled against the murder of Bertham, and for the first time he realized that he couldn't just hire the job done and forget it. He hated Bertham, they had hated each other for a long time, and it would be politically expedient for him to die. On the other hand, something told him intuitively that there was more to this than could be resolved by a few drops of poison or a sharp-edged blade. Bertham had to be faced, dealt with, grown through, he realized, and not for Bertham's sake but for his own. It had never occurred to him before to kill Bertham, and he was sure that, under it all, Bertham's attempt had been meant to fail. Bertham and Tiernon needed each other in some strange way, in some working of the Planes that could not be denied any more than it could be explained. He and Bertham were mirror twins.

Cataia sensed Tiernon's consternation at her suggestion and dropped it immediately. He was absolutely right. There was nothing else she could do. "But what if he is involved with 'Kleppah and Lechefrian's attack? Shouldn't we be expecting another?"

"Of course," Tiernon answered jovially. "You think the Eater of Souls would give up after one halfhearted try? Not likely. This doesn't even have anything to do with Lechefrian. And I think we have some time. By historical evidence, at least, Lechefrian tends to wait a long time, to let people get sloppy." He reached unconcernedly for a fat green fruit in the bowl at his side, enjoying Cataia's manifest confusion. She took things too seriously.

"By your leave, Highness, I am extremely tired," he said. "I must go to sleep. I cannot help it. If there should be any further developments, I will inform you immediately, but at the present I have other business to attend to.'' He grinned broadly.

Cataia's face softened a bit as she nodded her assent and rose to leave.

Tiernon held the long-handled brush away from the paper as he thought. His mother was going to be very surprised at the recent increase in the volume of her correspondence. Yet this time, more than any other, he had to be careful. If nothing else, this letter could be intercepted, and he did not like the idea of decapitation overly much. Public execution was demanded for high treason, and it was in such bad taste.

He began to write in long broad strokes, not quite the fine calligraphy required for Court and for the joy of the eye, but a straightforward hand that Asirithe would judge honest and true. He admonished her to follow the Temple in *all things,* something she would read twice and understand.

He tried to imagine her, but he could not. There had always been an abyss between the strongly materialistic Asirithe and her mystical son. If she had any religion it was common sense, Tiernon reflected, although she was a stalwart supporter of the Temple; that had been political necessity. It was expected, and Asirithe always did what was expected of one with her responsibilities, at least outwardly. She was as stable as the Great House they had grown up in, the House built before the War by the people who were now nomads in that barren waste called the Nestezi.

It was impossible to believe that the tribes were really primitive, at least not from that House. It was a model of proportion and line; splendor and restraint showed at every turn. The great central Tree, formed of colored glass and enamel, had withstood the ravages of time and countless generations of children without a blemish, and was considered one of the greatest art treasures in the world. Surely the creators of such beauty could not have entirely forgotten what they once were.

The note finished, he stamped it with the glyph-stone of his House and rank. The more personal glyph-stone had been used infrequently, and lay neglected in the brush box waiting for some personal need. He barely noticed the underused glyph-stone rolling against the fragile brush handles.

&SEVEN

JOSTLING AND PACKING, Valnera managed to keep up a nearly uninterrupted flow of conversation to anyone who would or would not listen. She was excited, and enjoying the packing, going over Cataia's wardrobe for perhaps the seventeenth time, deciding what should be taken and what should be left. Of course, there was always that horrid little box Cataia insisted on, but Valnera did not worry about that. Cataia sat in the middle of the dishevelment of preparations entirely unmoved by Valnera's constant outpourings and rhetorical questions about clothing.

For three days they had known, and the Court was in a bustle to get ready. Asirithe had a granddaughter, first of a generation from her eldest daughter, Tiernon's sister. The child had been acknowledged by three father-rugs, all of them the finest quality, all knotted with the Bietehel Tree in indigo to honor the future Mother of the Rei. The entire Court must be present at the naming of such an important heiress.

Cataia was rather amused by the whole thing. It would be

interesting to see Tiernon taking part in the Star ritual. As nearest male kin to the child he had no choice.

"My sister and I were never close, but I never thought she'd do a thing like this to me," he had exclaimed in mock despair during the banquet at which it was first announced. The entire Court had laughed with the Councilor, who couldn't possibly be that unconcerned about the succession of his own Rei, and Tiernon had laughed with them. It wouldn't do, he knew, for them to have any inkling that he was honestly upset at having to return to his home Rei at this time. The expected attack from Lechefrian could take place anytime, and it would be more than inconvenient for it to happen in his mother's house. First, there would be no Abbey nearby to call on if help were needed. Then, as he had explained to Cataia, his mother and sisters were cut from a single mold, and did not quite believe that there was anything in the world that existed besides the land and fishing fleet and towns owned by the Rei. When he thought of her, it was more difficult to recall her face than her massive ledgers.

On top of it all, although he did not say this to Cataia, he had not seen his family since he had entered the Abbey. It would be uncomfortable enough to have to renew their acquaintance in private, but with the whole Court looking on it would be practically impossible.

And all of that would make it a perfect time for Lechefrian to attack. The high emotion involved, the weariness of late hours from the round of parties, and the crushed, excited milieu were just the right edge.

Cataia wasn't worried, but she was curious. Of course, it was possible that this would be the perfect moment for attack, but she was interested to see Tiernon's family home. There were probably hints about him there, almost as if the place that had seen his birth could tell her what was in him. Cataia admitted to honest curiosity about that, and also the desire to see the richest Rei in Avriaten, and the most famed and beautiful Great House. She hadn't traveled much in life, and it was rather exciting. Tiernon's misgivings were his own problem.

It was a bright fleet that left the wharves of Tsanos on the Entelle that afternoon. Each of the ships was brightly festooned with ribbons and streamers and flags of the Major

Reis. Cataia was forced by protocol to ride with Lathanor in the flagship, brilliant with its identifying white Aandev pennants. Tiernon's ship was next in line, more festive than the rest and filled with courtiers whose Reis were not sending a full entourage. The colors of all those on the ship were flown, so it looked like some majestic rainbow had descended. The Temple ship was the most beautiful, though. Ayt and at least four Priests and Priestesses and a bevy of novices and acolytes were preparing for the ceremony on the red-painted deck. The trim was black and silver and brass, which shone brightly against the red. The large collection of Temple people was necessary for the naming of such an important heiress. Hugging the coastline, the small flotilla expanded as the ships bearing Rei Mothers not in residence in Tsanos joined them. Even the Minor Reis were represented, and several of the Guilds, the masons and woodcutters and jewelers, had sent delegations.

The weather was beautiful and the long sun-drenched days were ones of enforced relaxation. Music floated lightly across the waves, and after dark, brilliant torches silhouetted dancers in the decks.

Nothing, however, was as spectacular as their arrival at Bietehel'Rei. The Great House had been built for seafarers, and merged with rock and shore. A long staircase led from the dock straight to the Eastern Terrace and the front door of the House. It was rather amazing, Cataia thought, to disembark right at someone's front steps, and those being right on the sea. There were some similar arrangements for the Palace and the Temple along the Entelle, but nothing quite as spectacular as the great grey ocean and the exposed rock hills with this incredibly civilized monument between them.

Asirithe Rei Mother was on the Terrace to meet them all, obviously proud at the birth of her granddaughter and that the entirety of Avriaten's nobility had come to acknowledge her.

Cataia, studying Asirithe, could find no trace of Tiernon in her face or form. She was tall and lovely, and though she was well past sixty her hair was still iron-grey. She seemed to belong with the land and the deceptively docile sea at her door, rising up out of the Terrace as though she had been planted there by some sculptor trying to depict the mother-right.

Lathanor and Cataia first, they were ushered into the large central hall of the place, the hall of the Tree. The Tree really was a marvel. The glasswork was unlike anything Cataia had ever seen before, spun of pale tints and half-lights, the enamel delicately giving depth to the work as a whole. Here, certainly, was one of the great art treasures of the entire world.

Tiernon and his mother exchanged formal greetings, each surprised at the other's appearance. To Tiernon, his mother seemed much older and very much smaller than he remembered. It was almost as if she weren't his mother at all.

Asirithe had a hard time identifying Tiernon. She had last seen her son as a boy of ten, and before her stood a man with an expression of maturity stamped on his face. It was disconcerting, and Asirithe gave him a look meaning they'd talk later. It struck her that Tiernon seemed puzzled, he didn't know her looks or moods anymore. She wondered again, as she had wondered almost every day since she had sent the child with the quiet Orange-clad men, if she had done the right thing. She pushed it from her mind. What was done could not be undone, mistake or no. They would all have to live with the world as it was.

Light refreshments had been laid out for guests and most lounged while an army of intrepid servers found rooms and unpacked belongings. There was an ambassador from Salsatee among them who had arrived a day earlier, but no one noticed that representation from the Nestezi was severely short. This was an international event.

Tiernon found it easy to pick out the Rei Mothers, who grouped together in a corner and were speaking quickly, obviously about something important. In a strange way they all looked something like Asirithe, he thought. At first he did not recognize his sister Pelynne, present heiress to Bietehel, among them. She too had the solid look of a Rei Mother, and was distinguishable only because her hair was still black.

Tiernon found himself crushed in from all sides, receiving congratulations on the birth of his niece. He fended them off courteously, moving imperceptibly closer to the knot of Rei Mothers grouped around a tray of cheese.

"It's this rumor of war. What do you think they're going to do about the new tax? Take blood? It's been too wet for the chiena orchards, I'll tell you that."

"The Treasury is dry. Flat bottom, and they're not paying their debts."

Tiernon wished he could turn and identify the Reis speaking, but that would give him away, and be no use at all. The topic would change immediately.

"I'm not at all sure it's just the Aandev, I mean the Aandev in general. Under Eltion things weren't like this, or her mother before her, for that matter. It's the Regency, and a Minor Rei like Tonea speaking for it."

There were grumbles of assent until another voice could be heard. "No, not just the Regency, it's too easy to blame a single person for the mistake of a system. Giving the Aandev some advantage was the problem. They were always too perfect for my taste to begin with. And their Rei is really a Minor one now. It certainly doesn't produce much in the way of revenue."

"Aandev'Rei Minor?" One of the women laughed.

"Think about it," the other speaker said. "The city hasn't been the center of anything except historical tourism and beggars since Tsanos became the capital. The land is played out and the only sea access they have is the Cleindron River, and that without fishing rights. What has the income of Aandev'Rei been, not counting Crown taxes and the like?"

No one answered and Tiernon suddenly became worried. They were going further than either he or Ayt had expected. Perhaps they didn't know what Salsatee had its eye on, or perhaps they did. And perhaps personal power was more important to some than the ambitions of a nation that would have to cross the Nestezi and the mountains to make good their attack.

Then a terrible thought hit Tiernon. The Salsateans, of all people, would not have to bother with mountains or deserts. They were a merchant society with a fleet so vast that the sheer numbers alone were astounding. All of Avriaten's important cities were on the sea or navigable waterways, and it would be a simple matter to sail a few ships up the rivers to deliver troops.

They would get very little trouble on the high seas. Avriaten was mainly an agricultural nation, and most of its boats were small fishing vessels. Too, they did not have large ship works and master builders; most of their ships came ready-made from Salsatee, and the Salsateans would be one step ahead in design.

Tiernon found himself making a snap decision. He didn't like to decide things quickly, without all the facts at hand, but suddenly it became very important that Avriaten have a navy. The Salsateans did, and if they had any designs on the bread-basket northern country, the issue would be decided at sea. A navy. It was his own idea, but Lathanor might like it. He'd make sure Cataia and Ayt did. They could import shipwrights from Condele Port, or even better, apprentice some of their own young people there. Then the ships would be built, ready to protect the country against invasion and compete with those snobbish Southerners in the exploration of the Western Lands. And Bertham would buy it.

It was all so simple. Bertham wanted to war against the Nestezi. Aside from the question of money, arms, troops and training, there was the matter of transportation. The Vellne Pass was too narrow and steep for an army, and to go around Maddigore would strain both provisions and time. But ships could be landed at the coasts and the army would have to travel only a short way. Bertham would surely buy it, and pay for it too, while Tiernon would outwardly build the greatest navy the world had ever seen.

And then, when it was built, and his shipwrights and mariners were ready, they would be well trained and conversant with his viewpoint. And they would be loyal, just as Ayt's Temple troops were. A private army and a private navy, just ready to turn around and put Cataia on the throne. The scenario pleased Tiernon greatly, and he filed the idea in a place where it would be easily accessible, sealing it with one of the images on the Wheel. Already he had missed much of the Mothers' conversation.

The room was small and overstuffed with cushions and papers. The writing case lay out and open on a simple polished wooden table, and several half-dried inks were beginning to flake on the smooth ceramic mixer. Tiernon sat quietly, taking in what the room had to say about the woman who worked there. Here was the heart of Bietehel. Here were the large ledgers covered with neat figures of income and outflow, the volumes of correspondence and the records of recent years. Here too were the notices of debt, and the small grey abacus sitting sentinel over it all.

Asirithe would arrive soon, Tiernon knew. His mother was nothing if not prompt, and it was only the necessity of seeing guests to their quarters and comfortably settled for the night that kept her. He did not mind that the task might take longer than expected, since there had been little time during the voyage and the overwhelming meal to prepare for this meeting. He dreaded it.

Not only was he finally meeting the stranger who was his mother, but he was also reporting in to the power base. There could be no deceptions here, and that worried him. Then too there was Asirithe herself. She was, if he remembered correctly, both fair and shrewd, a good judge of character and extremely intelligent. In short, she would not be an easy enemy, and would make an uncomfortable ally at best. Bietehel could not be bought. It was both Tiernon's pride and his sorrow that this was true, and that he could not quite trust his own mother.

She relied on him, had given him her authority in Court and listened to his advice, but what kind of tie was blood? Tiernon wondered. They had not seen each other in twenty-three years, not since the Order's searchers had found and taken him when he was ten. Now he understood that they were guided by the Wheel, and that they could already see his potential running through the energy-net of his body. There were other marks too, so the Father-Priests of the Abbey had told him, but he was not a searcher and could not read the energy-net like a page of plain writing.

He wasn't entirely sure that Asirithe had cared much for him as a child at any rate. First, he could never give her grandchildren, on whom she counted like cash, and second, he was not like the others in the family. He had often wondered, when he was a child, why all his sisters looked like junior versions of his mother and why he looked like no one at all. Asirithe had stated on several occasions that she wasn't even sure who his father had been because he resembled none of the men who had presented her with birth-rugs.

The Priests of the Abbey had explained that this was generally true, and that it worked to their advantage. Asirithe had made very little fuss about his leaving. He remembered now too that Keani had seemed only pleased to be relieved of her responsibilities for her child.

Tiernon thought that he was beyond the hurt of his leaving by now, but viewed with his Abbey training that seemed unlikely. There were times when his bitterness and anger had surfaced, although he had managed to keep it well hidden. After all, why otherwise would he have avoided any visits home at all costs, preferring instead to send a messenger? Why was his breathing irregular and his pulse a little too strong, if not with nervousness that didn't bother him at all with Bertham, who had tried to kill him? It wasn't anger now, he realized. It was hope that Asirithe would want him for himself, apart from his useful functions, and the fear that she would reject him again as she had when he was a boy.

She had never inquired as to his activities or his reading, believing that he was perfectly well enough left alone. And once, when two fishermen had some argument to be settled by the Rei Mother, she had told him crossly to be silent, when the men and the argument had been well-known to him.

The memories brought a certain anxiety, and he closed his eyes and went into a light meditative state to regulate his heartbeat and breathing before his mother arrived.

Asirithe came in silently and watched for a moment from the door, almost frightened at the sight of his light trance state. Tiernon opened his eyes and rose quickly to give her the respect she deserved, and he noticed the tiny hint of apprehension in her stance. There was an awkwardness between them, a not knowing how to act or what to say, or even what relationship to call on. It would be far more comfortable to simply be Rei Mother and Court Ambassador, but that was not possible. It would be dishonest, and Asirithe hated dishonesty more than anything else she could name.

"Welcome home, Tiernon," she said quietly. "It has been a very long time."

"Yes, Mother, it has. I wanted to consult you on several matters, concerning the state of the country, and the Rei Mothers in particular."

"I had no doubt of that," she said. "My decision is made, and the others will follow me no matter what they prefer, follow or be consumed by what comes. It is no longer your concern."

Tiernon could only nod, trying to keep the misery off his face. Asirithe had not changed. "Will you tell me, then?" he asked.

"In time," she said. "First, I want to know you better. It isn't natural for a mother not to know her son. What have you become?"

For a moment Tiernon was shaken. How could he explain

to Asirithe about the Abbey, the Orders and his own recent involvement in the turning of 'Kleppah? Asirithe didn't even believe in 'Kleppah, or magia, or secret Orders. "I wasn't sure you'd be interested. I don't know what you want to know."

"You still believe in secrets," she said. "You live in some world I can't perceive, and I'm not sure I want to. I've heard reports from Court, from Tsanos, and I was afraid that you'd become one of those courtiers who cared for nothing but style and impression, and I worried. I worried that you were not yourself. A child reveals more fully what he is than an adult does, and I was afraid that you had been changed in some way. I'm glad I was wrong."

"I don't understand," he said.

"Of course you don't. As a little boy you used to sit quietly for hours on the Terrace, not moving at all. You'd tell me that you'd been thinking, and not the things you'd think about. And then the reading. Normal seven-year-olds don't read like you did, and I have your sisters and the knowledge of others to support me in that. But you'd never show me what you'd read, or tell me what you thought like your sisters did. You still read secretly, don't you? And you still think things you won't tell. I'm glad of that. It means I can trust you."

"I'm amazed," Tiernon said with puzzlement.

"Very simply this, then. If you were not the adult version of the boy they took from me, I could not trust you. It would mean that I didn't know who you were or the fiber of your being. I am not a mystical person, Tiernon, but I know a fraud when I see one, and you're no fraud. That was all that concerned me. The rest I can handle."

"Are you sure?" The words began to flow, and Tiernon wasn't even sure of what he was saying. He knew that it was wrong somehow, and that it didn't matter. She had sent him out as a child, had never invited him home, not for any of the holidays in the thirteen years since he had been Initiated. He wasn't even sure if he wanted to hurt her, or make her accept him. "You asked me what I am, but I'm not even sure you believe that I exist. I am an Adept, Mother, in the ancient Orders of the Seven. I am a Priest. I have seen colors that do not exist in this world, and I've created fire from my hands. I can call the wind up at sea. No poison can touch me. I can call armies of spirits from the earth and fire to be my servants and do what I command. I have done these things. And I have very little personal stake in the outcome of the political games in the Court, and the only political end I serve is the fulfillment of the Prophecies.''

Asirithe was dumbstruck, but she held her ground. "I cannot believe these things. I cannot believe they exist. The Prophecies are a lovely poem, no more. But in the end, they're a better goal than the constant bickering I hear from Court, and I'm glad your classical education has not been neglected. I'm sorry they gave you gods, though. That demands a lot and returns very little. On the other hand, better the Seven than 'Kleppah, even if it is only an allegory. I can trust you, you see, because you aren't a liar, although I'm afraid you've been lied to, and now you do it to yourself.''

"Not at all, Mother, not at all.''

Asirithe shook her head. There was intelligence there, and he could have hardly managed in his position at Court so long, rising so high, if he were not hardheaded. Yet he had always been strange, distant, too mystical for her understanding. She wondered how he could be her son at all. Now that was not important. They were too far apart. "Blood is a tie," Asirithe said wearily, "and it cannot be broken. You are Bietehel and always will be, and will be treated as such in this House. But don't ask me to understand you. Don't even ask me to try. Just promise to give me the truth, and let me weigh matters. You are not loyal to Bietehel the way the others are, and that might be bad for us. So then, what is the meaning of this cryptic note you sent me?''

"I thought you had made your decision.''

"I had. I decided to trust you.''

Tiernon began outlining what Ayt had said to him, giving his own observations both of the Court and the Salsatean situation. Asirithe considered for a moment and spoke. "Good. That is acceptable. We would be too weak to stand individually against the Salsateans if it came to that, and if you offer us some way out of the domination of this Regent and that Tonea upstart who wants our wealth and our traditional rights, I think the others will join me. But there must be no war, do you understand? None of them will stand for a war.''

Tiernon nodded, understanding her fully. Her tone had been more professional with him, and he knew that now they were mother and son in name only. Well, so be it. It had been that way since he had left this hall, and while the acknowledgment of it was final and painful, it was at least tinged with trust and respect, which also could have been withheld. Obviously she valued him as her advisor on Court matters. And maybe, just maybe, if he needed her she would come through. After all, she had acknowledged his right to the House, and that was indicative of her intentions. Tiernon paused to realize that they might well need her help before things were quite over.

"Well, we'd both better get some sleep," Asirithe said. "We have a long day tomorrow, and if you find the ceremonies even half as boring as I do, then you'll need plenty of sleep to stay awake during them."

The thing started at dawn. Pelynne sat on the Terrace with the baby in her arms, surrounded by the rich father-rugs, presented almost a month ago. The possible fathers must be in the crowd, but Tiernon wasn't in any mood to speculate. It was certainly of no importance, as the rugs showed the quality of men involved to be high enough for the future Rei Mother of Bietehel.

Ayt, resplendent in her black-and-silver ceremonial robes and surrounded by the Priests and Priestesses and novices, led a processional onto the Terrace, where she began the long chants to the Stars for the infant and read the child's horoscope to the crowd. It was too good to be possible, but Ayt had told him once that she read only the best parts of the chart at a naming. It would be rude to do otherwise. The sun was becoming very hot and the guests started to look uncomfortable. Tiernon wondered when the long chants would end. Finally the moment was at hand when Asirithe came forward and claimed the child from Pelynne.

"This is the heiress of my House, one day to have possession of this Rei and the goods therein and the keeping in justice of all its people. And for that, and the glory of this House, I name her Eltion, for memory of a good and just Queen. May she rule her Rei as this Queen ruled her people."

Tiernon almost gasped aloud. It was not just the councils of the night, taken over some cup of wine, where political announcements were made. Here Asirithe had declared not only her support of the Aandev, of the concept of central government, but her dislike of the present Regency, and had let the Rei Mothers and the Salsateans know it in powerful, if subtle, terms.

Tiernon, now at Pelynne's left, collected the birth-rugs, and with a small oil lamp symbolically singed the fringed edges. "Belong to no House but this, and may no other claim you but the Rei you were born to rule." Asirithe's voice rang out clear, as she managed a quick wink at Tiernon.

The baby, now Eltion pra Pelynne rei Bietehel, was laid in the arms of a nurse and the company returned to the shaded depths of the hall where a feast worthy of the occasion had been set. There was a satisfying roar of conversation and Tiernon was by no means innocent of its contents. The Rei Mothers, the ambassadors and Bertham, too, must have taken the hint. At the center table, reserved for the family and royalty, Tiernon quickly squeezed his mother's hand. She caught his eye and they were engulfed by a wave of mutual understanding. Tiernon had never suspected that he might have gotten some of his ability at subtle manipulation from the materialistic, pragmatic Asirithe. He was glad that experience had proved him wrong.

Intoxicated with his newfound knowledge, the festivities of the day and a good supply of exceptional wine, Tiernon required three or four tugs at his sleeve before he could be induced to turn. Valnera, looking drawn and concerned, stood away from the festivities with beseeching eyes.

"The Princess wants you immediately. She's in her room. I'll bring you to her."

Cataia waited for Valnera to finish her fluttering and leave before she spoke. "Tiernon, I have a feeling we may have a problem. Chervan is missing. He wasn't at the ceremony this morning, and Valnera heard some rumors about a horse being readied late last night."

"Chervan? Maybe he had a patient to look after. He's Batter and a physician. What could he have to do with anything?"

"I don't know. I have no idea what this means, but I know it's important. Do you remember how easily he bought that story of the attempted assassination? And he's not seeing a patient, Valnera said his rooms were cleaned out!"

Tiernon shrugged. "You set it up well."

"Except for one thing. How in the world would you end up

with claw marks from a knife? There's no way he could miss it, Tiernon. He's mixed up in this somehow."

"Lechefrian?" Tiernon asked.

"I have this feeling that there won't be an attack until we reach Tsanos. You're right, the atmosphere here isn't conducive to magia of any stripe. I'd defy Lechefrian himself to try anything in this carnival."

Tiernon laughed deeply and eased himself from a sitting to a reclining position. "I suggest then that we use this interval to gather strength and a lot of rest. Also, to be relieved of each other's company."

Cataia raised an eyebrow. "Relieved of each other's company?"

"When we return, there will be no way of knowing when or where the strike will come. We can't afford to be out of rhythm, and even though physical proximity is not necessary, it would certainly be useful in these matters. Like it or not, once we return to the Palace we'll have to be sewn closer than a seam. I, for one, relish the prospect, but given that Your Highness has had so little regard for me in the past days, I would assume that you would prefer to enjoy your freedom now." Tiernon smiled jovially.

"Oh, stop smirking," Cataia said. "At least try to earn your position. What can you tell me about Chervan, and not the obvious trash, either. I already know he's Batter, and educated at Volenten in the Faculty of Medicine. Tell me something new."

Tiernon thought for a moment. He had never really paid much attention to the physician, he had never considered it important. Closing his eyes, he concentrated on a simple pattern, a pattern that could aid the memory in times like this. Tiernon knew that nothing was ever lost from the mind, and that even information not registered consciously will be stored, if only it can be dredged up. The process was one of the most minor forms of magic, but one of the most useful. After a few moments he had several shards.

"A few, a very few things about Chervan don't exactly follow the pattern," he said. "It's not a lot to go on. Valnera may well have more, and better information on this than I do."

"Very little is better than nothing, and I don't think I can really trust Valnera for this."

Tiernon nodded his agreement and continued. "Well then, to start, there are rumors that he's half Nestezian. Not big rumors, you understand, just little hints now and then. But if I remember correctly, the story goes something to the effect that his mother never received a birth-rug for him, but a large Nestezian jewel. That isn't proof by any means, even if it is true, and it could just have been set off by his features."

"So many people look Nestezian," Cataia mused. "It means nothing."

"Second," Tiernon said, "have you ever heard his matronymic used?"

"His what?"

"His full name. Have you ever heard Chervan's full name?" he repeated. "We don't know for a fact who his mother was, do we? We don't even know if he's directly related to the Rei Mother or the member of some collateral branch of the family, or even if he is noble through adoption. But it does strike me as odd that I never did hear anyone ever use his full name."

"Now that you mention it, it's true," Cataia said. "I never did hear any mention. It never occurred to me as important."

"And it wouldn't. It wouldn't occur to anyone. He wasn't important in any official sense, and it's very easy to assume that his name must be written down somewhere, when he first came to Court or Volenten or something. But it's an interesting omission nevertheless."

"Are you suggesting that he might not be Batter at all?" Cataia asked, aghast.

"No, not really," Tiernon replied. "I'm just saying that he was not publicizing who he was, and that might lead to several very interesting conclusions. Third, how old did he appear to you?"

"Oh, about forty-five or so. Not old, not young, nothing really in particular," she answered.

"Funny," Tiernon said, "because that's the age I would have put him at when I met him, only I met him thirteen years ago."

"Yes, but you know that change is so gradual, and people don't really show their age at that point, not until they're older."

"What I'm saying is this," Tiernon said thoughtfully. "We have no idea of his age at all. He doesn't appear to have aged in the thirteen years since I met him, and that's all I can judge.''

"Is there anything else?" Cataia asked quietly.

"Let me think for a moment. . . . Yes, how could I have forgotten? It's the most outstanding thing. When I had first come to Court, I invited him for an after-dinner. I invited everyone at the time, trying to meet people and sort them out. Anyway, I served pastries and wine, an ordinary after-dinner, you know, but he mentioned the pastries. And he knew that they had come from the shop on Dier Street.''

"Then why didn't you remember?" Cataia asked excitedly. "That's a real clue. He couldn't be one of us? He doesn't wear a ring.''

"No, and that's just it. That's why I forgot. The pastry shop is known to gourmets throughout the city, but at the time I didn't know that Chervan was not at all a gourmet.''

"So he knows Dier Street," Cataia muttered. "Well, it's not exactly secret, but if he grew up in Batter'Rei and studied in Volenten and isn't a gourmet, it does seem a little suspicious. Only I never felt anything from him, not the faintest flicker.''

Tiernon turned half a shade paler. "And you wouldn't, nor would I, if it was 'Kleppah. Lechefrian is on a different length from the Planes, a length that only Aken monitors," Tiernon said.

"Great. We can ask Aken, then," Cataia said bitterly. Then her face fell. "Oh, no, Tiernon, no. When I went back to the Abbey, they told me one of Aken had been watching me, in the flesh.''

Tiernon stared at her in shock. "You should have told me," he whispered. "You should have told me at once. And it makes sense. Of course he didn't look any older. Those of Aken don't age, and they live until they train a successor of their own Order. And they were trained in the Abbeys on Dier Street, each one of them, until they were tapped by Aken.''

They stared at each other in shock, realizing just what Chervan had been, and who he was. "I wonder where he went?" Cataia thought out loud.

"If it's Aken's business, we're not going to know," Tiernon replied. "Aken does as it pleases, and doesn't bother to tell us mere other magicians what they're up to, as long as we follow orders. Look, we still have two days until we return. And we'd

better go down and enjoy the party before they send out a
patrol. We can at least have a look at what Bertham and the
Rei Mothers are up to. Did you like what my mother pulled
this morning?''

"And the way it was done. Tiernon, you are truly your
mother's son," Cataia said a little too loudly.

"You're the first person who's ever said that," he said.

They walked down the halls to rejoin the feasters in silence.
They knew, only too well, that Aken had been more than just
interested.

ꙮ Eight

IT WAS GOOD to be back in Tsanos, Bertham thought. It was bad manners for Pelynne to have that baby now, when his work was just getting underway, bad manners and bad timing, but there was no help for it. After Bietehel'Rei, the Palace seemed to be a bastion of cool and quiet. There were no crowds anywhere but in the most public of rooms, and they were decent enough to keep their voices down so a person could think. Southerners. All they thought about were parties and more parties and food and more food, and even if the Rei was on the water, it was too hot. Bertham never thought he'd welcome Tsanos, but after five solid days of pleasantries it was nice not to be expected to make another comment about someone's food or wine or crops or baby or other nonsense.

Besides, five days of the Rei Mothers was more than he could bear. That Asirithe had certainly done it when she'd named the baby Eltion. As if that were not the most stupid move she could have made, and all those petty little queens so jealous of their domains, ready to follow at the slightest word. It was sickening.

More than anything, the setback irked him. It was impossible, absolutely impossible, to keep up with the System from the *Rituals of Lechefrian* in that atmosphere, and he feared that he had lost far more than five days. It would take time to get back to where he had been when they had left, and then there was still a little ways to go before he could bring through the demon.

Funny, in all the stories of the magia that had survived, it seemed like the whole thing took no work at all. Not that Bertham had been that innocent. He knew that the more power yielded, the more it would have to be worked for, but the level of dedication demanded by the magia was far and beyond anything he had imagined. No wonder they were able to wreck a world, he thought grimly. If the rewards are half of what one puts into it, there should be power enough to bring both moons down to the sea and stop them dead short on the roof garden besides. It was worth it, he decided again. It was the kind of thing that had to be redecided often.

The dream was going to fall into his hands. That he had never doubted for a moment. If he had, he thought bitterly, he would never have left Tonea in the first place, never have had the sheer gall to present himself at Court. But the dream had driven him, always just out of grasp, always there in front of him just waiting to be plucked. And now the ripe fruit was starting to fall into his hands, and all by his own efforts, too. Maybe magia wouldn't be necessary. Maybe only shrewd plotting, careful planning and nerve would serve him again as it had in the past. And it had served him very well indeed, but the dream had grown.

At this point it had grown so vast that no one could conceive of it, and Bertham smiled grimly with the realization that the vastness of it concealed him. They were not universal, not daring enough. They hid behind an outdated provincialism. Avriaten, Nestezi, Salsatee, what were they really? Different languages, customs and histories did not affect Bertham's vision, nor did the very physical boundaries between them, the Sky Mountains and strips of desert that even the tribes wouldn't cross. To Bertham, this was nothing against his vision, and if it clouded others it was to his good fortune that it did. Well and good.

The dream was now far too great to be accomplished by good politics alone, at least in one lifetime. A little help would come in useful, and Bertham felt he fully deserved it. Who else at Court deserved help? The overfed children of the rich Major Reis? The Aandev? The Temple of the Stars, which he thought behaved like it could make or break any policy with the merest nod of approval? How could they know what work meant, work and hunger and hard rocks at your back? The whole Court, born to glitter and comfort, to rich food and soft amber rugs—how could they ever conceive of his ambition? Fools, the lot of them!

For a moment Bertham gave full vent to his hatred, shaking with the poison of it pent up for so long. It had all been so obvious at the naming that they still considered him an inferior in some way. Oh, no one dared snub him, or speak impolitely, or any one of the million things that could be done. Nothing so overt as a breach of good manners. But it was there all the same, on their faces, in the way they hushed their voices as he went by, in the naming of the child itself and in the covert glances of the Rei Mothers. Upstart, they said, all of them. When revenge came it would be sweet. He had promised himself that, it would be long and perfectly planned, and he would enjoy every second of it. He had not been born to be second to anyone. A burning heat began to consume him as the hatred grew, and he felt it and fed on it. He imagined what they would look like, those Rei Mothers and courtiers, when they were hungry as he had been, when their hands were raw and split from hauling boulders, when their preciously scented bodies were filthy and full of vermin. He wondered how they'd feel, and he hated them all the more.

The fantasy caught him up and took him. So lost was he that he didn't hear the soft, almost loverlike voice crooning gently in the background.

"Wait, wait and save it. Save all of it, deep within you. Don't waste it on shadows, it can be used."

Startled so strongly by the voice, it was the shock and not the message that brought Bertham back from his well-loved hatred. He pivoted quickly to the corner where the voice had come from, and thought he caught a bit of smoky trail out of the corner of his eye, but nothing was sure. Around him the room almost glowed. The light was far too clear, the edges of things too sharp and the shadows too precise. It was almost as if the room were a painting and not a habitation. Bertham stood stock-still, not wanting to destroy the effect. The intense clarity almost hurt his eyes and then he knew, and a joy as warm as the hatred had been now filled him.

It must be Lechefrian. The lost days had not been lost. "Wait," the thing had said, and wait he gladly would. It was all true, all the stories, all the half-hidden rumors, all were true, real. Lechefrian was real, magia was real, and it worked. The clarity started to fade a bit, but the joy and overwhelming confidence it gave him were still full to exploding.

"I await your call, Master," he said softly to the empty room.

The room faded back to its normal state and Bertham was left stunned by the implications of what he had said. He had never used the word *master* to anyone or anything, not even when imploring the gods. Yet he knew from some deep instinct that Lechefrian would always be the Master, and it chilled him to know that he'd meant what he had said. The Eater of Souls could never be anything else, and the sigal had been burned so deeply into his mind that now it moved in him and through him without his knowledge.

Bertham pulled his katreisi around himself, mute in the knowledge that he had exchanged freedom for something greater than he had ever thought existed. He almost thought he heard soft laughter, but the room did not brighten again, and for a moment he considered the bargain he had made. No, it was not quite made yet, not sealed and formalized, but it was made all the same. He wanted to run from it, from the Master and from the dream that had driven him so hard.

Then, when the moment had passed, he turned to embrace it. There was a shining edge of destiny in the evening. Who else had done what he had done? Who else in the world could call up powers so ancient that their very names had been forgotten? Was it insane not to bend to a force that could rip a continent in two and toss up mountains like froth on a cake?

He was with them now, one of them, and he imagined how they must have stood, dark and stony in their fortress on the island. They had not succeeded, and Bertham knew that where eleven of the greatest Adepts ever to walk had failed he would succeed. It was that simple. He was the fulfillment of the Prophecies, and if he served Lechefrian, then Lechefrian in the end would serve him. The Eater of Souls would be satisfied, and Bertham would claim his share, eventually to the being of the Master.

How he knew this he could not say. But Lechefrian was something made out of souls, and when the time came, his might be eaten but not consumed and the thing called Lechefrian would hold Bertham immortal. The hints, the half truths of the old stories came back together suddenly and became whole cloth. Lechefrian was no more than those who chose to become Lechefrian! An exultation filled Bertham, filled him so that he could barely sense his body. Already he could taste the fright and fear and small joys of those morsels of earth, sweeter than any fruit and more burning than wine.

Cataia looked pale and drawn, Tiernon thought as he reclined against the thick green cushions in the Princess's apartments. Not that he wasn't feeling the strain as well. There had been a twinge the first night, hard and demanding, wrenching at him almost to the body, but since then, nothing. Cataia had not spoken much since their last meeting at Bietehel'Rei even though they had not been separated since.

Tiernon found the whole thing maddening. It reduced their political activities, and it had totally annihilated his personal life. That was to be expected, but for how long? It could be days, or years, or centuries before the time came, and now he suddenly wished he could forget the whole matter. They would in time, anyway, and that was what Lechefrian must be waiting for, the time when they slackened their guard and forgot how precarious life could be. Lechefrian could afford to wait. Waiting for a thousand years makes one pretty good at it, Tiernon supposed. A few days or years wouldn't matter.

Suddenly Cataia's face contorted with a scream that never left her throat. "Tomorrow night," she managed to whisper.

Half-terrified, half-exalted, Tiernon called Valnera and spoke quietly for a few moments, and then laid Cataia in what he hoped would be a comfortable position to bring her out of the trance. There was all of tonight to relax, then, and all of tomorrow to prepare. How very thoughtful of Lechefrian to warn them.

Bertham faced the thing without fear, and certainly, in these circumstances, it did not inspire fear. It was far more like having a visitor, if one could forget the deep blank eyes that held centuries. Bertham could not forget them.

"Now," it was saying in the most seductive voice Bertham had ever heard, "we make a Watcher. You know what a Watcher is?"

Bertham nodded, having come across a description in his reading of Eskenese manuscripts.

"Good. It would be tiresome to explain it, almost as tiresome as to build one. You have not, I hope, permitted yourself any free range of feeling in these past days? It is emotion that fashions Watchers. Lie down."

Puzzled, Bertham did as he was told.

"Now," the voice continued, "just use your imagination. You were doing a fine job when I cautioned you to stop, but the energy was simply being dissipated. Now we will use the same method, but control it. Now imagine, Bertham, imagine what it was like at Tonea when you were a small boy. Remember how hard you had to work, and the kind of work you did. Feel the stones you had to rip out of the ground, feel them tearing your hands. Think about the Court, about people like Ayt and Tiernon and the little Princess and Lathanor. Think about their easy lives, how they never had to eat things crawling in the mud to still the screaming in them. Think of their fine rich clothing and cool stone houses while the heat in your house killed your mother. Think of it, imagine it clearly. Think now, of what they had and what you had, and how far you've come. Think of how you've worked, slaved for your position, you, better and more intelligent than they."

Bertham could feel the hate beginning to rise. He knew that Lechefrian was not hypnotizing him as he had done to others. The demon was merely instructing, helping him to get down to the real core of emotion, and now the imagination began to do its work. Bertham began to reconstruct all of his grievances with a depth and clarity so refined that he could almost smell the food wafting off the well-laden tables while he starved outside. He could see them with water, great jugs of water, and his throat felt parched and dry as it had so long ago. He had almost forgotten, but it came back even more clearly than it had happened, and his anger grew. Spiral after spiral of hatred came from those images, and most of those images were of Tiernon. More than anyone he hated Tiernon. Tiernon, who had been so very rich, so very refined and so very, very intelligent. Tiernon, who was probably as unscrupulous as himself and just as canny. He hated Tiernon because Tiernon was exactly what he would have been if he had been as well born and as well loved. And then he really let the emotions fly.

It was summer and there was plague. *Mother, don't die, please don't die.* Strana holding his face in her lap; *Mother, don't die.* But she had died, and the house had smelled of blood and it was summer. Blood dripped from everything. He bit Strana, although she was his favorite sister, and Strana screamed and struck him, and screamed again. Then there was Mother, lying there. Get up, get up, he had told her, and she would not get up. She couldn't die. She hated him. He knew it. He had killed her because she hated him, and for a moment he had hated her back, had taken the long black hair caked in blood, taken hanks of it in his hands and beat her head against the wall. Hatred, blind rage, consumed him. There had never been rage like this for all fury, and he trembled with the greatness of it.

Lechefrian was smiling when he finally opened his eyes. The trembling had not yet stopped and he felt weak and cold, as if he had been wounded.

Lechefrian poured a glass of wine and handed it to Bertham. "This will make you feel better. I hadn't known."

Bertham took the glass and could not avoid spilling a few drops before he got it to his mouth. It did not occur to him as odd that a sheer energy force would pick up something as solid as a jug.

"But see what we have made," Lechefrian said.

Bertham's eyes followed that all too material-looking claw, and in a dark corner stood a large beast. Unconsciously he drew away from it and Lechefrian laughed. "How can you be afraid of it? It is you."

Bertham looked again. It was grey and pale, connected to him by a thin cord of light. Large with great jowls and teeth, the mouth lined in scarlet and the eyes blank sockets, he had never imagined a creature so utterly evil, so utterly ugly.

"It will serve well," Lechefrian's smooth voice continued, "but it functions only after dark. Perhaps tomorrow night. . . ."

"What do you want done?" Bertham asked hoarsely, but already Lechefrian was becoming misty and less solid. After a moment, had it not been for the Watcher leering in the corner, Bertham would have believed it had all been some fantasy.

• • •

Cataia lay awake watching the grey creep into the sky. How Tiernon slept so soundly she couldn't guess. Absently she reached out and stroked his hair, half smiling to herself. It was really insane. Here she was in bed with the man she wanted, and she couldn't do a thing about it. Celibacy, like fasting, was necessary before the kind of ritual they were going to perform. Not that they knew just what ritual it would be, or how Lechefrian was planning to attack. Only, Cataia thought with grim certainty, it wasn't going to be anything small.

He seemed so calm. It would be unreasonable to be calm, she thought, unreasonable in this time and this place, without knowing what they would face. That was the worst part, now that the waiting was over.

Then she chuckled to herself. Tiernon's face had not softened in sleep; he must also be apprehensive. There was so much to do, just in case, so much to plan and prepare. Red was beginning to streak the cold greyness, and soon Tiernon could get up and make a good pretense of having slept the night in perfect comfort.

"Oh, my baby, I knew you'd be awake," Valnera said, bustling in with a tray. "Here, have some warm milk. There are hot rolls just waiting, and we'll have a nice restful day."

"No, Valnera, no milk, no rolls, nothing today, just water," Cataia replied.

Valnera's face fell, and Cataia knew that she had just disrupted Valnera's whole philosophy of food dissolving any crisis. Noting the older woman's stricken face, Cataia softened her own.

"You can be of great help to us, Valnera," Cataia said. "First, we have to make sure that no one sees us today, no one we don't specifically ask for. And, when it's all over, you can help. We'll probably be very tired, and need a good meal and wine and no questions asked."

"What is going on today? Is the Council voting on the Nestezi?" Valnera demanded.

Cataia laughed so loudly that Tiernon opened his eyes and sat up. "No," she replied, "the Council is not voting on the Nestezi today. Bertham doesn't have the support he needs quite yet for the motion to pass. Don't worry, I can't explain it, but it will be over tomorrow."

Valnera turned to Tiernon, who was wrapping his katreisi

around himself against the early chill. "What have you got her involved in now?" the older woman asked. "Not to eat all day, that's plain unhealthy."

"Valnera, please, things might not be very pleasant tonight. I have a request," Tiernon said. "We will be in my apartments. I don't want us disturbed. Tonight, when things are over, there's a chance, a very slim chance, that we might not be entirely well. I have already discussed the matter with Ayt. Sometime today, I want you to go to the Temple. She'll give you instructions, and if circumstances warrant, follow them to the letter. I warn you, we may seem dead, but no matter what, do as Ayt instructs."

The coldness in Tiernon's voice precluded any reply other than Valnera's whimpered "Yes." Pale-faced and silent, she retreated.

"What do you mean, you talked with Ayt about this?" Cataia demanded after Valnera left. "What, exactly, did you tell her, and when, and what is going on?"

"I didn't tell her anything, except that we might be in danger at some point. She knows about Bertham's plots, if not his magia, and is not fond of them. In case, just in case, we need a place to hide for a while when this is over. . . ."

Cataia wanted to ask more, but then thought better of it.

"Bring your sword. I think you'll need it," Tiernon added as they prepared to leave.

Cataia brought the sword, and the other ritual instruments as well. There was no point in being unprepared. When they entered the ritual area, she took each one out and began the long process of cleaning, partly because it was required, and partly because it was something concrete to do. As she unwrapped each piece, she thought of its legend.

First the Earth-sign, which must be found. She had found hers half-buried on the banks of the Entelle one day when she and Dacia had slipped away to go wading. The heavy metal disk had glowed dully in the sunlight, smooth and unmarked. Where Dacia found hers Cataia never guessed, and it was a constant source of wonder that they were found at all. There were suspicions that they were planted by the Order to fulfill the old requirements. Cataia dipped a rag in a bowl of scented oil and began to polish, noting again how well the engraving had come out. Her names and sigals were well drawn, a feat that had taken the Princess many long moons.

The Cup was given by one who loved, and that had been given by Dacia, and was as beautiful as all the things that Dacia chose were. The sword had to be won.

Unwrapping the long, straight sword, she remembered the fight that had brought it to her. No ordinary manner of winning was permitted with this: it had to be in a battle close to the one she was ready to enter now. She had won the sword on the Hunting, when they had discovered three who had tried to gain forbidden access to the Planes and had had to be destroyed. It had not been a pleasant matter, and even now Cataia trembled, thinking of those poor mutilated souls who'd had no choice but to fail. Stupid, misguided fools, when would they ever learn? She had won the sword in battle, and it had been forged at the Red Abbey, where they knew such things. It had taken her almost a year to purge and engrave it, and Cataia was only thankful that it was not required to make one from scratch. Her motto was engraved in Eskenese on the long, straight blade: *Abratne tha Qtrn Nye,* Eternal Justice is all Mercy.

For a moment, Cataia averted her eyes from Tiernon's blade, so plainly open before her as he sat with the rag and oil. Then she couldn't resist and when she had read it she lowered her eyes. It was a strange motto, as mottos went. *Dinantrame Mekt,* From Suffering, Strength. For Tiernon that was especially strange, she thought. He did not know his past lives. How could he have chosen as he had?

He noticed her surprise and shrugged. It would be the worst possible form for her to ask, she knew, and just as bad for him to offer. The real meaning of a motto was only for the one who had chosen it, or for those who could appreciate what it expressed, but Cataia still wondered. She never imagined that Tiernon might find hers just as obscure.

By midafternoon, all was ready and laid out on the altar. Now, Cataia knew, it was time to prepare *themselves*. Emptying her mind, she took off her garments and slipped her Green Initiation robe over her head. It was the symbol of her identity as Priestess, and as she felt the thin silk envelop her she felt overshadowed by her entire Order. She unbound her hair and pulled the circlet low on her forehead, meditating on concentration. Then she buckled the belt around her waist, the physical counterpart of the limits she set in her mind, so that the forces she called would not overwhelm her control. She

herself was now just one more tool. She looked to the altar
and found Tiernon, robed, already seated and ready to begin.

They took some water and began the meditations, Litanies
of Being and the silent songs that would create the right mind-
set for whatever they would need to do. A deep calm settled
over them, and when the three slow knocks came, signaling
sunset, Cataia felt ready, which meant she hardly felt at all.
They performed the small banishing ritual and then invoked
the four elements in the quarters, preparing the ground, and
settled to focus at the mirror.

She could not tell the time, or how long her awareness had
been pitched and focused into the dark mirror-wall, but slowly
it seemed as if something were beginning to form. At first,
taking it for clouding vision or wavering attention, Cataia
imposed a sigal. No, her focus was not wrong, there was definitely a grey mist growing out of the mirror and starting to
take form.

Even before the lines were final, she knew what it was. A
Watcher, a thing of pure emotion, a thing more dangerous
than all the Hunting missions she had ever fought combined.
In the back of her head she could hear Mother Daniessa's lec-
tures running as though she read them from a book.

"There is little chance you will ever meet a Watcher, but
there is only one way to destroy it. First, it is necessary to
understand the nature of the emotion being used; second,
meditate on the opposite; and third, absorb the power through
yourself and transmute it. This operation is dangerous and the
dangers are as follows. First, if you lose control and cannot
transmute, it will cause a burn-out; second, if your attention is
not absolute, it could gain mastery over you; and third, you
are acquiring energy from the sender, whom I can assure you
means you no good." Damn, how Mother Daniessa loved to
enumerate points.

It was not difficult to discern the emotion concentrated in
the Watcher—the hatred could be seen almost as clear ripples,
unable to penetrate the enclosure of their seals. It could not
come in, but by the same token they were trapped. Cataia suddenly realized that something had never been included in the
lecture, and that was the simple problem of . . . how do you
absorb a Watcher? It cannot come in, and it would be very
stupid to break the seals. Cataia was afraid. The seals would
last until sunrise, but the Watcher would come back night

after night until it got its prey. It was infinitely patient and after the first sending the sender didn't even have to bother, the thing would return on its own. They could live behind seals after sundown every night for now, but for how long? . . . Cataia wanted to cry.

"We'll use the swords. They'll pierce the seals, but not break them, and then we can use the swords to draw," Tiernon said.

Cataia only grunted in agreement. Of course it would take one of the Orange to discover the trick so quickly; that was their function. Cataia did not envy Tiernon's alacrity of mind; the Orders were what they were, and each had its own talents.

Again they went into a meditative state, but this time it was extremely pointed. If the thing was hatred, then it was necessary to have only love. Cataia began as she had been taught, from the most to the least recent, thinking first of those she loved, and then she focused on those she hated with full concentration, feeling the link between them, feeling compassion, and finally . . . yes, it was there. That spark of Unity created it, and they were all within her, her children. She became Ge, the Primordial Mother, the absolute, for whom none can be hated or scorned. "Dark and deep, my children, return, that I may be given and drunk, for you are thirsty and I will nourish you."

Cataia, who was now Ge, turned to Tiernon and smiled. She saw that he had invoked Megraha, the Bright Sacrifice, and the tenor of the room changed subtly as the invocations took effect. Now there were four and not two to face the Watcher, and the two who stood in bodies had ceased to be afraid. They were linked, the four, the Adepts, the Megraha and the Mother, in the Unity that underlay all eternity, all the Universe and all its evil as well.

The Watcher did not look so dangerous now. Conscious thought suspended, Tiernon and Cataia picked up their swords and pierced the seals, then the Watcher. Carefully, tending to it, reassuring it, they began to draw its energy through the long blades and into themselves.

Transmute, transmute, love it, the poor thing, come to me, it will be better, it will be all right, don't worry, we'll care for you.

It began to diminish. Great as it was, the grey seemed a little less dense. It was so easy, so very easy, and then it broke. The

Unity would not hold, they were not strong enough to hold it and fight the thing at the same time. Personality broke through, broke free of the Unity, and suddenly it was only Tiernon and Cataia again, and the thing was still huge. Love it, love it, Tiernon commanded himself. The memory of the Unity sustained them, but now they could feel the intense emotion of the Watcher in the seconds before it was transformed.

Love it, damn it! Tiernon screamed at himself. Already it was noticeably smaller, smaller. The Unity. How had it looked from that perspective, from that high place? How had they seen it then? Again, transmute, transmute.

Tiernon felt it hit deep down in the base of the spine, the lowest energy center. He almost imagined Bertham's face, and then, as he quashed that, his mother's. The rage had taken hold. It was there in a knot down at the bottom of the spine, being fed by the emotion of the thing. It would grow. It would grow and run up the central nerve until it hit his brain and then he would be lost. That was the function of the thing. The hatred, the damned rage.

Again he thought about the Unity. Ignore the hatred, think of the Megraha, the Perfection of the Shining Beauty. The image almost faltered in his mind, but he managed to hold it firm. He could feel it now in his back, and there came to him an urge to smash, to kill anything present. It was almost to the heart center. It was happening too fast! Discipline! Nothing at all is better than giving in to it. Love. Think of the ones you love. The old Master of Novices at the Abbey sprang to mind, and Tiernon grabbed the image and began to build it. The white hair always askew, the perpetually hurried air, the delighted smile whenever a pupil came to him with some new discovery. Tiernon had loved him, and poured out this love to the image that he had created. The hatred stopped spreading, but the image was growing thin. Another. Anros, the little novice who had cried for him when he was denied Volenten, who had saved him from Lechefrian as an Adept. Anros, standing there at the retreat house, joy pouring out of him; Anros, who had cut the tie to Lechefrian. For a moment he was safe, secure in the warmth and joy of that memory; but the image began to shatter. Quickly, another. The fishermen and the boats and the great ocean and the fish. The desperation did not leave him enough time to build as carefully as he would have wished.

The thing was less than one-third of its original size now, and shrinking rapidly, but it had affected him deeply, and he knew that he could not hold off the raging fury that was capturing him for very long. The fishermen, their seamed faces, the stories and yarns and the knots they had taught him. He tied knot after knot, neither love nor compassion coming through now, but only the coldness of the types of knots and where they were in the rigging.

There was no more love. Concentrate on anything but hatred. Do not let anger get in the way. Only a little more now, double hitch, clover, lashing on the mast. He glanced at Cataia and noted with fear that she was shaking. He could see the greyness growing in her as it was in him, taking over. In her it was further along. The damn Green training. Soft! The hatred passed the heart center, and, panicking, he began to name the sails one set for storm conditions.

Cataia lay on the floor as his sword pulled in the last burst of energy from the Watcher, and in that last blast he saw Cataia and his half-held control went wild. In utter rage he smashed the mirror with the heavy brass hilt, seeing bright shards of glass drift down as the rage ate and overpowered him. By the time Tiernon hit the floor, his consciousness was severed.

It was the noise of the shattering glass that brought Valnera running. She didn't care that Tiernon had given her specific instructions to stay out until dawn; the noise seemed to have no part of what she had been told to expect and she didn't hesitate. The seals were still flaming around the ritual area, and Valnera worried about passing through them, but Cataia lay on the floor looking at least half-dead. Still, the seals were there. Valnera hesitated again at this thing she did not understand.

It would be better to send for help, the kind of help that would take care of this. She rummaged through the apartment quickly to find the writing case and handed the note to a servant. "Run," she said. "Tell them to wake the Priestess if necessary, this is an emergency!" Valnera shooed the already fleeing servant out, and then waited the eternity of seconds before Ayt arrived.

With Ayt came a detachment of guards in the uniform of the Temple. "Don't worry," the Priestess said quietly, "they're loyal to me."

Ayt made several passes with her hands and chanted in a language Valnera couldn't understand. The seals blazed brightly once more, and began to fade. Ignoring the Adepts on the floor, Ayt completed the ritual of the four quarters, and although Valnera did not know what was being done or why, the atmosphere in the room changed and seemed more normal. The seals were gone.

Turning her attention to the two unconscious magicians, Ayt checked with a broken sliver of mirror to see if they were even breathing. "Valnera, I'll need two rugs, and the guards will take them to the Temple. You clear up this mess and seal it, and then send over some clothes. I think they might be needed. And on no account tell anyone anything! You were asleep in your own room. You heard nothing. You saw nothing. You know nothing."

"And what will happen to my poor little Princess?" the older woman wailed.

"It's better for Cataia that you don't know. I don't know at this point, but they'll be safer with me. Valnera, for the Princess's sake and your own, you weren't here tonight. Guards, lift them onto the rugs. Carefully, there are injuries."

"But Ayt," Valnera began, "the square is full of people, they'll see you."

"Valnera, do as I told you. I can take care of the rest. Go now. They'll need clothes and money, and I want it all at the Temple before sunrise."

Valnera went. Ayt signaled the guards and they followed her through a maze of corridors and small back halls between the laundry and the kitchens. Ayt was not going to risk the square, but both the Palace and the Temple had doorways down to the river. The small boat they had come in was tied up at the steps and Ayt engaged the guard in conversation as the Temple loyalists carried two rolled rugs down to the boat.

"But why do you come this way, Priestess?" the guard asked, more conversational than concerned.

"I have no wish to be disturbed by everyone in the square. At every step someone wants to know what Megerai's phase is, or if Vecheiel is in a good position to pursue a love affair. They won't ask one of the acolytes or the lower Priesthood, or come to the Temple where these things are read aloud daily, but they'll stop me in the square."

The guard clucked his tongue understandingly. The great

had far better things to do than to be bothered, and for his part, he felt more honored that the High Priestess even deigned to speak to him at all.

When Cataia and Tiernon had been installed in her private quarters at the Temple, Ayt sat down and studied the Star charts she had kept of them, as she had charts of every important and powerful figure.

They seemed dead. She had not told Valnera that the mirror had not fogged. But here, the charts showed it clearly, it was not yet time for them to die, either of them. Three days she would wait. In that time something should change, and there should be some indication of what was meant here.

A tear ran down her face. So this was what had driven Tiernon away from her. Like water running over her fingers, she felt what could have been slip away again. There was no place in life for "if only." Gathering the sorrow and slightly tarnished pride of her profession around her, Ayt slipped away. The Orders had forgotten too much.

Bertham couldn't decide whether or not to be disturbed. The Guard had searched all day, and the secret room in Tiernon's apartments had been found, but there were no bodies. If the bodies couldn't be found, there was no proof that Tiernon and Cataia were dead. On the other hand, he had seen them die, and that memory was fresh. On the positive side, the disappearance of the bodies could be called kidnapping, and if they were found dead, well, then some anonymous kidnappers, probably Nestezian spies, had done the dirty work. Here was a clear-cut alibi, so perfect that it could not fail to gain support for both the war and Lathanor.

Besides, where were the bodies? They had searched everywhere, facing the smirks of servants and kitchen maids who seemed to think that being missing might have explanations other than danger. Valnera claimed to have been asleep the whole time, and it was impossible to doubt her, especially when she began describing her dream.

The Guards' failure at the Temple didn't annoy him too badly. First, by tradition the Temple was inviolate and he had never expected to penetrate it, and second, Ayt was on his side as far as this went. Why, he had not exactly figured out, and he wasn't idiot enough to trust her, Priestess though she may be. But she certainly wasn't a logical party to be hiding two bodies, not when it might mean her downfall.

Besides, Ayt was neutral. She always had been and there hadn't been much change recently. Of course, he had seen her with Tiernon, but that wasn't important. They had been lovers and Ayt was still attractive. He couldn't begrudge her her pleasures. But that was still no reason for her to risk herself hiding a dead man. No, until other courses had been eliminated, it was best to believe Ayt.

There was another possibility, a possibility that played at the back of Bertham's mind, a possibility that he did not want to face and knew he must. Tiernon and Cataia might not be dead, or only one of them might have died and the other, or both, were in hiding. He had only felt Cataia fleeing from the Watcher as it took her body, and though he was sure that Tiernon couldn't have survived the final blast, there was always a possibility. Lechefrian would know, but it took energy to call the demon and Bertham had no energy left.

That would be the final resort. Other options were still open. The Guard was searching, and they might well find the bodies. He knew, he had felt it, they must be dead. Bertham was worried, but not unduly so.

All was warmth and darkness. It was rich with rest and nourishment, and Tiernon was content. It was pleasant in a womblike way. The darkness was nice, comforting and thick with palpitations of beingness all around. He knew where he was, not from a clear memory, but from some primitive instinct. These were the Caverns of Ge, the Place of the Dead. Then he was dead.

Being dead seemed far nicer than being alive. It was too bad he had never remembered in the Abbey about this place, about the comfort of it.

He felt movement around him. There were others here, others newly dead. There was Judgment, of course, but it was not a Judgment he feared. He had died doing what had to be done, to the best of his ability. The Judgment wouldn't be too harsh. He searched for Cataia and couldn't contact her. Maybe she was not dead, or in a different place. He was not concerned. Nothing concerned him, and he drifted with pleasure in the great Caverns of Ge the Primordial.

Perhaps it was time to go. He sensed a figure in front of him, cowled and veiled and indistinct. The Guide? Was it time for the Judgment, then? He hadn't seen any Guides before, not like this, not with the authority of the figure before him. Perhaps Adepts got special treatment. He sensed a patience and a sadness about it, and became more alert so it might speak.

"You must return. It is not time, and there are things to do and things you must know before you can approach Judgment."

He did not exactly hear the voice. It permeated his being, and he felt it and understood in some mute way exactly what was meant, far more so than if he had simply heard the words. It felt feminine and the figure seemed familiar.

"You have been given rest and strength to go on and finish, but you cannot remain here. Tiernon, we watch for you to return. Take care of your soul, or I shall not want to guide you to Judgment."

He understood what was happening. He was going to be alive again. The darkness began to shimmer and take on hues, the strong glistening colors of the Planes, and he knew he was passing through them, but it was smooth and easy and there was no effort required.

Then the pleasantness stopped. He felt ill and weak, as if the energy drained by the defeat of the Watcher and the days in the Caverns of Ge had opened a door to something, and that it had taken over. It was too hot to breathe, to exist, and his back and legs ached.

"Thank the Stars," he heard a voice say, and risked opening his eyes to the brightness. It was Ayt, followed by a young novice with a water-jug. "You're safe here, for the time being, anyway," she said. "You have some fever, but I was afraid you were dead."

"I was," he croaked, reaching for the water. Parched as he was, Tiernon obeyed Ayt's instructions to drink slowly, and he noted that the water was not cold.

"Bertham's guards have been searching. They won't be back, at least not for a while, but you have to do something. It would be death to walk into the Palace now, if you were well enough to walk," said Ayt. "I think we can manage to hide you both until you regain some strength, but I don't know what to do after."

"Cataia?" he asked.

"She isn't much better than you. Sleep now. You'll feel better and we can make plans."

The rugged little pony was slow, but Chervan didn't mind in the least. He was enjoying the scenery and the air far from Tsanos. Looking back on it now, the city seemed an incarceration, albeit a far more luxurious one than that which he was heading for. Still, it was almost done. He had served and waited a very long time, and would have waited longer had it been necessary, but the time was right.

First, there had been the ten years' novitiate, and then all the years as an ordinary Priest of his Order. And then Aken, and the training there and the work, until it was time for this. It had been twenty years at Court, waiting and watching, until the orders had come from Aken.

When they had come, there in Bietehel, he had been both relieved and unhappy. He was caught in history, in the unraveling of events that he had seen and prepared. Now all he could do was play out his role like one of the heroes of the ballads; but, like the singer, he knew where it would end.

He had been asked three times if he would accept the honor of Aken. He had been so young then, although not young by the way it was counted here, had jumped at the greatness and glory of it, even when Degevan had told him that it was a sacrifice and bought with pain. He had not understood that then. He understood only too well now.

The pony shied and Chervan awoke from his reverie. A slight, veiled figure, heavily swathed in black, stood in the middle of the path. It was one of the Guides, one such as had brought the message that it was time to leave the Court, that his work was about to begin. Now he dismounted heavily and fell into step with the veiled figure, knowing that the orders would come. The Guide waited for him, and wasted no time in preliminaries.

"You must hurry. They have been sent back, and now the real work begins. If necessary, call every night while you're out on the trail, all night, every night. Remember, they must not know, none of them. Forget the other until you have reached the Caverns, he hasn't as far to travel. But the two up north are urgent, and you're far enough south for even a general call to be effective."

Chervan bowed the deep, stiff bow of novice to Master as the Guide passed into a small glade and disappeared in the shadow.

The prologue was over, Chervan knew. Now it was time for history to reveal itself. He could change things, if he wished. He could refuse to give the call, could refuse what would come after it. But he knew that he wouldn't. He was Aken.

The path was good here, hard-packed and wide, and if he could get some spirit from the pony they should near the mountains by nightfall. He knew a good place to camp, if it hadn't been destroyed in the years he had been away from his native mountains.

Then he would call, and they would come. He had no doubts. He and they and Lechefrian himself, they were all only players within the great plan of the Universe. They had been born to come to that call, as he had been born to give it. And after, maybe, there would be release.

🎗 NINE

TIERNON WAS SURPRISED when he awoke. Although he felt weak, the fever and the pain were gone and he could remember quite clearly what Ayt had said the night before. Next, Cataia was standing over him, dribbling drops of water on his face from the glass she held. He should have known; she was an early riser, and if she had dreamed as he had, she would be impatient.

"Hurry up. We have things to get ready, and the sooner we're gone the better. Here." She flung him his clothes, which had previously been neatly folded in the corner. "Get dressed. There's some breakfast in Ayt's receiving room, and we'll have some privacy before she returns if you hurry."

Surprised to find that he was hungry, Tiernon dressed quickly and met Cataia, who was already munching on bread and a strip of dried fish. She was lady enough to swallow before she began talking. "We have to leave here. Ayt told me before she left that the Guard have been here twice, and she had to challenge one of the captains to a duel before he'd leave. Do you think we should brazen it out at the Palace? I can just see their faces, especially Bertham's, if we just walk in.''

"It would work," Tiernon said slowly between careful sips of broth. "Bertham couldn't do much once we arrived. He would have to act as if he were wonderfully happy to see us. But, given what happened with the Watcher, he is probably certain that we're dead, and we might be able to use that to our advantage.''

"What do you mean by that?" Cataia asked.

Tiernon took a few sips of broth, collecting his thoughts. It would be very easy to return to the Palace as if nothing had happened, but there was Ayt's plan and the Rei Mothers. Bertham thought they were dead and Ayt knew they weren't, and the Rei Mothers would be far more inclined to believe Ayt.

"It depends on Ayt," he said slowly. "If she could let the Rei Mothers know that we're alive, then we've lost nothing and gained some time. With us apparently out of the way, there's nothing to stop Bertham now, and Ayt's plan would go into effect, with one simple alteration. He wouldn't know that a revolution is fomenting, since there's no longer an obvious rallying point. Not from his point of view, anyway."

"You mean like throwing the Brilliant Sun in the last hand at tiles?" Cataia asked.

Tiernon smiled. He knew Cataia was no gambler, but she had the idea. "Pretty much," he agreed. "The thing is, we have two choices, or one, don't we?"

Cataia gave him an angry look. So she had dreamed. He had known it, it was too strong to resist, that call, that urge to move south. Even now he could barely remain still, the need to go was so deep in him. His voice shifted slightly. "We have to go to the Nestezi, don't we?" he asked.

"I dreamed," Cataia responded. "I think it's even more important than Bertham or Lathanor or even Avriaten. I can't describe it. It's a compulsion. And I'm afraid. I'm scared it's 'Kleppah, trying to give Bertham a clear field, getting us out of the way.''

Tiernon had a sudden impulse to hug her and reassure her. With her hair still down, fingers tearing off bits of bread, she looked like the young girl barely come of age that she was, unsure of herself, and not the Initiate Queen she usually affected.

"I think not," Tiernon said in a warm voice. " 'Kleppah made a stand with the Watcher. My mind says we should go to the Palace, but there are ways of using the situation. And even if the call is from 'Kleppah, can you resist?"

She shook her head and looked down, ashamed. Tiernon took her hand and stroked it. "Neither can I," he said softly. "I dreamed too, and it still moves in me. Even now, I don't feel right sitting here." He hesitated a moment, some scrap of memory playing around the fringes of his consciousness. "I know," he said suddenly. "We can ask Ayt."

"Ayt?" Cataia almost dropped her glass. "How in the deadly sun could she know anything useful in this kind of thing? What in Ronarian's name does she know about magia?"

"You know what the Temple is, and was," Tiernon said quietly. "She's an astrologer and she has our charts. If I had a Wheel with me I'd consult it, but we don't. No, she's got to be good, she wouldn't be High Priestess if she weren't."

"Tiernon, please be sensible. We probably know more about the uses of astrology than she does. The Temple became profane ages ago, when they went public. And since they've been named the State religion I wouldn't trust a thing she says. They've forgotten."

"Maybe, but it doesn't hurt to ask her opinion," Tiernon said. "Besides, if the second possible plan is to succeed, Ayt is a major factor. It would make her feel better if we consulted her, instead of just ordering her. She may even have some useful suggestions herself. And even if she knows only half as much about astrology as she does about the Court, it would be useful."

"You're right," she agreed grudgingly, "it can't hurt if we don't tell her too much about the other."

"Then stop eating so much fish and drink some broth," Tiernon chided laughingly. "Broth is good when you've been sick."

Tiernon supervised as Cataia drank most of a bowl of the salty broth. Even if he hadn't pursued advanced training at Volenten, he still knew that after a high fever, salt and fluids were important. He knew that Cataia was watching to see that he took his own advice. They were just finishing when Ayt came in.

"Ayt," Tiernon began, "we're going to need your help, if

you have some time and would be willing. In your official capacity, that is, and not as ministering angel."

"I'd been hoping you'd ask," Ayt said quietly. "The Temple has always been at the service of the Orders."

It was only with the greatest control that Tiernon kept his face impassive.

"What?" demanded Cataia, the near empty bowl of broth nearly dropping into her lap.

"I know what you are, Princess, and I know what the Councilor Tiernon is," Ayt said softly, "but I'm afraid you have not been as well informed. The Inner Temple knows, and has not forgotten, what our science really is, although we cannot serve except under request. We have never forgotten that we serve the Orders of the Seven, although it has been a very long time since you have come to us."

Tiernon could not meet Ayt's gaze. So much lost, not only to the Orders, but in his own life. To have rejected Ayt because he couldn't disclose . . . and then to hear this. He understood now why heroes in romantic poetry raged against Fate.

"Perhaps I should explain," Ayt continued. "We give comfort and guidance to the people, as Ronarian intended when we were founded. It is a function the Orders will not and cannot discharge, it is not their function. But like the Orders, we cannot tell the full truth. And is it wrong to worship the Stars? Isn't the Creator within the Creation? We don't teach lies, only simple truths. In any event, that is not important, although please remember it when you come to the throne, Princess."

"How long have you known about us?" Tiernon asked, his voice tight.

"Since the night of the ritual," she answered. "The seals were still blazing."

The soft, sad tone of her voice pierced Tiernon. Looking at her now he knew, and knew that she also knew, that there was no longer any hope for them. Unspoken there had been a narrow crevasse between them; opened, it had turned into an unbroachable chasm.

"What is it you need?" Ayt asked Tiernon simply.

"Priestess," he said, "there is a decision to be made. Either we return to the Palace now, or leave for the South as soon as we are fit."

"It has crossed my mind that you can't stay here forever," Ayt said, smiling. "Bertham is certain you're dead. You could go directly to the Palace, but that would only put you back in danger. And if I may remind the Princess, her safety is paramount. Without her, there is no hope of removing Bertham and Lathanor, at least not without Salsatee moving in."

"The Rei Mothers know that you're linked to our camp," Tiernon added quickly. "They would believe you if . . ."

"Yes," Ayt agreed. "It's much simpler, and we're all safer, if you're in hiding. I can deal with Bertham from a much stronger position if he thinks you're dead. Right now he doesn't trust me, or any deals I might make. But if he couldn't see any ulterior motive, if there weren't another obvious candidate to support, then I would be in a better position to move. As long as the Rei Mothers know, this brings our plan one step closer to fruition." She hesitated for a moment. "I have also been studying your charts since the night of your ritual. Usually I don't do that, it's a breach of privacy, but astrologically all the signs say that you must go. I don't want to bore you with the technicalities, and your charts are very different from each other, but I've done the progressions and transits, and there are indications of great change and journey for both of you. Funny, I've never seen anything that alike in two so different charts, but it's there. I rechecked the mathematics three times."

"Can you tell us any more about it?" Cataia asked.

"No, not really. The Stars reveal trends, not specifics. Just that you will travel far, very far, and that there will be difficulties. Other than that, I can't say anything."

Cataia smiled and tore the roll she was holding. Offering Ayt half, she said, "May this life be your last."

Tiernon nodded. It was the formal greeting of the Adepti, used in the Abbeys.

"Live in Unity," Ayt replied.

"Valnera is not going to like this," Cataia said suddenly, laughing.

"She'll like it better than Bertham will," Tiernon replied.

"Now," said Ayt, "for some serious decisions. You shouldn't leave for a day or two yet. I shouldn't have any trouble holding you that long. But it's not going to be easy for you to get out. Just because Bertham says you're dead in public doesn't mean that he believes it, or that he's acting like he does. His men are watching the gates and the wharf. I can think of only one way, and it isn't very good."

"Wait a minute," Tiernon interrupted. "The Temple has an entrance directly on the river, doesn't it? And it will be hard for him to reach us magically on running water. We take a small boat and head downstream to Batter."

"But they're patrolling the river!" Ayt exclaimed.

"Wait, wait," Cataia said, "I know it will work. Look, they can't really inspect every boat that passes, can they? But if we leave at around dusk, there'll be a lot of small craft in the river, fisherfolk and tenant farmers who have spent the day selling at the market. There should be a good number of boats, and it's hard to see by twilight. And remember, they're looking for a Council Lord and a Princess. They're not looking for a couple who've come to the market to sell fish. Poor clothes, a little dirt to disguise our features a bit, it shouldn't be too difficult."

"We can try," Tiernon said. "But I don't like it."

Cataia looked at him sharply. "Disguise, image and reality is part of the Green training," she said authoritatively.

"It's not the plan I don't like, it's Bertham running the country without me to check on him," Tiernon replied.

Ayt looked uncomfortable, and then spoke softly. "But Tiernon, that's the idea. It could actually be to our benefit. Without your influence on the Council, Bertham will go ahead with his war, his taxes and his jurisdiction reforms. The Rei Mothers will be more than ready to rebel when they're presented with any alternative, let alone the rightful Queen. Let me arrange things, please. You both still need rest to recover."

Still sitting, Tiernon bowed as if he were in Court. "Then I leave things in competent hands."

Eryah watched as SiUran stuffed six days' worth of dried meat into a pouch. The Great Ones had spoken and it was time, she knew. He wore the yellow-and-green-patterned plekas of a shaman tied around his headdress and trailing down his back, bestowed when the call came. Eryah thought it was funny that he, the War Leader of the Atnefi, should be protected from attack by other tribes by the shaman colors, but he was on the Great Ones' errand and deserved protection.

"Please let me go with you. I heard the call, I told you

about it, why can't I go?'' she pleaded again, without hope.

"No, Eryah," SiUran said. "The shaman said no. The vision smoke said no. I say no, and the answer is no. Hearing and being called are different, and you need the discipline. Besides, the war band needs you. What if we are attacked by the Qaludi?''

"But you're the Si," Eryah protested.

"Yes, and so I have the authority to order you to stay, and stay you will, unless you want to join the outcasts. I can assure you that they are not particularly interested in this matter."

Eryah became quiet. To be cast out of the tribe would be death. All outcasts died—they could not use the wells or gather food from the tribal places, and they did not have the use or the hospitality of a tent. They died, and Eryah didn't want to die, not just yet. The Great Ones would need her war band, of that she had no doubts. To do what had been promised, they would need every warrior in the Nestezi, although the idea of joining with the other tribes was faintly disgusting.

SiUran had turned his back to her, and she knew that he wouldn't listen to any more entreaties. Perhaps he was right. She got up and left without a word, and walked around the perimeter of the camp.

"I vow I will never again be left out of this work. For I have dreamed and I have spoken with them, and I will have my chance, and those who oppose me will be as dust in the wind. This I vow," she said, chanting in the old High Language.

"Not a very good idea to make vows concerning the Great Ones. They have their own ways, and it is not for us to decide."

Eryah turned on her heel, her knife at the ready, only to face SiUran laughing behind her. "Save the tanning stick for someone else's hide," he said.

Embarrassed, she laughed and he laughed with her. SiUran never failed to amaze her, never failed to be right. But the vow, spoken and witnessed, could not be withdrawn now.

"If you wish," he said, "I will wait, and go to the fire with you and have this set down. If you wish."

That was strange. No one ever said "if you wish" about a vow, but that didn't matter. It was made, and Eryah felt she had spoken correctly. At least she felt none of the pain or the shyness she did when she said something wrong.

"Let's go to the fire, then," she said.

Eryah had never made a vow before, but she knew the rules. Everyone did. SiUran led her to the small fire outside the shaman's tent, a fire too small to cook food or to warm, and never permitted to go out. Here they stood, SiUran yelling no-words until there was an assembly. Then Eryah stepped out.

"I have made a vow," she said. "It was witnessed by our War Leader and the Great Ones."

SiUran then repeated what he had heard her say at the edge of the camp, and then there was silence.

The shaman looked at her. She was young, but she wore the red pants of a warrior and the bracelet of a band leader, and the profusion of small braids indicated that she was a grown woman. She had the right. He cast a handful of dried herbs into the fire and the vision smoke rose lazily.

Eryah inhaled deeply and began to chant the Prophecy. Then her voice changed and she began to speak, unintelligible things, not really words at all. Then she laughed, and in clear High Language said, "It is done."

The war band carried her back to the young women's tent because the smoke had plunged Eryah into a trance. Her visions were her own, and none had the right to disturb her.

No one watched as SiUran took Feln and left the camp.

Feln was a good hannart, not a racer by any means, but strong and full of endurance. The great desert beasts, resembling their horse-cousins in form and beauty, were the fastest animals in the world, and natives of the harsh desert climate.

SiUran knew he would make it to the mountains in time for the greeting and guiding. He knew they would come to the Pass, the Dreams had told him so, and the Dreams had never been wrong. He had asked the Great One whose face he could not see why he, an old man, had been chosen, and the Great One had not answered. The question had been impertinent and SiUran had been afraid and anxious, but now that the tents were dwindling behind him he felt only relief. There was plenty of time to go by the well-way, and SiUran grinned, thinking of meeting his former enemies while wearing the shaman's plekas.

Sailing the small boat wasn't as easy as Tiernon thought it would be. First, he hadn't sailed in a very long time, and the old reflexes were half-forgotten or worse, mixed up, and it took time to readjust. Then, too, Cataia couldn't sail. She had never been in a small boat in her life, only the large royal barge, and it was merely luck that the weather stayed calm and the wind steady so that her stomach remained in its proper place. He was pleased to see her enjoying it, though, and he soon began to enjoy it again, too.

Ayt had been very clever getting them out of the Temple, right in full sight of the Palace guards. She had sent them down in the robes of Temple novices, along with two real novices and a tar bucket full of rags, clothes and jewels. No one had bothered to notice that they stayed very late, and that only two returned to the Temple. It had been well done, and he had to give Ayt credit.

On the third day out there was a strong wind, and in a sudden, uncharacteristic burst of recklessness Tiernon decided to tack into it for speed. Cataia screamed in pleasure as she threw her weight over the windward rail, clinging to the heavy line of the mainsail as the little boat plowed the water. The mast seemed almost parallel to the river and the speed of the boat cast up great sheets of cold spray, thoroughly drenching both of them.

When Tiernon brought the dinghy up into the wind, Cataia moved along beside him and put her hand on the tiller. He noticed a glow to her eyes that he hadn't seen before, filled as they were with warm contentment, which reminded him of warm milk and early spring.

"Come on," Tiernon said, suddenly jovial, "I'll teach you to swim."

He dove over the side, the water stinging his hands, which were raw from the tiller, and did a lazy backflip, motioning her to join him. He noticed that she showed no fear jumping into deep water, although she didn't know how to swim. He towed her for a while as she kicked gamely, laughing and swallowing water and sputtering the entire time.

Soon tired, they pulled the boat out on the bank and collapsed on the grass. Tiernon found himself watching her, strangely, as if she were a stranger. And she was. He realized that he had only thought of her as the Princess, the Priestess, and not simply as Cataia. Suddenly, he realized that he liked Cataia, her spunk and her willingness to try to swim and the way she trusted him. He had seen that courage before, he knew, and the mind behind it, in the midst of Lechefrian's attack. But she had been the Princess then, something he had always been too aware of to see beyond.

When she turned away shyly from his gaze, Tiernon had an impulse to say something, but he didn't know what. He had been unfair to her, and resolved to change that.

By the fifth day the land began to change around them. It was no longer the great flat green plains of the Entelle floodland, the floods that silted the great river basin and brought Avriaten its wealth. Now the pale, rippling steema fields gave way to the chiena and geri trees that loved the deep heat of the southern tip of the country.

The river narrowed slightly here, and the branches, heavy with fruit, reached out over the rushing water. The banks were higher now, getting higher still, and they were often in deep shadow as they sailed.

As the ancient chiena trees arched over them, Cataia found herself looking deep into the water, trailing her hand in its coolness. She felt deliciously relaxed and lighthearted. She enjoyed learning how to sail and swim, the feeling of Tiernon's hands guiding her through the water and his laughter. They had both laughed more, she reflected, than they had at Court.

She hadn't had any skill in catching or skinning fish, or building fires out in the open, and Tiernon had been patient and uncritical teaching her.

"Take the helm for a bit," he said.

She moved easily to the back of the boat and placed her hand on the smooth, weathered tiller. At first it had been frightening, but now she took it firmly, letting the slight breeze on her cheek direct her.

"Your hands are all raw," Tiernon said.

Cataia looked up at him and smiled. It had stopped bothering her, and she liked the easy feel of the boat gliding beneath them, so responsive to her directions. It surprised her more when Tiernon went rummaging through the pack and came up with a soft, overwashed wide pleka.

Bracing the tiller against his elbow, he tore the pleka in half and began binding her palms very gently. Cataia sighed with contentment as the river rushed past and Tiernon tended her.

Very likely they had entered Batter by now. In any case, Tiernon said gently, it would be necessary to take to land soon. Not only were the banks getting higher and steeper, but the current was getting stronger. They were getting closer to the mountain tributaries and further from the placid Entelle itself.

They beached the boat near a small village high up on the banks of the river, and traded it for two sturdy plow ponies.

Tiernon did the trading conscientiously, and Cataia wondered where he had learned such skills. Certainly not in the Palace. But the Palace felt very far away now. She smiled at Tiernon as she stroked the nose of one of the ponies.

"It was good to relax, but now that we're off the river we're back in Bertham's field of perception," Tiernon said gently. "He might have lost us by now, but it would be very easy to pick us up again. I suggest that we keep well off the main roads and stay away from the likes of any inns, or, Powers forbid, nobility. We should be able to purchase food or lodgings from the farmers around here—and if not it's warm enough to sleep out."

Seeing the way Cataia's face became tight at the mention of Bertham and the Palace, Tiernon felt almost bereft. He had hurt her, he knew, just when the tension of Court life was beginning to dissipate for both of them.

"Where did you learn all of this, Tiernon?" Cataia asked. "It seems as if you are experienced at running."

"No"—he grinned broadly, trying to save the moment— "but what's the good of reading modern romantic poetry if you don't pick up some good advice?"

They chuckled together at the joke and the sense of history behind it.

"You know," Cataia said as they walked through the rich lands, "this is the way it should be. The people are honest, judging from these ponies, anyway. No wonder Timesa Rei Mother doesn't want to give Lathanor any power here."

"That's the whole way of it," Tiernon agreed. "The Rei Mothers are as much a part of the land they rule as the peasants. More so, even. You know, I worked like any child of the fishing village before I went off to the Abbey. The Rei Mothers, the people, the land, they all depend on each other."

"But Bertham," Cataia continued, "I wonder why he doesn't see it." She turned to Tiernon and he saw an intensity burning in her face. "I think I understand now," she said. "I felt that you and Nikkot and Ayt and even my mother were pushing at me, saying it's time to move, that I had to make a bid, that I had to have the power. And now I understand the reason for it. It's for me to be to all Avriaten what Timesa is for Batter. But it frightens me.''

Tiernon stopped and took both her hands. "I'm frightened too," he said bluntly. "Something is waiting for us over the mountains and there's only the beginning of an uncertain coup at home. Ayt will do her job, I don't worry about that. I only hope we can trust my mother. Maybe," he said as much for himself as for her, "maybe we should stop trying to rely only on ourselves and trust the destiny of the Universe. Like when we were little children in the Abbey, they taught us that." He looked at the sky and dropped her hands. "It's getting dark. Even supported by Lechefrian he can't work by day, but . . ."

"In theory," Cataia said.

Tiernon shrugged helplessly. "Theory is all we have to go on at the moment. Anyway, I suggest that we set the Dark Cube tonight, and that means we should find a place to sleep."

Cataia agreed with some trepidation. It would take some memory work before she recalled how to set that kind of protection, a thing she had never done before, or needed to do. Tiernon looked so distant that Cataia wondered. Yes, he was older and had been at Court for longer than she had been a novice, and he had done far more magia than she, but this situation must be new to him too. Yet she had leaned on him and made demands. She saw the weight of it in his eyes and in his walk. Even when he smiled there was a burden there, and she felt it as a stab of pain.

She had used him. She had constantly demanded things of him and had given him little except grief and contempt. She had treated him as if he could take care of everything for her, if he only would. Now, facing herself squarely, Cataia saw that he was a man. An Adept to be sure, but still only a man, and being asked to take on more burdens than any man could reasonably be expected to shoulder alone. She wanted to tell him something, perhaps that she would carry her own weight and not rail at him anymore, but the words stuck in her throat.

There were small farms along the cart path, and they managed to find a barn to sleep in before the red had completely faded from the sky. It was better to stay in the barn away from prying eyes and potential sensitives. They stabled the ponies and climbed into the loft with as few provisions as could be considered adequate.

The Dark Cube, set at countercorners to the major directions, was designed to camouflage. Any normal invocation, Cataia knew, protective as it might be, would be easily traceable on the Planes. Now the whole idea was to hide. It was the only protection they had, she knew.

They worked quietly together, drawing cubes and circles in the air, not daring to light any incense over the flooring of dry hay. Over, crossing under, sealing every possible crack, building walls and floor and ceiling in their minds until it was more solid than stone. It was not a very difficult thing to do, and once they found the orientations and recalled the first line of the chants, Cataia found that it all came back to her easily, as if this ritual were one that she had done often.

Tiernon seemed subdued, as if he were trying to forget and couldn't. She had never seen him like this, not after the attack, not while they were waiting for the next move—she had never seen his face so drawn or melancholy. With her new awareness of Tiernon, she realized that he must have looked that way before and she hadn't noticed. Something in her went out to him, wanting to cradle him against the terrors that lay both behind and ahead.

As the feeling grew in her, the training of ten years took over. She was a Priestess of the Green Order. The Priestess. The essence of Woman, a thing very ancient, and though she was his junior, she was also his mother and the Green One who brought dreams and inner life to men.

Cataia was aware of herself on two levels, the Priestess and the girl. And the girl who was simply Cataia was a little frightened about what she was doing. Frightened of herself, but glad too. Tiernon had become so much more real, so much less an abstraction, these few days on the river. She acknowledged that she had wanted him for a very long time. Grateful, she surrendered to the Priestess in herself.

She reached out her hand and touched him lightly on the shoulder, and when Tiernon raised his eyes he found himself looking into a face that was the summation of all Cataia had been and would be. He felt compassion for his weakness lance

through and wound him, the weakness he didn't even know he
had, and the sadness they shared, and he knew that she understood.

It was frightening. The loneliness that he accepted and
railed against alternately was a familiar companion and he
hesitated. If he touched her something in him would die, but
the hand that rested on his shoulder was not the hand of the
Crown Princess of Avriaten, not the promising girl who managed Council meetings and threw cosmetics. This was some
manifestation of the Being in feminine form and it could not
be rejected, not even when he knew the price would be his
loneliness and the nakedness of his soul.

He reached out and touched her cheek, her throat, her soft
shoulders, amazed at the change in her. She laughed deep in
her throat, the laugh of the courtesan, and drew him to her
languidly, using her hands and lips like a woman who had
seduced many men. Tiernon's mind reeled as his body began
to respond. She was a virgin, he knew, and yet she was no
virgin. She was the Primordial Mother, the mistress of every
man. For once he forgot himself as the perfect sensualist, the
skilled lover, and gave himself over to the hands of the Bride
of the World.

For the first time in many mornings, Tiernon awoke refreshed. Cataia lay beside him, her dark hair tangled in the
straw, her face so very innocent that for a moment Tiernon
wondered if he had indeed taken her the night before. Or had
it been something else, something not a woman at all? Then
her mouth curved into a small, knowing smile before he bent
to awaken her with a not-so-chaste kiss.

Cataia smiled, feeling a little shy, but glad that the magic of
the night before had not been sealed apart, away from them,
as magic could be. It was not only magic, then, she knew, but
something more. Contentment filled her, soaking in with the
buttery light stealing in through the slats in the wall.

Then the call began again, now so strong and urgent that
there was no thinking, no resisting, no waiting even to say the
Chant to the Sun. They did the daily ritual on the road, and
munched the thick slabs of bread as they walked.

It became more rocky around midday, and slightly cooler.
The boulders poked through the packed trail, and it was ob-

vious that they were reaching the mountains and the Pass would not be far off.

"We'll have to risk the main road," Tiernon said, "or we'll never get to the Pass."

Cataia nodded quietly and they turned onto a second, larger cart road that would bring them to the approach. Neither needed to affirm that this was the right road or to ask the farmers with wagonloads of chiena when they would reach the approach. Cataia found it vaguely strange that even though she had never been in this place she knew without asking that they were on the right road and would reach the narrow path to the Pass before sunset. She knew there was a glade near there with a nice spring that would be perfect for their camp. It was not good to question such knowledge.

Chervan held the picture steady in his mind as he sat in the Caverns. It was working, he knew, and they'd be across the Pass sometime the next day, just exactly on schedule. He carefully constructed a picture of the glade, the campground he had found so pleasant, and using the technique he had learned as a novice on Dier Street, threw it out to those waiting minds. He could sense the fear and trouble in them, and it saddened him. He knew what was to come, leading them on, forcing them forward on this task that would eventually . . . Chervan didn't want to think about it. Their fate was beyond anything he would have to face. He called, but he also grieved.

He threw his mind to the southeast, searching well into the desert for the open mind, waiting. Things were going well. All parties were in position, exactly as planned. Still, he kept the image strong, sending with all his might, not because it was necessary, but because it kept him from feeling the dampness of the Caverns.

Perhaps the cold, wet place had suited the Seven after they had bound 'Kleppah, but then penitents tend to prefer discomfort. Or maybe it was the sheer beauty of the immense, natural structure, the clear glistening lake and the mammoth pillars of green and red and white and orange, created by the minerals of the cave itself. Chervan could admire the lovely fabriclike folds of stone, which hung translucent from the ceiling and the muted, long arcades, but for himself, he would choose a drier place to live.

This was the last night he would call. Then he had only to wait, and to prepare the third part of the plan that Aken had devised. Part of him still rebelled, thinking about the final operation, but he forced himself to think as he had learned to over a century ago at Volenten. Sometimes it was necessary to cause a patient some pain to save his life. It was a single, wrenching operation he would perform, traumatic for the patient, but more easily overcome than the disease itself.

In his years at Court he had come to know and like both of them. He remembered Cataia as an infant, and Tiernon at just twenty years old, newly Initiated a Priest and just come to Court. He knew the grief he would cause them. When he had first taken this operation on, he had not thought that he would become fond of those he was to guide. The first rule of being a good physician was never to get emotionally involved with the patients.

But soon, soon it would be over. He could take his chosen successor, a young Initiate of his own Order who now resided at the retreat house in Tsanos, and train him. Then, finally, he could shed this too old flesh and enter the Caverns of Ge. How he longed for it! Already he had lived twice the normal span for a man and more. He was tired, so very tired, but all great works of magia had their price.

As he stretched out to sleep, he knew the dampness was no slight complaint. His joints ached immeasurably these days, and as a doctor he knew that it wouldn't be very long before they would stiffen terribly and it would take years to lose the pain.

In a strange way, he was glad for the justice of it. His pain was a small thing compared to what he would cause his two fellow Adepti, but it was there nonetheless. And if their pain would be greater, it would also last a far shorter time.

The view from the Vellne Pass was something that deserved a reputation. If it weren't the border between tacitly hostile groups, Cataia was sure that there would be crowds every summer to picnic and take in the scenery. At this height the mountains were stark and grim, new mountains that had not yet had the time to round off a little on the top and grow deep moss and large-rooted trees. These were young mountains, so young that there were maps of the world that did not show them, so young that the rocks were still ragged and raw, unworn by wind and rain.

From the top of the Pass both great plains could be seen. Behind lay the rich greenery promising shade and water and luscious food. In front lay the Nestezi, an expanse of nothingness that not even height or distance could disguise. But the barrenness was beautiful in its way, beautiful in its perfect pristine splendor. The unmarked white sand stretched on forever, reflecting the brilliant white sun overhead, a world still unformed. It was molded by the wind, dunes that were rearranged as if they were the work of some painter not yet quite sure of the palette, to be erased and done differently another day.

They stood and looked for a long time, awed by the magnificence of the view, by the symbolism of this place. This place between the mountains was the only doorway into this different world. It was easy to wonder again if they shouldn't go back to the Palace, back to the green lands that lay temptingly at their backs. But they had come too far and the call had been too strong.

"Well, let's do it," Cataia said quietly, leading the laden pony out between the twin peaks of Cheya and Leit mountains. She had been aware of Tiernon squeezing her shoulder as she surveyed the scene, the perfect hermit's retreat on top of the world and alone.

Across the Pass and down the other side, not quite as steep as it looked from the top, they kept up a good pace. Tiernon was glad that the ponies were steady creatures, bred for these mountains and not particularly worried by the grade of a hill. In fact, the animals were more sure-footed than any person could be on this road. By midafternoon they were tired and the ponies weren't, so they mounted.

The beasts were small, so small that Tiernon's feet almost touched the ground, but they seemed not to notice the extra weight of their riders. The sun was lowering behind them, and the desert was already mostly dark when they were in sight of the bottom.

"Tiernon, look!" Cataia whispered. Out on the face of the featureless sand something was moving rapidly toward them.

"A rider, and on something faster than I've ever seen. I wonder if it's one of those desert beasts?" Tiernon said.

"Stop speculating. If it's human, it's a tribesman, and you will remember that they're not fond of us. Also, they like to fight," Cataia said caustically.

"Yes, so I've heard."

"Well, if we can see him, he can see us, and two against one isn't exactly fair odds, but they're in our favor and I won't complain."

"You want us to fight?" Tiernon asked, a little taken aback. Not that he had not been trained to fight, although he had never had the talent for it. It was just the idea of the thing. "Fine. What happens if we lose and you get killed? The whole country goes heirless."

Cataia stared at him hard. "All right, you go. One on one is fair, and I've heard that you're not bad with that thing." She glanced at his scimitar.

Tiernon thought for a moment. It was hot and he was already half-soaked with perspiration, and bathing facilities couldn't be that common in the desert. Besides, charging into battle might be fine in romantic poetry, but it was a little lowbrow and well beneath his dignity. On the other hand, under the circumstances it did have a somewhat noble ring to it. All right, he thought, it's better than sitting here.

Drawing the heavy scimitar from the saddle scabbard, he reached back and slapped the pony hard on the rump. The pony whinnied its indignation and promptly sat down, spilling Tiernon and four rug-rolls of supplies onto the rocks. That was too much. The whole thing was ignoble, undignified and totally unacceptable. Heroes in ballads simply did not end up on their backsides surrounded by spilled loaves of bread and workclothes. Besides, the figure was now too close to charge in any case. Tiernon picked up the scimitar and tried to find some good footing on the rocks.

Cataia was trying with all her might to keep from laughing. She already had her long knife in her hands and had quietly slipped off the pony to avoid Tiernon's fate, but she couldn't help thinking that nothing dangerous could possibly come from a situation like this.

SiUran had seen the movement on the hill and, knowing the precise location, ascended quickly. They stood before him, armed and ready, and he was pleased. The Great Ones fulfill prophecies in strange manners, and he had been afraid that he had been sent to meet children or cowards. It was good that they were warriors, it suited his nature. He held out empty hands, controlling Feln with his knees. Slowly they lowered their blades and, without taking their eyes off him, re-sheathed.

"I have been sent to guide you," he said in the High Language.

Tiernon and Cataia kept the shock off their faces. It was Eskenese. How had the nomads learned the language of magia? . . . They couldn't wonder about that now.

"We mean no harm in your lands," Tiernon said.

SiUran smiled. It was right that they spoke the language of the Great Ones, one of their many gifts. And it was good that it had not been lost among the Atnefi. Perhaps it was the reason his tribe had been chosen. "I have been sent to guide you," he repeated. "I have been given a Vision. My people will welcome you and you will be guests in my tent."

"Those we all serve have provided. So be it. We are honored by your hospitality. I am Cataia pra Keani rei Aandev, Queen of Avriaten, and this is Tiernon lar Asirithe rei Bietehel. May we have your name?"

"I am SiUran, Vision Man, War Leader of the Atnefi. Come, the sun is hot and my tent offers shade."

They mounted the ponies, who seemed to know that the danger was over, and followed the old man. Cataia wondered idly if these people—the Atnefi, he had called them—were always so formal. Well, that remained to be seen.

Tiernon was not so relaxed. So this War Leader had heard the call, the same call they had heard; but he seemed to know much more about it all, seemed to expect a series of events, as if the ballad were already written and the whole story already told. What did the old man know? Tiernon felt that he had been entrapped in some way, enticed into this situation without his knowledge or consent. It was all too pat. Ayt's chart, which probably did say exactly what she insisted it did, the need to go south with no plan or idea whatsoever as to what they'd do when they got there, Cataia's campground last night, and now this meeting, obviously arranged and timed very carefully. Something or someone was behind all this, and there were only a very few forces Tiernon could imagine that could do it. His Order, or all the Orders combined maybe, Lechefrian and 'Kleppah with a certainty, and above all Aken. Which of the three it was he wasn't sure he wanted to know, although that knowledge would come soon enough. And Chervan had disappeared.

They traveled the well-way, SiUran explained. It was longer but more comfortable, and it wasn't until the third day that they reached the Atnefi camp. Tiernon's heart sank when he saw it, a motley collection of sand-colored tents interspersed with cooking fires and dirty children. It didn't look good.

SiUran led them into his tent, and after the severe glare of the sunlight, Tiernon found himself blinded by the shade. There were oil lamps, to be sure, but he wasn't sure if he wanted to see what they revealed. The outside of the camp had been barren and poor and depressing, and what he craved most was a bath and a few days' sleep. A woman came out of the darkness and poured cool water over his hands. It felt good.

As his eyes adjusted he found that while the exterior of the camp might reek with poverty, the inside of this tent had a richness and elegance of its own. Perhaps this place would not be so bad after all, he thought. The rugs were fine, the finest he had ever seen, in deep midnight-blue patterned with brilliant red and orange. The wall-rugs were knotted in silk and gold, and set with gems. They depicted a wild grove of trees with strange flowers and birds throughout. The low tables were lacquered dark-red and inlaid with inscriptions from the Prophecies in fine bronze. There was a great water-jug, cloisonnéd in a manner so perfect that there was no doubt as to its antiquity. Obviously, the outside of the camp had been deceptive.

The woman came around again, this time handing him a thin cup, so thin that the heat of the liquid inside burned his fingers through the ceramic. He waited, watching what the others did, uncertain of manners in this place. The woman settled herself next to SiUran and took a cup herself. Then she was no servant, and as if to verify that, SiUran said, "This is Eryah, the war band leader of the kefti age-set."

Tiernon nodded at the introduction, and noted that SiUran and Eryah began to drink. The stuff was bitter, but that was hardly noticeable beneath the heat. Tiernon had never encountered anything so hot in his life. It took all his control to swallow the drink, feeling it burn not only his mouth, but all the tubes down to his stomach. It was rather remarkable that the desert people drank quickly and seemed unaffected by it.

He resolved to wait until his hosts spoke first, to give some indication of what they were expecting. There was a momentary fear that Cataia might speak, but experience in the Council had taught her caution. They waited.

Eryah refilled the cups twice. There was no doubt in her mind that this was a three-cup meeting, but when they had not said a word by the time the third cup was empty, she poured again. There had never been a four-cup meeting, never in all the songs or mysteries put together, and she was almost frightened. It must be the fulfillment, nothing less would merit four cups of ghena, and she was glad that enough had been brewed for the momentous occasion.

Finally, halfway through the fourth cup, SiUran spoke. He could not bear it going to five cups, and was certain that the visitors would take it to that extreme. "You are welcome here for as long as you wish to stay. I will not ask your plans, not yet, but my people are anxious. We have waited a very long time."

Cataia shot a glance at Tiernon, half wondering and half commanding. Obviously something was expected, then, something was necessary here, and neither of them knew what. It was starting to make a pattern and Cataia didn't like it very much. It was all too neat, too obvious, and there had to be a graceful way out of the thing.

"We will stay for a while. We have no plans yet, and it is among your people we will make our plans, and then things will be as they will be. But now it is necessary for us to rest, and later to learn your ways. Then, when we can tell you, we will speak of these matters again. Until then, it is best that we do not speak of it at all."

"It is said, 'Silence does more than talk,' " Eryah said quietly. "My grandfather's home is yours. Rest, if it pleases you. The Atnefi are proud to have been chosen."

Eryah left, and SiUran showed them through the hangings that divided the main room of the tent from the sleeping rugs, and left them.

"Tiernon," Cataia whispered, "we're going to have to do something. . . ." But he was already asleep, and Cataia decided that he was right. At the moment, a good nap was the better part of strategy.

Ayt and Bertham sat calmly facing each other across the

polished bronze table in the Council Chamber. A bowl of red
and green and yellow fruit, chosen to accent the colors of the
room, separated them. Ayt had refused to enter Bertham's
rooms and had also refused him access to the Temple. They
stared at each other unswervingly, and their voices were so low
that ominous silence seemed to cloak the room.

"I'll ask again, why?" Bertham said.

"And I'll answer the same way. The Temple never has been
ruled by the Palace, and it won't be now. You have no rights,
that is all," Ayt replied softly.

"Why did you challenge the Captain? Everyone knows that
a Priestess does not challenge," Bertham hissed.

"What everyone knows and what is true are two different
things, as they so often are. In fact I am permitted to defend
the Temple, and its integrity, by whatever means I find necessary."

"You can't fight," Bertham said.

"No one has ever informed me of that fact," Ayt replied
archly. "My arms master said I was quite good."

Silence reigned. Ayt remained impassive. She had found
that no expression at all was better than acting, especially in a
bluff.

"Well," she said conversationally, "perhaps we can come
to an agreement, a bargain if you like."

"No. I want those two. You know where they are and I
want them," Bertham replied coldly.

"Oh?" Ayt asked, feigning innocence. "I thought they
were kidnapped by Nestezian spies. As a matter of fact, it's
better for you if that remains the story. It will create far more
support in return for some small favors."

"I am willing to listen," Bertham said evenly. "I assure you
it would be quite convenient for you if you saw it my way. Tell
me where you hid them and where they went, and the Temple
has all the immunity it wants."

"The Temple has all the immunity it wants no matter what
you do," Ayt said. "And I have never said I'd seen them, let
alone know where they went."

"You're lying if you expect me to believe that," Bertham
said.

"I don't expect you to believe it," Ayt replied. "That isn't
the point. We don't trust each other. But I am offering you
over two hundred warriors to defend Tsanos, all armed,

trained and mounted at the Temple's expense."

"To do what?" Bertham asked. "March on the Palace?"

"You yourself have said that Tiernon and Cataia are dead. I believe you. They were dead. I saw the bodies."

"Where?" Bertham demanded, breathless.

"In Tiernon's apartments," Ayt replied. "So you see, you've been wrong about me. Now, it's all very simple. Without Tiernon and Cataia, the Rei Mothers trust me far more than they do you. I know what you're planning. Let it go, Bertham, and you've got my troops, ten thousand zertin for the campaign and my blessing on the army. And if you think they will fight without my blessing, you are mistaken."

"And what," Bertham asked archly, "am I planning?"

Ayt sighed. She hadn't wanted to use it, not quite yet, but she didn't want to be boxed in, either. "Your niece, Bertham. Cataia is dead. Lathanor can't provide an heir. Give me the power to convene the Rei Mothers. I know them, and they will never accept Tonea against the Aandev. They would take a second daughter of one of the Major Reis, and you know it. And so will they. I'll tell them about your plans once your back is turned in the Nestezi."

Bertham stared hard at her. He had a strong desire to kill her; she knew too much. Yes, a very young Tonea dynasty in Avriaten and himself as Emperor of Salsatee; she almost had the entire thing. Maybe she even knew the entire plan. And he had no doubt she would inform the Rei Mothers, which would give him a rather nasty rebellion right here, just when things were going so well. "I see," he said in a softly threatening voice. "And what do you want for yourself, Ayt?"

"Just what I told you. The power to convene the session that will choose the new dynasty. You might control the Nestezi and Salsatee, but I will be First Councilor of Avriaten," she said.

Bertham understood her only too well. He would have to give in to her, or she would inform the Rei Mothers of his plans, and they would never stand for it. Never. They were close enough to rebellion as it was. "I could kill you right now," he said softly.

"I know," Ayt said.

Bertham was startled by her quick movement as she left the red cushion on the floor and flung open the balcony doors. Even from deep inside the room, he saw that there were too

many workmen for this time of day. All of them were staring
at the figure of the Priestess framed in the balcony. Bertham
had to congratulate her on her acumen. She was more wily
than he had thought. He understood a threat when he saw
one.

"Could you kill me now?" she asked him without turning.
"They'll tear you apart. You'd better keep your knife in your
sleeve. No telling what this rabble might do, is there? But my
bargain still stands. Give me what I want, give up on your
niece as the next Queen, and you get the troops, the money
and the support of the Temple."

Silence hung like bitter incense between them. Finally Bertham nodded. "You've made your point quite clearly, Lady.
But if the Rei Mothers get any notion . . ."

"Oh, they won't," Ayt said softly, not moving from the
balcony. Then she raised her voice. "Guard, open the door."

Bertham watched her as she left, watched her striding across
the square between the Temple and the Palace. He should
have seen it, of course. Funny that she had figured it all out
and Tiernon hadn't. Well, he thought, there would be some
way to work around this later. But he couldn't afford the Rei
Mothers knowing. Besides, there were the troops and the
money. Ayt would not be able to go back on that. And once he
had her Guard and her treasure . . . Well, he would see about
that later.

Once well into the shadows of the Temple and out of Bertham's sight, Ayt burst into giggles, releasing the great tension
she had held. Second bluff, done. Idly she wondered if she
could have made a fortune at tiles. It had been done. Still, she
couldn't help but wonder about her safety, and the safety of
the Temple. Physically she wasn't worried, but after seeing
what he had done to Tiernon, she had to admit some fear.
Would he dare to attack her magically? In theory it shouldn't
be possible to set a magical attack against the Temple. There
were protections, reenergized daily for generations by hundreds of the ignorant and the superstitious. Well, they would
have to work. Ayt knew she couldn't run, could no longer
even leave the Temple. Her army must be ready for Cataia's
return, swift and sure and ready the moment the Queen
crossed back within her own borders.

An acolyte ran up to her. "Lady, will you be taking the Sun
service at noon today?"

"No," she said. "Tell Miraln to take it for me, and then run up to my rooms and have a bath prepared." She needed the bath. When in doubt, some people rode, some slept, but Ayt bathed. It wasn't even noon yet, and already it had been a long day.

Tiernon was glad to be left alone. SiUran, with his respect for the Sent Ones, as he called Tiernon and Cataia, did not press him. Cataia spent much of her day practicing with a scimitar and becoming acquainted with the Atnefi. It suited him that they left him to his own devices, to think and sort things out. The basic gift of the Orange Order was logic, and now there was a simple question he must answer. Well, two questions, really, and one not quite so simple.

Tiernon knew that their disappearance would be the signal for Bertham to start really pushing forward to war on the Nestezi. Ayt would be encouraging him, as they had planned. But, Tiernon wondered, should he alert SiUran?

By the laws of hospitality, he was bound to tell the Atnefi War Leader that he was in danger. On the other hand, Tiernon thought, it would take Bertham some time to mobilize. In that time, he and Cataia would prepare to return to Avriaten. He would be telling SiUran about a ghost, something that would never materialize.

Seen from SiUran's standpoint, Tiernon understood that the Nestezians would have to attack first. They couldn't risk an invasion. He had learned enough to know that the tribes were constantly fighting each other, and it would be only too easy to pick them off individually. Only if they united and launched a major campaign into Avriaten would they stand a chance. Tiernon knew that SiUran was not blind to that necessity.

But why should he bring war to his country, the thing he had sought to avoid, when the invasion would never occur? Still, by honor he was bound to protect his host, and that included intelligence that would assist in that protection.

Much as he hated to admit it, Tiernon found himself thinking of Avriaten, beautiful Tsanos, the Great House at Bietehel, overrun by the Atnefi. It didn't matter that he had found them civilized and intelligent, they still were Nestezian. In the Order, they had suspended idle loyalties, and any loyalty to those except the Powers was idle. But home was . . . well, home. It belonged as it was, without Nestezians camped in the square before the Palace and kicking his mother and sisters out of the house he had been born in.

It was too painful to consider that question, and there was still the other one. What exactly did the Atnefi expect them to do? It had been obvious from the first that SiUran and Eryah and the entire camp expected something from Cataia and himself. But what? They hadn't been given a hint, a clue, beyond the fact that they were expected. And whatever they expected, it was being guided by Aken.

His mind twisted and knotted like a skein of wool. There were pieces, but he couldn't put them together to form a picture, a pattern. And he suspected, deep inside, he didn't want to look and see the pattern they would make, and that bothered him most of all.

Cataia appeared at the entrance of the tent. She had taken to wearing desert clothing, and he had to admit that she looked more . . . well, regal than ever. The harsh blue-and-grey-striped tunic over the red pants was inelegant but defiant, and the fullness of the cut made her look less fragile. She had abandoned the white Aandev katreisi as impractical in this dust, and had adopted pale-grey, as well as the tindi headcloth of the tribes. There was something to be said for the tindi's practicality; it reflected the worst of the sun's rays from the head, but it also emphasized the burning expression in her eyes. *Dangerous* was the word that came to Tiernon's mind.

Surprising, he thought, he really wanted to consult her, needed her opinion and her support. It was almost as if her presence were a relief. Her Order was Green, her training intuitive. Where reason failed and conflicted, she might have the answer.

Or she may be the answer. Tiernon's thoughts swam so quickly that he was almost dizzy. Of course, Cataia was the answer! She had named herself Queen to SiUran, and by law she was Queen. There was Ayt, inside the city walls with her Temple army, ready to support Cataia's claim. And if the tribes accepted that Cataia had a claim over them, and SiUran certainly seemed to think she did as a Sent One, and accepted her as their Queen as well, then . . . It was too much. The Prophecy said, "And reinstate the Western Lands," didn't it? The Nestezians were the original inhabitants forced out of their homes. It had been the promise of the Seven. The whole thing was suddenly very clear in his mind.

"Your Majesty," he said quietly.

"Tiernon, what is this? SiUran told me that you weren't eating." She touched his cheek lightly, tracing the line of the bone, and another pattern resolved itself.

"It's all right now," he said. "Please, atore, do you know what we have to do? We have to organize the tribes and drive Bertham out of Avriaten. The Nestezians and our people both will accept you as the lawful Queen. It's a little thing."

Cataia turned white. She had avoided thinking about it, she realized. Losing herself in sword practice with Eryah, she had permitted herself the luxury of not facing anything at all. "Oh, no, no no no. Tiernon, do you know what you've just said? Do you know what that makes us?"

"Just the people we've all been waiting a thousand years for," he said lightly. It was almost the old Tiernon, but not quite. "You see the pattern."

Cataia shook her head sadly, her eyes clouding. She had known all along in that curious way that prevents knowing. It had been an easy pretense, pushing aside all indications that she was not a typical Aandev monarch. It was too much, too big, too presumptuous to presume. She held his hands so hard that his fingers turned white and neither of them noticed. It was like being on the top of a mountain, far from any others. Somewhere between sinking and flying, she clung to him, hoping for an anchor.

"Ronarian of the Seven, help us," Cataia whispered. "We need all the help there is."

"And then some," Tiernon added.

Even with the whole thing clear before him, Tiernon found it a little difficult telling SiUran about Bertham's plans. He was grateful that the old War Leader only listened quietly, showing no emotion or reaction at all. Now it felt better. It had been like stepping off the edge of the Pass, but now it was done and could not be recalled, and the shape of what would come would now be decided by others. Still, he knew somewhere that the burden was his alone, that the fulfillment of the Prophecy meant more than a few battles. The world had changed overnight, and whatever happened next would be his responsibility.

Tiernon found himself wishing that he were seven years old again. Life had been easy at seven, when everything had been taken care of and his mother and the fishermen filled all his needs. Now there was only the vague possibility that Cataia could understand, but she had her own share of the burden and could not be expected to carry it for both of them.

It honestly amazed Tiernon to see how she reacted. After the initial shock, Cataia had been reserved and even serene. She had not sensed the overwhelming power of responsibility that burdened him at all times.

"What do you mean?" she said when he confronted her with it. "If you think I like this, that I don't wish it were a good bit easier, then you're less wise than I thought. But what is to be done, anyway? There's nowhere to run, no way to get out of it. And besides," she said, softening, "I've been trained all my life to be Queen. I never considered another option. There never has been anyone else for me to blame. Tiernon, I wish I hadn't dragged you into this. I wish you were free of it all."

"Thank you," he said softly. "But it is my own responsibility. I made the choice to enter the Abbey, to come to the desert and to tell SiUran. And every one of those choices that I made, was also made for me. But I don't have the luxury of that anymore."

"You did not choose the Abbey," Cataia said quietly. "They choose you, we know that. There's no changing it. And Aken forced us into the desert, through no will of our own. And the pattern itself forced you to tell SiUran. We're pawns, that's all, story characters put here to do what has to be done and put aside when the story is over. We just have to trust that whatever is guiding us is greater and wiser than we are."

Tiernon smiled at her slowly. He knew she was right, that he might be the messenger but had not decided the contents of the letter. That had been done long ago in the Caverns of Ge when the world was spun. Suddenly he began to laugh. The freedom of the retreat came over him, that total freedom that let him cast himself out, willing servant of the Powers.

Joyfully, he picked up a handful of sand and threw it into the wind, then turned back to the camp. It was almost time for dinner and there was a lot of planning to do.

They were halfway through the meat when Tiernon finished explaining everything to SiUran. The old man nearly choked on a mouthful of broiled ferri.

"But the Swanimir? All thieves!" he sputtered, trying to

swallow. "And the Qaludi? How could we have anything to do with them?"

"It isn't a matter of how, it's a matter of must. Certainly they must see that too. After all, the Prophecy did not specify one tribe," Cataia said reasonably.

"But it's impossible!" SiUran bellowed. "It is more than impossible, it's unthinkable, it's intolerable! Besides, there are the feuds to be considered," he added quite reasonably. "SiLevernal of the Itesi swore a blood feud with the Qaludi over the death of her brother, and the Tororer Anerim will kill any of the Swanimir on sight. That one's been going on for six generations. The Swanimir always get into trouble, because of their greedy, sticky hands. They stole Qaludi stock back then too, and the Qaludi have no love for them."

Tiernon smiled slowly. "So do you see, SiUran, why it was the Atnefi who should be our hosts? You are the only ones who do not have a running blood feud with anyone. Why, you are almost neutral, which makes you the perfect person to decide these things and this camp the perfect place to meet."

If SiUran could have killed a guest, he would have at that moment. Indeed, he had never been so tempted to bad manners. The very idea of those others in his camp was sickening.

"There is also the fact that you are senior to all the War Leaders of the tribes, if I am not mistaken," Tiernon continued, "and, by the power of holding the position so long, they are bound to respect you. Therefore, we should invite all the War Leaders for a meeting here."

"Well, maybe it should be some neutral place," Cataia said. "Surely there must be a neutral place, and we will guarantee the safety of everyone there."

"The whole of the world is neutral," SiUran said. "It is only the people who are not. One place is no different from another, and the Atnefi will not leave me in any case."

"So we must send out messengers," Cataia said. "Is there a way to get a message into one of the other camps, without the carrier being killed on sight?"

SiUran nodded slowly. There was a way, with black-and-white plekas and the striped tindi. They would know it was a messenger and unarmed. The status was supposed to have protection, and among the Atnefi no one would dare harm one in black-and-white stripes. But who could trust the Swanimir or the Tororer Anerim?

SiUran gazed at Cataia and then at Tiernon. They were the ones the Great Ones had sent. No matter how crazy their scheme, he would support it. Prophecies were, of necessity, fulfilled in unforeseen ways. "It shall be as the Sent Ones command," he said stiffly.

"If our riders go out tomorrow, we should sleep now. There will be a lot of questions, and they should be answered all at once. Eryah should stay here with us," Tiernon said.

"Do you think I can't keep quiet?" the junior war band leader demanded, speaking for the first time that evening.

"No, not at all," Cataia responded smoothly. "It's merely to keep from arousing suspicion when you won't talk, which will avoid unpleasant speculation. It would be best not to have rumors."

♪TEN

IT WAS CLEARLY WAR, thought the Emperor of Salsatee as he reviewed the reports brought back from spies in Avriaten's Court. The formation of the militia in Tsanos and the gathering of peasants for military training worried him. Lathanor would not be doing that simply to spend money, the Emperor knew. He knew, also, just how distressed the Treasury of Avriaten was.

Too bad; war was not good for business, and there were the Western Lands to consider. There was still too much to explore in the West, and the promise of gain was great. Already his captains had brought back a treasure store of gold and curiously cut stones, with tales of wealth that seemed to come from the old stories.

If Avriaten and the Nestezian tribes were set on destroying each other, then further exploration and expansion would have to wait. The Emperor knew that Avriaten had her eye set on Salsatee. The war would not stop with the submission of the barbarian desert tribes.

"I assume you have read the report from Tsanos," the Emperor said to the Admiral, who had just appeared in the doorway. "I want your opinion. Do we sit here and wait, or do we join in the fight? And on whose side?"

"Well, Sire, peace is always better than war for trade, but with the Nestezi and Avriaten involved in a full-scale conflict, waiting wouldn't help our position at all. Avriaten owes us food, a lot of it, and money. They can't pay and I don't think they intend to. It isn't pleasant to think of the population of Condele Port hungry. The people have grown used to prosperity of late and they'll take its loss badly. Then, too, the idea of one country, no matter which it is, having access not only to the growing potential of Avriaten, but to the desert jewel caves as well . . . That would put us in a bad bargaining position."

"So you suggest?" the Emperor demanded.

"I haven't had time to think the matter over carefully. The report came only last night, but in any case, it does us no good to stay out. We gain nothing and stand to lose a great deal. If we enter, we could throw the balance and emerge in a good position to negotiate for part revenues in the jewel caves. Now, I don't think we should go and get killed for either the King Regent or the so-called Queen of Avriaten. We should give just enough to ensure their goodwill and their material indebtedness."

"So we have only a limited commitment," the Emperor mused. "I don't want to commit troops, and the Avriatenese would insist on it."

"No," the Admiral countered, "I was thinking quite differently. The Nestezians are a good match for Lathanor's troops. They're seasoned fighters and seem to believe that they have a holy cause. They wouldn't need troops. They need ships. Either they go the long way around the mountains or they take the Vellne, which is useful for a few but won't do for an army. No, with transportation by sea, they would have a real edge. And they would be much more deeply indebted to us than Lathanor and for less."

The Emperor shook his head. "No. There are political reasons. To support the Princess against the King would give some of my own cousins just the opening they are waiting for. It doesn't make good policy to support a usurper."

"But Sire," said the Admiral, "by Avriatenese law, Lathanor is the usurper. His cousin Cataia is Queen by tradition and custom, and has been ever since she came of age. No, you are supporting the rightful Queen against a usurper. You are upholding the most sacred right of a monarch, the succession. Recognize her as the government in exile, and no one can use it against you. It's very simple."

The Emperor looked up at him. "Then there's only one problem. Do you honestly think the tribes can work together? It's been their disunity that has let us get good prices from them for so long."

The Admiral lowered his eyes. He had thought of that—it was the only catch in his scheme. "I don't know, Majesty. For our sakes, let us pray that they can. If it looks likely, then we can approach them. If not, we contact Lathanor. But if they can, Sire. Think of what would happen if they can."

To the vast surprise and chagrin of the Atnefi, the tribes came, camping around the Atnefi site and enlarging it to a great ring which extended as far as anyone could see. Those junior age-sets on the perimeter had to ride to get into the center of the camp; it was now too far to walk before breakfast. Four large tents, War Leaders' tents, had been pitched around SiUran's, making the central circle and the heart of the Nestezian people.

If Eryah had been surprised at the four-ghena matter when Tiernon and Cataia arrived, the joint discussion of the War Leaders of the five tribes needed at least six cups, twice what had ever been required for the most serious affair. They gathered in the evening around the fire in the midst of the War Leaders' tents on rugs spread out on the sand—an unusual luxury, but no one was sure what kind of manners were necessary at a meeting of this type. There was no way to know since it had never been done before.

SiThereti of the Itesi was the first to speak. "It is SiUran who summons us. Perhaps he should give his reasons now, and explain these actions. Ever since I was a child I heard stories of his Vision Quest and the strange things he saw. He is either mad or loved by the Great Ones, and since there has been truth to his visions I don't think he's mad. So tell us, SiUran, what is it that required breaking off blood feuds and going against all tradition?"

SiUran looked over them, men and women of the desert, with the lines of leadership etched in their faces. How much alike they looked, he thought, the proud carriage and vague mistrust mirrored in their eyes. War Leaders, as he was himself. And he knew that except for the signs of age, he could be taken for the brother of any one of them.

He told them what had happened in the long, formal way that left nothing out. He started with his Vision Quest and his dreams, well over fifty years ago, and told them of the call and the meeting with Tiernon and Cataia by the Pass, and what had transpired since.

"Are they here? We must examine them," said Matea, shaman of the Qaludi. "After so long, it is reasonable to think that we could be mistaken and you are old, SiUran. Your eyes are no longer good."

"I could see well enough to cut you to plekas," SiUran responded.

"Then why won't you see that the Repreni well is ours?" asked SiLiasryn of the Tororer Anerim.

"Because it isn't and never has been," said SiThereti.

"And talking about eyes, the Swanimir still mistake our hannarts for theirs, and I want to know when half our herds will be returned. We won't eat with them otherwise," said SiJerti of the Qaludi.

"If you don't have the sense to guard your herd, it is no wonder they prefer a tribe that knows how to treat fine animals," the Swanimir War Leader retorted.

"Stop this!" The voice was so clear and loud that for a moment everyone froze in silence, more startled than obedient. Tiernon stood in front of SiUran's tent, examining the tribesmen. "We came to offer you a land where you don't have to fight over wells, and there are great plains for the raising of herds with good grass. And all you do is sit and fight over ills that would have been forgotten if your singers had not recorded them forever."

The silence had settled now, and all eyes were firmly fixed on the dark-clad Adept who still stood motionless in the shadows. Cataia held her breath without realizing it, afraid that Tiernon might overstep the bounds of what these people could bear. One wrong step now, a single word, would destroy everything, including the greater part of the population of the Nestezi.

Tiernon's voice changed, became lower and more seductive, drawing the quarrelsome Nestezians to his image. "You were given a promise. What is time to the Great Ones, who know neither time nor death? From them, from their Caverns, you have had proof of that promise and kept it, and always knew that it would be fulfilled. They know and they are glad. There has never been doubt among you, and that is good. You have kept your end, and now the Powers will keep theirs, if it is your will. But if you prefer to live as you have been living, to ignore the fulfillment of the Promise and deny the Prophecies out of your hatred for each other, that is your choice. The Great Ones are understanding and we are all free to choose. For myself, and I am a man as you are, I choose to ignore old ties and make new ones for a new age. Do as you wish. But remember, the offer comes only once.''

He disappeared behind the tent flap almost magically, and as Cataia watched the faces of the War Leaders around her, she sighed.

"He is real,'' declared Matea solemnly. "I have seen. I am willing to put aside my quarrels with you. Doubtless we can renew them in a pleasanter place.''

There was short, terse laughter, laughter that seemed out of place. A consensus had been reached, but there was still tension. Perhaps they could decide to work together, but would it be possible to do so? Cataia, listening, hoped so and feared it at the same time. It seemed possible, almost, for this thing to happen.

As they spoke, slowly and softly, Cataia began to feel anxious. They were serious, these men and women, but Cataia knew people all too well, and she had not spent time in the women's tent for nothing. She knew how deep the feuds and hatred ran. It would take more than an evening of consideration to bind forces like these together, and while the effect Tiernon had had on the group was phenomenal, by morning they might well doubt the wisdom of their decision. They might even doubt the fact that they had reached an agreement at all: there was a miragelike quality that would eventually give the night the aura of a dream or fantasy.

In the flickering of the great fire, faces were thrown into high relief and shadow. The night covered the dark stains on the rugged clothing, picked up the brilliant colors of the pleka that bound their heads. Firelight reflected from the sparkling eyes of all those gathered, from the War Leaders down to the most junior observer. The desert seemed lightly scented, and the dry, hot breeze could be smelled over the deeper, more subtle scent of water and rich brown earth.

It was a scene from a wall hanging, the sky the color of the deepest blue the Salsateans could produce, the reds of the rugs glimmering like crimson ponds, and millions of stars set like random knots of precious metal thread through a carpet, the better to proclaim the wealth of its owner.

As Cataia watched the scene before her, she understood that they would not be sure come morning, and they must be sure. They must awaken knowing that something had been done and that it was real, not simply a figment of an overwrought imagination. She rose quickly in the firelight and all eyes turned to her expectantly.

In a single motion she let down her hair and then slipped her mother's knife from its wrist sheath. The effect was calculated against Eryah's expectations, the young Nestezian's image of what Chevaina of the Seven had looked like. They must have something they could hold, feel, something physical to remind them that this night had happened.

She held her long hair in her hands, feeling the fresh-washed smoothness of it falling down over her shoulders. It had never been cut.

"So we are bound," she said carefully. "I am bound to you as the representative of Chevaina and Queen of Avriaten, the land that is mine, and yours by promise. And I am in mourning until our land is ours again."

Feeling a deep stab of regret, she gathered the long black hair in her fist and slashed it off. The knife was sharp and cut the thick tresses easily. There was a gasp from the crowd as she held the hank of hair in her hand and began to braid. She was glad of the training in the Abbey where she had braided her own hair, and she worked deftly as the War Leaders looked on.

She counted five long braids, tied them into loops, and dropped one over the head of each War Leader. "Wear these in remembrance of our dedication tonight, of your oath to the Great Ones and of our love." She sat down at the edge of the group, wanting to be inconspicuous and still needing to observe. She felt the eyes of the entire assembly on her, and she bowed her head, not wanting them to see her eyes.

SiLiasryn was the first to rise and cut her hair, throwing the discarded locks into the fire. "The Sent One's hair is enough for me," she said, abashed. One by one they followed suit, and if the area stank of burning hair it also reeked of awe. The gesture had been successful, Cataia decided. Even if they didn't care to keep her offering, their own shorn heads would remind them in the morning of what had passed. Unobtrusively she crept to SiUran's tent, exhausted. Tiernon sat just behind the front flap, waiting for her in the dim light. His face fell as he saw her, and in an instant Cataia comprehended. He had withdrawn to some degree while he waited, so now her shoulder-length hair came as a shock to him.

"Cataia," he faltered, "was it really necessary?"

"I couldn't think of any other way," she said as her face contorted. It hit her then, mirrored on Tiernon's face. Her beautiful hair, which Dacia used to play with and envy and which Valnera loved to dress and comb, was gone.

Tiernon thought for a moment. "Well," he said brightly, "I suppose I'll have to join you. Who knows? Perhaps we'll start a new style."

She didn't know what possessed her, but she found herself sobbing on Tiernon's shoulder. He held her gently, patting her on the back as her breathing became ragged. "Enough, enough," he crooned, "or you'll have a headache when you wake up." She quieted a little, and he ran his hands over her, down the long line of her spine, over her ribs. If it was comforting at first, it did not remain that way long as his experience elicited other responses from her.

As they lay together, the oil lamps giving a soft glow to the color of the flesh against the deep rugs, he ran his hand through her ravaged hair. "It needs to be straightened a bit," he said, "and you'll look so wild, so fierce—"

She drew him into a long kiss before he could say any more, and then he drew away. Holding her head against his chest, he cut carefully around the nape of her neck, and when he had finished he took the knife to his own mane.

As Cataia had anticipated, even in daylight the shorn heads brought back memories of the night before. Not that the bickering had lessened among the various tribes, but the tension had eased, as if it were accepted that no new feuds would be started now and no old animosities settled. The serious work of planning began in SiUran's tent in the typical fashion, although a bit amplified as befitted the occasion. They shared food and ghena, trying to make small talk and avoid all mention of anything that would set off antagonisms, which left very little to talk about. Cataia was pleased that Eryah had been chosen as one of the junior leaders to attend, and while it was obvious that she was placed uncomfortably close to AlDied of the Itesi, they seemed to be trying to converse.

"Well," said SiUran, "are we going to waste all day eating and drinking? I think, my friends, that we have some business to decide, and that should be far more enjoyable than pretending that we are all the best of friends."

"And who gave you the authority to lead this session?" asked SiJerti.

"It's my tent. Or you can ask the Sent Ones if you want."

SiJerti darted a glance at Tiernon and Cataia and bowed his head. "A man may do as he wishes in his own tent. Still, I think it would be wisest to hear from the Sent Ones first. After all, they have promised to get Avriaten and they must have something in mind."

Cataia swallowed hard. From what she had gathered in the past few days, the tribespeople were far better strategists than she would ever be. She turned to Tiernon and he understood that she would say nothing. Well, that was to be expected. At least he had some knowledge of what Bertham had been planning, and if the plans hadn't been changed so far, there was a good chance, given that intelligence, that the War Leaders would find a suitable strategy.

"Avriaten has been preparing," he began. "They have enlisted a large number of forces, far more than we have at present, but these are young men and women who have no training. Not that they won't be taught—Lathanor is not stupid—but they can't compare with seasoned veterans. We have an advantage there. Then, the majority of the force is to be sent to Maddigore, so very close to the desert. There's another advantage. But remember, they will be fighting for their homes, their families, and that's their advantage. There will also be troops in Tsanos and Aandev'Rei, and in order to take the country it is necessary to take those cities. Actually, if you control those places it will be quite easy to take the rest of the country, but those cities and Maddigore constitute the heart of Avriaten. And the cities are well defended."

Outside, on the perimeter of the camp, a hannart was being saddled. The young woman, a Swanimir, made sure that she was far from the eyes of the camp before she turned her mount to the South. This was the information they were waiting for, the miracle that just might save them. She kicked the hannart again, increasing its speed a fraction. Every second counted. If they could only rely on Salsatee, there would be no question of the outcome.

Two short moons after their initial hesitation, the camp was in full preparation for the coming action. Strips of meat were hanging out in the sun to dry, and the constant sound of grindstone on blade had become a background noise, at first accepted and now ignored. Tiernon found some pleasure in walking through the dusty lanes created by rings of dull brown and grey tents, turning to talk or to inspect some work currently under progress. There was a row of bootmakers he visited frequently, hoping to get a pair as fine as the ones Eryah had presented to Cataia; they were truly fine boots, with a thick band of tooling at the top and dyed with red and green and gold colors. But the bootmakers were too busy with harnesses and saddles and sheaths, and an occasional pair of boots for some warrior who was not already well shod. It was disappointing and exciting at the same time, watching the fervor of the workers all vitally involved in the process of production. The leather smelled good along the ring of tents where the cutting and stitching were done, and Tiernon imagined them in Tsanos in a row of houses, their wares being sold in Salsatee. They treated him with the utmost respect and swelled with pride as he inspected the lovely bits of harness and scabbard that lay around in various stages of completion.

He could sense the difference in the camp. There was no longer veiled hostility between the tribes, although he realized that to say there was no animosity would be to ignore the reality of the situation. No, but he had seen Eryah and AlDied argue about the deployment of several bands around a fictional Aandev'Rei, the kind of argument that only people working for the same goals could have. It was good.

Still, he was troubled. Once, he remembered, he had dreamed of ships, many ships, and what they could mean to Avriaten. Now, again, he realized how bound they were to the land. There were only two choices available, and both were bad.

The Vellne Pass would be the best route, direct through Batter'Rei, which just might accept Cataia's claim, and then up the river to Tsanos. If they could only get to Tsanos and crown

Cataia there would be little trouble with the Rei Mothers.
After all, the Reis had not been doing well, and the last thing
they wanted was a war, especially on home territory, on the
fields and through the orchards, destroying fishing fleets and
herds. But the Vellne was too narrow for an army to pass
without many days' march, stringing out the line to an in-
defensible position. Tiernon was not so innocent as to assume
that troops would not be stationed around the Pass, and the
Avriaten side of the approach was the perfect place for an
ambush. No, there would be far too many risks, and Tsanos
would have to be taken with a major force, no matter how
many loyalists Ayt had ready.

Then there was Maddigore, where Bertham's troops were
massing, a long march around the mountains and hard fighting across the countryside to reach Tsanos. Cataia could not
be crowned a day too soon to rally the support not only of the
Rei Mothers, but of the commoners who would be making up
the bulk of the army.

It would be necessary to take the country with as little
fighting as possible. SiUran had refused to understand that the
night before. "A good fight," he had said, "a long campaign
to make epics from and sing for hours at night, that is what
this will be." But SiUran did not know the Avriatenese, did
not realize there would have to be some semblance of unity
between the two peoples under Cataia for the tribes to settle in
the North. If only there were ships he could get through,
perhaps to Asirithe, and then to all the major points without
once marching on, and destroying, the land itself.

Every major city in Avriaten was on the sea or a major
waterway. If they could get ships, they would be able to strike
quickly and without terrible resistance. Bertham had lived on
a small rural Rei in the center of the Plains, far from any har-
bor or port. He did not naturally turn to the sea, and he would
not expect attack from that direction. No, if only there were
ships. Or no mountains.

Well, much as he hated it, he would have to suggest Maddigore to the War Leaders. The Vellne was more direct but put
them in far too much danger.

Cataia was surprised that Eryah had asked, shyly, for her
presence in the kefti women's tent. The others were out, at-

tending to their weapons, their mounts or the usual camp duties.

Used to SiUran's mobile palace, she was momentarily taken aback by the interior of the women's tent. Worn old rugs hung on the braces, which served only to highlight the only really good hanging; sleeping rugs were still unrolled wherever they lay; and piles of clothes were randomly draped over what Cataia assumed must be the one or two tables necessary in a nomad home. Only the weapons were carefully sheathed and hung on the four large central poles.

Eryah dropped to a sitting position and gestured for Cataia to do the same. The Atnefi woman's eyes were curiously averted, and Cataia sensed something strange. Usually, Eryah was only too direct.

"Lady Sent One, I . . . well, could I ask for your advice and assistance?" Eryah asked.

From her tone, Cataia believed that the tall woman was embarrassed, and this puzzled her. "Please," she responded, "there's no need for you to be worried."

"Well," Eryah said, "it's AlDied. I mean, I think, that I never thought of anyone not Atnefi, and I'd never thought about, and well, if you would be so kind, well . . ."

For the first time in many days, a smile played around the edges of Cataia's lips. "I think he likes you," she said slowly, "and you would like him to like you better."

"Well, it would be good for the sake of the combined forces," Eryah replied defiantly. "I've always been a warrior, an Atnefi. I'd never really wanted to attract any notice before, but . . ."

Cataia really did begin to laugh. Eryah looked hurt, so Cataia tried to keep her voice low. "I'm not the greatest expert in these things myself," she admitted. "But let me think a minute."

The Princess's hands began to play with Eryah's heavy butter-colored hair. "Hmmm. Do you think you could find another tunic? Something red, or bright-blue? Pale-grey doesn't suit you really. Do you have any cosmetics?"

Eryah shrugged helplessly. "Someone here does. I think I could find some. But I only wanted to ask. I didn't think . . . I mean, you're a Sent One. You shouldn't, I mean . . ."

Cataia had already begun undoing the myriad small braids

that Eryah wore. "Don't be silly," Cataia said firmly. "It's fun. My good friend and I used to do this all the time, just to pass an evening. It would be pleasant for me."

Eryah turned to Cataia, her face bewildered. Cataia knew that she wasn't relaxed, but decided not to think about it. How she and Dacia had loved to play with each other's hair, trying various adult styles! It was Dacia, with her ability to understand subtleties of color, who had taught Cataia the use of cosmetics; muted, careful hues of paints that would never show, only highlight or tone.

"It's a good night for such things," Cataia said firmly. "Everyone feels good. The alliance is working. And I enjoy being just another woman again, not always the Sent One."

Eryah looked like she would gag at the blasphemy, then shrugged and began to burrow under a pile of clothing. "I think the cosmetics are under here somewhere," she said, resigned.

Just as the camp crier announced dinner, Cataia's work was done. Critically, she stood back to judge her handiwork. The brilliant-red blouse brought out the pale-pink in the Atnefi's complexion, and her hair fell softly, framing a face that seemed just slightly more delicate than it had when they had entered. Eryah glowed with excitement.

"It is a rather plain form of magic"—the desert woman laughed softly—"but if it works . . ."

Cataia smiled with delight. "I only hope you really want AlDied. For the alliance, you understand. Or you might just serve to sever it tonight."

They both laughed again, softly, and Cataia saw something new in the way Eryah looked at her. She had become something a little less than a Sent One, perhaps, but also something more. Friendship, she remembered Mother Daniessa saying, was a far more potent pledge of loyalty than awe.

The crier came around for his second round.

"Come on," Cataia said. "If we wait any longer, there won't be any food left." Boldly, she led Eryah from the tent to the central fire.

By dinnertime everyone was hungry. Alunan age-set served the unending spiced stew and doughy bread that had been dinner every night since they had come to the Atnefi camp. Once Tiernon had asked SiUran if he ever got bored with the same fare, but the War Leader had looked shocked. "But it wouldn't be dinner without stew and bread. It's nice to know that there's the same thing waiting and that it will be just the same, and that home hasn't changed." Tiernon hadn't pursued the matter and now found that he hardly noticed the flavor of the meal at all. Food was food, and if it provided strength and socialization, it had done all that could reasonably be expected.

Enlarged as the great central fire was, there was still not enough room for the entire population of the five tribes to gather, not even when all the uninitiated children had been put to bed. It had become a tacit agreement that only senior age-sets and shamans were to eat with the War Leaders and the Sent Ones, although some juniors, such as Eryah and AlDied, were accepted. They belonged to the Sent Ones and so it was their right, although it disturbed the sensibilities of many senior to them.

Just as the youngsters brought in the dried fruit covered with honey and chopped nuts, Matea brought out a long thin instrument. The reed pipe had a hollow, high sound, haunting in the cool shadows of sundown. The tune was obviously familiar to the Nestezians; even the War Leaders hummed along, and AlDied began to sing.

He had a good, strong tenor, and a true ear. Tiernon found that he could follow the words in the High Language, pure, classical Eskenese. It was something sad, about two young people in love from different tribes who found themselves involved in a blood feud. SiLiasryn took up the harmony in a surprisingly lyrical soprano, and as the ballad went on even Tiernon found himself joining in on the chorus.

"But that's such a sad song," SiLiasryn said when it was over. "Why don't we sing something more lively, a well-raiding song, perhaps."

With that, Matea began to play again, only this time the beat was lively and SiJerti produced a skin drum to keep time.

"How, how the water sounds, when it's ours all around / How the children splash and play on the day we raid."

After perhaps fifteen verses, no one could remember the rest, and the chorus became a ragged round, drawing juniors from the other fires. The music became faster as the singers clapped, and Eryah stood close to the fire.

"Fire dance," someone yelled through the clapping and

drumming, but it seemed that Eryah had in mind to dance in any case. She pulled off her tindi, and her now short hair fell in hundreds of braids around her shoulders. The first steps were easy—skip, skip, kick and turn, again and again as the music became even faster. As she whirled around the fire other shapes came up and joined her, and if the original dance looked easy, there was now a display of gymnastic pyrotechnics that would have impressed the acrobats in Tsanos. Eryah leapt over the fire, touching her toes, and when this brought shouts of admiration, SiNioni spun a full circle in the air. Only the singers and the musicians were left around the tent circle with Tiernon and Cataia, who were clapping and singing as loudly as those who had known the song all their lives. The circle of dancers started to thin, and outlined in the fire they could see two junior warriors fighting. One of them was AlDied.

Cataia held her breath. All they had worked for, all they had tried to achieve could be torn to shreds by these hotheads, but no one called them down and the singing and laughing continued. Soon it could be seen that they were not using swords at all, but long sticks, and that the battle was a dance, showing off more and more of the dancers' ability. When the battling dancers fell, exhausted, they were doused with vinegar by SiUran, to the great amusement of the now panting crowd.

The song had ended, but no one made a move to leave the fireside. "A story," came the shout from between the Swanimir and the Itesi tents. The cry was immediately taken up by all present, and Matea got up and passed the flute to Cataia. There was an immediate roar of approval, although Cataia, holding the flute, was worried. What kind of story should she tell? A story about herself, a funny story. Fine, everyone loves funny stories and there was definitely a mirthful feeling in the crowd.

"Well," she began, "once very long ago in Avriaten there were two junior novices who loved mischief. They had already hidden books and painted rhymes on the walls, but they were almost old enough to be Initiated and so they felt they had to do something really impressive. They thought of many things. They thought of putting soap in the soup and watching the seniors as the soup became bubbles. They thought of running wires through the halls and making the rugs fly around the building. They thought of everything they could, but nothing was exactly right, until one day, in the middle of the garden on a fine afternoon, one of them said, 'Let's steal the Queen's underwear.' Now, you have to understand that the sacred coronation underwear had been around for almost eight hundred years and it's terribly old and dirty and probably smelly, but the Queen has to wear it at her coronation.

"It is kept in a deep vault in the Temple of the Stars, locked and guarded, but that didn't bother these juniors. Oh, no. That just made it all the better. Besides, they had a plan.

"On the Feast of Nayra, the feast of the founding of the Aandev line, all the coronation garments and regalia are put on display in the Temple of the Stars in Tsanos. There are guards and large crowds, but the festival goes on all night, and at all times there are visitors to the Temple. But of course the underwear is the least interesting part of the display and is in the back, so the novices formed their plan. They would go late at night to the viewing and slip into the display area. From there they hoped they could pass as cleaning women, perhaps, and get the garments.

"So they went into the night with cloths and buckets, pretending it was part of their masquerade. They walked through the streets and the parties and the bonfires until they came to the large central square of Tsanos, between the Palace and the Temple. Here is the best partying in the city, with a huge bonfire and free food provided by the monarch. There were all kinds of sweets, cakes and seed pastries, and dried fruits and whole bowls of nutmeats. Well, ask any youngster to pass all that by. It was impossible, so our young novices had to stop and sample the goodies, all of them. So they ate and ate and ate.

"Finally, when they had eaten enough and had stuffed their pails with extras to take back home, they joined the crowd that constantly marches through the Temple on the feast day. The crowd was so huge that it was a long time before they got to the back where the underwear was laid out on a table behind the ropes and guards, and here one of them finally collapsed.

"You see, it seems that she had eaten a few too many of the sweets and drunk a little too much of the wine, and all very quickly to quell her nerves. Her stomach wasn't up to the task, though, and in the middle of the crowd she sat down with her head over the bucket. She was green and purple and a few colors that I will not name, moaning and crying between bouts of nausea.

"Although it was not planned, it turned into the perfect diversion. The entire crowd and several of the guards, especially in that area, rushed over. She might need help, she might need a physician, she might need someone to make sure she got home. The whole crowd gathered around the little girl losing all her sweets into the pail. What a good idea those pails were!

"The other junior, knowing her companion's weak stomach well enough not to be worried, snuck around the edge of the mob and under the ropes. As her friend cried in misery she grabbed at the clothing on the display table and stuffed it in her pail, covering it over with the many fruits and pastries gathered outside.

"Just then, the sick girl looked up and shook her head. She seemed well enough, having passed the point of needing a bucket, although still a little weak.

" 'I'll get her,' the junior thief said, and the crowd was quite relieved. As she led her friend from the Temple, people resumed their viewing of the treasures. But as I said, no one is very interested in underwear, so it was not for several minutes, until the girls were well away from the Temple and the square, well into the side streets and on their way home, that the theft was discovered.

"And that is how they stole the coronation underwear. Later they hid it behind the barrels of torrigon in the pantry, a deep and dark place where even the housekeeper would not look, and to our knowledge it lies there to this very day."

The applause was loud, and Cataia beamed in the firelight. She ignored a piercing stare from Tiernon. The Nestezians thought it was wonderful. It was a good theft, well executed. Thefts in the dark of night were uninteresting, but those done in the full glare of a public feast—there was nerve and cunning.

Matea began to play again, this time a bright and lively tune that had no words, or at least not any words anyone sang. There were three or four drums going now in different but complementary beats that moved right into the blood and shook the body. The entire area around the fire became a dance ground, and even Cataia and Tiernon joined in, the drums indicating their movements with remarkable accuracy.

More food was brought, and wine and vinegar-mint drink jugs provided an obstacle course for the dancers. It was almost dawn before they retired to their tents, reeling more with exhaustion than with drunkenness.

When they returned to the tent, Tiernon turned to Cataia with a strange look on his face. "Tell me, which one of you got sick, you or Dacia?"

Cataia laughed and dropped down onto the rug. "I never said it was a true story, did I?" But the mischievous gleam in her eyes was proof enough.

Lechefrian was lying across the cushion in Bertham's private study when the First Councilor came in. Bertham tried to mask his expression, which the demon picked up and bared his teeth at.

"So you think you've eliminated Tiernon and Cataia?" the demon asked pointedly.

"Ayt told me she saw them dead. We're still searching for the bodies," Bertham replied.

"They are not dead, Bertham," Lechefrian said. "They are a definite threat to your position here. To say nothing of your position with me. I want them destroyed. I have told you that before, and you have not succeeded, even with the most powerful weapon you could summon. You let them out of your grasp when they were weak and helpless. You have failed, Bertham, and I don't take that lightly. I have been generous to you. They are in the Nestezi. I want them dead."

The tone of Lechefrian's voice turned Bertham's hands to ice. The crimson claws plucking at the ivory cushion contained just enough threat to rouse him.

"If they're in the Nestezi, they're no problem. They can't live in that desert, and the tribes will kill them. If not, those tribes are going to stop polluting the jewel caves in a very short time," Bertham said too quickly.

Lechefrian chuckled unpleasantly. "I want them dead, Bertham, very, very dead. Of course, if you do not see fit to keep your part of our agreement, I could cancel the rest of it. But I have decided to be generous. You have one last chance. I suggest you take it very seriously."

The figure faded quickly into a grey mist and then disappeared. Bertham was hesitant to sit on the cushions where Lechefrian had lounged in case some residue still lingered, or worse, he was still there. Bertham was frightened. Very frightened. Lechefrian was capable of making his life more horrible than even he could imagine.

Damn Ayt! She had lied to him, had held the Guard Captain off. She was responsible for the trouble he was having now. If she had not hidden them, gotten them out of Tsanos ... Of course it had been Ayt who had managed it. They had no other allies in the city, unless one counted that idiot Valnera. Fury grabbed him. He would eliminate Ayt before anything else. She, even more than those two, deserved it.

And there she was, with her own army barricaded in that fortress of a Temple where worshippers could go in but she would not come out. He knew he needed a suicide assassin, and he could not trust that type to do this job. That, or a professional.

Quickly he glanced at the water-clock. If he dressed and hurried down to the wharf, he just might be able to catch Nadraw before the evening's work. In certain matters the years of drinking with Lathanor in the roughest section of town had had its advantages.

Tyas Nadraw was the best assassin in all of Avriaten, to be sure, but he was not a boastful man. For grandiose claims, however true, seemed to alienate clients. Certainly his office did not. The back table at the Spice Barrel was kept for him from sundown until whenever he chose to leave, and even then no one else was permitted its use. Who knew when Nadraw might return, and no one wanted to make him angry. That might be dangerous.

The proprietor of the Spice Barrel often wondered about Nadraw. It was said that his fees were phenomenally high, but that was hard to believe. He had sat at the same table for fifteen years, and his clothes were always shabby. Nor had the owner once seen him spend money on a prostitute, although there were plenty to be had in the neighborhood. No, Nadraw was not the typical death-for-hire type, and no one complained. He could not be faulted, as he paid his rent and bar bill. And there were worse characters. Nadraw, at least, had a trade.

Dressed as a commoner, Bertham entered the back room where Nadraw had his table. It was good there was little business as yet and Nadraw was alone. It would not do well to disturb him with another client. Bertham found it insulting that the assassin treated every tradesman with the money to pay as well as he treated the First Councilor of Avriaten. Damn egalitarianism, he thought. But Tyas was alone that night, waiting for business.

The usual drinks having been ordered, Tyas began to question the Councilor in his usual manner. "Who?"

"The High Priestess of the Star Temple, Ayt."

Tyas made a little noise in his throat. To be honest, the assassin thought, he enjoyed this client. The jobs were definitely interesting and usually high-class, attesting to the truth of his reputation. Still, Ayt would be a hard assignment. There was nothing to do but pursue the matter; the challenge of the Temple was more than Nadraw could knowingly resist. Certainly it would take him from prince of hired death to king. It wouldn't be bad for business, either. "When?"

"As soon as possible. I leave it to your discretion, but certainly not more than three or four days."

That was the thing Nadraw did not like about this client, or any of the nobility, for that matter. They acted as if art could be performed on command. "I leave that to your discretion, three or four days." That rankled. If it weren't for the infinite challenge, the high stakes and the position of the quarry, he would be sorely tempted to turn the job down. It would serve this hot-nosed noble right if he should have to seek out some lesser assassin who would botch the job and talk besides.

"It will be twice my usual fee, part for the danger involved, and part for the rush. I'm used to one short moon at least. And half in advance, half on completion, as usual," Tyas said.

Bertham hesitated. The usual fee was more than high enough, and twice that was unthinkable. Besides, that money would be needed for more equipment if his soldiers were to be well armed in this war. Still, the value of Ayt's Guard unit transferred from the Temple might just do it. In any case there was no choice. Bertham handed over the purse of gems he had assumed would be the full fee, paid in advance.

Nadraw spilled it open on the table and fingered the jewels carefully, inspecting them in the small flame that sat in the center of the table. "These will do. Negotiable and nontraceable. For your protection, you understand, not mine. Well, then, the second half when the job is done. No doubt you will know," Nadraw said.

"No doubt," Bertham agreed. He was anxious to return to the Palace. Nadraw was too crude, too unwashed to be considered a proper companion. It was uncomfortable.

Nadraw eyed him carefully, watching him squirm. Well, money and an interesting job and an enhanced reputation made up for the unpleasantness of dealing with the nobility. As Bertham walked out, Nadraw speculated professionally on how much his death would bring. A rather good price, he surmised.

The assassin retired upstairs after a decent interval. There would be no more clients that night, and the challenge of this job was fascinating. He had kept a building plan of the Temple, taken from some low-level cutthroat, and had kept it in readiness for such an opportunity as this. The Temple, a fortress and full of well-trained, well-armed loyalists, would not have been easy in any case. To get the High Priestess, unnoticed and alone, would pose problems. Well, he had four days, plenty of time to find a solution.

Bertham shook with anger the whole way back to the Palace. Dealings with Nadraw always left him in this state, furious at the fellow's calm assumption of superiority. He had seen it in Nadraw's eyes. The fellow would wait the full four days until he made the attempt on Ayt, just for sheer spite, just to prove who needed whom. Once again Bertham found himself wishing there were another competent, silent assassin for hire in Tsanos. He had felt the same way when he had paid for Nikkot's death.

✿ELEVEN

THE ADMIRAL WALKED into the Nestezi camp at mid-morning and seated himself at the central firepit, disgusted. The day was already well along and there were no signs of productivity in the tent city, and the ground was littered with cups and rugs and dried bits of bread.

There were times when he could honestly question his own judgment, and this was clearly one of those times. He had set out immediately upon receiving word that the tribes were indeed managing to find some common ground, and had ridden hard to get here and offer Salsatean support, and what did he find? A lazy, sleeping camp littered with what were the unmistakable leftovers of a party. Not that he didn't approve of parties, but not on the eve of war, not when there was so much to be done.

Barbarians, probably. If only for the cause of civilization, they might have been better off with the Avriatenese. Still, he had journeyed all this distance, and he would make his offer and have his answer. In a moment of despair he truly hoped that they would reject Salsatean support and he could deal with the Aandev court in Tsanos. If they were treacherous, they were at least civilized about it, and he knew how to handle that. Laziness was beyond him.

Careful of his garments, he sat down on one of the less dusty rugs at the firepit and waited. They would have to get up sometime, he reasoned, and they would certainly find him here.

He was not disappointed. The sun had not quite marked off noon when the first War Leader stirred from one of the large tents and entered the central area, staring at the Admiral as if he were an hallucination.

After all, thought SiThereti, what could it be but a mirage? There it was, big as day, covered from head to foot in bright-scarlet cloth embroidered with pearls and small bells hanging from the shoulders. What SiThereti found really objectionable, however, were his shoes. They were not boots made from good strong leather, but embroidered cloth slippers for which no purpose in humanity could be found. They were useless for walking on the sands, riding or dancing—in short, for anything for which anyone would go shod. SiThereti became suspicious. Had this apparition dishonored them by arriving in sleeping clothes? The concept of wearing garments to sleep in was alien, but he had heard of such things in places like Salsatee. Certainly the man, if he was a man, did not look fit to do anything but sleep.

"I wish to speak to the leader of this camp," the Admiral said imperiously in the language used for trade. Unused to such patois SiThereti did not really understand his meaning. Or maybe it was because the man's accent was so bad.

"I am SiThereti, War Leader of the Itesi, one of the Council of this camp. Perhaps you will speak to me?" SiThereti said politely.

"I will speak to the Queen, if you would be so good as to summon her," the Admiral replied. Already he regretted having influenced the Emperor to join with these tribespeople. And if Cataia consorted with them it only spoke badly for her. How, how could any Aandev be involved in such a sordid affair as this? It was depressing.

More and more of the tribespeople came and gathered around to stare at the strange figure seated in SiNioni's place at the fire. They wondered if she would be angry and challenge him, and then they could have a duel that was not forbidden by the pact with the Sent Ones. That would be exciting, and it looked like this overstuffed bit of bunting needed some lessons.

For his part, the Admiral ignored them. He had made up his mind that he would speak only with Cataia and would remain in that spot until he did so. He was regretting everything he had ever said, had ever thought about the Nestezians. A pack of rabble, no more. They would have done better to go to Lathanor.

"You wish to have some conference with me?" a voice spoke from behind. Cataia stood in the flapway of the tent dressed like a Nestezi warrior, not at all like a Queen.

No, she's gone native, thought the Admiral. It was like entering a nightmare. He devoutly hoped he would wake up soon.

"This way," she said. "We'll be more comfortable."

He had not planned to give in to her in any case. As an ambassador, he was entitled to the same respect that would have been shown to the Emperor himself, and he strongly doubted that the Emperor of Salsatee would be treated like a commoner by the Queen of Avriaten. Of course, if this were all a bad dream, it didn't matter. Besides, it was getting very hot and he could see the wisdom of her words.

The interior of the tent shocked him. The drab, dusty exterior had prepared the Admiral for anything but the luxury that surrounded him now. The deep pile rugs and cushions were of the best manufacture and artfully arranged, and the shade alone was more than welcome.

When his eyes adjusted to the darkness he saw that they were not alone. Two figures sat motionless in the shadows, and with their tindi-covered heads he could not make out their features.

"My words are for you alone, Majesty," the Admiral said.

"Please. This"—she gestured to one of the figures—"is my advisor, Tiernon lar Asirithe rei Bietehel, Third Councilor of Avriaten, and this is the War Leader of the Atnefi, SiUran, who is presently our host."

The Admiral digested this information. He had heard of the young Bietehel, very intelligent, very subtle, if the information was correct. It usually was. It was surprising to find him in the baggy shirt and full trousers of the desert instead of the fine

Court dress he had heard this Tiernon was so fond of.

Almost as if reading the Admiral's mind, Tiernon said, "This is far more suited to the climate here. You would be happier to adopt it, if you are planning to spend any time here."

"I am not planning on spending any time here at all," the Admiral fumed. "I have an embassy from my Emperor, and I shall discharge it with such alacrity as is possible in these circumstances."

"Will you share food and ghena with us?" SiUran asked neutrally.

The Admiral assented. There were always native customs that must be taken into consideration, and as a man of civilization he could not appear unmannerly, even to savages. Besides, it would be bad policy to offend a host, especially when the host was a War Leader of one of these notably ferocious tribes.

There was silence as the ghena was sipped and dried fruits sampled.

After waiting what seemed a proper amount of time, the Admiral took out a sheaf of papers and presented them to Cataia with a flourish. "My credentials."

She glanced at them and put on her most winning smile. "Unneeded in this case, Admiral. Your reputation precedes you and we are greatly honored by your presence. Please, speak plainly about your mission. It is not the practice here to be elegant, I'm afraid, and in any case we haven't time for long speeches. So please, feel free to state your mission in brief terms, and then we can discuss it at length."

Well, thought the Admiral, she might have become half-savage, but there was still a degree of grace. "Majesty," he began, "esteemed Councilors, the Emperor of Salsatee sends his greetings and wishes you to know that he is mindful of his cousin's dire position. That the rightful Queen of Avriaten should have her seat in Tsanos, most lovely of cities, torn from her by a usurper, has caused grievous pain in his heart. To remedy this, he wishes to support his most royal kinswoman in her coming just struggle to regain what is rightfully hers."

Cataia nodded graciously. "We are most gratified that His Majesty takes note of our poor plight."

"His Majesty is most concerned for the safety and welfare

of Avriaten," the Admiral continued. "He is most anxious to reassure his royal cousin that he is willing to be most helpful to her. Salsatee has a great fleet, the most marvelous armada in the history of the world. He is aware of the grievous transportation problems around the mountains and would be most happy if you would accept the small offer of his fleet to expedite the movement of fighting troops. He knows Your Majesty will look upon this action favorably and would help him were the unfortunate positions reversed."

Even across two large rug lengths Cataia could see Tiernon's eyes gleaming. "We are deeply moved by the great generosity of our royal kinsman," she said. "Please convey to him our deep regard and eternal gratitude, that he would think of us in our misfortune. But now, worthy Admiral, we must confer with our advisors, and it is plain that the long journey and the hot sun have wearied you. Please do us the honor of accepting our poor hospitality and avail yourself of this time to refresh yourself."

Cataia clapped, and Eryah, who had been behind one of the interior rugs, came out and motioned the Admiral to follow. There was at present a shaman's tent, particularly fine, which had been vacated for use by the Salsatean Ambassador.

When the Admiral had left and was well out of earshot, SiUran spoke for the first time. "What did that overdressed bag of wind say? Why can't he speak to the point like an honest creature that walks on two legs and carries a sword?"

Tiernon laughed aloud. "SiUran, from his point of view, he was being almost rudely abrupt. But listen, he offered ships. Ships! We don't have to go by the Pass or Maddigore, we can sail around the mountains and it will take less time, and we will have the element of surprise. SiUran, this is better than we could possibly have hoped for. We have everything we need now. There is no doubt any longer, there is no way they'd think of ships."

SiUran remained surly. "I don't see where ships are any better than hannarts."

"One thing," interrupted Cataia. "I don't really like it. I don't trust them. Why didn't he offer us troops too? No, they just want an easy commitment, and I wonder what they want in exchange. Knowing Salsatee, it won't be something small. They never act without a hefty profit involved."

"Obviously," Tiernon agreed. "But we need the ships.

Cataia, I've been lying awake nights thinking about ships. We can negotiate the terms later. This will turn things for us. Anyway, if he's going to betray you, what says you can't double-cross him back?''

SiUran smiled his approval of Tiernon broadly. Here was reasoning he understood.

Cataia frowned. "You know perfectly well what, or have you forgotten your vows as well as your clothes?" she asked Tiernon harshly.

"No, you misunderstood," he replied. "We know they want something. Let's see what it is. The treaty would have to be negotiated and written and rewritten, and finally it could be made so that we don't really make any major concessions. And you never know, the Salsateans are funny about some things. They may want something we won't mind giving. Don't cut it off.''

"I'm not that stupid," Cataia retorted. "I just don't trust the whole thing. It smells worse than a ferri in heat."

"Agreed," Tiernon said, smiling. "What doesn't?"

"Tiernon, I think you have ships on the brain," Cataia said. "I see you sitting there and looking out into space as if you could see it all. Besides, even if we managed to get the ships, knowing the Salsateans, they'd probably sink."

Tiernon laughed and shook his head. "Well, Cataia, we still have to get the approval of the War Leaders on this. We can't take the Nestezians on ships if they won't go."

Then the catch in the plan became plain to Cataia. These people had no conception of ocean, or ship, or anything vaguely resembling them. And the War Leaders would be conservative, if not about strategy then about what they well might consider outlandish means. "SiUran, what do you think about this?" she asked cautiously.

The elderly War Leader thought for a moment. "Well, what good are ships? Why do we need them? How do they work? Do you really think they'll sink? But wait, one thing I do know is that if I know anything before the others we won't have a unified force left. That's certain."

More ghena was brewed while the War Leaders drifted in, looking suspicious.

"What was that?" asked SiJerti. "Some ghost out of the Caverns?"

They were not impressed with Tiernon's answer.

"I don't think that ships are useful things in the least," Si-Nioni said adamantly. "After all, can't hannarts run fast? Don't the ships have to go all the way around the mountains? Aren't the Salsateans a bunch of beggars and thieves, anyway?"

"Please," Tiernon said quietly, "this opportunity has been given to us so that we can be assured of victory. Ships are faster than hannarts because they run night and day and never need a rest. And our war bands would be spared a long hard ride. Yes, we must go around the mountains, but we will enter the important end of the country. Taking the East would mean little in terms of real gains—we must get to Tsanos."

"So we ride like kings on a desert of water that cannot be drunk and never wiggle our toes until we land at the site of the battle? I don't believe it," SiLiasryn said flatly. "But if it is, and I still don't believe it, but if I'm wrong, I'll go along. After all, everything else is crazy, me talking to a Qaludi and sharing food with an Itesi, why not? One thing makes about as much sense as another."

They looked at each other and silently gave their assent. SiLiasryn had spoken for all. What did more craziness matter at this point?

"Still," said SiThereti, "a major force is in Maddigore. We will have to attack there in any case. Each warrior may have a choice, Maddigore or the ships. I am sure many will choose the ships for novelty, and many others will wish to go to Maddigore because it is familiar. I myself would prefer not to ride on one of those things."

SiUran looked about himself with amazement. Of all the things he had never thought to see in his long life, this was the most unthinkable. Here they were gathered in his tent, the Sent Ones and his worst enemies, sharing food, and all agreed on a single—well, dual—course of action. It was amazing, all of it, and if they never set foot outside of this great five-tribe camp, it would become a song that would be sung forever. But they would go, there was no question now.

"We must send for the Admiral." SiUran gestured to the others. "It will amuse you to hear him talk. He can't be understood at all."

As they voiced their agreement, Cataia spoke up. "No, not yet. After sunset. Let him worry awhile and try other plots out in his head. He may tell us more that way."

There was an air of expectancy in the camp, an undefinable current that ran to the youngest age-set. Something big was going to happen. There were rumors. As Eryah wandered through the camp she heard at least four versions that had the Admiral as everything from a ghost sent to oppose the Promise to the spirit of Ronarian. However, there was one magic word that permeated all of them—*ships*. Suddenly everyone was an expert on the subject, and it took the greatest discipline not to break out laughing when firmly reassured that the ships were either winged beasts that ate children or great caverns that slid through the night powered by the light of the moons when their beams hit the correct angles. After a few hours of amusement, Eryah decided that anyone who had even the slightest idea of the truth never said a word.

"So Salsatee wants the jewels," SiUran said slowly after the Admiral left them for the second time. "What good will the jewels do them? What harm will it do us?"

"SiUran, please stop talking in questions," Eryah requested. It was frustrating to hear him, after so many cups of the Admiral's useless speeches.

"We should do it," SiNioni said. "We must give them exactly what they have asked for, after a reasonable time, of course."

Cataia was aghast. The resources of the jewel caves, even a few of them, would make bargaining with Salsatee far different from what it had been in the past. They would have entirely too much power, too much wealth, and who knew how they'd use it in the West?

SiUran looked at SiNioni quizzically and then smiled broadly. "If anyone could have a plan of this type, it is the Swanimir. After all, if they can take half a herd from under my nose, they can take a few caves from the Admiral."

SiNioni bristled. "We did not take what was yours. What was ours has always come to us. We are not thieves." She spat out of the tent flap to underline her disgust. "But the Swanimir, being more intelligent than is usual, do come up with good plans far more often than the rest of you. Now, what did the Admiral ask for?" She raised her cup and sipped the hot ghena slowly, savoring the tension in the tent far more than the bitter beverage. "The jewel caves, right? Or, actually, rights to half of our cavern holdings. But did he ever mention jewels? Never! Only the caverns, and there are those lovely caverns near Chotd Mountain that would be just perfect."

There was mirth on SiLiasryn's face. "You mean the ones that are pretty much played out, don't you? The ones that aren't profitable anymore."

"Well, he asked for jewel caverns," SiNioni said innocently. "These are famous. He never did say they had to have jewels in them, did he?"

It was perfect. If SiUran could have chosen a moment to die, it would have been then. Trust the Swanimir. He, the old fox, the master of the double-cross, had never thought of the Chotd caves. At that moment he wanted to take out a drum and dance with SiNioni. She was beautiful and more than beautiful.

"Of course," she was continuing, "there would have to be a condition that they could not take full possession until after our Queen is firmly established in her government or something like that, and we'd better salt the caves a bit, too. A few little stones from the working caverns should do nicely, some of the ones that are not quite jewel grade."

SiJerti was gazing at the Swanimir War Leader with awe. She was too smart to bother fighting with, and for the first time since all this craziness began, since the messenger had arrived from the Atnefi, he saw just how great the advantage was. Why, all together they would be invincible! Combined, the War Leaders of the five tribes had more battle experience than any army ever assembled, or so he felt. How fortunate not to have SiNioni as an enemy any longer! No wonder the Swanimir seemed to have better wells than anyone else.

"We should make them sign a paper on it soon," SiNioni was saying, "before they know what's been done."

"I'm not so sure this is entirely ethical," Cataia whispered to Tiernon.

"Since when are any of us concerned about that?" Tiernon replied. "Besides, as far as politics goes, SiNioni is far more ethical than I ever was. Didn't anyone ever tell you?"

" 'Politics is the art of getting as much as possible for as little as possible for as long as possible as quietly as possible.' " Cataia quoted from the Eskenese.

"Those ancients knew what they were doing," Tiernon said quietly.

"So should we get the Admiral? He should be told as soon as possible," SiThereti said.

"No!" Cataia exclaimed, jumping to her feet. "No, we must let him wait a full day at the least. He must think we have considered this deeply and that we had trouble giving up something cherished."

SiJerti clicked his tongue. Having a Queen was not something he quite understood, but she was a Sent One and for the moment he was grateful. It was so stupid, making someone wait when the thing was decided. It was unnecessarily cruel, and perhaps that's why these Salsateans were so strange. If their customs included this form of torture, there must be many others that they had devised. Besides, he wanted to see how the foreigner reacted to their offer. No tribe would trust anything as generous as the caverns, and the Qaludi had a strange feeling that the Admiral might. Just like a child. It would be so very amusing.

The Admiral was not happy with the news, with his mission or with the Nestezians in general. Rabble, he thought. How could a great Empire like Salsatee treat with a collection of barbarians? The very thought of it was enough to bring on a dizzy spell, and dizzy spells were not good news, according to the physician. Still, he had managed to get more than he expected—the famed Chotd caverns. Unless something was wrong, unless they never intended to keep the bargain.

He sat and breathed deeply to avoid the dizzy spell he could feel beginning at the nape of his neck. And that Queen Cataia wasn't much better. Gone native, by the look of it, her hair chopped off at the shoulder, wearing a scimitar nearly as long as she was.

The Admiral wanted to go home. The sun and strange food must have turned his mind. Indigestion did evoke unusual responses in people, or so he had heard, and perhaps it was having an effect. It would be impossible to believe that he would honestly . . .

Well, it was no matter. They would win, Salsatee would, whether anyone else did or not. Avriaten would need the Empire far more, and trade terms could be bent to favor Salsatee heavily. A few boats, what was that compared to the great Chotd caves? And a sea attack could always be blamed on independents or adventurers, if worse came to worst. Thinking back on the camp, the Admiral had no doubt that it would.

❧ TWELVE

IT WAS VERY LATE, and there would be an early service in the morning, but Ayt was still awake. It was the only time she had alone since the city had begun to swarm with Bertham's troops. She liked to sit in the dark stillness even though the summer heat curled the little hairs on her neck and plastered them to her head. Perhaps it was hot enough and the chiena crop would be large and full of oil, and trade agreements with Salsatee could be honored. She didn't like to think of what would happen if they were not.

Bertham had been in an unusually conciliatory mood in the Council that morning, offering Ayt command over her Temple Guard and offering them a permanent post in Tsanos. "After all," he had said, "the city needs to be well protected, and your people are already here. Why not?"

Why not indeed? She found this attitude more disturbing than if he had been openly hostile. Bertham smiling was worse than a double moon eclipse and those were disasters. Ayt had no illusions. He had to be planning a trick of some kind, something so nasty that it satisfied his requirements for pleasure. He looked like a hunting animal not quite hungry yet.

Suddenly she snapped her head around, aware of a whisper of air just outside the door. No one should be up now, she had given orders that they were to prepare for a crowd tomorrow. She had given even more explicit orders that she be left thoroughly alone. Straining, she listened again. It was there, almost silent, almost unnoticeable were it not for the nervous state that peaked her awareness. It had stopped just outside her door. Ayt held her breath, waiting for it to move on.

If only it would, she prayed, if only it went down the corridor, if only it was just some restless novice. No, she could not fool herself. There was no sound.

Think, she commanded herself, what must be done? What was the most logical thing? To go to the door and fling it open? No, whatever was outside must see the flickering of the oil lamp under the door. Blow out the lamp, then, and let it come in?

Terror rested in her throat. Bertham had been too pleasant and there were strange noises in the Temple. Yes, blow out the light. She knew the room, every step of it. But first she must have a weapon of her own, something that could be used for defense. She leaned down over the lamp, solid brasswork with deep relief carving. Holding it in her hand, she judged it heavy.

Ayt blew out the light. Maybe it would have been better to leave it on, and whoever was outside would wait and go away. No, that was not Bertham's style. He had known something this morning, and now Ayt dared to guess at what it was.

She sat motionless on the cushion for a moment, an eternity. Another eternity passed and she needed to breathe again. It was hard to remember to breathe. She lost track of time.

When the little moon could no longer be seen through her window, the door opened slowly and a figure glided in, a shadow of a figure that seemed to merge so deeply with the dark that it was just another shadow.

It turned toward her and she readied the lamp for one good throw. It moved toward her so quickly that she had no time to judge her action but threw as hard as she could and let out a shriek.

The shadow dodged the heavy lamp and came at her again, this time so fast that she couldn't think. Instinctively she crouched and began to roll just as the dagger ripped into the cushion. There was a soft curse in the darkness. She screamed again, afraid to scream and sure it was the only way. Ayt was no fighter. She had never been hit in her life, and the only time she had ever kicked anything was the time the door to the bathhouse had jammed.

There was light coming from somewhere, and without realizing it, Ayt headed for the source. Life, light, warmth, people. Without warning she found herself out the door, her screams echoing up and down the hallway. Now she heard running footsteps and she hoped they would not be too late.

It seemed as if the intruder had not decided immediately to follow her out into the light, where it might be all too easy to get caught. He hesitated; she did not. Taking one of the large torches that lined the hall, she heaved it through the door with more force than she had ever imagined herself possessing.

The Temple Guard was just in time to see the figure leap out through the flames and into the courtyard.

"Wait," Ayt said, breathing raggedly, "to the roof. It's the only way out of there."

Hand-picked, trained for years for such a situation, the Temple Guard reacted reflexively. They immediately left room for Martlel to throw the small singing stings at the rapidly retreating shadow. Martlel never missed, and she was not about to now. The figure was already starting to scale the wall when the singing sting brought it down.

It was not the first time Ayt was glad that Valnera had moved into the Temple after Cataia's departure. The fire had been put out, but all the High Priestess's quarters and personal possessions had been damaged beyond recovery. What had not burned had been destroyed by water, and only the heavy stone walls had kept the rest of the inhabitants of the Temple safe. Ayt sat trembling in Valnera's small suite, gulping cup after cup of hot milk without noticing. She hadn't permitted herself to break down until then, but now the tears ran freely down her face and she could not stop shivering. Valnera had wrapped her in a heavy quilt, and despite the heat Ayt still felt terribly cold and horrified.

Valnera was comforting, providing nourishment and support in the only way she knew how. Ayt ate five pastries and two fruits before the older woman was satisfied. But Valnera could not satisfy something else, the need to talk about the ex-

perience and understand what to do next. They had recovered
the body of the assassin, and when Ayt heard his name she was
amazed.

Should she even show herself in the morning, now only a
breath away, or should she throw Bertham off the track?
There was no one to ask, no council to tell her what would be
best.

The palest light began in the east and Ayt's terror turned to
anger. How dare Bertham, how dare he? More from fury than
policy she decided to appear as if nothing had happened. Let
him see that he would have to be a little more creative if he
wanted to rid himself of her. Had he really expected to control
her successor? Bertham knew too little about the Temple, Ayt
decided. She would take her chances. No one besides Nadraw
could get into the private area beyond the guard posts, and
Bertham wouldn't be so stupid as to try the same method
twice, not when it had failed.

Martlel came into the small chamber. "We would like to
know what you wish, Lady Priestess," the guardswoman said.
"You asked us to wait until dawn, and the sun will be over the
horizon shortly."

"Take Nadraw's head," Ayt said coldly, "and hang it on
the Traitor's Fountain. As for you, by nightfall you will be my
personal bodyguard. I have some suspicion that I will need
one."

Martlel tried to hide her smile of pleasure at the promotion
by passing her open hand across her face, as was proper in the
presence of a superior.

"No, please go, I will sleep here, and suddenly I find I am
very tired," Ayt said. Martlel nodded and readied the cushion
in front of the door.

"No," Ayt said, "attend to Nadraw's head first, please. I
wish the sight to greet a certain party when he wakes. It is of
the greatest importance."

Bertham did not like the view from his balcony that morning. He had always thought it fortunate that his balcony faced
the Traitor's Fountain, one of the smaller and more ornate
sculptures in the square. It had pleased him to think of the use
that lovely filigree had been put to in the past, and he had considered his people very clever. The Salsateans hung traitors'
heads from the walls of the city, where they bled all over
the ground and smelled. Now with the fountain it was kept

washed and clean, and all the blood was nicely drained into the sewers. Stupid Salsateans.

He had not been prepared to meet Tyas Nadraw's head on the fountain as he came out to breakfast. How could it have happened? he mused. Ayt? It was impossible, but there was the head, facing him with a dead, mocking grin. It was an unpleasant way to begin the day. He vowed it would improve, and his spirits lifted enough to finish the large breakfast that had been laid. A good breakfast and a good plan, someone had said once. Or maybe not, but that was not important. What he decided to do next was.

It was a magnificent sight to watch the camp pull up. There was an underlying order to it all as the tents were dismantled and packed in what seemed to be a festival atmosphere. There were singing and drumming to help with the work, and before the haphazardness of the operation sorted itself out there was barren sand where the first Nestezian city had stood. Tiernon marveled at the feat, far more impressed with the offhand manner of the workers who had nevertheless gotten everything packed and stowed without any overt supervision. Like a moving sculpture, he thought, or some dance, the internal rhythm of life in some large amorphous animal. It was pleasing, almost as pleasing as the memory of Cataia the night before. She stood joking with Eryah now, the hard, bitter Atnefi jokes that neither of them found funny but participated in just the same.

The rhythm of the drumming changed into that strange compelling sound that dominated the blood and even the heartbeat. The tribes were ordering their march to the sound of it, and it began to come closer. Eryah propelled Cataia to the head of the line of march where she was placed next to Tiernon and the five War Leaders. Behind were the drummers, beating out the rhythms with what seemed to be frenzied zeal. The tribes were singing in their own language and Tiernon could only pick up words here and there, but the tune set the feet marching. It was surprising, Tiernon thought, but no one was mounted. Led by SiUran they started to move out.

"No," Cataia found herself saying, "we're going in the wrong direction. We're going north. . . ."

"To the Caverns, the true Caverns," SiUran said. "I dreamed a dream last night, and we must take you. It is for the sake of the Promise. The Great Ones want you to enter the sacred place, and so you will.''

Cataia nodded and tried to suppress the thrill rising along her spine. The Caverns of the Adepti still existed, then, and they would see them. Perhaps, just perhaps, they would learn something important, something to make up for the delay, for the days lost by the long trek northward.

The sky was crimson and indigo when they reached the foothills and the party stopped. There were activities that spoke of camp-making even though they should not be long. The shamans and War Leaders did not let them stay and watch, however. Surrounding the two Adepts, drums and sticks weaving with the hypnotic, wordless song they sang, they propelled Tiernon and Cataia up the hill and onto a ledge. Here, yawning in front of them, was a great black hole in the mountainside. The drumming and singing stopped. "We will leave you now," SiUran said in a whisper.

The great Cavern drew them in. It reminded Tiernon of a dream, the deep cool darkness smelling faintly of water.

There was a long tunnel that opened onto a great chamber, greater in size than the entire city of the tribes, yet neither of them felt surprise. Always it had been there, waiting for them, just as the Promise had been spoken. Lights were flickering far off, and the smell of the water was strong. There was a lake, he knew, a treacherous lake whose bottom had never been found. And the lights, they must be on the island, the place of ceremonies. Half-dazed, Tiernon found himself seeing the Cavern as it had been when it had been used by the Seven, bright torches flaming around the chamber and on the island in the center, and on the boats that ferried people back and forth throughout the sacred night. Even then, with all the bright lights, the ceiling had disappeared in the gloom and the great stalagmites and columns of glorious greens and reds and pure white could barely be seen.

It reminded him of another cavern, a warmer place, a place for dying, and it amazed him that it could exist here.

"There should be a boat or two tied up a little to your left," Cataia said, startling Tiernon. In some strange way he had known that too, but had wanted to wait a little, to look and feel the great loneliness of the place. So she also knew. That was as it should be, coming home. There was none of the strangeness of his return to the House in Bietehel'Rei, none of the feeling that he no longer belonged. The lights on the island were beckoning, and Tiernon and Cataia went silently to the place where the boats had once taken on the crowd at the shore.

There was a boat there in good repair, although it could not have remained from the time of constant use. It had been placed there for them. Someone had prepared for their arrival quite thoroughly.

The sound of oars in the water was comforting, the slight splish-splash locating them in the vastness of the chamber. It was a long time and a very short time before they reached the island, now bright with the illumination of the torch path to the major seat and the figure that sat there in shadow.

He didn't see the robed, hooded Adept who waited for them at first. His eyes, his entire mind was drawn to a seat in the far deep-red stalagmite. There, on the hollowed part, glistened a great sword. Tiernon knew how it was made, how the soft wire had been braided for the blade in an intricate filigree delineating an Eskenese motto. The hilt was a simple crosspiece set with strong sigals, and he knew the weight of the sword in his hands and its purpose. Internally he quivered, recognizing what was about to occur, and denying it at the same time.

He had felt fear before, cool, rational fear, but this was something different. This was something primordial, a point of movement in the stillness, a fear that came from knowledge he would have given anything to ignore.

"Welcome, Cataia, Queen of the Aandev, Priestess and Initiate, and welcome to you, Tiernon of the Bietehel, Initiate Priest. You have rights to this place which is yours, and in the name of those who have the care of it I greet you."

The voice was masculine, deep and mellifluous and strangely familiar. He wore the white robes of Ronarian's Order, the Seventh, Aken. Of course Aken would be the keepers of this chamber, Tiernon thought, but to his knowledge they rarely left their fastness in the Western Sea. Still, the familiarity of the voice brought him back to the days at Court, an eon ago.

"Take your places," the Adept of Aken commanded, and Tiernon shuddered. He knew that voice. Chervan! "Take up again what has been left for this time, as it has been prophesied. . . ."

Tiernon found himself before the slab seat and grasped the

sword, then settled himself, kneeling as he did in front of the mirror. The sword rested across his thighs, his hands at either end, as he began the long-count breathing. The clammy chill of the Cavern dissipated, and he was wholly within the darkness of the single point of being.

Without warning, his mind was flung back on itself, into the deep recess that he had never been able to breach. The Cavern dissolved, and Tiernon knew that this was his own memory taking over, calling things up from the depths of himself. *It was very early in the morning, so early that the light in the sky could be mistaken for illusion. The others were sleeping. Good. Silently he slipped the Orange robe over his shoulders and belted it with the cord of power. He slipped behind the glass screen to the ritual area. There on the altar lay the demon sword. It had been made recently, open and braided, a link to Lechefrian.*

How long had they been fighting Lechefrian? Tiernon was not sure. He knew it was three, maybe four years, but it felt like forever. And now they were so very close to victory, after all the suffering and destruction he had seen.

Three days ago he had received the letter from Chadeer, begging him for aid, begging him not to destroy 'Kleppah. Chadeer had been afraid, and had promised to abandon all magia, if only they were spared.

Tiernon picked up the sword and fastened it to the cord at his waist. He couldn't leave Chadeer to the mercy of the others. They would condemn him beyond all hope of salvation. There had to be hope. It would do as much to bind Lechefrian as to destroy him. How many times had he argued that with Ronarian and the others, who had never listened? But now his old friend, his old teacher, needed help. He would not leave him.

He had gone to Tyne early, when it was still grey. The small island faced the fortress of 'Kleppah across a small rough strait. He could almost make out the outlines of the structure on 'Kleppah. He could feel the salt wind in his face as he called, bellowing his voice hoarse, swinging the sword through the air, calling Lechefrian. Lechefrian, the demon, Chadeer's master. And Lechefrian had come, crimson and sparkling, alighting on the harsh rocks of Tyne.

The demon, the Laughing Master, had smiled at him, a cruel smile, and had reached out a great vermilion claw.

Flames had engulfed him, flames of all the colors of the rainbow, fire that burned like ice and ran through him, sparkling with glory. Power, pure power.

Images flashed into his mind. What he could do with this power! He saw cities, wrecked by magical battles, rise again, shining and new. And he saw the land itself, ravaged by the blasting fury of both the Seven and 'Kleppah, green and gentle once again, rich fields and orchards giving food and life to the people who had fled and now returned.

His heart twisted. "Yes," he had told Lechefrian, "yes." He had laid the sword on the bare rock of Tyne as Lechefrian had laughed. Taking up the new energy, the energy of 'Kleppah itself, he had begun to weave and build, a wall to keep the new land safe, a wall to keep 'Kleppah safe. The Seven could not enter here. It was his own. Far away he saw the island of 'Kleppah glimmer and smoke, and he knew what he had done. Agony filled him. Chadeer and his followers, all there, were dead. He could see Lechefrian laughing, and Tiernon knew that he himself was lost.

When he returned to the Hall, the others looked at him as if he were one of the evil. Chevaina had laid a knife between them on the rug they had shared for so many years, and had asked him to kill either himself or her. In her eyes he could see both love and revulsion.

The next morning he had chosen. He had gone into the forest and collected wood. Chevaina had watched, taking note and saying nothing to him. She was forbidden to speak, he knew. None of them would speak a word to him. His name was gone forever. And when he had built the pyre of hard and well-seasoned wood, Chevaina had lit it for him.

He could feel the fire through him, burning, stripping him. The agony in his body merged with the agony in his mind, and he understood what he had done, and begged for forgiveness, for a chance to win it. He remembered Chevaina's face through the wall of flame, softening.

And then he was in the place of the dead, not the Caverns of Ge, but the place of punishment. Ronarian, harsh and sad, stood before him. "Chevaina pleaded for you. You will have a chance to undo what you have done. But first you will have to pay."

And in the place of punishment he had paid, and paid, in terror and loneliness, he had paid, but the payment had been *joyful. He had hope. He would have a chance to undo what he had done. He would have a chance to rejoin the others.*

When Tiernon opened his eyes in the Cavern again he became aware of the taste of salt in his mouth. The torches were burning low and the figure no longer sat in Ronarian's place. His muscles were badly cramped, the limbs colder than they had ever been. He had never been out of his body for so long, not since his Initiation when he had been well prepared for the ordeal. The pain of the cold, lonely place of death, the knowledge of his rejection, was still with him. So this was what he had not dared remember for all that time, that time when he would have given anything to remember.

Closing his eyes, he carefully brought his body back into balance, slowly forcing the blood into the toes and fingers. He felt something on his head, and when he opened his eyes he found Cataia gazing at him as she rubbed his scalp and neck, relieving some of the cramping. There was no need to say anything. Every gesture proved that she knew all that he did and more, and he was grateful for her silence. Of course, that had been true of Chevaina too, knowing deep within and always keeping silence.

She took his hand and led him to the small boat and they crossed the lake again, not looking back. The torches of the island had burnt out now, dead, and soon cold, and there might never again be reason to rekindle them. The Cavern felt lifeless now, no longer a place of wonder, but just another place that could be left behind.

The ledge was bright with midmorning sun when they emerged to find SiUran and Eryah waiting with food and ghena. If they saw any difference in the Adepts they said nothing and quietly led the way back to camp where the drums had been silent for many days.

The approach to Condele Port was a hard one to miss, SiUran thought miserably. How anyone could live within walls was beyond his imagination, but it was the stench that made him sick. The dyer's guild was so situated, or so they had been told, that the sea breeze blew the smell over the walls and away from the city, but it seemed horrible to have to actually enter the area where the odor originated.

They had said good-bye to the Maddigore attack force several days ago at the well, and even though none of the

Atnefi had chosen to ride with any but their own War Leader and the Sent Ones, it was a joyless parting. SiJerti would have said something funny about the stink pouring over the walls in the distance.

Cataia called a halt. It had already been decided to enter the city in the morning, and camp had to be set up within sight of the walls.

The stench did not lessen with evening. Camp seemed too quiet with the Maddigore forces gone. Cataia lay on her sleeping rug wide-awake. She was aware that Tiernon was not sleeping either, but he feigned it well enough that she knew he wanted to be left alone. She was afraid, she decided. It was a creeping, silent type of fear, the kind of fear that was strongest at night. Hard practice with Eryah had given her some ability with the scimitar, and the Salsatean Court couldn't be more difficult to cope with than the Court at Avriaten. Cataia sighed, rolling on her back. It was a gathering of so many strands, so many pieces of history in the very moment, and that awareness itself overwhelmed her. If only Dacia were here, she thought. If only there were someone to confide in beside Tiernon, who had been a stranger ever since they had left the Caverns.

Not that she had rested peacefully there. The memories, horrible in their intensity, had hit a chord deep in her soul. There had been those days, the smoke and the emptiness and the sensation of being flung around the Cavern. Watching her mouth babble words that she could not comprehend, regretting the decision Tiernon had made on Tyne and the decision the Seven had made after that. There had been terrible loneliness then, when she sat in the chair of the Oracle, knowing he was in exile not only from the group, but from their being. The deep link, the psychic connection, had been severed and there was a bleeding wound in the place where it had been. Still, there was the Oracle, the chair over the smoking leaves, and the scent of the bitter resin, the drug that released her knowledge.

It had been knowledge that she hadn't wanted, had never sought, and having it was more painful than before it had been discovered. And somewhere in there, Cataia knew herself for both Cataia and Chevaina, in the memories when the Prophecies were given, when she had seen this time now. There were still moments when she lived in both times, in both images, and neither of them was pleasant. Worse still was the knowledge that she could not remember the final outcome of what they were doing now. It had been there once, and she had seen it in the Caverns, but now it failed and the edges were fuzzy, as though a simple dream had replaced what she had found.

The dye smell was wafting around her, irritating her nose and insisting on fixing her attention in the here and now. But which here and now? She reached over to stroke Tiernon's back, wishing that he would tell her what he had learned. He had been distant since then, never outwardly acknowledging what he was going through. The worst of it was when he looked at her, when his eyes would get soft with some memory and he'd half touch her neck as if he somehow expected a different face or neck there.

Then he turned and held her desperately as if anchoring himself. It hurt. She could barely breathe and there would be bruises in the morning from this terror, so like that of a child but delivered with a man's strength.

Suddenly Cataia noticed that it was cooler, the deep chill before dawn. The entire night had passed, would finish soon, and they could pretend that this night, with its terrors and waiting, had never been. Tomorrow—no, today—she would ride through the streets as the acknowledged Queen of Avriaten on her way to battle, the true Aandev heir in the true Aandev way. It didn't matter, really, what they would see. It would only be show, and inside there would only be emptiness.

Condele Port was something made for the Nestezians to gawk at. There were people dressed even more luxuriously than the Admiral. Actually, compared to what they saw on the streets, he had been a model of restraint. There were too many colors, all clashing and jarring, enough to make any Nestezian, or any Avriatenese, nauseated. The houses had been thrown together with no thought at all as to how they would look with their neighbors, and all had been painted bright colors, each trying to outdo the next. There was constant noise from the street, as the bells sewn into the women's wide skirts jangled incessantly. Small chips of bright materials and metals were fastened to the ends of plekas, making even more noise. On one corner a man in four shades of blue mixed with red and yellow slashes beat a large drum and called to the crowd to buy his nuts. Two small boys scurried along in the throng, and there was no doubt as to their intentions. Their knives flickered gracefully and soon they had gathered enough to eat themselves sick for days.

Of course, the entry route had been prepared ahead of time, with the proper complement of soldiers to keep the marchers safe and the obligatory number of workers to cheer their new allies. Cataia did not set much store by the cheers or the bright displays or even the showers of kyrili blossoms. Simply the manners of a State visit, nothing more, and even perhaps a little less. There had been no nobles at the gate to greet them, no sign of the Emperor or Admiral, although in Tsanos she would have selected at least one Councilor to greet her allies on their entrance to the city.

As they marched farther, Cataia became more and more suspicious. They could not be far from the Palace now, she judged from the slight change in architecture. Houses were larger and grander here, and there was more garden space. Still, no sign of any official welcome besides the troops, who could as easily have been guarding them or imprisoning them as acting as ornaments to the reception of foreign dignitaries.

It wasn't until the formal reception that night, however, that Cataia found out just what the Emperor meant by their somewhat cool reception in the city. The hall was blazing with oil lamps and mirrors, the decorations perfect in every way, but the Emperor sat alone on a cushion on the dais on the far side of the hall. Cataia approached quietly, feeling somewhat somber in her Aandev-white, in contrast to the brightly dressed courtiers. Three steps down from the Emperor stood an older man who, with his large belly, looked like nothing so much as an overstuffed cushion from a second-rate brothel. A smaller cushion sat on the second step, presumably for her, Cataia decided. Her face was perfectly controlled and she hoped that her body was not reflecting the rage that she felt. So. For his minor help in this campaign Salsatee wanted the honor of overstate?

Standing before the Emperor, Cataia drew her hand across her body in the manner of equals. He did not rise, but gestured to the small cushion at his feet. Cataia froze. She could not accept the symbolism of that gesture, the insinuation of a different type of relationship between Salsatee and Avriaten. On the other hand it would be unwise to provoke an incident in a foreign city, especially now, before her coronation and acknowledgment by the Rei Mothers. She stood woodenly, staring into the Emperor's eyes.

"I see no place of honor for Avriaten," she said quietly, pitching her voice so that none but the Emperor and those closest to him could hear. The Emperor's smile became hard, but Cataia stood firm. A moment passed, two moments suspended, while the two rulers stood their ground and measured each other. Then, breaking the silence, the Emperor said, "Why has no proper place been prepared for the Queen of Avriaten, my dear cousin?"

A large cushion appeared on the high dais, and Cataia stepped up to take her seat. Tiernon, without apparent thought, took the lower cushion that had been originally provided for Cataia.

The Emperor stared at the young woman, fully aware of what she had done and not sure if he approved. Perhaps it would have been better if she were easily threatened, from his point of view. On the other hand, a strong ally was better than a weak inferior. He reviewed the history of the relationship between the two countries, the constant suspicion, the few wars, the need for trade. And now there was a new factor, the Western Lands to be explored. He felt an idea bubbling at the back of his mind, an insight that was not quite ready to be born yet, but the vision was there. Safe trade, truly friendly relations with Avriaten, would free Salsatee to fully exploit the Western Lands, and the food supply that Salsatee could not provide for itself would be used in this endeavor. A triangle, in which Salsatee would be free to pursue its interest across the sea while remaining safe at home. Perhaps she was as just and pragmatic as she was strong, and his friendship would be important to her in the near future—not just in the war, but in the change of power that would follow.

He decided that he was glad she had passed his little test.

✎ THIRTEEN

IF THE FIRST two days at sea weren't bad enough, SiUran thought, this was beyond all evil imaginable. A squall had broken out several hours ago, and while the Salsatean seamen made light of it and laughed, SiUran lay below in agony. His stomach was complaining fiercely and his head would not stay steady. Malaise grew, isolating his body in its own litany of miseries. All he wanted was to be still. If only they were on solid ground and not here in the middle of this desert of water, if only they could stop, he would be all right. They would not stop. Every second seemed interminable, every moment another agony was added. The ship pitched and lurched once again and SiUran felt his stomach turn in place.

This was hell. This was what the shaman meant when he talked about the place of punishment for those who lived badly. What have I done, the War Leader wondered, to deserve this in life? What terrible thing have I done or not done?

The ship heaved again, and now it was no use. He did not want to move. Moving would be difficult, if not impossible, on this surface that would not stay put. Still, there was no choice. Groggy, half reeling both with discomfort and with the roll of the ship, SiUran made his unsteady way to the ladder. Perhaps the fresh air up on deck would relieve his misery.

It was worse on deck. Water poured out of the sky with no regard to those below, and the air smelled thick. A sailor waved his hand, pointing to the stern. SiUran followed the motion and found himself at the rail with almost half the Nestezians on the ship. One view of the grey sea released his control and he found himself vomiting over the side.

Even that did not relieve the pressure, the misery of his vainly protesting body. He staggered back down the ladder and into his bunk, praying. This could not continue much longer. There could not be so much water in all existence as was pouring out of that sky.

Finally the ship stopped rolling, and SiUran learned that the storm had lasted three days. Three days of all that water and fury, he thought, water enough for all the Atnefi for five generations. Still, there was a long time left to journey on this strange desert, and there would be no real return to comfort until they hit dry land.

Tiernon looked out over the starboard side, watching the other ships moving together across the sea. There were thirty of them, an armada greater than any he had ever imagined. He wished there were some word from Maddigore on how the battle was going there. They must have reached the city by now. And then, in a few days' time, this fleet would break in two, one group going down the Cleindelle to Aandev'Rei. SiNioni was on that flagship with the maps he had drawn of the ancient city. She had a plan and, SiNioni being Swanimir, Tiernon was sure it was both crafty and ingenious.

As for this fleet, it would be three, four days at most before they sighted their objective. Cataia had wanted to sail straight into Tsanos and take the city immediately, but he had argued with her far into the night and she had finally agreed with his idea. They would land at Bietehel'Rei, where he would meet with his mother. If the Rei Mothers were in agreement and would support Cataia, they would disembark and march to Tsanos. Militarily, Cataia's idea was better, but the Rei Mothers were a power to be contended with, and if they were firmly committed, the transfer of power would be simplified. He was glad that she had agreed. His plan would not work well without Asirithe, and he had to get to her before anyone else did.

Now they were so near, Cataia thought. The whole journey had seemed unreal, full of tension with nothing she needed to do. Now it would all come to an end. There would be a sign or no sign from Asirithe. Cataia almost didn't care. Anything was better than the waiting wearing on her nerves.

It was cold predawn when the ship turned into the small cover that the Great House fronted. The others remained hidden behind a rise, waiting for an answer from the Rei Mother. Tiernon shivered as the stingingly cold air whipped his skin. He could barely see the house from this point—the swim would be a long one and the water would be colder than he had ever encountered. He heard the mate shout, a shout half-lost in the sound of the waves. He checked the knotted ribbon holding his hair away from his face, dropped the thin katreisi from his shoulders and stood poised above the port rail. Then, with a long and graceful dive, he entered the grey water and began to swim.

The frigidity of the sea numbed his legs, but he disregarded it. Swim, and the blood, the warmth, will return. Swim, or freeze to death. He could no longer see the shore. The swimming was a purpose in itself, and all sense of direction was lost. He followed the tide, trying to keep moving in a straight line, and watching out for the undertow that was strong in this cove. He heard nothing, and after what seemed like an eternity in the water he lifted his head to regain his bearings. Both the ship and the shore seemed an interminable distance off, he could no longer make out the House. Readjusting his aim toward the point of sand, he set out again, aware that there was no choice. The sun had risen and the surface of the water became warmer. When he was a boy he had enjoyed diving deep and watching the fish that swam in the colder layers, but now he had no energy for such a dive. His lungs were aching, gasping desperately for more and more air as he moved. The swimming became harder and harder, as though something were dragging him downward. That would not be permitted, not even the heaviness of his muscles would be allowed a moment of rest before he came up to dry land again. He could no long see the ship. Either it had moved behind the cliff to await word of his mission, or he had drifted dangerously far from his original line of movement.

The dragging feeling was overwhelming now; his arms were barely able to pull through the thick murk under him, or so it seemed. Murk and tiredness could no longer be distinguished. Again he looked around, and saw that the shore was no longer so far. That gave him new hope, and he kicked deeply, trying to make land before he gave in to exhaustion and slept.

His toe found something with one of those deep kicks, something hard, and Tiernon maneuvered his body into an upright position. Then, tired and disoriented as he was, he could not resist laughing. When he stood the water came below his knees—no wonder swimming had been so hard.

But even walking was not easy in these waters. The under-tow was still there, little but fierce, constantly threatening to knock his legs from under him. There was the matter of place too. All sense of direction was lost, and even though he had focused on the strip of land in front of him, he found himself drifting to the side. His head spun.

Fifteen paces above the high-water mark he collapsed. He wanted to sleep, to do nothing but lie out in the warm sun, but that was not possible either. He had no knife, nothing that would serve as protection should someone come upon him. Before, in the comfort of the ship, that had been seen as a matter of policy, to come unarmed, and besides, he should need no arms in his home Rei. Still, there were peasants around who would distrust a stranger who seemed to have washed up on shore.

Again observing the sun and the beating of the waves, Tiernon realized that he had drifted far to the left of his planned goal. Slowly and carefully he set out, half-hidden by the trees, and he could just barely discern the outline of the House. A little rest, a little water, he thought. A short rest would do no harm. But where were the fishermen and their boats? He had not seen one since he'd begun this swim. And where were the farmers on the terraces, and the netmakers? The place seemed strangely deserted. Well then, a little rest would be in order.

Tiernon awoke to find himself lying on a thick sleeping rug. There were voices murmuring around him, and as he experimentally opened one eye he saw a pitcher of water already laid out. Burning thirst flamed in his throat as he reached for the pitcher, aware of the ache in his arms. Suddenly his whole body began to ache and itch and his head throbbed. He groaned softly and fell back against the deep pile.

"You cooked yourself in the sun," he heard a familiar female voice say. "You have to drink all the water, the physician says so. And you should be careful. Anyway, when you feel like it, what is this all about?"

Again opening his eyes, Tiernon saw Pelynne sitting over him, pouring the liquid from the pitcher into a large enameled glass. "Here," she said, "and then tell me what you were doing. I mean, I never in my whole life even considered that I would one day find that my brother had been washed up on a beach. You looked at least three-quarters dead. Well, hurry up. Asirithe wants to know what this is all about. You can imagine the rumors that are going around, even though we have tried to keep things as quiet as possible."

Tiernon dutifully gulped the cool water. "I must speak to Asirithe. I have a message for her."

"Hah. So my brother is now demoted to messenger, and he doesn't even trust his own sister, not even when she's the heiress of the Rei. Don't think I won't remember this, Tiernon." She only held the frown for a moment, though, before she broke into a sad smile. "My little brother, my strange little brother who gets stranger all the time. Fine. Asirithe told me to wait with you. She had some business with one of the overseers. I will decide if this is important enough to disturb her."

"It is," Tiernon replied. "It is probably the most important thing that has happened in the past hundred years."

He lay back and thought of nothing until Asirithe arrived. Pelynne's insistence had bothered him. His mother, at least, he could trust. Pelynne was an unknown. Besides, his sister had not been particularly kind when they had been younger. He saw no reason to trust her now. When he opened his eyes for the third time Asirithe was in the room.

"Rei Mother," Tiernon began formally, "and representative of the others, this is a time to make a decision. Cataia, Queen by right and blood, is leading an army that will land here, at the steps of the Eastern Terrace, in a day's time. Whether we come as liberators from Lathanor, or as enemies, is your decision, but come we will. There is a fleet in hiding, waiting for my signal. For the good of Bietehel, I suggest that you welcome and acknowledge the Queen."

"That sounds like an ultimatum," she said softly. "But you are badly burned, and are in no condition to talk much. I have heard that there is fighting around Maddigore, if the rumors are true. I heard that you were dead too, although Ayt sent me very cryptic messages that said otherwise. I will admit that I am confused. And why do you come to me?''

Tiernon took more water. He was parched, and it was difficult to talk much. ''The Rei Mothers follow your lead, and Cataia will rule with the support of the Rei Mothers or not at all, and she knows it.''

''Why did I hear that you were dead?'' she asked softly. Tiernon waved a hand weakly, trying to wave the question aside. ''You know that the Nestezians have attacked Maddigore. They would gladly rip Avriaten to bits, but they have decided to follow Cataia for their own reasons. She needs your support, as I have said. This will be a chance for you to demonstrate publicly that you have broken with Lathanor, which will affect the reactions of the other Rei Mothers. As I have said, we do not want to fight on productive land. This is crucial. But if the Rei Mothers remain with Lathanor, or do not declare for Cataia, the Nestezians will be only too happy to fight anywhere. Have you ever had reason to doubt my judgment?''

''Why did I hear that you were dead?'' she asked again.

''It is not important,'' Tiernon rasped, exhausted. ''I have explained the politics of the situation, and there isn't a lot of time to act. And there is more. It is not just you, or me, or any of us. There's more here than meets the eye, far more, and it's all at stake.''

Asirithe filled the glass again and handed it to Tiernon. ''It is very important for me to know who tried to kill you, if that was in fact the case,'' she said softly. ''The people of this Rei come first. From myself to the fishermen to the House servants—it is these people who are first in my mind. It is this Rei that I serve, not a country or political goals of one cousin or another. Who warms a cushion in Tsanos is none of my concern, except in the way it affects this Rei. That is something you have never quite understood. Tell me, why did I hear you were dead?''

Tiernon sighed. ''Bertham tried to kill me. He very nearly succeeded.''

Asirithe nodded. ''And, if I have read your reports correctly, Bertham is the power and Lathanor is the figurehead.''

Although it was not a question, Tiernon nodded.

"Then for me, it is really quite simple. Were any person of this Rei attacked, it would be my duty to defend that person. You are of this Rei. If to help Cataia is the only way to attack Bertham, to get retribution, then there is no choice at all," Asirithe said softly.

She rose to leave, but when she reached the door she turned back. "It isn't a game, Tiernon," she said. "At Court, for you, maybe you see it differently. But here, it's no game. Explain this to the Queen. No ultimatums, those I would reject if it meant every tree on this earth were scorched. But it is my duty to defend the Rei, and you are also of this Rei. Remember that. Tell Cataia. A country isn't a real thing. The people who make it up, the people who are loyal to each other and have a duty to each other, that's real. And even if you were not my son, and even if I hated you, it would still be my duty to defend you. Explain that to Cataia. It is something the Aandev need to remember. When you have finished the water, tell the servant to bring you more. And tell Pelynne how to signal your ships. You have my support on one condition. Make sure Cataia understands where her duty lies."

With that, Asirithe left. Tiernon sank down into the deep pile of the rug. Asirithe had always lived by duty, he knew, and he understood her reasoning, could find no flaw in its simple logic. But somehow, when he told Pelynne to hang a red banner on the cliff, he felt dishonest. He knew that he was using them all, and he also knew that he had no choice.

The ships came in, docking and discharging their passengers at the steps of the Eastern Terrace. This was a far different occasion from the one Cataia remembered so fondly, and now there was a feeling of threat to the way the house fronted the water. There were sullen looks on the faces of the daughters of the House, she noticed, and the few proper welcoming speeches were little more than the necessary formalities. It would have been better, cleaner, she reflected, to have fought and gained Tsanos straight off. None of these faces would stare reproach then, none of these sullen glances would warn her that she was merely the lesser of two evils for them.

How little they knew. Cataia looked closely at the faces that remained closed and angry, realizing their misunderstanding. How could they know? The Prophecies, the fight with Bertham and the Watcher, Chervan being an Adept of Aken in the Caverns—how could they know that all of them, herself included, were simply little stitches on a garment called history?

There was little beyond veiled hostility at the feast that night, and Cataia was glad that they were moving on in the morning. She would not be sorry to leave this place, and even Tiernon had seemed puzzled. Word had been sent ahead to Volenten, and Cataia held the formal written reply in her hand.

Bertham's troops would not make a stand there, she knew, and she had so informed the people of the University city. They themselves had no soldiers, and most of the fit students had already been recruited into Bertham's army either to serve in Maddigore or to defend Tsanos. With only old scholars to defend them, and Asirithe sitting at their backs, they would open up.

So it would be the straight road to Tsanos, Cataia thought. It was better that way. The less fighting the better. But something in her quailed at the sight of the Volenten letter, so obviously fearful. She would have a lot to prove once she won, she knew. And it frightened her.

They started out early the next morning, the Nestezians keeping in disciplined lines, controlling their mounts. Cataia glanced at Tiernon, who seemed a little stiff but able to ride. She herself headed the column, and it was with little regret that she gave the signal to move on. Once she glanced back to find the Great House of Bietehel had faded into the distance.

They encountered no travelers on the road to Tsanos. The fields and trees on the sides of the road looked unkempt, and the dwellings had an air of desertion. Cataia felt as if she were seeing a ghost of the country. This land had once been productive, even what was left of the crops showed that. Then maybe there were people here, people who locked themselves behind their barn doors, not sure of what army this was and not caring.

No life could be seen except birds and small rodents, scuttling away from the marching sounds. Cataia lost track of time. The nights they made camp were little relief. The march tents were not the lovely residences she had become used to in the desert, but far simpler affairs. And it was not only the tents, but the feeling of the Nestezians themselves. Cataia felt isolated, cut off from the army and from Tiernon, who had been so close and now spent most of his time alone in meditation.

It was on the fifth day, Cataia judged, that they could finally see the thin glazed spires of Tsanos reflecting in the sun. Cataia was startled as they drew nearer. She had never seen the city from this perspective, and it was beautiful, clean and peaceful. There was no hint of the plotting behind the Palace walls, the poverty down near the gates, the outlawry of the wharf.

As the spires resolved themselves into colors and became sharp, Eryah pulled up next to Cataia. "If we can see them, they can see us. I suggest we advance at full speed from this point."

"Not quite yet," came SiUran's voice at her shoulder. "Distances are deceiving, and we don't want to tire our mounts. There, when we reach that rock." He pointed to a large boulder, a landowner's marker, at the edge of the road, a little more than a third of the distance they still had to travel.

Cataia nodded. They rode on, but Cataia could feel her belly turning over, and her throat was clogged. She had never fought before, never tried to kill anyone, and now she would have to battle her own subjects. She wanted to run, to hide someplace. She saw the peaceful sweep of the plain in front of the city gates, and it chilled her. Any moment those gates would open and Bertham's troops would swarm out, intent on nothing so much as killing her. Fear coursed through her body, numbing her brain.

She passed the boulder and SiUran nodded at her. She pulled a long white scarf from her sleeve and held it up to flutter in the breeze, the charge signal.

Ayt stood on the highest balcony of the Temple, squinting to get a good view. She knew that Bertham was also watching; she could see his Rei colors on the high balcony of the Palace. From here it was easy to see across the city walls and out onto the plain where the Nestezians massed. The only sound was the beating of hooves against the hard ground. There were no battle cries or songs. The grim silence of that force chilled Ayt to the bone. It was as if a body of phantoms had appeared. And then the city gates opened, spilling forth guards in red and grey and the city militia.

There were over three hundred desert warriors, Ayt figured,

mounted and faceless. They wore their headdresses tied around their noses and mouths, only their eyes showing. They held long curved scimitars above their heads and the metal blades reflected the bright sunlight, becoming a molten river in the sky.

The defending army drew itself into ranks, uniformed Palace guards in front. Their banners flickered feebly in the languid air. Ayt heard a hoarse order and a volley of javelins was released in unison at the onrushing host, falling well short of the Nestezian army but meant as a brave show.

The Nestezians came forward, pressing the attack. There was no lessening of speed and still no sound, but the distance between the two armies was quickly diminishing.

The Guard, already mounted, rushed toward the desert force. As they approached they split into two groups, leaving the center open and throwing their full strength at the flanks. It cost the desert center some time, as they overshot the defenders and had to pull in and wheel around to join the battle now in progress behind them. Ayt wondered whether Cataia was in that center group. She could clearly see the indigo of Bietehel, and her heart ached. Tiernon did not belong in that carnage, she thought.

But she could not find Cataia. Without Cataia there was no hope at all, but it was very far from the Temple to the field outside the walls. Perhaps she had just missed Cataia. Perhaps the Queen was not in Aandev-white.

Ayt pressed her back into the solid wall. Behind her, down in the Temple courtyard, stood ranks of fighters in midnight-blue, awaiting her command. But if Cataia were not there, Ayt told herself icily, that command would never come.

A brilliant glitter was reflected momentarily from the field. Ayt looked again to be sure. Aandev-white. Grimly the Priest-ess smiled and a movement of her hand brought an acolyte in yellow.

Tiernon felt as if he had been split in half. Part of him was raising the scimitar and bringing it down in a smooth curve with a beautiful through motion. The other part seemed to retreat to the back of his mind and watch, horrified. The part of his brain that controlled the fighting was thankful for the desert tindi that absorbed the sweat before it could reach his eyes and shielded his nose and mouth from the dust, and for the lovely balance of the sword he held. The scimitar descended again, and was countered by the small circular shield of a guardsman. He crouched to dodge an intended blow and then swept underneath into the other's rib cage. He felt resistance as the blade sliced into the guardsman's abdomen, and he twisted, pulling up through hard muscle.

In the back of his mind, Tiernon could hear Father Anertin's voice quite clearly. "Always follow through with a blow. Snap at the wrist. Let it come from the back, not the shoulder. Put your whole body into it. Let gravity help you. Let the weight of the scimitar help you." And he could feel his body responding without thinking, reacting as he had been taught to react. There was no need to consider, just function.

With his knees he controlled his mount over the ground now slick with blood and entrails. The rational part of his mind, horrified as it was, turned its concentration to keeping him alive. Under the tindi his mouth curved in a grim smile. It was working to his advantage now and Tiernon watched for sloppy openings. The Guard were well trained but had never been tested in battle and had a tendency to fight as if it were a practice match. Tiernon did not bother to consider that he too had never fought in a battle before.

He noticed an enemy with a drooping shield and somewhat slow reactions. A fast blow and the head was connected to the body by a thin strip of flesh. He almost wanted to yell, to express his pride in his own ability and his anger at the guard's stupidity.

Now another uniform was on him, obviously a natural who was superbly trained. He rose to the challenge with excitement. The guard was fast, able to block with the shield and deliver a blow at the same moment. Tiernon pulled away, missing her edge by a breath. They slashed at each other rapidly several times, and Tiernon realized that he could not wait for her to make a mistake. He thought quickly. Pulling back in the face of her onslaught, he began to see a subtle rhythm to her movements. There would not be much time. Keeping his ribs covered, he raised his arm just as she began her downward stroke. The top-heavy scimitar did the rest, slicing through the joint cleanly. The woman was as good as dead. Tiernon scanned the crowd swiftly in search of his next opponent.

Bertham could not resist the irony of the situation. Here

they were, he and Ayt, standing on almost twin walls, watching the same battle from the same position. He could not kill her. But it *was* interesting that she had never attempted to eliminate him. Had she, he had no doubts that she would not have succeeded. Twins in a way, he thought wryly. Like himself and Tiernon.

Suddenly he found his attention riveted by the action below. While moments before the sides had seemed fairly equal, now there were definitely more fighters wearing the desert tindi than those in red and grey.

On the Temple wall, he watched Ayt smiling, whispering to a young priestess in yellow. There was movement in the square, noise of clattering metal and marching. So she had given the command for her troops to take the Palace. He had known that Ayt would do that, ever since she shut herself up in the Temple.

There was still a chance that Tsanos's force would win, that Cataia and Tiernon would be dead shortly, but in any case Ayt did not intend that he live to know the outcome.

Ayt was too predictable, thought Bertham. She should have realized that he would have a contingency plan. That was the first thing he had learned: back up all your moves. Teth was with the force in Maddigore, and Lathanor was lying in his room, drunk as ever. The marching men and women could be seen coming across the square, a blot of midnight against the blazing white pavement. There was no time to be lost. The boat was waiting on his orders behind the Palace. That the others hadn't any means of escape was no business of his. They would only slow him down.

As the boat moved away from the steps of the Palace, Bertham looked over at his former perch. Yes, the Palace was overrun. There was probably some fighting in the halls, but none of them had noticed him. Just as well—and he had not left a moment before it was necessary.

The fisherman who owned the boat had turned white when Bertham told him, "To 'Kleppah."

"But sir," he finally found the courage to say, "this is a coast hugger. She's not built for the open sea. I can take you to one of the Reis and you can get a larger boat there. The *Little Wing* just can't make it."

Fury washed over Bertham. He wanted to punish the man, and would have if he knew how to sail. "She can make it," the

First Councilor replied coldly. "She had better if you want to see home again."

Eryah had never felt so free in all her life. The long years of training had shown profit, since she was alive and anyone who had dared challenge her was not. Her movements were automatic as she swung into the uniformed guards opposing her. Only her eyes were visible behind the tindi, glowing with excitement and joy.

Liquid fire flowed in her veins. She felt invincible, and in truth she seemed so. It was as if she had been charmed, protected in some arcane manner.

Always from the corner of her eye she watched for the flash of white that was Cataia. Sent One, yes, but pitifully unprepared for war. All the hours of training had not made up for years of their absence.

A glint of light alerted her suddenly, and she turned her mount with her knees, her hands already controlling the scimitar and small round shield. From the direction, she perceived that this warrior was headed straight for Cataia. Fear flashed suddenly, not for herself, but for the other.

She intercepted the guard well before he reached Cataia's position. His scimitar was already arcing over his head, and his reach was long. Urging her tall desert-bred hannart, she lunged forward, under his reach, inside his defenses. It was one trick a woman fighter had to learn.

His blade bit deeply into the heavy leather layers of her saddle. It was not the sword she used as he spent precious moments trying to tear his own blade free, but the wicked desert knife. Almost by magic it seemed to jump into her hand, and it was only a short thrust into his ribs, under and up, piercing the diaphragm.

She pulled back quickly and again she surveyed the field for the white that would mark Cataia. There would be others who would attack the Sent One. Eryah wasn't going to permit them to get far.

A paean rose in her throat. This was life. This was what SiUran meant when he said he was Atnefi. She too was Atnefi.

Things had not gone well for Cataia. She found it hard to kill the guards who were supposed to be her own subjects, to fight and take the city that she had grown up in. It had slowed her sword arm on occasion, and there had been consequences.

The guardsman who had come at her had been tall, tall enough to hint at desert blood. He had charged at her but had brought his blade down too soon. That, and his height, had resulted in a mere glancing blow. It had, however, given Cataia the time and opening to bring her own blade up, slicing into the ribs before he had even completed the carry-through. Her relief at his death was abruptly cut short as she felt moisture spreading across her face and dripping down her neck. A paroxysm of fear caught her, and as she trembled she did not dare bring her hand to her face. In the core of her being she knew what had happened and that knowledge nearly broke her.

The tindi covering her face was torn and dried blood clung to the edges. It was hard to continue fighting after that, faced with the possibility of more pain and disfigurement. She had to force herself forward, force herself to strike and defend, force herself not to turn and run. Every nerve in her body screamed. It was only by a supreme act of will that she managed to stay in the battle at all.

She also felt deep shame. Too often Eryah, or Tiernon, or some other whose name she did not know, had saved her from a sword more skilled than her own. She was aware of the fact that if it were not for her position she would have been killed long ago; at times she wished she had been. With every move she thought about her face, and about the fact that others had to do some of her fighting for her.

Still, an Adept with a trained will could manage things that others could not. Cataia pushed herself forward, grimly determined to fight until the battle ended. She would not disgrace herself when the others had died, no matter how afraid she was.

Another uniform loomed in front of her, and Cataia felt again the tightening knot in her midsection screaming to leave by any means possible. She lifted her scimitar again, the weight reminding her of the weariness in her arm. The weariness was becoming unbearable, and her muscles rebelled against the strain. Cataia never really knew when she dropped the sword and backed off from her attacker. He followed. Cataia bent down to hug the saddle, hoping to protect herself from the blows she knew would follow. Her hand slid over the loose leather thong looped there and pulled it free. It was reflex more than design that controlled her now. She was like an animal fighting on instinct when there was no place to run. The hours she had spent with Eryah's war band had been imprinted directly into her muscles and there was no need to think.

She lifted the weighted thong and swung it around her head. She did not even let it loose when it connected with her enemy's ear, breaking all the small bones leading into the skull. He toppled over, unable to balance, and was crushed under the hooves of his own frightened mount.

Cataia turned her head, wanting to cry, but knowing that tears would cloud her vision. She grasped the sling tighter and kept swinging, hoping that the activity would keep any would-be attackers away from her. She had no strength left to fight. Eryah and Tiernon, always close, closed in around her and acted as bodyguards. She lost all sense of time, not even noticing the slight chill that indicated the end of the day.

There were screams and shouts now in the strange desert accent, and Cataia trembled, fearing the worst. She rode unthinking, letting herself be led by Eryah and Tiernon, and it was not until they were at the gates of the city that she realized those had been shouts of victory. She was too tired to care.

They drew up in front of the partially completed barricade, and several Nestezians cleared a path through. It was not hard, for the barricade had been built with little time and less effort. They found the trench only partly dug with the sharpened spikes neatly piled near the wall. They had no trouble jumping the unfinished defenses and riding straight into the city.

Cataia glanced back. The field behind them resembled the scene of a massacre more than a battle. Only a third of the desert troops had survived, and only a handful of the guards. Already a mass of flies had settled and the stench of old blood tainted the ground.

The wounded were moaning, and Cataia dispatched a few riders to build the pyres for those who would choose them. The thought of it made her blood curdle, but it was better than what waited for them now, and would be recorded and sung for time to come, proper compensation for those who chose to die.

They rode straight to the Palace, and at the sight of the Temple Guard now occupying the space, they drew in. Cataia uttered a small cry. No more, she thought, no more. But there was Ayt in the doorway, veiled in her ritual robes and surrounded by a pack of fighters, all obviously fresh.

"Welcome, Queen Cataia, to your city Tsanos. The Temple gives you this place as your home, that you might be near us and remember us sometime," Ayt said.

Tiernon nodded his approval. He knew that Cataia was too tired to care, but his mind turned to Bertham. The wily First Councilor certainly must have escaped; it would have been too easy to ʹ d him in Ayt's restraints.

Tiern studied Cataia again for a moment. She was in some kin ʹf shock, he thought, probably from the wound. It wasn't se‿us, he noted, but she had lost blood. He himself wasn't feeling well. The smell had penetrated the walls, and the stench of bonfires was carried in the air.

"Can you help the Queen?" he asked Ayt. She would, of course, and Eryah wouldn't leave Cataia's side. Grateful for that fact, unconcerned with the soreness in his back and the sweat stiffening his clothes, Tiernon remounted. He needed to be alone.

Heading back out the gates, Tiernon found himself on the battlefield again. Beneath him he saw the mangled intestines of something once human, whether Nestezian or Avriatenese he could not tell. There were insects covering the winding trail of gut lying open, and screeching carrion birds had landed, their long beaks thrust into communion with the dead. Far off, embers glowed and thick black smoke floated over him, the last remains of those who had chosen to die with grace.

So this is what he had wrought a thousand years ago on Tyne, when he had made his pact with Lechefrian. He could not escape seeing himself everywhere he turned, his own hand forcing these events to happen. Shame flooded him, and he turned his head and retched uncontrollably.

It was not fear but disgust at himself that kept his hands trembling. He wanted to scream, to howl, as the small moon became visible over the horizon. What good, he asked himself, were refinement and learning and power and wealth if this is what he had done with them all? What good? Tomorrow they would burn the dead and celebrate a victory, and there was no victory. The greater moon rose, the long moon that kept time and the tides. It illuminated the field, turning it into a collection of cold, colorless shapes that defied identification. Were it not for the smell, he would have been able to believe that he had entered one of the ancient places of power.

The chilling moon could be cleansing, and as he watched it the violent disgust left him. The Prophecy was fulfilled. Their place had been won, the Promise to the Nestezians had been kept. That was enough for the moment. There would be other times to think of it all, to understand. Tiernon suddenly found that he didn't care now, he was as one of the dead. They had been joined, he and they, by some sort of marriage in the blood, whereby he could never be free of this night on the field. He returned to the Palace and fell asleep in Cataia's apartments, thankful for the brief respite.

Cataia awoke in the predawn. For a moment she was confused, her deep sleep distancing her from the events of the previous day. Eryah and Tiernon were asleep on rugs and cushions they had tossed around the room as if it were one of their campgrounds. The stinging on her cheek brought back the events of the battle, and, careful not to wake Tiernon and Eryah, she groped for a mirror. She only glanced at it before she began weeping. She had been so proud of her beauty, and it was gone, slashed, sacrificed like her hair so that she might bear more responsibility. She looked over at Tiernon and wondered if he would abandon her now that she was no longer beautiful.

Then Cataia thought of Dacia. If only Dacia were here, to comfort her and try to laugh. Dacia was the only one who hadn't been touched. She lived in her own world of form and color, undefiled by Palace politics and murder. All, all the others had been forced out. Only Dacia remained clean.

Casting one look at the sleeping forms behind her, Cataia slipped out of the room. Dacia's house was near Dier Street, where the fruitman would be coming soon and the pastry shop would open. Nothing could have changed, not there, and Cataia covered her head and began to walk down to her old home to try to find some peace.

In the early dawn, the neighborhood around Dier Street seemed to have been untouched by the battle the day before. Cataia noted several houses where, already, children were at work scrubbing the stone steps. Wars may be fought, she thought, governments fall, but the steps must be washed every day. So Mother Daniessa had taught, and now the evidence of it comforted her far more than any words could have.

It was early enough that Dacia should still be home, not yet teaching at the Abbey. Her house wasn't difficult to find, a tiny place overgrown with myriad creepers squeezed in between two larger structures in a little alley. She and Dacia had passed this house many times. It was usually occupied by one of the Priestesses. Dacia had been pleased when she had been assigned to live there.

Cataia made her way carefully up the fragmented walk and threw back her hood before knocking. Dacia, bleary-eyed, opened the door.

"Cai! You? At this hour? Well, come on in."

Dacia, a katreisi thrown over her nightdress, led the way through the airy parlor into the back room, where pastries and a pitcher of water were laid out. "I'm sorry there isn't more," she said, "but I usually eat at the Abbey."

They each ate a pastry and drank to clear their throats.

Dacia seemed to need to clear her mind as well. It made Cataia feel at home. Dacia had never been a good riser.

"Oh, my, Cai, your face," Dacia exclaimed after her eyes had come fully open. "Have you seen a doctor? Is it going to be okay?"

Cataia shrugged. "Someone put some salve on it, but I think it will scar. Dacia, I hate it."

Cataia began to sob violently, hunching over on the cushion. Dacia stepped over to her and took the smaller woman in her arms.

"It's going to be all right, Cai. I know it is. Really. And you can fix that up with cosmetics. And it's all going to work out. Only now there's just a lot, right? So you have to sort it out into neat piles, and look at them one at a time. It isn't so bad. It can't be that terrible. Do you want a handkerchief?" Dacia disappeared momentarily and came back with a soft cloth, stained in the jewel colors of her palette.

"Dacia, do you know what we just did? Do you *know*?"

"Well," Dacia said sensibly, "someone had to."

Suddenly, Cataia had to laugh. Someone, after all, did have to. And Dacia looked so blasé about it all, the water pitcher in her hand, refilling the cups.

"Let's look at it in pieces, all right? What's the next thing you have to do?" Dacia asked.

Cataia felt calmer. Dacia was guiding her in the way they

had been taught, one step at a time. "The next thing," she said slowly, "is to get Lathanor's abdication. Then there's the coronation."

"Don't you have to appoint a Council or something?" Dacia asked, more curious than guiding. Cataia had to remember that she really knew very little of the inner workings of the Court.

"No, for the time I'll leave things pretty much as they are. Tiernon will be First Councilor, of course. When he stands as swordsman at the coronation, everyone will know. That's the official appointment to First, anyway. And I think I'll add one or two of the Nestezians, but I'd better wait for that, maybe only a few days."

Dacia nodded. "And after that things have to be finished with Lechefrian."

Cataia dropped her head.

"Oh, come on, now," Dacia chided. "That's not really your job, anyway. You don't even have to be there, although I suppose it's right if you go. And stop looking so morose. I can't let you into the studio like that. You'll cry into the colors, and that'll spoil the mixtures."

The pale light, patterned by the window insets, turned rosy and crept across the tiles between two rugs on the floor.

"It's getting late," Dacia said softly. "It's even time for me to get dressed. And you'd better get back, Cai, or they're going to miss you. And you don't need any more mess than you've got."

Cataia hugged Dacia once more before they parted. She had been right. Dacia's sense, and a reminder about cosmetics, had helped a good bit. And it was good to see this part of the city, outwardly untouched by the events of the day before.

Heavily hooded, Cataia walked through the streets again, now full of people about their morning business. The fruitman pulled his cart up Dier Street, yelling, "Geri, ripe alonti, fresh vonioes, ripe, cheap." Lazier children than she had seen out on her approach were now kneeling on white or red stone steps, scrub brushes working furiously. Two small girls, too young to be novices, were playing pick-up-the-stones in the street.

Much had changed in Tsanos, Cataia reflected, but the important things had not.

ಶ FOURTEEN

AANDEV'REI LOOKED almost enchanted in the pale light of the false dawn. The city was still sleeping, with only a few guards walking the outer walls, and the guards themselves were tired.

SiNioni noted with satisfaction that the city was not protected from the river. Indeed, that would have been impossible, as it spanned both sides with four large bridges linking the banks. The horror of water travel had been well worth the effort, she thought. The small boats were lowered and filled with fighters, the oars muffled by hides.

That was almost too much for SiNioni. The large boat had almost been overwhelming; these smaller ones were simply hideous. They were far too close to the water and bounced up and down on the slightest swell. Just looking at them made SiNioni's normally strong stomach turn. She felt a tug at her sleeve and found a Salsatean sailor directing her down the rope ladder into one of those miserable things, and she gulped hard for air.

Death she had faced in many forms, but never, never in her long life had she faced such fear. The small boat sat low in the water and she could reach over the side and immerse her hand in the river. The small boat dipped and swayed under her. She closed her eyes and concentrated on an old chant she had learned in her mother's tent. It did not stop the horror of the river and the rocking. Once they hit a bit of wind and the river turned choppy, and SiNioni thought that she could endure no more. Only the chant in her head now, she tried desperately to overcome her rebellious stomach and the pangs of fear from the occasional spray.

Silently she watched as the small boats discharged their loads under the bridges. There was a faint warmth under the night chill, and SiNioni shivered with apprehension. It would soon be dawn, and all her troops would have to be deposited in the city before the day started. Bit by bit, under each bridge, the army grew. The War Leader could not repress a sigh of relief when the last group was safe on soil.

They needed to act swiftly. Each group climbed both banks and pilings to get onto the bridges, cutting the city in half. If they could hold the bridges, they would push outward like a star.

The first cart came into view. A scream emerged from its occupant, and very few minutes passed before the first Guard detachment reached the river, mounted and racing forward. SiNioni thought quickly. The Swanimir were known for quick thinking and cunning plans. The animals, the animals were the key, she realized, and she swiftly tore off her heavy overrobe and lit it with the flint and steel she always carried. The others followed her example, working with desperate haste, feeling for the dry areas under the sleeves and behind the knees of the garments where the fire would catch first. A barrier of flame erupted across each bridge before the Guard had time to reach it, and nobody can control a horse in the presence of flame.

The animals bolted to the banks, jumped in the river and trampled each other and their riders in their frantic attempts to avoid the blaze. One unfortunate beast, hide glittering with oil as the jars it carried broke, was hit by several sparks and caught fire. SiNioni could see it running down the wharves and through the marketplace. Insane with pain, it rolled about and hurled itself through the narrow streets by the river, throwing sparks into the barrels stacked for shipping. The living torch shrieked as it crashed through the tar barrels and plunged into the river.

Now the fire was raging at the riverbank. Those guardsmen still alive after the stampede found themselves facing a group of armed, fresh warriors backed by a raging fire. Those who could surrendered, and in less than an hour after the battle had begun, the defending army was routed.

The city now belonged to the Nestezians, but SiNioni was deeply troubled. The city they had won was fast being reduced to ash, for the fire raging at the wharf was spreading. It was almost impossible to move in the streets because panic had struck and the alleys, quiet such a short time ago, were now choked with a mob.

The fire effectively barricaded the Nestezians from the panic-stricken populace and held them prisoner on the bridges. SiNioni cursed. There was nothing she could do but watch as the city burned and people ran. She saw children die, trampled under the feet of a heaving mass of humanity, and the light breeze carried the cacophony of their terror.

The screams and smell alerted others in the city too. In the retreat houses the long dawn service had just ended, and during breakfast the rule of silence was broken. Three masters and three mistresses rose and quietly informed the residents of the situation.

SiNioni sniffed the air. Was the smell of fire and river distracting her, or was there really a difference? It seemed heavier, thicker, and the sky was growing dark. Looking up, there was no mistaking the grey clouds floating purposefully through the sky. Then the first drops fell.

"Are the abdication papers ready?" Cataia asked brusquely.

Tiernon handed them over, worried by the tone in her voice. She seemed hardened somehow, bitter, ever since she'd awakened from that deathlike sleep after the battle. He could understand that she must be tense. Demanding Lathanor's abdication was a terrible strain and she was reading her own doom in every line. Still, there was no choice, and many another would have had him killed. Cataia would not even listen to that line of reasoning.

"Is he sober?" she asked.

"We've had him under guard since the Palace was taken," Tiernon replied. "Ayt's troops have been monitoring him, and then Eryah took over. He hasn't seen a drop since you entered the Palace."

"Good."

Tiernon took her gently by the arm. If anything, she seemed more vulnerable to him. He recognized that she needed what he had taken for himself the night he had ridden back to the battlefield—some moments alone to assimilate what had been done, and some time to face what she had become. She had had neither.

"To the garden, then," he said.

She nodded, carefully composing her features into a mask-like calm.

The roof garden was warm and fragrant, and it was easy to forget here that there had been a war. Yellow and pink and pale-blue blossoms turned eastward as if following the Adepti in their morning Chant to the Sun. There was no wall, only a small ledge around the garden, but the abundant growth obscured the sights and sounds of the conquered city below. The last words of the chant had scarcely been uttered when Eryah came in, Lathanor in tow. He looked ill, his hands trembling more from alcohol deprivation than fear of what awaited him.

"Greetings, cousin," Cataia began.

"It would have been kinder if you had killed me drunk," Lathanor said. "Do you honestly think I didn't know what was going on?"

Tiernon looked at Cataia. "We ask only that you abdicate in favor of Cataia and retire to Aandev'Rei. We had no thought to kill you; rather the opposite," Tiernon said gently.

"I don't want your mercy," Lathanor responded.

"Lathanor, cousin, please sit down," Cataia said, softening. "I'm sorry we could not permit you your wine, but we had no wish to manipulate you as Bertham has done."

"I should see the city, see what has been done to it," Lathanor said.

"Will you abdicate?" Cataia asked.

Lathanor looked at her searchingly. "Does it matter? Do I have a choice? I could have told them who killed Eltion, but that wouldn't have changed things. Bertham set it up very

well, and Keani was a terror. But I would never stoop to what
you have done, Cataia. I would never destroy my own country, my own people.''

"Will you abdicate?" she asked again.

Lathanor gazed at both of them harshly. "I don't suppose
you will permit me a chosen death, will you? With the proper
honors that should go with it? No, I don't think you could."

"Lathanor," Tiernon said gently, shaken, "we don't want
you to die. There has been enough death. I don't think I could
face it, for you to burn alive. Don't ask it."

Lathanor smiled coldly. "Yes, I knew you couldn't. There
was no choice but to refuse. But I was still a King, however
bad, I was a King." He walked over to the ledge slowly, Tiernon and Cataia following. Then Lathanor swept his hands
over the high bushes, indicating the city. "That is my legacy to
you, cousin. All the destruction your mother could have
wanted. Enjoy it."

He laughed almost insanely, and Tiernon pulled him back.
Four large bronze lamps were glittering around the fountain,
throwing bright-golden reflections into the soft and peaceful
water. They were full of oil, having been refilled just before
dawn. Lathanor sat in front of one, running his hands over the
bronzework.

"At least I can do one thing right," he said quietly, gazing
into the flames.

With speed that startled Tiernon into inaction, Lathanor
hefted the large lamp and poured the fresh oil over himself,
completely saturating his garments and hair. Then, quickly, he
touched the still burning wick to his hem.

Cataia jumped forward, her eyes on the water in the fountain, but a hand on her shoulder held her back.

"He has the right," Tiernon said in a strained voice, the
flesh around his jaw tightening. "It is well done, with two
witnesses of proper rank."

Cataia stood transfixed as the body that once held her
cousin charred black against the fragrant trees and the setting
sun.

The messenger was young, probably not even of age yet,
Cataia thought as she paced across the room. Not that the
news had not been good, but she had wished to leave Tsanos.
It would have relieved her of the vision of Lathanor burning in

the soft garden. She could not go to the roof anymore.

But tomorrow the combined armies of Maddigore and Aandev'Rei would be arriving, and she must show proper respect for those who had won her country back for her and for themselves. She ordered food to be made ready and places prepared in the Palace for the generals.

Cataia wished she could speak to Tiernon, but since this morning's incident on the roof garden he had retired for a day of meditation. She had no such luxury, although she was aware that the suicide had affected Tiernon even more than herself. True, it had been the only proper and kingly thing he could have done, but she couldn't figure out why it had affected Tiernon so badly. He had made the same choice himself once, she remembered. She had done everything except join him in meditation, which would have been an unthinkable breach of privacy. Now she had to prepare for the generals, hoping that Tiernon's meditations would be over in time for her to consult him, and plan for her coronation. Ayt was even now readying the Temple for the ceremony.

As if on cue, Ayt burst into the room, flustered and almost in tears. "They're missing. Everything else is there, the robes and the katreisi and the crown and the belt, but they're not there."

"What's not there?" Cataia demanded.

"The . . . the unmentionables," Ayt blurted out.

Cataia couldn't control her laughter. She hadn't laughed so hard in ages and her ribs hurt and she gasped for breath but the laughter wouldn't stop. "Don't worry," she managed between gasps, "they'll turn up." They were still in the hiding place in the Abbey, behind the torrigon barrels in the cellar.

Still laughing, Cataia dismissed Ayt and sent a note to Dacia asking for the underwear back. To see Dacia receiving that note! It would be the funniest thing in the world. Her laughter shrieked down the hall, hinting at hysteria, but the dam had broken and Cataia released the hardships and terrors of the past days in a well of giggles.

The horn sounded in the early light outside the Palace gates. The victorious generals were demanding entrance. Cataia, already awake, stroked Tiernon's neck. The second blast was louder, and he started, coming to consciousness suddenly. The horn was reminiscent of war, and the strong culture that they had become used to. She smiled slowly at him. "Just our victories," she said. There was a third blast, as protocol demanded, and at that the two disentangled themselves, dressed and raced at the fastest pace decorum would allow in order to enter the large audience chamber just before the War Leaders were seated.

In accordance with the old customs, food was served as an offering of peace and there was real desert ghena in honor of the new alliance. Cup after cup was drunk in silence, four cups at least to celebrate this victory, five for the Promise, six for the unity of the Nestezian tribes. After the sixth cup had been consumed each War Leader lifted a voice to tell a different story, and the cacophony was deafening. Finally Cataia called them to order.

SiUran spoke. "Boats. Newfangled foreign idea. Here I am, old, waiting for this battle all my life, and what do I get? A ride on a boat, sickness, misery, surrounded by water, only to find that my dear friends have dispatched as many of the enemy as I. I will never, never go against my better judgment again, and permit such as these, of thieving tribes all, to steal my glory."

"And what a battle you missed, old foeman," said SiJerti jokingly.

"So you said, so you said, and I'm sick of it," SiUran responded.

"Perhaps it was for the best that you missed the action," SiJerti continued. "After all, such a battle for a man of your years ..."

"I can still outfight any of you," SiUran exclaimed. "I can outshout, outplan and outfight all of you combined and I'm willing to prove it."

If Cataia had not intervened, she knew that he would have proved it right there in the middle of the hall. She finally had to call up the fact that they had sipped ghena to quell the argument, and even that did not lessen the enthusiasm. After all, it was only going to be a friendly fight, no hostility involved. Luckily, a servant arrived with a tray of mint drink and pastries. This diverted attention for the moment, but it was long enough for Cataia to be assured that peace had been restored.

After sampling a fair number of the pastries, SiUran gestured expansively to the group and spoke good-naturedly. "So they are my children. It is always for the child to surpass the parent, that is the parents' dream. I apologize for their behavior, but children can be ill mannered. It shows their spirit."

Cataia smiled and nodded at SiJerti. He stood proudly, proud for himself and for the Qaludi, to be called on to speak first. After all, the Swanimir were thieves even if they were cunning, and the Itesi were mere scavengers. As for SiUran's Atnefi, they were the worst, a band of puling moderators who had no stomach for a real fight. So SiJerti, while not surprised to be called on, started quickly before the Swanimir could steal this bit of precedence from the Qaludi too.

"We waited until the appointed day, after our groups had split, and then we journeyed west against the sun. We followed the mountains to the north, and the desert favored us with many wells. On the seventh day we found a stand of neth trees heavy with ripe fruit. There was enough for all and more besides, and it was firm and sweet and we took it as an omen.

"From there the land began to change. The cacti grew more thickly, and on the fourteenth day, twice the sacred seven, as we awoke we witnessed another omen. There were many cacti here, and all had bloomed with large and strange flowers, flowers that I have never seen before. Their smell was sweet and light and there were colors that no color should be, pale-violets and greys with the reds and yellows."

"That," said the Itesi War Leader, "was because the sun was not up and you could not see the colors. They were probably pale-yellow and pink, but of course it sounds better for the telling if there are many omens."

SiJerti glowered before he continued. "At the moment the sun came up, the flowers wilted and died, and we were frightened for what this portent really meant. But the shaman said that victory would come only after a long and hard fight with a chance for glory for all, and it did.

"On the eighteenth day we first caught sight of Maddigore, dark walls against the green of the mountains, and we approached carefully. We came quietly to the very gates of the city, which we found closed and well guarded, and we called them to come and fight. But they would not open their gates and meet us openly, oh, no. Those honorless cherzi threw javelins from behind the walls, while they sat protected."

"And?" prompted Cataia.

"We simply moved out of range. They did not think that we

would figure that out. We just backed off. But"—a wicked gleam came to SiJerti's eye—"they did not know that they were still in the range of our slings, and even the smallest target is enough to hit. And they did have to show their heads occasionally to see where we were. Even they were not so stupid as to throw a javelin blind. We started a good fight there at the Western Gate, and soon we saw more and more guards up on the wall. We were sure that they believed we would sit there all day throwing stones at them.

"They believed in their walls too well. We sent several of the junior war bands around the back to scale the walls there. Most of them are excellent climbers, and the youngest bands could cover with their slings."

"I assume," Tiernon said, "that they learned their skill in climbing mountains, into Avriaten, perhaps?"

"Perhaps," SiJerti agreed. "It does not matter. Their objective was not really to climb the wall, but to draw the enemy to that side of the city. Now they were busy protecting two ends, spread far from each other. We had planned to split again, by tribes, and further confuse them. It should have been an easy victory."

"If one believes in omens," said SiLiasryn caustically. "But it was not. There were several boats moored upstream, and this we had not thought of, that they would come by river. Their boats had weapons on them and stayed in the river while they fired at those trying to scale the walls. We did not know what to do, how to get rid of them. It was almost dark, and we retreated quickly to think about this menace. Perhaps if we could get to them and set them on fire, we could destroy them, if they would burn in the water. But we could not get to them."

Here SiLiasryn had to breathe, and SiJerti took advantage of that small pause. He reminded himself to never, no matter what, trust the Tororer Anerim. They were snakes, hiding in the shadows waiting to strike. He spoke quickly before any of the others could take the narrative again. "We thought of throwing barrels of burning pitch at them, but the air is strange around the river. If they would come on land and fight us, it would be different, but they stayed in their boats as the others stayed behind their walls. We decided to keep up the attack from the land side, and stay well away from the water, which is what we did the next day. They must have some system to communicate with the boats, for as we were attacking from the front of the Western Gate, they came off the boats.

"There were hundreds of them and they used great stealth, for they had sneaked up behind us while we were in the midst of battle. We found ourselves surrounded.

"We were far outnumbered, and when we turned to fight those off the boats we were exposed to those on the walls. We had no choice, and cut through as best we could, although it cost us greatly. We did not think they would fight so well, those boat people, and they had a strange kind of sword, poisoned perhaps, that did not kill cleanly.

"It must have been poison, because we lost more to infection and dirty wounds than in the fighting itself. Still, cowardly as the trick was, it was their own undoing. A wounded fighter, though poisoned, can still kill and will be more vigorous about it. Brasia, before she died, said that she could smell the poison. Those who are already dying have nothing to lose. Perhaps they thought they'd trick us. I don't know.

"We slashed our way across their lines and managed to retreat deep into the mountains. We lost half our warriors that day, and not to clean death. The boats had been defeated, but there were many more behind those walls, and there might have been more boats that we knew nothing about. There could even have been a second army camped across the river and able to sail across. We didn't know.

"We were deeply troubled that night and felt that all we could do was win a proper death, if they used no more poison. We said very little that night, but we could not sleep. We left a fire burning for the light, and just after it started the young shaman of the women's mysteries entered our circle and began telling us a story from when the world was young.

"It is a shaman's duty to tell stories, to instruct, but we could not understand why she chose a story about the youth of the mountains, nor did we feel like listening to instruction. This shaman is very young and not trained in war, and we did not think she could help anything except our souls. And we weren't worried about our souls at that moment. Only SiLiasryn listened," he said, gesturing to the Tororer Anerim War Leader.

"I listened because I knew the story and I like it," SiLiasryn said, pulling the honor from the Qaludi again. "It was only later that I began to see the shaman's meaning, not until after she left.''

"That story is not often told in Avriaten," Cataia said. "I would like to hear it."

"That's because it's not really your land," SiLiasryn said softly, careful not to offend. "You don't know all the secrets of it, nor would you try to preserve the knowledge. The mountains and the city of Maddigore were ours long before you knew there was land to the west, and to our advantage this time. A great river once flowed beneath these mountains, and much of the rock has been carved and hollowed by it. The Caverns of the Adepti are the greatest of these chambers, but there are others that run the entire length of the range. No one has explored them fully, although many have tried and never come back.

"The city of Maddigore was founded when our ancestors were caught in a cavern and the mouth fell in. They wandered through the chambers and corridors, and many died. Finally they came to a place where they saw light, and cut their way through to the sunlight. There they founded a city, on the site of their salvation."

"So there's an underground route into the city that no one knew about?'' Cataia asked.

"It was not so easy to say," SiThereti said. "First, the original opening had caved shut. Second, the caverns are treacherous. It is only by great luck that the first party found their way out. We have learned some things since then, but we know enough to respect the danger. If we did not find the escape route we could be wandering the caverns forever, and there are no paths, no stars to guide. There are great crevasses and places no one can pass, and water that looks no deeper than your finger can drown you. But we had no choice. For four days we sent out search parties, trying to find the opening to the cave, or some indication of one. Finally, on the fourth day, a small crack was found.

"We had to dig into the mountainside to make a hole wide enough to crawl through, and then we had to mark the passages. Each day we went in, three warriors, bound to each other and to us with a long rope. They carried limestone and marked the way. Every day we went farther, starting from the point where we'd left off before, but we still did not know if we were going in the right direction. After a short moon we found a small opening with light shining through, and we posted guards to see if they could hear anything, to see if we had come to the right place.

"I think it was fate, the fate of our people, that we came to the right passage; others think it was luck. That no longer matters. The small opening we found led into the Star Temple of Maddigore, the Temple that was built by our ancestors to the dark gods under the earth before the Seven came to this land. We listened constantly and finally made out a pattern. There were several hours a day when the Temple was not in use, and it was not being guarded. Indeed, from what we overheard, the army of Maddigore already thought themselves the victors and ourselves in defeat.

"Little by little we worked at widening the hole in the Temple in the hours when no one was there, being careful to cover our work with loose stones that could easily be removed.

"One night the hole was large enough, and we waited until well after the city had gone to bed, and then we came through. We stationed ourselves at various places in the city where the concentrations of troops were the largest and waited until morning."

"Why not kill them when they slept?" Cataia asked. "That would have been the safest thing, with your forces depleted."

"Killing someone in his sleep is the work of an assassin, not a warrior," SiJerti said stiffly.

Cataia nodded, thinking of the many assassins in the Court of Tsanos.

SiJerti continued with his narrative, although it might be argued that it was his no longer. "Although we were outnumbered, we had the advantage. They had grown lazy in the time we had been absent trying to find another way into the city. They felt their victory had been won and were spending a lot of time in the public houses. On top of that there was the surprise of seeing us already in the city. That disheartened them. They were also disadvantaged because they relied heavily on the skill of the spearthrowers and the boat weapons, both useless in the city. So even badly outnumbered we held a good edge.

"The battle within the city was not long. After the first hour most of the Avriatenese surrendered and we had only to deal with the commanders."

"It is easy to see why they surrendered," said SiLiasryn.

"For most, Maddigore was not their native city, and we spared all of those who submitted to us."

"That, of course, was pure expediency," SiThereti interjected. "First, we did not wish to take a dead city. That is useless. And when those others saw that we killed none who surrendered, more were willing to do so. We did not have the numbers to take the city if everyone in Maddigore had been committed to the fight, so the more who came over to us, the greater our chances.

"We had the city by noon, with the exception of a few outbreaks where the King's stalwarts still resisted. It took several days to make sure the place was secure, and although some looting must have taken place, we did manage to hold it to a minimum. We left a small force behind to ensure that there would be no reversal, and then we marched to meet with Si-Nioni's group from Aandev'Rei. There were a very few encounters on the way, mostly old people who were afraid that we would slit their throats. As we marched farther north there was no resistance at all."

"Truly, that should be made into a story by the best teller we have, and be told over and over again," Tiernon said, careful of Nestezi pride.

"But perhaps not right now," Cataia said quietly. "It would not be good to remind the people that they are defeated. It would make things difficult."

"You are becoming wise," said SiUran. He leaned back against his left heel and took another gulp of ghena. Turning to the other War Leaders, he said, "We did not take this land to crush it, but to live in it. To make it ours again. There is enough here for both peoples, if we can make good policy."

Cataia had no wish to extend the meeting further. "I thank you for coming so quickly to bring me this good news, but you must be tired. Your quarters have been prepared. I hope they suit your tastes. If there is anything you require for your comfort, it will be provided immediately."

Cataia and Tiernon returned to the Queen's chambers. When they opened the door, Tiernon froze. Things were wrong, and there was a good chance that a spy or assassin lurked nearby. A stupid one, Tiernon thought, for no one else would bother to put away all the clothes or plump all the cushions.

Glasses of hot milk sat on the low lacquered table in the

middle of the room. So that was the ploy. Poison again. Tiernon dashed at the cups as if they were an enemy and poured the contents out over the square.

As Tiernon replaced the cups on the table, Valnera walked in.

"How very nice, I see you've both drunk all your milk," she said. "Milk is good for you when you work so hard. Now, your bath is ready and nice and hot and scented just the way you like it, Princess. Oh, I mean Majesty."

Cataia flew across the room and hugged Valnera hard. "What happened? Where have you been? Oh, it's so good to see you, Valnera, hot milk and all. I don't care," Cataia rambled, tears running down her cheeks.

"Well, well, good, that's nice," Valnera replied, seeming a little lost. "Lady Ayt told me this morning that you'd been here for some time. I've been in the Temple, embroidering some very nice ceremonial garments for her. She'll wear them for your coronation. 'Ayt,' I told her, 'do you mean to say that all that noise was my pretty little lady coming home with her war and you didn't even tell me? Phooey on you.' That's just what I told her."

Valnera held Cataia at arm's length and stared before she noticed Tiernon in the room, looking on with some cross between amusement and disbelief. "And Lord Tiernon back with you too. Well, I knew he never had a philandering heart, no matter what the kitchen wenches said, and they said a lot. Our whole old family, just like in the days before all this terrible stuff started to happen. But enough of that. Cataia, your bath will be cold soon, and you both look like you could use it. Oh!"

♪FIFTEEN

IT WAS STILL COLD on the field outside the city, and Cataia shivered under the thin white shift. For the first time since her coming of age her hair was loose and her feet were bare in public. Thus did an Aandev monarch enter the capital to be crowned. In the Palace, thought Cataia, Tiernon would already be dressed in his somber indigo, preparing for the ceremony. He would be holding a razor-sharp scimitar over her for part of the proceedings, the official duty of the new First Councilor. She wondered if he would have to let it drop, and then her blood too would stain the shift. It had happened before. A very long time before, she knew, but it had happened and for far less than she had done.

The sky was slowly streaking with pink and the air began to warm imperceptibly. Suddenly the great gate of the city swung open. Cataia breathed deeply, took a few moments to calm herself and then entered.

The streets were lined with people, people with grim faces. They were silent. Cataia knew they were examining her closely, a young woman in an old garment, alone and without any protection. They could set upon her if they wished. Once before Cataia knew they had so wished and a monarch had not lived even to see the blade raised above her head. The color drained out of her face and she looked more resigned than proud. Perhaps that was why, she thought, they let her pass unmolested, moving aside quietly to let her through the crowd.

"The Queen of Avriaten has no need to fear her children, as a mother does not. In exposing herself to them, she proves her trust in them, and they in turn can trust her." Cataia remembered the words not from the night before, when Ayt had read them to her, but from Mother Daniessa's ceaseless repetitions. Mother Daniessa had tried to prepare her for this, but no amount of preparation could adequately ready anyone for this day. She felt frightened and very much alone. Every callow face that studied her was another burden, another test. She wanted to bolt and hide, maybe in Dacia's little cottage. There was no one to help her here.

Perhaps that was what it was all about, Cataia thought. From now on, she would be alone. All decisions would finally be hers. Something in her screamed that she did not want to be Queen, and she squelched it. Then she exhaled slowly, trying to empty her mind and find some form of peace.

Looking up, Cataia was startled to find herself in the courtyard of the Temple of the Stars. She had carefully averted her eyes from the crowd and could not recall a single face, a single landmark, not even Dier Street, which she must have passed on her way. Here people were welcoming, unlike the hostile multitude near the gate.

The carved latticework threw strange patterns of light and shadow down the central aisle. Cataia walked slowly, noticing the intricacy of the patterns etched into the floor and the warmth of the stone against the soles of her feet. Above her, spread across the great dome, was painted the vault of the heavens. The entire Court, ambassadors from Salsatee, War Leaders and the Mothers of the Reis sat on the small patterned rugs to both sides of her. Their rich garments were subdued for this occasion, even the brilliant rainbow of the courtiers muted for this solemn event. In front of her was the cushion on which she was to kneel. Tiernon stood near it, sword in hand. Farther up, Ayt, in her richly embroidered ceremonial garments, stood motionless, waiting.

She did not sit on the cushion but knelt in the formal position, heels tucked under and back straight. She bent her head forward and the shadow of the sword fell over her dark shoulder-length hair.

Ayt raised her arms and began the ceremony. First there was a long incantation and dedication, and then the question. This was what Cataia had been waiting for.

"Is there any that finds Cataia pra Keani rei Aandev unworthy to rule until the end of her days?" Ayt intoned.

Cataia's heart skipped a beat. Surely someone would take this chance to accuse her of treason, or Lathanor's death at least, not to mention her mother's supposed regicide. She glanced up and noticed that Tiernon's face was tense. No one had spoken yet, but the question must be repeated three times before he could withdraw, and others in his position had been forced to sever a royal head.

Ayt repeated the question for the third time and there was a hush, as if the entire assembly waited for the one who would dare speak. The silence was overpowering. Cataia's pulse was racing. Ayt was her friend, her ally, had supported her in the capture of Tsanos—surely she could make the intervals shorter, not give so much time for them to evaluate Cataia's unorthodox behavior. It seemed an eternity before Ayt motioned Tiernon to put the scimitar aside.

Cataia stayed in place to repeat the interminable vows and oaths, and in her relief she had very little idea of what she was saying. Finally she was wrapped in the heavy silk embroidered robe, and after a few more incantations the serpent-and-sun crown of Avriaten was placed on her brow. Immediately she was surrounded by members of the Council, who escorted her across the square back to the Palace to take her place on the throne.

All in all, it had been an exhausting day, but Cataia and Tiernon sat up late over supper in Cataia's new apartments, the royal suite. Weariness had not affected either of them yet. Indeed, neither of them could sleep.

"I was afraid someone would speak out against me, I really was," Cataia said.

Tiernon laughed heartily. "Do you really think that Ayt would permit it? A royal execution would be rather untidy, don't you think, and blood is so hard to wash out of white stone."

"Don't laugh at me," she retorted. "I saw you and you looked petrified."

"Petrified? Not in the least. But it would have appeared bad if I had not seemed somewhat tense. Besides, I was worried that the drape of my katreisi might not have been flattering."

"You would have to say that," Cataia said, exasperated. "I don't believe you. Well, I do believe you about the katreisi, but you know that there could have been someone who might have spoken. . . ."

"It has happened exactly twice since the Aandev were more than Rei Mothers, and then only because there was trouble between the Aandev and the Reis," Tiernon explained as if to a child. "You knew that as long as the Rei Mothers supported you there was nothing to fear. That's one reason it was so important to stop in Bietehel. And I rather think they approved of your choice of a First Councilor. They know where my interests stand. Besides, Lathanor was drunk at his coronation and no one challenged him."

"That's different. *He* didn't invade his country," Cataia countered.

"He might as well have," Tiernon replied.

"I don't know. Besides, I'm not feeling very political right now."

"I am," Tiernon said, leering comically.

Cataia was confused. He was playing again, and she wasn't sure what the game was.

"Oh, yes, my love," he continued, "now that you are Queen it's even more your duty to provide an heiress."

Cataia broke out laughing. "Schemer. All this time, and I never even suspected that was the reason you wanted me."

"I just believe in doing my best for my country. You understand."

Both laughed, and Tiernon pulled Cataia to her feet and led her to the next room.

Tiernon awakened, disturbed by something he couldn't quite define. He glanced down at Cataia lying beside him. She seemed so peaceful, so safe. But he was not able to shake the anxiety. He touched Cataia's hair once, gently, and then wrapped his katreisi around himself and headed to his own quarters, to his private ritual room. Bertham was on his mind, Bertham and Lechefrian.

As he entered the ritual room he immediately perceived a difference in the atmosphere. Someone had been there; he could still sense the residue of that passing. And lying on the altar was the sword of the Caverns. His first reaction was anger. How dare anyone enter this place and touch his ritual items? Even Cataia would not do that without specific permission, and they were highly attuned to one another. They had certainly worked enough rituals together. Besides, by now he could identify her residue, and this one was definitely different.

Different, yes, but familiar as well. He tried to place the feeling, the frequency, and realized that he had felt it in the Caverns. The one who had spoken for Aken had had the same texture, and that one was Chervan, a friend as well. Well, it was enough to know that it was one of his own kind, and of a higher Order at that.

It was useless to pursue Aken, he thought angrily. It was bound to lead nowhere. But that feeling—let it go, let it wind back, back.

Entering a state of full concentration, he focused on the feeling and let the associations flow. There, bit by bit, he saw the same face over and over, harsh and gentle at the same time.

"Chervan has returned to Aken, his work in your place is done. But your own work, your own . . ."

The rhythm of the voice from Aken brought to mind the rhythm of the Caverns, and that scene lay before him with all its emotional content. Tiernon winced, but the voice went on, dragging him back to the image. Fighting it was painful and was bound to do no good, anyway. But it was harder to go with it, knowing what would come, knowing there would be no escape, now or ever.

The insane lust, that controlling need awakened in him as he took the braided hilt of the sword and found himself staring into the shattered remains of the mirror. The reflection was and was not his own. The robe was different, the same Orange but of an archaic cut, and the hair was slightly paler and still untouched by grey. The body was basically like his own, but moved more forcefully. Yet even as he saw its differences, he knew it to be himself, and suddenly it seemed that a thin veil in his mind had been torn open and the memory that had been fragments of understanding became whole, complete.

It invaded him again, the terrible paradox of craving power and wishing peace. And the conflicting loves and duties, his old friend turned to 'Kleppah, enticing him, pleading. He felt the war in himself burn and tear through his flesh, driving for oblivion, driving for desire, pulling him apart. In the center there was pain, the great wrong he had committed. Again he saw himself sign a paper, and he remembered what that paper had contained. His own damnation.

The hell in the Caverns of Ge, the place of the dead, where he had wandered cold and alone with his agony since he had chosen the pyre, the last warmth he had ever known. And he fought against it, the bastard son of Ge the Mother, the Dark One, raging in that empty echoless pit. Screaming, his spirit suspended over the yawning plain of oblivion as the Dark Mother stood there, silent, immobile, cold and hard, glorying in his tearing grief.

No, *he* had gloried in it, in his rebellion. Power and pride burned like the flames he had fueled, his body burning alive until there was nothing left but ash. Pain was not important, only the pit, and the struggle against it. And he had chosen, he remembered that part well. They had come to him, the Guides of Judgment, and let him choose, this life and death or oblivion below him. And he had been grateful. Even now the possibility choked him, that it was possible to escape after he had signed his own doom. He had signed, but he was permitted this single time, just once, to try.

And he had chosen. He had had that choice then, and now he knew that he faced it again here. He had always faced it. He knew that this time he would use the sword on the enemy it had been forged for. He had been granted this one chance and he was not going to let it drop away from him like the mirror he had shattered in its frame.

He felt as if his skin were burning hot and fevered and his breath was short. The insignificant part of him, the part that would be destroyed, that would feel the fire lick at the sinew, cried and screamed and pleaded. It rejected what it had not known, but the deep recesses of the soul stood fast.

Again he stood before the Primordial, the Dark Goddess. He dared not ask for her mercy, for even the strength to die as an Adept and not give himself living to the fire. Already he had been given more mercy than he deserved. Lathanor, dying, came to his mind. Lathanor had done evil from weakness, not choice. Lathanor was surely his better in all these things.

He, Tiernon, was dishonored. He must earn his mercy, for he did not deserve any. He did not even deserve this chance to escape from the pit. What had been granted was charity, unearned. It was only by Chevaina's intercession that he was allowed even this much hope.

He bowed low before the great image of the Goddess of Death, accepting the task. His task, the one he had been born for, great and horrible as it was. It was his alone. He gazed into her eyes and assumed his burden with the fullness of his self. The Dark One, Ge the Bringer of Death, echoed his smile.

The ritual room reformed around him. He was deeply shaken and more deeply afraid.

And then Tiernon began to laugh. Oh, they all knew him well enough. It was so neatly done. All those years, when he had suspected he knew that Tiernon of the Seven would be punished. And how had Tiernon of Bietehel thought of it? Poverty, of course, that would hurt the worst, poverty and no position. Now that knowledge of reality flooded him, he saw the irony of it all. Not to be denied what he sought, far from it, but to have to give it all up of his free will. Every attachment had to be renounced, abandoned, flung away by choice. It was the perfect punishment, the perfect plan, a work of art in fact.

Silently he congratulated those who had set it up, his own self among them, for the perfection that had been attained. Even with the pain it required, it was a beautiful thing and as such must be acknowledged.

His hands grasped the hilt of the sword and his knees buckled under him, but the outcome of the battle was already decided. Before he hit the floor of the ritual chamber, his parched lips managed to pronounce the Oath of Ge, and he lay still.

Tiernon did not reappear in Court until dinner of the next day. He had spent most of the night on the floor of the ritual room until he could gather enough strength to drag himself to his sleeping rug. The long sleep had done some good, but he was still pale and had little appetite.

After the meal he invited Cataia to join him in his own apartments briefly. It seemed strange to him, when they arrived in the private dining room, that the colors no longer delighted him as they had in the past. He watched Cataia, feeling distantly sorry for her as she waited for what he would say, her hands quietly folded in her lap.

"I must go to Tyne," he said as gently as he could. "I must go now. It is the only thing there is left for me to do, and every day I stay, every moment I linger here, will draw me back. It's time to make an end."

Cataia held her face rigid, masking the terror that passed through her. It was not Tiernon speaking, she knew, not the Tiernon who had been friend, advisor, Councilor, lover. The words gave him away, and the slowness with which they were spoken. He was only the Adept now, the personality she had known so well locked away. It was no longer of service to the magician who stood before her.

"Tiernon, please," she replied, grasping for something. "You're not ready to fight Lechefrian, anyway. You can hardly stand straight. And I'm not ready to face it."

"You don't have to be there," he said, talking more for his own benefit than hers. "You are the Queen now, and you're needed here."

"I'm an Adept first," she replied angrily, "and I am going. I was witness when you made your bargain with that demon, and I can witness you unmaking it."

"As you wish," Tiernon replied, bowing his head. She was right. Chevaina had been there before, and she must be there again, even if he were only to throw himself into the abyss. She was his witness.

"You can wait at least a short moon," she pleaded. "You know there are things I have to settle here before I can go. Please."

Tiernon nodded his acceptance and showed her to the door. He was honored that she would come and bear witness. And he was relieved that she would not try to hold him here.

There were several things that Cataia had to do before she departed for Tyne. First on the list was the scheduling of a ceremony that was long overdue anyway. It took place just after sunrise of the second day, after the Chant to the Sun had been completed and the full white disc rested on the horizon. It was a stately event, the raising of Eryah to SiEryah, a full War Leader.

Cataia's throne was set in the square between the Palace and the Temple of the Stars. She did not like the throne. The large

cushion was on a high carved platform, and kneeling in the
formal position required at State events was insecure at such a
height. Cataia constantly wished for the firmness of the floor
and a less impressively stuffed cushion, but tradition was tradition so she put up with it.

The square was crowded with people dressed in bright
colors, which gave the place the look of a market, and it was
twice as crowded as it was on marketdays. The outer walls of
the Palace and the Temple had been hung with bright banners,
giving everything an even more festive air. The Council, in all
their Rei colors, stood on either side of her, and the undercurrent of noise stopped when Eryah entered the square from the
Palace in the ceremonial dress of an Atnefi warrior. She was
accompanied by her war band, who played rhythm sticks and
finger cymbals and sang old songs about warriors long dead.

The pale-yellow tindi was tied with two scarlet plekas, the
ends of which hung down her back in tassels. The desert robe,
slit front and back for riding, was of a glittering gold-
and-white-striped fabric, belted with a bright-red sash that
matched the red of her pants and plekas. Cataia knew that
among desert tribes that shade of red was worn only by
women, although where the custom had started no one could
say. The most popular story was that, vain of their clothes, the
women preferred a shade that would not show the stain of
blood. Eryah's boots were exceptionally spectacular, with a
band of tooling at least four fingers wide around the top, dyed
red and blue with hints of gold. Actually though, thought
Cataia, she looked a little odd. Eryah wore no weapons.

When Eryah reached the throne the singing stopped and the
senior storyteller of the Palace listed Eryah's deeds and virtues
to the point where the blood rose in her face and her cheeks
matched her crimson pants. Cataia knew that this was considered a good sign, an open testimony to her modesty. Cataia
handed her her new weapons one by one in the specific order
required by the Nestezi traditions. Each one was newly made
and the best that could be obtained.

First came the long curved scimitar with fine calligraphy
etched into the blade, the primary weapon of the desert. Then
the knife was presented, curved and etched to match the
sword. These were thrust under the red sash so that their hilts
crossed in the middle. After that came a wrist dagger in an or-
nately tooled leather sheath, and finally the humble but deadly

sling. Members of Eryah's war band fastened the dagger to her forearm and secured the sling in a special pocket in the lining of her boot. When they had finished, Cataia called Eryah to turn to the crowd, as she and SiUran named Eryah SiEryah from this time forward.

The crowd cheered, although for the native city dwellers it was more a matter of form than real enthusiasm, and the newly made War Leader, the Queen and their entourage crossed the square back into the Palace. Behind them servants were distributing food to the throng, a policy Cataia had revived from the time Eltion had been Queen. A little popularity would not hurt her position, especially now.

♪ SIXTEEN

EVERYTHING WAS READY to go. The last few days had been spent mostly in Council meetings and gathering the few supplies needed to prepare for the ritual. Just that day they had finally obtained the thin bitter juice that would provide their sustenance for the last few days of the journey. Their robes were freshly laundered and packed into soft hide cases. Meat pies were readied in the kitchen, as were dried strips of meat with torrigon and fruit beaten in.

Making the preparations, Cataia realized how much she owed to the tribes. Having learned to love a nomadic life, she found that she still had not forgotten how to roll her sleeping rug with thongs, or how to case all the small fragile vials of oils and ritual ointments so they would not break.

"You don't have to come," Tiernon said, his face tense, as Cataia made up her final pack. "It's pointless, anyway. You've done what Chevaina promised to do. You didn't make any bargains with 'Kleppah, and you're not responsible for mine."

"What's pointless is you trying to talk me out of it," Cataia replied, stubborn for all the softness in her voice. "I just wish you could have waited a little longer, that's all. At least until my power was secure. Maybe until I had a daughter to follow me."

"And then there would have been another reason, and another, each very important, why it should wait a little longer," Tiernon said. He paused and looked out over the city, smelling the food from the kitchens and with it the sewage from the slum down by the wharf. It was all wonderful to him. Then he turned and faced her again. "Cataia, I don't want to do this. I'm afraid. I've never been so afraid. I'm not proud enough, or stupid enough, to think that I'm a match for Lechefrian. But the only other choice is the pit, and that's no choice at all. And I'm lucky to have this much."

The bitterness in his voice pierced her. She reached up and her fingers fluttered across his face. She could see both of him now, the past and the present, as she could see herself as both Cataia and Chevaina. There was a new stillness about her. "We have both grown," she said, "more than we know. You are never given more than what you can do, at least that's what Mother Daniessa used to say all the time."

"I have my doubts this is what Mother Daniessa had in mind." He thought a moment, and then changed tacks. "Cai, I don't think I ever told you that I love you."

"No," she said softly. She remained silent for a long time, but she knew there wouldn't be another time. "There are things I didn't tell you before, either. I'm going to have a child."

The resolve on his face melted and he only barely held himself back from tears. That was the final cut he had to endure. No other punishment could be quite so complete. His body, bent as if against some sharp desert storm, held little of his customary languid grace.

The pain seemed to pass through him, as he let go of this as he had let go of everything else. Everything was gone. He raised his head and the face was again the one that Cataia found familiar. He leaned back on one elbow and let his fingertips brush the ends of her hair.

His touch was different than it had been in the past, even in the worst of times. He studied her face as if trying to fix it in his memory and caressed the narrow livid scar healing across her cheek. They both noticed details of texture that had been passed over at earlier times, prolonging every moment. The coolness of the predawn breeze surrounded them with silence.

Tears ran down Cataia's face as she realized this would be the last time—not only the last time to love, but the last time to be human with him. The moment they left the Palace they would be entirely Adepts on a mission, and all other things would cease to exist. She did not want to think about the homecoming, about her return. Now there was only one goal.

They did not sleep that night. As the first ray of light appeared they began the Chant to the Sun, the center where all roads connect. For the first time Cataia actually felt the fullness of that chant, felt the centeredness of her own inner being with the oneness of the Power. She could feel the oneness in Tiernon too, and for a moment she knew the fusion of their souls at the center. It was over far too soon, disappearing as the words of the Chant died with the full birth of the white disc, but the memory strengthened her. There was one more thing that must be done before they could set out on the road to 'Kleppah.

The appointment of Ayt and SiEryah as co-Regents in the absence of the Queen was done in a closed Council meeting with as little pomp as possible. There was little debate on the subject, as Tiernon, who as First Councilor would have traditionally filled this role, had tendered his resignation the day before. Besides, all saw the wisdom of appointing both the Star Priestess and a Nestezian War Leader. No one could argue favoritism, and each was held in high regard among her own people.

Cataia cut the meeting short after the appointments had been approved. There had been no questions about her instructions, painstakingly detailed, about what was expected during her absence. On the way out of the Council Chamber she was waylaid by Ayt.

"There is no reason for you to worry about the country, Majesty," the Star Priestess said. Then the tall woman in the heavy black robes lowered her voice. "I have looked at both your charts. Like you, I wish it didn't have to end this way, but he has no choice." She stopped for a moment, realizing that she had been speaking to herself. Cataia was nodding in agreement. "Just, would you tell Tiernon that I wish him well? And that I'll pray for him?"

Cataia clasped Ayt's hand quickly and then turned away. They were in the courtyard now, Tiernon checking on the last of the packing. Cataia saw the tears in Ayt's eyes before the Star Priestess turned abruptly away and disappeared back into the Palace.

They mounted, and as they rode out Tiernon gazed at the city carefully, seeing it in its fullness. They took the main route through the marketplace and were soon at the gates, overlooking the fertile strip created by the Entelle's spring floods.

On the other side of the city walls they were hailed by a young woman in a brilliant-green katreisi. As she ran up to them, Cataia recognized Dacia. Cataia jumped from her horse and ran to embrace her old friend. Tiernon remained aloof, but Dacia came up to him and laid her hand on the bridle of his horse. She looked at him sorrowfully for a moment, and then said, "We are with you. All of us."

Her voice was so soft that Tiernon was not sure he understood, but before he could say anything she was already treading the road back to the city.

The land held a strange serenity and sweetness—wide open plains filled with short stubble grass and grazing herds that took flight when they caught the scent of humans. There were several small towns on the road. There were inns along the road too, although many of them had been closed until recently for lack of travelers and local patronage.

Tiernon had decided against staying in the inns. This must be a time of purging and purifying to make him ready to meet what was to come. They had rationed their meat so that there would be no more than enough for two days and the return trip for one. After that, they would eat only vegetable foods, and during the final three days they would refrain from food altogether, drinking the bitter raw juice of torrigon mixed with herbs. This was not a penance, but a preparation of the body to endure heightened energy levels. Solids, most especially meats, would dull the body and affect the delicate flow of power through the spine. In most cases this precaution would be unnecessary, but for the amounts of energy Tiernon would be handling it was absolutely vital for the pathways to be as clear as possible. Not only the body, but the mind too must be cleared to be at its most efficient. They spent most of their time in the saddle doing exercises in concentration, strengthen-

ing control of the energy levels. In this they kept a narrow
focus on their final goal. During rest stops they did other exercises, connecting with the earth and stretching out to the life
around them. They did not venture out onto the Planes, however, in this scourging discipline of the self.

The land changed. They passed over the bridge and the flat
plains became rolling hills. The earth became hard and stony,
and the plants were fewer and of unusual varieties. Finally the
air itself became moister and they knew they were approaching
Aandev'Rei. The next day they camped within sight of the
walls.

The smell of burning had not yet settled, and the black scars
near the river were clearly visible from that distance. The city
was grey with ash. It colored everything and swirled through
the air. Cataia and Tiernon soon matched the color of the
walls. The entire place reeked of defeat and despair.

The horses picked their way through the charred streets.
They passed the retreat houses and Tiernon pointed them out
to Cataia, but their destination for the night was quite different. Now they let instinct and fragments of a thousand-year-
old memory guide them as they passed through the cluttered
maze of streets and alleyways, trying to find the great Hall
where they once before had rested before confronting 'Kleppah.

In the back of his mind, Tiernon felt the nagging fear that it
had burned, although its position at the edge of town was
reassuring. It seemed to take too long, and things looked different. Tiernon kept reminding himself that the city had both
grown and burned since that time. The open spaces were now
filled in with clay huts that leaned together at precarious
angles.

Then the great doors appeared before them, untouched
since the morning remembered out of a legendary past. The
deep carving had rounded at the edges, and the great rings had
been smoothed by thousands of hands tugging lightly to see if
the doors would open. They had not opened in all that time;
the Hall was kept as a sealed shrine and there was a rut worn in
the stone just before the door from those who had come over
the years to pay their respects.

A key, a few words and a moment of concentration had the
huge metal doors swinging open for the first time since Ronarian of the Seven had closed them behind her. The air smelled

musty and the floor was covered with dust.

The interior of the Hall was simple. There were no windows; Cataia lit a torch to see in the darkness. It was one long room, one end walled with a dark mirror and a large black stone slab which formed an altar about two-thirds of the way down. The near walls had many niches that held small clay pots of oils and foodstuffs, now disintegrated, and chests storing robes that would now dissolve with a touch. Tatters of rugs still hung from the walls, and others were neatly rolled up near the trunks. In the center a magnificent screen, made of lead grillwork and enameled glass depicting the Wheel and its symbolism, separated the living and working areas.

Cataia went through the pots on the shelves, trying to find if there was anything left that had not rotted. She came across only one survivor, a fine dust of gold such as was used to paint the hands, face and feet of the candidate for Initiation. Tiernon came over to see what she had found, and a strange expression crossed his face when she showed it to him.

"It's used at times other than Initiation," he said softly.

They brought in their gear and unrolled their sleeping rugs on the dusty floor. No broom had survived to sweep the place out, and neither of them had thought to bring one. They laid their Initiation robes over the chests in one of the alcoves and measured out a cup of juice apiece. Before retiring, Tiernon dragged a heavy stone basin to the center of the living area, and Cataia visited the well to fill several buckets of water. Then she poured salt and herbs into each to let them steep overnight, and they retreated to the sleeping rugs and fell into oblivion.

When Tiernon awoke it was not yet dawn. He stood in the stone basin, sluicing the now tepid water over his head, letting it take all negative thoughts and emotions from him as it ran down his legs and collected at his feet. For a moment he smiled, remembering his first experience with this type of bathing in the desert. Quickly he forced that thought out of his mind. Today he could afford no thought that did not focus on the task at hand. He tipped the basin so that the water flowed into the grillwork on the floor, and stood to let the warm air dry him.

When Cataia had awakened and bathed in a similar ritual fashion, Tiernon had already marked his hands and forehead with oil and stood dressed in his Initiation robes. The braided sword had been fastened to his cord belt with a thin strand looped in an intricate manner. He would be leaving the soft bag with his books and other ritual implements behind.

Cataia took the oil and began drawing the appropriate figures on her hands, though when she finished Tiernon took the vial from her. In the single last gesture permitted between them, he drew the sigal on her forehead in the sweetly scented oil. Already they were beginning to rise, only half aware of their bodies and what was needed, yet still efficient. Tiernon retained only the things he needed, the single book and the sword.

Cataia made sure he did not see the small vial she secreted in her sleeve. He would understand, she thought, but it would be better if he were not distracted now.

They walked to the boat that would take them to Tyne. They sang the Chant to the Sun as they walked, and fell into silence after that, a silence that would be broken only when the task was behind them.

Tyne appeared across the bay as coldly grey as it had appeared that other morning so long ago. The narrow fishing boat pitched across the choppy water, and the two Adepts were occasionally doused with spray, but did not seem to notice. They handled the ropes, trimming the single small sail to tack into the wind, but their concentration was not on the craft. The landing was not pleasant as the small boat beached on the sandy outcrop. Cataia gathered the ends of her robe up and tucked them into her belt, and they stepped out into the water to drag the boat high up on shore.

The eastern end of the island was a series of slabs of granite laid one on top of another so that it looked like the work of men. It was not, for it had been uncovered when the earth had moved so violently and the tops of the hills had been shorn off by torrential rains. The granite was surfaced with obsidian here and there, formed during an attack of Lechefrian, but the blast had not been strong enough to level the heap. Tiernon and Cataia climbed to just below the top, a wide ledge with a central altar slab that looked out to sea.

It was when they had arrived at the top that Cataia noticed that Tiernon wasn't wearing his Initiation ring. Even that, such a simple and meaningful gift, was denied him. She clutched the hidden vial of gold dust and hoped silently that the Powers would grant that he merited it. She desperately did not want to light the pyre under him while he breathed, but she was prepared for that as well, should he demand it.

Bertham would be coming soon, Cataia thought. She perched on a low ledge watching the tide, aware of life now as she had never been before. In this last battle she would have no part, and that she accepted quietly. Chevaina had not bargained with the demon, and neither had she. Things were as they must be. Somewhere within her she heard Dacia's voice, soft and comforting. But now Cataia was beyond support or need, beyond thought or rationality. Nothing moved, nothing had changed, things *were* and they had been and they would be. That view of eternity would have been comforting, but her awareness was beyond even comfort.

The sea beat the rock below her, and they were not separate, any more than she was separate from the ledge that held her, or from Tiernon far above. With him she reached out into the air, poised for flight, waiting for the first updraft. There was no time. Who was Cataia? Chevaina, Cataia, the others, all the others, and Dacia and both Tiernons, all were there and she was aware of them all as she was aware of the body that belonged to her looking out to the incoming boat.

They, the single entity that was they, knew it was coming long before the small dark spot appeared. The boat bounced over the choppy water as theirs had done, coming from another angle. Exhilaration filled them. On the horizon it was possible to make out the rising stones of 'Kleppah.

He knew what had happened in 'Kleppah. Tiernon could see Bertham now, eyes as set as his, robed in the same manner but with the sigal of Lechefrian hanging from a chain around his neck. It was good to meet an equal, but there was sorrow there. Power flowed through Bertham, almost physically enveloping him with the smoke that was Lechefrian. They were together now; the Eater of Souls resided in that body, taking on the personality that had been Bertham's.

Tiernon smiled. Bertham had not been Eaten, and that was good. They were still two there, living in some type of symbiosis that had not existed since 'Kleppah had first been sealed. The boat had disappeared, and Tiernon knew that Bertham would be on Tyne now, making his way from the sandy beach area to the rock altar. He saw Cataia below him, and they broke the link gently. The child could not be a witness to what was to happen. No matter how it ended, they had no right to involve those who had not asked to come. That was the Law.

Tiernon rose from the ledge and made his way back to the altar. Taking the sword, he traced first a circle and then a triangle around the slab. He opened the book he had brought to the old invocation for the Laughing Master, but the formula of the invocation seemed small and trite. Suddenly words came from nowhere, and he spoke in Eskenese, but with a slightly different accent from the one he had been taught.

"Lechefrian, Eater of Souls, the Laughing Master, Enigma of the Wheel, I bid you, Lechefrian, guardian of 'Kleppah, bound and bargained for, Prince of the Old Ones, the time has come. Lechefrian, older than morning, King of Lies, Ruler of Dissipation, the place is appointed. Lechefrian, my enemy, you know who I am and what is my purpose."

"I am here."

The voice was Bertham's, low and measured, and the robed Adept of 'Kleppah stood in the triangle Tiernon had inscribed. Tiernon met his eyes as he began to speak, and it was Bertham and Lechefrian speaking with one voice.

"Tiernon, listen to me. I, Bertham, am still myself, but I have learned what you are and were to my master. Think, Tiernon, of the power. You and I together—what the two of us could do. We are so very much alike, Tiernon. I always felt that in some way you were my brother. Think of that power, changed and grown greater. Taste it. Not just one place, but the world. Not just now, but forever, beyond Judgment. You know the Judgment you face. Lechefrian will keep you safe from it, and from those who would cast you into the pit of obliteration.

"How many times have I asked you to join me. How often I saw what we could do, be, together. Even after all this, Lechefrian still wants you. He would still honor the old agreement, and there would be more, immeasurably more, than there ever was. And no Judgment, but power forever, for eternity.

"I could be your friend. I offered once before and you would not have me. I have wanted it, Tiernon, and I still want it. Together there would be nothing, nothing, that we would not be able to do."

Tiernon was trembling. The hilt of the sword felt cold in his hands, a cold that grew up over him. He forced himself to look at it, and it brought back memories of the Caverns, of what had happened to him after he had accepted that proposition once before.

Bertham looked sad and his voice was heavy. "Is that what you want? You? To die a servant to an old sword and a dead cave? You, a servant? You could have everything"—and then his voice turned to stone, Lechefrian's voice—"including a very nasty death. And what would you accomplish by it? How could you even think that we could succumb to such as you? Don't be hasty. What have they promised you? What have they ever given you, except a millennium of misery?"

The coldness in the sword had become Tiernon's focus now, and from it he drew a small point into himself. Coldness, running so it burned. For a second he remembered the final moment of his Initiation, of that Unity with the absolute that had been freedom from all things. He began to feel it again, at the base of his spine, entering with the ice from the sword. It crawled up his back, that seed that had been planted on Dier Street. Striving, stretching, it reached his brain, and Tiernon no longer existed.

Or the Tiernon that was no longer existed. That Unity, which he had become once before, now exploded in his skull, and the dead weights of want and need and desire dissolved like dirt in hot water. He took the sword and touched it to Bertham's breast.

Things changed rapidly, and Tiernon was not sure if what he saw were one place or another, only that it was true. Bertham lay before him in a heap, his face like clay and all the fire gone. Lechefrian, form and claws, now regarded him carefully.

"If you insist," the demon said graciously.

Lechefrian threw energy through the braided metal, appealing to the animal in the man. He created terror, drawing on the loneliness in the Caverns of Ge, creating Tiernon's fears from his own mind. More energy he threw, weaving fantasies of lust, of strange and exotic orgies. The thought-form half smiled, thinking that it had been almost too easy. He had known Tiernon long enough to know his two greatest weaknesses. He had already resisted one, but could he resist the other?

The Unity held within Tiernon. Lust was no more than a physical expression, and if there is no body . . . at this moment

Tiernon was not aware of his body or his surroundings. He was enveloped in a great mind, a soul that was a million souls, and all that existed was love. He was not lonely anymore. He opened his mind to welcome the demon into the Unity. He drew Lechefrian gently through the sword, reassuring him constantly.

Lechefrian, revolted, thrust at the Adept with everything he was. He entered the sword in a single stroke, determined to burn Tiernon back to the young man he had bargained with before.

The hilt of the sword burned and the shock of it brought Tiernon back to the body. No longer part of the Unity, he still felt within him the reverberations of it through the rock and sea and sky. Yes, he wanted, yes, he needed, yes, he desired. But for that short time he had loved Lechefrian, and he fought now to retain that love. It was the only way to destroy the demon.

Tiernon could smell the flesh burning, could feel Lechefrian as an energy force under his skin, in his bone, fighting, beating, dragging him down. His mind was fully occupied trying to resist the visions the demon spewed through his mind. Something within him, the reserve that was his true identity, that was Tiernon of the Seven, was not tempted. The promises were false, were pain, and they were necessary. No, he thought with calm amusement, no, that was a misjudgment. A strange joy, a kind of peace, took hold of him as he realized that, yes, they were wrong. He was the master of himself, and he was above what he had thought himself to be.

In the midst of this revelation, this mastery, he thought to thank that which had tested him. It was the way of the Abbey, and with his full heart he was grateful to Lechefrian for permitting him to prove his humanity. The gratitude overwhelmed him, and he surrounded the demon with emotions of love and bliss. Yes, he could do it himself, even without the Unity.

Lechefrian recoiled. So much energy spent and he could not find a hold anywhere. He was slipping, his reserves being drained off to protect himself from Tiernon. More than anything, he hated the fact that he had actually kept his promise by bringing Tiernon to the Bridge. Even his enormous energy reserves were being drained, filtered through Tiernon's rapture and annihilation. Finally, Lechefrian could tolerate no more, and in a last suicidal blast he released himself to the

Plane where Tiernon was hovering near the Bridge.

The Adept was already on the Bridge, halfway across that strange place in the Planes where the highest Initiation took place. Very few, perhaps only a handful in all history, had been able to pass that point, to embrace their own oblivion. Lechefrian rushed across the pale glowing landscape, trying to catch up to Tiernon. If the Bridge failed he would remain suspended between the Planes, so weakened that he would simply disperse. He had to get to the other side before Tiernon could gain the power that traversing the Bridge imparted. He sent out a final thrust of energy, trying to catch the Adept before it was too late, but Tiernon had already placed a foot on the other side.

When Tiernon stepped off the Bridge, the pale glimmer died and the chasm was sealed. There was almost the echo of a shriek and the shreds of what had been Lechefrian for thousands of years simply failed to exist.

Tiernon wanted to walk on in the warm and comforting darkness, through it to see the endless boundaries of light that he knew lay beyond. The Bridge, he realized, was something he himself had had to create, create by the rejection of illusion by immersion in that other reality. He felt a faint tugging at the back of his mind. He tried to be rid of it, to reassure it, but it would not leave. He heard words spoken in him, words formed so softly that at first he thought it was memory speaking, but the words laughed and he knew they were and were not of his own being. He had to return. There was one last thing to do, to experience.

Cataia had waited on the lower level until she felt the pang that told her that Lechefrian was gone and 'Kleppah was no longer a Citadel on the Planes: a ruin now, and as she felt the dispersion of what had been there she knew the battle was ended. Only then did she climb the slick rocks to rejoin Tiernon.

His eyes were open when she found him, crumpled where he had stood in front of the slab. Closer in, by the ledge, she saw Bertham as well, quite obviously dead. There was no reason to pay attention to Bertham; he had been true to himself and was where he belonged.

Turning again to Tiernon, she noticed the look of pain on his face, but could not see the reason for it. She had smelled the burning, but from the angle at which she stood she could see no mark on him. Something fluttered within her. The Prophecy was wrong, he was still alive and, so far as she could see, unhurt. She rushed closer in amazement and bent over him.

It took all of her control not to retch. The levels of energy he had been working with were too much for flesh, no matter how well prepared. The palms of his hands, where contact had been made, were entirely burned away, and the metal of the sword hilt had melted and fused with the exposed white bone. This, Cataia knew, was only small evidence of what must have happened internally throughout the body. All the transfer points, so carefully kept open, had been overloaded and burned out.

Even beyond the agony, however, she could feel the change. Something had grown in Tiernon, and she could see from the expression in his eyes that he was accepting the pain for a reason. Surely otherwise he would have walled off his mind from the physical, at least to some degree; but he was experiencing all of it. She did not pretend. She started to cry.

Tiernon looked both puzzled and hurt at her tears. "But I was granted grace," he said. "And when does an Adept show grief over death?"

"I'm selfish," she said, but stopped crying and tried to match his smile. "After all, you're getting out, while I have to face who knows how many years alone, making decisions alone. It was hard enough before."

Tiernon gestured to the altar with his eyes. "Please, now," he said softly.

Cataia held herself straight and nodded. It was the only thing that could be done for him, and it was a great honor that had been hard won. She took the book off the altar and spread her sleeping rug across it. Half lifting, half supporting, she managed to help Tiernon onto the rug and straightened his robes so they fell smoothly. She found the small jar of powdered gold and brushed it lightly over the soles of his feet and his face. There was nothing she could do about his hands, but she sprinkled some of the dust where his palms would have been. His eyes showed that this was doubly painful, but there was an unspoken agreement between them. It would be done correctly, to the letter. The letter stated that the preparations must be exactly the same as for Initiation, both of them life and death and life. Even much of the text was the same. Cataia picked up the book and found the proper place.

"Your feet are on the corridor that leads to life, for we live in illusion and all things are illusion."

"Life and death are illusion," Tiernon responded.

"Have glory and triumph, be guided by the truth, be guarded by knowledge." Cataia felt others around her as she spoke the ritual words. Their strength and support flowed into her, and she knew that every Adept was aware of what had happened and what was happening, and there were many others there with them.

"The truth and knowledge are one, as all things are one."

"As we take the symbol of the sun as it rises."

"To the East," Tiernon responded, and Cataia felt him destroy the energy-net on that side of himself.

"And as it sets."

"To the West." There was another tear in the net, and the life-force was beginning to flow away in the directions named. Cataia felt a hollow pain, but held steady. The First and Final Rite was far less painful than most types of death. It was an honor, a grace, and could only be chosen when an Adept had fulfilled destiny and had attained the Bridge.

Cataia hesitated, and then went on, "As the burning sands of the desert and the cold mountains."

"To the South."

"And the sea."

"Dark Mother, who is our Mother beyond the Bridge, I thank you."

"Cradle him against death."

"Bitter Mother, for it is bitter, accept this for your halls, a sacrifice."

Cataia felt the final thrust of energy as Tiernon willed the net of his body to collapse, freeing himself to disappear beyond the Bridge. Cataia went with him through the Planes, as was her right, until they came to the chasm and Tiernon stepped into the unsupported void. Under his feet a brilliant path of light opened up as the Bridge again came into being, accepting one of its own. Cataia was filled with joy. She watched him cross to the other side into the conscious care of the Unity, before returning to the ledge.

The walls of Tsanos glowed pink in the predawn light.

Cataia stopped outside the gates and waited for a moment. It had not been possible to put down her grief on the long road back. Many times she had wanted to follow Tiernon, but his destiny had ended on Tyne, and she had a country to look after. A country and, soon, Tiernon's child. A guard saw her, recognized her, and the gate was opened. She touched her heels to her mount's flanks and started into the city. She would be in time for the first Council meeting of the morning.